BOOKS BY RUTH KRAUSS

 The Carrot Seed

 The Growing Story

Bears

The Happy Day

The Backward Day

The Bundle Book

A Hole Is To Dig

A Very Special House

How To Make an Earthquake

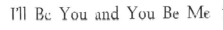 I'll Be You and You Be Me

I'LL BE YOU
AND YOU BE ME

By Ruth Krauss

Pictures by Maurice Sendak

HarperCollins Publishers

Thanks to Nina, Lynnie, Chris, Pat, Carmen, Doc, Judy, Trisha, Joel, Davey, Stephie, Emily, Mimi, Tommy, Danny, Normie, Git, Ruthie, Bert, Seth, Lucy, Stuart, Suzy, Petey, Margie, Kathy, Larry, Linda, Nancy, Guiseppe, Mary, Dos, Jackie, Harriet, and Ursie

she is waiting
for her friend,
waiting and
waiting

—He runs

—I run

—He jumps

—I jump

—He dunks his toast

and I dunk mine

—He calls 'Watch out, Lady!'

I call 'Watch out, Lady!'

He's practically my brother.

We take walks

and hold hands

—We trade things

—and if he didn't have a squirt-gun

and he wanted a squirt-gun

and I didn't have a squirt-gun

I'd get one for him.

And when I go away

he gives me a present

and ties it up special with ribbons

and it is to keep.

Oh, thank you very much!

You look just
like an elephant.

a horse that's lost could be dreaming
of the girl that's going to find him

Blup!

He means
'Goodby!'

he can't talk yet
but I can understand him—
even when he's over at his house and he yells
and nobody knows what he means—
I know. I could tell other people for him.
If someone draws a horse for me,
I say 'Draw two saddles, one for me
and one for him. He's my friend.'
And if I fell through a hole in the ice,
my friend would help me get out.
He can't talk yet
but he answers when I call.
I call 'Honey, come here, Honey'
and he comes.

poem by a tree for some bugs

I'm a big strong tree—
see my green leaves
—I look down at the grass and say
'I wish I was all that other green stuff too.'
The bugs come in me
because I am so much green and their favorite color
is green.

love is when you send postcards
more than to other people—
love is they could push you down in the grass
and it doesn't even hurt—
love is the same as like
only you spell them different—
only more of the same, sort of—
Love has more stuff in it!
love is you give them
a leg off your gingerbread man.
No, two legs.
And the head!

All I want is
sugar off a button

The Doll In Pink

a play

SCENE: There's a little girl and a big doll and it's snowing. It's snowing hard. The doll is all dressed up, but no coat. Then a big girl comes along.

LITTLE GIRL: Hi!

BIG GIRL: Hi!

LITTLE GIRL: My doll has on her Best Dress. See. All over shiny stuff. But she doesn't have a coat.

BIG GIRL: Oh.

LITTLE GIRL: I'm not big enough for her to fit under mine. Would you carry her under your coat for me?

BIG GIRL: Sure.   (*She takes the doll and puts it under her coat*)

LITTLE GIRL: You're my friend.   (*Then they all go along together holding hands*)

THE END

I WENT THERE

a mystery

I went to you.

I went to me.

I went to

every where.

And I went

THERE.

I think I'll grow up to be a bunny before I grow up to be a lady.

I think I'll grow up to be a steam-shovel.

shoes shoes
little black shoes
little black shoes
with little black bows—
someday someday
little black shoes
with little black bows
on the toes—

someday

Dance For A Horse

White Stallion,
White Stallion,
Where are you, White Stallion?
Here's an apple for you.

I'm coming. See!
I can run faster than Anything—
I'm stronger than Anything—
Open the gates!
I'm coming!

White Stallion,
White Stallion,
· Here's an apple for you.

a new holiday and a good song
if you have a monkey for a friend friend friend

You are my friend, little Monkey,
and I'm going to make a special holiday for you
like, for instance, Mother's Day—only Monkey Day.
Then everyone will have an extra holiday. We'll
have George Washington's Birth Day, New Year's Day,
Valentine Day and the others—and Monkey Day.
And here's a song for you with it.

Happy Monkey Day to You,
Happy Monkey Day to You,
Happy Monkey Day, dear Monkey,
Happy Monkey Day to You.

special talk
for talking to monkeys

Cheep cheep cheep  Cheep-cheep

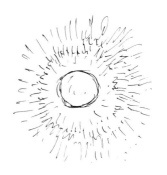

I love the sun
I love a house
I love a river
and a hill where I watch
and a song I heard
and a dream I made

a dream for you

and a dream for you

and a dream for you

and a dream for you

The Chicken And The Princess
a fairy tale

One day the chicken

was going to town.

The chicken got lost.

But a princess found him.

She was nice.

And she was poor, the princess.

So he took her home to his house.

We want to be like twins
with shoes like twins, and coats,
if one is plaid, the other
should be plaid too, like twins—
and when we go to spend the night,
we take all clothes the same, like twins.
We phone up each other ahead of time.
—little pajamas alike, with flowers, we have
—and make our milk come evens in the glasses
—and when we pass a cemetery, we both
hold our breath alike, like twins,
even when we're not together.

She's wide
and I'm thin—

her hair's short
and my hair's long—

I hope I widen out
as she grows narrowed and

my hair should get shorter
as hers gets long—

we'd be like twins.

I had a little elephant
—Bibo's what I called it—
I loved it so much
I thought it was a flower.

And I lost it.

I found another elephant
—someone threw it out I think—
with one ear bit
and it had an only eye
and I loved it so much—

Bibo's what I call it too
I love them both
I love them both the best—
I love you both, my honeys,
I love you both the best.

two little houses
and their smokes are joining

the monkey is in the beauty-parlor
getting his toes blacked

dopey

You are dopey
I am not
You are dopey
I am not
dopey dopey dopey dopey
You are dopey dopey dopey

You could even
have a dopey
for a friend.

You sit on my cold feet and

I'll sit on your cold feet and

You sit on my cold feet and

I'd come to your party
even if you didn't have a cake.

I have a little bear-friend.
He wears a little sailor-suit
and sleeps with me every night.

in a little hole and
out a little hole and
in a little hole and
out a little hole and
sometimes I like to crawl in and look out
and sometimes I like to crawl out and look in.
crawl crawl

a friend means Joe

see my new shoes. See.

see my new coat. See.

see my new hat. See.

with a little red flower
with a little red flower

I'll sit on your cold feet and

You sit on my cold feet and

I'll sit on your cold feet—

Skippy skipped over the rocks—

Hoppy hopped over the rocks—

together they both

jumped over the world.

I wish I was a mouse
so I could run over the table!

No More Woxes

a short Tall Tale

There was a wolf
and there was a fox and
they ate each other up.
And that made the wox.

Then the wox
ate himself up and
that's why there are
no more woxes.

You take my name
and I'll take yours.

There are six friends

and they all put on each other's

coats. It is winter

and they run in the snow.

Then they begin to fight.

Then they are unfriends.

Then they yell at each other

"You give me back my coat!"

It is winter—right in the middle—

and they are running in the snow.

Is there something you want to
say to Dickie?

Yes! I want to say
I want to put him in
the garbage can.

I used to love monkeys more but now I love horses—

just my one ear is a monkey's now and the rest of me is a horse.

I can sleep standing up because horses do—

but I can still live in a tree or hang by my tail

if I want I can give it to a friend

some grass
and some ocean
and some dark for daytime
and some sun for nighttime
and a hug—
I put them down together
on a piece of paper
—I could hold it in my hand
—I could keep it in my pocket

you could roll it in a little ball
and poke it in a shell

A LIKING SONG

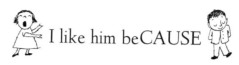 I like him beCAUSE

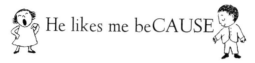 He likes me beCAUSE

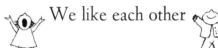 We like each other

beCAUSE

beCAUSE

—and here's the dance to it—

Because I say so!

Transforming RN Education:
Dialogue and Debate

Transforming RN Education: Dialogue and Debate

Edited by
Nancy L. Diekelmann
and
Marsha L. Rather

National League for Nursing Press · New York
Pub. No. 14-2511

To RN Students
and Their Teachers

Copyright © 1993
National League for Nursing Press
350 Hudson Street, New York, NY 10014

ISBN 0-88737-573-1

Library of Congress Cataloging-in-Publication Data

Transforming RN education : dialogue and debate / edited by Nancy L. Diekelmann and Marsha L. Rather.
    p. cm.
   Includes bibliographical references.
   ISBN 0-88737-573-1
   1. Nursing—Study and teaching (Continuing education)—Congresses.
   2. Nursing—Study and teaching (Graduate)—Congresses.
   I. Diekelmann, Nancy L.   II. Rather, Marsha L.
   [DNLM: 1. Education, Nursing, Continuing—congresses.
   2. Education, Graduate—congresses. WY 18 T7718 1993]
   RT73.T68 1993
   610.73'071'5—dc20
   DNLM/DLC
   for Library of Congress   92-48348
                           CIP

This book was set in Palatino by Eastern Composition, Inc. The editor and designer was Nancy Jeffries. Northeastern Press was the printer and binder. The cover was designed by Lauren Stevens.

Printed in the United States of America

Contents

Preface

We are losing our literature in nursing education. The number of new books in this area is declining rapidly. Enrollments in nursing are rising and the issues of nursing education are becoming more complex. This is a dangerous time to be without a diverse literature in nursing education that evokes thinking in teachers.

Realizing that they must design clinical research studies in order to get funded, and ultimately tenured, new faculty in schools of nursing conduct less educational studies. Limited grant monies also hamper the dissemination of any findings. Given this research climate, it becomes ever more important for educators to speak out about the importance of our work through books such as this one.

The intent of this book is to shape a dialogue among teachers who are committed to education for the returning registered nurse. Registered nursing students are a gift to nursing education: they return to school with the practical understanding of what shapes and guides practice. They have a commitment to enhance their thinking in order to transform the problems of clinical practice with new possibilities. In addition, it is often the case that these RN students are on their way to graduate degrees. As our clinical practice demands advanced preparation and nurses are called upon to expand their roles, the exploration of new approaches to RN education reveals a new future of possibilities for us all. It is timely to explore new approaches to RN education.

This book is a collection of papers presented at the Transforming RN Education: Dialogue and Debate conference sponsored by the University of Wisconsin-Madison, June 17–19, 1992 in Madison, Wisconsin. In response to the call for abstracts, teachers from thirty-seven states and five countries submitted presentations. Keynote speeches were given by Patricia Benner, PhD, RN, FAAN, Christine Tanner,

PhD, RN, FAAN, Sandra Eyres, PhD, RN, and Nancy Diekelmann, PhD, RN, FAAN. At the conference, participants were invited to submit their presentations for this book. Forty-three manuscripts were submitted and sent out for three blind reviews. This refereed collection of papers represents the current thinking of teachers and researchers in RN education.

The keynote speeches by Benner, Tanner, and Diekelmann present research funded by the Helene Fuld Health Trust. Issues in RN education are described by researchers and teachers from around the world. These thought provoking chapters provide both breadth and depth to contemporary dialogue and debate in RN education. Innovative approaches to curriculum and instruction include chapters on program evaluation, research and description of innovative approaches. Creative instructional strategies are described with rich illustrations. We hope this book extends the dialogue and debate toward transforming RN education.

It would have been impossible to assemble this book without the copious help of family, friends, students, and colleagues. To our colleagues who during the summer diligently and skillfully reviewed these manuscripts, we extend our heartfelt appreciation. Our students, friends, faculty, and support staff caringly and enthusiastically helped with all the invisible tasks to host the conference that produced this manuscript. The generous support of Alan Trench, Administrative Vice President, Marine Midland Bank and Chairman, Grants Committee, Helene Fuld Health Trust and the Helene Fuld Health Trust is acknowledged with profound gratitude. Lastly, we acknowledge the support and expertise given by National League for Nursing Editor, Sally Barhydt, RN. Her willingness to publish and efforts to sustain and create a vanguard literature in nursing education is a gift to us all.

Nancy L. Diekelmann, PhD, RN, FAAN
Helen Denne Schulte Professor
University of Wisconsin-Madison
School of Nursing

Marsha L. Rather, PhD, RN
Assistant Clinical Professor
University of Wisconsin-Madison
School of Nursing

Editorial Board

Contributors

Theresa Allor, MPH, RN
Assistant Professor
University of Michigan
School of Nursing
Ann Arbor, MI

Janet S. Barnfather, PhD, RN
Assistant Professor
University of Michigan
School of Nursing
Ann Arbor, MI

Patricia Benner, PhD, RN, FAAN
UCSF
Department of Physiological Nursing
School of Nursing
San Francisco, CA

Janalou Blecke, PhD, RN
Professor and Assistant Dean
Saginaw Valley State University
University Center, MI

Nina Bruni, MEd, DIP, Ed, BA
Senior Lecturer
Royal Melbourne Institute of
   Technology University
Victoria, Australia

Janet E. Bryant, BSN, RN
MSN Student
Saginaw Valley State University
University Center, MI

Judith Buchanan, MHSc, RN
Assistant Professor
University of New Brunswick-Saint
   John
Department of Biology and Nursing
Saint John, New Brunswick, Canada

Geraldine M. Chalykoff, MSN, RN
Assistant Professor
University of New Brunswick-Saint
   John
Department of Nursing
Saint John, New Brunswick, Canada

Genevieve E. Chandler, PhD, RN
Assistant Professor
University of Massachusetts at
   Amherst
Amherst, MA

Philip Darbyshire, PhD, RNMH,
   RSCN, Dip N (Lond.), RNT, MN
Lecturer in Health and Nursing
   Studies
Glasgow Caledonian University
Glasgow, Scotland

Sally A. Decker, PhD, RN
Associate Professor of Nursing
Saginaw Valley State University
University Center, MI

Nancy L. Diekelmann, PhD, RN,
  FAAN
Helen Denne Schulte Professor
University of Wisconsin-Madison
Madison, WI

Joyce Engel, MEd, RN
Assistant Professor
School of Nursing
University of Lethbridge
Medicine Hat College
Medicine Hat, Alberta, Canada

Sandra J. Eyres, PhD, RN
Professor
University of Washington
School of Nursing
Seattle, WA

Margaret M. Flatt, PhD, RN
Associate Professor and RN
  Coordinator
Saginaw Valley State University
University Center, MI

Joan M. Hau, EdD, RN
Associate Professor
Saint Xavier University
Chicago, IL

Pat Hayes, MHSA, RN
Associate Professor
Faculty of Nursing
University of Alberta
Edmonton, Alberta, Canada

Mary Hoenecke, MN, RN
Lecturer
University of Michigan
School of Nursing
Ann Arbor, MI

Christina D. Horne, MS, RN
Associate Professor of Nursing
Department of Nursing
School of Science and Allied Health
Kennesaw State College
Marietta, GA

Alice Kienholz, BASc, BEd, DipEd,
  MSc
Principal
Alice Kienholz Associates
Calgary, Alberta, Canada

Ann Kruszewski, MSN, RN
Assistant Professor
University of Michigan
School of Nursing
Ann Arbor, MI

Mary M. Lebold, EdD, RN
Dean, School of Nursing
Saint Xavier University
Chicago, IL

Cecile Lengacher, PhD, RN
Assistant Dean for Undergraduate
  Studies
University of South Florida
College of Nursing
Tampa, FL

Anne Loustau, PhD, RN
Associate Professor
University of Washington
School of Nursing
Seattle, WA

Rama K. Mishra, PhD
Researcher, Developmental
  Disabilities
Department of Educational
  Psychology
University of Alberta
Edmonton, Alberta, Canada

Claudia Moore, PhD
RN Student Advisor
University of Michigan
School of Nursing
Ann Arbor, MI

Sallie C. Nealand, EdD, RN
Assistant Professor
Lewiston-Auburn College
Lewiston, Maine

Darlene O'Callaghan, MSEd, MSN, RN
Associate Professor
Saint Xavier University
Chicago, Illinois

Betty J. Paulanka, EdD, RN
Dean
University of Delaware
College of Nursing
Newark, Delaware

Elisabeth Pennington, EdD, RN
Interim Associate Dean/Assistant
    Professor
University of Michigan
School of Nursing
Ann Arbor, MI

Marsha L. Rather, PhD, RN
Clinical Assistant Professor
School of Nursing
University of Wisconsin-Madison
Madison, WI

Marianne W. Rodgers, EdD, RN
Associate Professor
University of Southern Maine
Portland, ME

Catherine O. Rosenlieb, PhD, RN
Chairperson, Department of Nursing
Slippery Rock University
Slippery Rock, PA

Mary Lou Rusin, EdD, RN
Chairman, Nursing Department
Daemen College
Amherst, NY

Christine Tanner, PhD, RN, FAAN
Professor of Nursing
School of Nursing
Oregon Health Sciences University
Portland, OR

Mary Lou VanCott, PhD, RN
Assistant Professor
University of South Florida
College of Nursing
Tampa, FL

Elaine VanDoren, MSN, RN
Lecturer
University of Michigan
School of Nursing
Kalamazoo, MI

Carol Zenas, PhD, RN
Adjunct Assistant Professor
University of Michigan
School of Nursing
Traverse City, MI

Foreword

This collected and edited work of Diekelmann and Rather represents and captures a turning point in the dialogue and debate concerning nursing education in general, and Registered Nurse (RN) Education in particular. Moreover, this work provides a new turn to the so-called curriculum revolution, led and fostered by the National League for Nursing, and some of the leading authors in this seminal collection. For example, the pioneering narrative works of Benner, Tanner, and Diekelmann provide a phenomenological-hermeneutic lived world, inquiry-as-praxis frame, and methodological backdrop for this book (Lather, 1991). This frame and backdrop inform and invite us toward creative developments and new educational options for the returning registered nurse student—as well as those dedicated teachers who discern the special strengths, embodied knowledge, and talents of the RN student.

The prominent authors in this book consist of nursing leaders and scholar-teachers and researchers from around the globe. They help us to attend to both the distinctive talents and clinical knowledge of the RNs, but also the special problems of RN students, especially when confronted with the unexamined status quo in traditional nursing education.

This unique collection stands as a mirror for nursing educators worldwide who are committed to and concerned about the status of registered nursing education and educational research. Further, this work is somewhat of a milestone in offering a timely voice for this neglected area of nursing scholarship in our colleges and universities.

Because of the international focus of this collection, which emerged from a targeted conference at the University of Wisconsin-Madison, in 1992, it represents contemporary global thinking of educators and researchers in RN education worldwide and highlights the common issues and problems in the field.

Further, this work highlights the innovative leadership of the Helene Fuld Health Trust, which supported some of the flagship work leading up to, and included in, this volume, e.g., the works of Benner, Tanner, and Diekelmann. Such work has proven to be a critical contribution to the dialogue and debate about nursing as a practice profession and the unique knowledge embedded in practice.

This book confirms for us that nursing's knowledge must be experientially and critically explored in order to uncover and sustain the richly contextual whole, but perhaps equally important, it reminds us that it is only in returning to the lived world itself can we be truly reflective and critical in our practices. Understood phenomenologically, this work characterizes nursing educational research as a sort of hermeneutics of caring practice—awakening us to a deeper layer of experience—how we live authentically with our colleagues and students, (Pinar and Reynolds, 1992), especially when those students are more often our mature colleagues and expert clinicians.

Such a slant on RN education, with its particular embodiment of nursing's knowledge and knowing in the human self, allows for narrative, story as method, life history constructing, deconstructing, and reconstructing as a way to see, to relive, to return to the relation of self to knowing. Such pedagogical practices affirm, restore and create meaning—they seek to capture the hidden, the subtext, the behind the lines experiences, they seek to examine the curriculum as text—a story to be told and retold, while still recognizing the epistemological and ontological limits as well as authentic possibilities.

Lastly, this work makes real and tangible the "data" of human life of the RN student; it attends to teaching learning experiences which are often considered immeasurable and epistemologically (and even ontologically) unsound, allowing for a true hermeneutics of educational practices. Through the ideas in this book one's thinking and actions become inquiry, a form of praxis, a form of thanks for what is given. As Heidegger puts it:

The things for which we owe thanks are not things we have from ourselves. They are given to us. We receive many gifts, of many kinds. But the highest and really most lasting gift to us is always our essential nature, with which we are gifted in such a way that we are what we are only through it. That is why we owe thanks for this endowment, first and unceasingly (Heidegger, 1968, p. 142).

Thus the perspective this book offers can be seen as a gift of thanks, which help us to see, appreciate, and learn from that which is already given to us in our teaching and learning. This work is both calling us and leading us toward new revelations, a revolution in our thinking, and ultimately, transformations in educational actions and practices, all of which are now required at the turn of this century (Bevis and Watson, 1989).

Finally, cross-cutting work such as this offers nursing educational literature the latest thinking in this neglected field. Because of the national and international distinction of the authors included in this work, it has incorporated dialectics and richly diverse teacher experiences into nursing education's debate about epistemology, ontology, and language and method, allowing for a resurgence of nursing educational research, dialogue and debate. Thus, this book is a book for its time—a time of historic change and transformation in nursing education at the turn of the twentieth century.

Jean Watson, PhD, RN, FAAN
University Distinguished Professor of Nursing
Director, Center for Human Caring
University of Colorado Health Sciences Center
School of Nursing
Denver, Colorado

REFERENCES

Bevis, E. and Watson, J. (1989). *Toward a caring curriculum.* New York: National League for Nursing Press.

Heidegger, M. (1968). *What is called thinking?* New York: Harper and Row.

Lather, P. (1991). *Getting smart. Feminist research and pedagogy with/in the postmodern.* New York: Routledge.

Pinar, W. F. and Reynolds, W. M. (1992). *Understanding curriculum as phenomenological and deconstructed text.* New York: Teachers College Press, Columbia University.

Part I

Dialogue and Debate:
Understanding Experience in
RN Education Hermeneutically

1

Transforming RN Education: Clinical Learning and Clinical Knowledge Development

Patricia Benner

Nursing has a profound educational opportunity in having an applicant pool of experienced clinicians returning for baccalaureate degrees. This cohort of clinically experienced nurses allows for teaching toward clinical knowledge development and strengthening level of clinical experience. However, we typically have modeled RN educational programs on a re-socialization model, or on a generic baccalaureate program, ignoring the advantages of the experience-rich students returning for a period of scholarly development and reflection. We can design our clinical teaching to enhance reflection and knowledge development that builds on an experience-rich background of clinical learning, and first hand knowledge of the structural impediments to excellent nursing practice.

There are several impediments to developing truly innovative RN education programs. Academia typically privileges theoretical knowledge over practical knowledge. In clinical disciplines such as nursing and medicine, clinical knowledge development is eclipsed by science and technology (Polanyi, 1958). A notorious gap between theory, science and clinical practice is acknowledged, but the assumptions about the nature of the gap are typically unidirectional—practice is deficient

The writing of this article was funded in part by the Helene Fuld Foundation.

and hasn't caught up with theory and science. This cultural bias is lodged deep in our Greek and Enlightenment Traditions. Granted, there are many under-researched and unthought through areas of clinical practice, just as there are large knowledge gaps in theory and science. However, the technological myth is that it should be possible to construct a clinical practice from the ground up through theory and science. Such a scientistic view ignores the narrative structure and socially embedded knowledge nature of clinical knowledge in any practice discipline. In the technical view there should be a perfect one-to-one relationship between the theory and science and the practice. This ideal is based upon several false assumptions:

1. Nursing and medical clinical practice can be completely formalized. That is, in principle, it should be possible to spell out all that is known and relevant to clinical practice. This assumption overlooks the nature of caring for particular human beings and particular human populations. It also overlooks the dynamic historical and particular evolution of a clinical trajectory whether the outcome be recovery or death.

2. It assumes a one-to-one relationship between ideal static physiological states and embodied clinical realities. Such a static model cannot account for particular human accommodation and adaptation to altered physiological states such as decreased lung capacity and diminished cardiac output. Nor does the static model capture the clinical trajectories of particular patients.

3. Perceptual and configurational relationships can be captured in static formal accounts. This assumption overlooks the distance and disparity between actual clinical manifestations and all their variegations and that ideal prototypical accounts captured in strong cases are needed to augment formal models. Perceptual recognition of clinical manifestations is a form of skilled know how that is socially embedded and embodied. Most often multiple clinical observations and accounts are discussed, compared and adjudicated by a community of practitioners.

4. Finally theory, science, and technology address a small portion of the complexity of actual practice. Not every contingency in a complex practice can be researched or definitively

adjudicated by science, therefore a practical socially embedded wisdom of practitioners is required to carry out the knowledge work in a working, living tradition. This is not a claim for blind traditionalism. It is merely an acknowledgment of the necessary role of the knowledge embedded in a practice community that can be scrutinized by science and criticized by critical thinking (see, Lave & Wegner, 1991; Lave, 1988; Suchman, 1987; Dreyfus & Dreyfus, & Athansiou, 1986; Collins, 1985).

The returning RN student offers academia the opportunity to teach clinical know how and clinical knowledge development and extend our clinical teaching/learning powers because they come with a first hand acquaintance with the nature of clinical knowing and a direct understanding of the limits of formalism. This student population rather than being an insufficiently educated group that must be shored up has much to teach the open nursing educator. Returning RN students provide a powerful opportunity to make visible and extend our clinical teaching learning abilities so that we might overcome the eclipse of clinical knowing in our academic settings (Bourdieu, 1990).

ASSESSING THE LEVEL OF CLINICAL EXPERTISE

Not all returning RN students enter with the same level of clinical expertise, therefore an initial description of the types of clinical populations and the kinds of clinical learning and clinical certification brought by the student can provide a basis for assessing the clinical experience that might be extended and refined in the program. In addition to this description, students should prepare some key clinical narratives that will assist them in understanding their own level of clinical practice. Narratives of learning, narratives where they learned something new, narratives that depict their best practice and constitute their understanding of what makes the practice worthwhile, as well as narratives of disillusionment, moral conflict, or confusion (Benner, 1991) can help the teacher and student jointly identify areas of advanced clinical practice, and areas where clinical learning needs to be expanded. This entering portfolio can be expanded as the program progresses with new clinical experience. Learning is enriched for all when students publicly share some of their significant experiential clinical learning. This allows the faculty member to point up the commonalities in the stories and allows the students to experience first-hand the social embeddedness of practice-based clinical knowledge. Students frequently have similar and contrasting stories to create a discussion of practical know how and wisdom. Qualitative distinctions between clinical issues in similar and contrasting clinical stories can be drawn out.

Narrative accounts of clinical situations have an advantage over traditional case study presentation because learners present their own concerns, thoughts, and feelings as the clinical situation unfolds. This allows the notions of the good, the contextual and relational knowledge to be expressed and considered. The experience based exemplar allows story tellers to consider the nature of their own agency in the situation. Telling the clinical story is an experience-near way of giving language to clinical understanding. The clinical story teller's concerns organize the story. The nature of the clinicians' notions of the good, and understanding of the situation determine which stories are memorable, where they begin, what is the point of the story, the tensions, conflicts and discovery (Benner, 1991; Baier, 1985).

This form of reflection allows for recapturing the engaged reasoning or modus operandi thinking that is characteristic of practical knowledge (Bourdieu, 1990). The experienced clinician is in the best position to engage in engaged reasoning since clinical knowing requires immediate historical understanding, modus operandi thinking, and an understanding of the particular in relation to the general. The narratives allow the students and teachers to focus on the skills of problem identification. Why did this clinical issue stand out in this situation? It also allows students and teachers to focus on the skills of involvement. Why did the nurse-patient-family level of connection and understanding help or hinder the outcome? In our extensive study of clinical skill acquisition (Benner, Tanner, Chesla, 1992; Benner, Tanner, Dreyfus, Dreyfus, Rubin, in progress) we have examined the longstanding philosophical question of what kind of reflection increases the clinical learner's understanding of the human and clinical issues at hand, and what kinds of reflection create confusion through a proliferation of variables so that maximum grasp of this particular clinical situation is lost or deteriorates to a formal general analysis that sheds little light on the particular clinical situation. Sometimes it is a problem of the student having inadequate information to increase the understanding of the situation. In which case clinical learning can focus on uncovering the missing, relevant information. One of the impoverishments of a strictly nursing process problem solving approach is that the capacity to identify which "problems" count as the ones to be solved or addressed is often left out of the discussion. And it is this capacity to choose the most salient problems that is at the heart of clinical expertise (Benner, Tanner, & Chesla, 1992).

DEVELOPING A PORTFOLIO OF PARADIGM CASES

Experiential clinical learning can be captured by the student developing a portfolio of paradigm cases, clinical situations that taught them something new. These exemplars should be told in narrative form. When students collect a number of paradigm cases, they can begin to identify clinical knowledge themes and issues. If the students examine selected paradigm cases from their classmates, they may be able to articulate areas of clinical knowledge not currently well understood. For example, in my entering Master's level class, we found eleven distinct clinical understandings of patient advocacy in the student's exemplars. The common understanding of advocacy is that nurse mediation ensures that the patient gets treatment congruent with patient/family needs, concerns and preferences. However, the exemplars indicated that the students also understood advocacy as giving the patient his or her voice, standing alongside, and supporting the patient during a time of suffering, adjudicating and clarifying conflicting therapeutic intents and other qualitative distinctions. The exemplars helped the class enrich their understanding of the common nursing value of patient advocacy. Doing an interpretive analysis of the exemplars teaches the students clinical knowledge development skills, skills of reflection on their practice, and demonstrates an educational valuing of clinical practice.

REWORKING PAST CLINICAL UNDERSTANDINGS

Students come with experiential accounts that may not have been revised by their current clinical understanding. Hearing their own stories from their past clinical practice may make them recognize areas of change when they critically reflect on the exemplar. For example, in my class a student had told a virtually unedited new graduate story, complete with an excessive amount of self-focus and very little information about how her actions were understood by the other clinicians or patient involved. A few well placed questions demonstrated her blind spots as a new graduate and she developed more insight on her entering level of anxiety and closedness to human and clinical information. Such self-discovery is highly valuable for creating openness for future clinical learning, and recognizing changes in perception as a result of experiential learning and reflection on practice.

RE-EXAMINING THE SKILL OF INVOLVEMENT AND CARING PRACTICES

The skill of involvement and caring practices are developed over time through trial and error. Often they are slight modifications to basic familial relating styles. Through examining narratives of actual practice, the student can begin to identify clinical situations where they may not have been able to connect to the patient/family in a facilitating way. Through their own and other student's narratives of engagement they can begin to reflect on their skill of involvement. When might they be too detached to be helpful to the patient/family? And when might they be over-involved and thus ineffective? When might they be susceptible, due to their own anxiety, to leap in and take over inappropriately for the patient (Benner & Wrubel, 1989)? In our current study of skill acquisition in critical care nursing practice, we have found that the skill of involvement is crucial for going on to become an expert practitioner. Nurses who become excessively disengaged, do not develop the narrative memory to learn from their clinical encounters. Nurses who are too disengaged literally cannot remember specific stories, and tend to describe their practice as a series of events and tasks (Benner, Tanner, Chesla, Dreyfus, Dreyfus, and Rubin, in progress).

Re-entry into an educational program gives students an opportunity to reevaluate and modify their skills of involvement. This educational change could be one of the most critical changes for the nurse moving to expert practice. Expert nurses link advanced clinical knowledge and judgment with highly evolved caring practices. It is evident that they evaluate the ethics of heroic care from a perspective of caring practices. They place themselves inside the patient/family's community, as advocates, seeing themselves as persons who stand alongside, empowering patient/families to have a voice when they are weak and vulnerable. They talk about their commitment to be vigilant in ensuring that adequate care is given, that early warnings of patient change are given, that instantaneous therapies are given with an understanding of the particular patient's responses; and they describe themselves as persons who ensure that the health team and patient/family have a congruent understanding of the intent of care.

We have examined notions of good embedded in the stories, and the skill of involvement and skill of responsibility and the skill of conserving and preserving world and personhood of extremely ill persons. But we also heard accounts of breakdown, and inevitably in these accounts, the patient shows up differently and we do not come away with a rich story of person or world. When caring practices deteriorate there are stories of rejection, exclusion, dominance, control, and power struggles. The stance is one of objectification and disengagement and fits the descriptions of "burnout" or loss of human caring (Maslach, 1982; Benner & Wrubel, 1989).

TEACHING STUDENTS TO TRANSLATE EXPERIENCE-BASED KNOWLEDGE INTO THEORETICAL AND SCIENTIFIC INQUIRIES

When we stop giving a unidirectional privilege to theory and science we can coach students to engage in the lively and rigorous teaching/ learning that moves a student from clinical innovations, dilemmas, and questions to a search of the extant theory and science, engaging in dialogical thinking that can enrich both the practice and the science. We have so focused on moving theory and science into practice that we have neglected the equally innovative task of scrutinizing theory and science with our practical know-how and clinical puzzles. This form of active reflection on practice teaches students to be good clinical learners and engage in the kind of dialogue between practice, science, and theory that will make them good clinical knowledge developers. Actually this kind of reflection on practice is also relevant for the generic clinical learner, it is just that it is much more difficult for them to see the complexity in practice that would engage and challenge current theory and science.

EDUCATING FOR LIBERATION AND EMPOWERMENT

Many RN students return to school with the hopes of gaining increased power over the inequities and exigencies of their work life. It is not unusual for a nurse to re-enter school as a way of exiting untenable work conditions. In nursing literature this has been labeled the service-education gap. Transforming victimization, oppression, and hopelessness to hope, empowerment, and liberation is the opportunity but also the daunting challenge of RN education. Rhetoric and idealization that ignores the actual realities of the workplace will not address this educational need. Students should be encouraged to confront and name the sources of low power, victimization, and oppression. Tracey White gives a good, honest example of the reality of an evening shift in what is actually a relatively well managed community based hospital:

"On Nursing"
by
Tracey White

I am in charge tonight with five nurses and thirty patients. Two of my nurses are floats who have never been on the floor, one will be an hour late so I will have to cover her patients. Our medical-surgical patients have diagnoses ranging from system failure of the kidney, Stroke, Diabetes, Cancer, Sickle-Cell Disease, Hepatitis, AIDS, Pneumonia and Alzheimer's Disease. The average age of our patients is seventy-nine. We have five fresh post-operative patients and one going to surgery in two hours. As I come out of report one of our stable patients who transferred from CCU (Coronary Care Unit) yesterday is having chest pain. There is a doctor on the phone wanting to give admission orders and the anesthetist for our pre-operative patient wants the old chart, now. Down the hall in 4324 an elderly confused patient has just crawled over the side rails and fallen. Two of our fresh post-op patients are vomiting as a side effect of anesthesia, their families are very tense and need reassuring. One of the patients I am covering for has just pulled out his IV; another wants something for pain; another needed the bed pan and I got there too late. The Lab has called with a critical low hemoglobin level on the patient who pulled out his IV, he'll be getting a few units of blood as soon as possible. This condensed version represents the first two hours of my working day. The above description of a medical-surgical floor in an acute care hospital is no fabrication. . . . In the nine years I have been a nurse the most meaningful memories of patients and families are held in a delicate web of what I call my "love-hate" relationship with the profession of nursing. What is this dynamic, this tension which is a real component in my life as a nurse? Is it a shared quality with other nurses I know? As a matter of fact, yes, it is. We share this similar yet vaguely unarticulated frustration that there is much we are unable to do because of the bureaucracy of the hospital institution which dictates the volume of patients to be cared for by each nurse and increasingly forces us to accomplish the minimal and more obvious aspects of our care. . . . I must say that in dealing with the issues and conflicts in the nursing profession today I have been moved from a point of pessimistic detachment to a stance of wavering hope. I am remembering, once again, that caring is a profound act of hope and its hidden aspects may not be recognized by our health care system (pp. 1, 2, & 23; published in Benner and Wrubel, 1989, p. 365).

Tracey White's narrative models the kind of educational exploration I have in mind. She comes to grips with the dignity and demands of the work, and moves to a new point of personal hope. This hope is a beginning opening and must be augmented with actual organizational, political, and economic skills that can transform the untenable day to day realities of the nurse clinician. It is not tenable to suggest that nurses just abandon hospital work settings and flee to the community or solo practice. We must find ways to reclaim all work settings for human health care.

As White's essay illustrates, nurses encounter status inequities and many illegitimate stresses not actually tied to the nature of the caring work which has its own legitimate demands. Structural and organizational constraints that prevent adequate performance damage the nurse's sense of self-esteem and efficacy and offer few effective personal coping options. Status inequity, staff shortages, work overload, unpredictable floating or using nurses interchangeably, underpay, et cetera directly undermine the nurse as a knowledge professional and inhibit caregiving practices that are congruent with caring. Therefore nursing education must develop strategies for teaching nurses to design new systems and organizational resources for care. This is true for the generic student as well, but it is an urgent and more plausible educational goal for the returning RN who may have succumbed to adopting low power strategies of victimization and moral outrage. The transition to empowerment and asserting claims for change is a transformation in self understanding and character and not just learning assertive communication techniques, though these techniques are enormously helpful. This is a consciousness raising form of education that allows the student to see the forms of self and other oppression and deliberately take up the political, policy, and organizational development discourses that will transform the conditions of nursing practice. These are social, political, and economic issues that require:

1. The uncovering of the primacy of care and a societal and personal valuing of caring.

2. A transformation of the health care system so that it includes and bridges preventive and low tech care with high tech care.

3. Societal and organizational changes that support and value nursing care allowing the public health and primary care potential of the profession to serve currently unmet health care needs.

4. A revision of organizational structures that are commensurate with nurses' responsibility, and caregiving demands.

Nursing educational programs are places where nurses can learn to develop language and studies that uncover the knowledge embedded in caring practices that have been poorly represented as knowledge.

TOWARD EDUCATING THE NURSE AS A CLINICAL KNOWLEDGE DEVELOPER

If we are to give clinical practice its rightful place as a way of knowing and a form of knowledge development we will need to teach for clinical learning and clinical skill acquisition (Benner, 1984; Dreyfus & Dreyfus, 1985; Benner, Tanner, Chesla, Dreyfus & Dreyfus, & Rubin, in progress). This will require an understanding of the narrative structure of clinical learning and clinical knowledge development. We will need to create opportunities for interpreting actual clinical narratives for the notions of the good, and knowledge embedded in the narratives. Opportunities for observing different levels of practice are also helpful for understanding different stages in skill acquisition. As students progress they can examine their sense of agency, and the nature of their stories. For example, nurses at the proficient stage of skill acquisition begin to see changing relevance in clinical situations moving from an overly planful, analytic approach to being able to recognize and respond to actual changes in the situation (Benner, Tanner, & Chesla, 1992). Returning RN students may or may not have the ability to readily recognize changing relevance, but they are much more in the position to be ready to learn this level of skilled practice. Following narratives of clinical learning over time allows students to develop coherent lines of clinical inquiry and thought from their practices. As students add complexities and nuances to their clinical understanding their clinical performance may deteriorate, and this can be explored as transition into a new level of clinical performance.

SUMMARY AND CONCLUSION

Transforming RN education has the potential for transforming clinical teaching and learning for all students. The returning RN student offers possibilities for clinical learning that the generic student does not have, but this should not cause us to limit the returning RN student to the generic level. Where possible innovative programs should be developed to move the RN student from baccalaureate level to the Master's level. As educators, we should take the opportunity to increase the numbers of nurses who are educationally prepared to move into advanced levels of practice. The returning RN student offers a rich human resource for the profession, and a rich resource for improving our clinical teaching as well as our practice.

REFERENCES

Baier, A. (1985). *Postures of the mind, essays on mind and morals.* Minneapolis: University of Minnesota Press.

Benner, P. (1984). *From novice to expert: Excellence and power in clinical nursing practice.* Menlo Park: Addison-Wesley.

Benner, P. (1991). The role of narrative, practice, and community in skilled ethical comportment. *Advances in Nursing Science, 14*(2), 1–21.

Benner, P., & Wrubel, J. (1989). *The Primacy of Caring.* Menlo Park. Addison-Wesley.

Benner, P., Tanner, C., Chesla, C. (1992). From beginners to expert: Gaining a differentiated clinical world in critical care nursing. *Advances in Nursing Science, 14*(3), 13–28.

Benner, P., Tanner, C., Chesla, C., Dreyfus, H. L., Dreyfus, S. E., Rubin, J. (in progress). *The nature of skill acquisition and human expertise in a practice discipline: Nursing as a case study.*

Collins, H. M. (1985). *Changing order: Replication and induction in scientific practice.* New York: Sage.

Dreyfus, H. L. (1979). *What computers can't do.* New York: Harper & Row.

Dreyfus, H. L., & Dreyfus, S. E. with Athanasiou, T. (1986). *Mind over machine, the power of human intuition and expertise in the era of the computer.* New York: The Free Press.

Dreyfus, H. L. (1990). *Being-in-the-world: A commentary on being and time, division I.* Cambridge, MA: M.I.T. Press.

Lave, J. (1988). *Cognition in practice.* Cambridge, MA: Cambridge University Press.

Lave, J., & Wegner, E. (1991). *Situated learning.* Cambridge, MA: Cambridge University Press.

Maslach, C. (1982). *Burnout—The costs of caring.* Englewood Cliffs, New Jersey: Prentice-Hall.

Polanyi, M. (1958). *Personal knowledge.* London: Routledge & Kegan Paul.

Suchman, L. A. (1987). *Plans and situated actions: The problem of human machine communication.* Cambridge, MA: Cambridge University Press.

2

Rethinking Clinical Judgment

Christine A. Tanner

Like all nursing educators, I've done a lot of thinking about issues in clinical nursing practice, and how best to help our students develop into safe beginning practitioners, who could think on their feet, and make sound decisions. Like all of us, I've wrung my hands over care plans, knew they weren't doing the trick but was afraid to abandon them, because they gave at least some window into how students think about some things. The impetus nearly 20 years ago for my beginning the study of clinical judgment in nursing was my dissatisfaction with the academic care plan as a primary method of teaching and evaluating clinical performance. I had one experience that was a turning point for me.

I was instructor for ten students in various intensive care units in a large city hospital. The students were required to write care plans in preparation for their three days per week of practice and submit them to me at the beginning of their first day. I would review the care plans while the students in each of the units were getting the end of shift report. One student who was caring for a patient post craniotomy wrote as a potential problem dehydration due to diabetes insipidus post craniotomy. The scientific rationale was well-developed. However, to prevent this dehydration her intervention was to clamp the foley. Well, I dashed up the eight flights of stairs to the neuro ICU to find that fortunately she had not done the interventions as written on her care plan. When queried about her care plan, the student responded "Well, Chris, at 2:00 this morning, I needed to come up with an *independent* nursing intervention to address this potential problem, and that was the only thing I could think of." As I reflected on this experience and numerous others, I began to think that the care plan may not be the best method to foster the development of skill in critical thinking and clinical decision making, much less be a reflection of what students actually do in practice.

As an entrant into a doctoral program some 18 years ago, I began a program of research on clinical decision-making/clinical judgment in an effort to find more effective teaching and evaluation approaches. Those years have taken me over interesting, perplexing, and highly convoluted terrain. As a student of cognitive psychology, most of my early research focused on use of rational models—information processing theory, and its methodological derivatives of simulation and verbal protocol analysis. After several studies aimed at describing how beginning and experienced nurses do clinical reasoning, the limitations of the rational models became increasingly clear. They simply could not capture some of the important aspects of skilled nursing performance. For the last several years, I have had the privilege of working with Patricia Benner using interpretive phenomenological approaches to the study of expertise in clinical nursing practice. I don't yet have the answers I started out seeking so many years ago. But through this work, I have new understandings of this highly complex practice we call clinical judgment. In this paper, I will share with you some of what I've learned about the nature of nursing practice and clinical judgment.

The paper is in three parts. In the first part, I will explore some of the nursing literature on clinical judgment, and attempt to show how the rational tradition has influenced the way in which we conceptualize nursing practice and has shaped the ways in which we teach students. In the second part, I will continue along this theme by illustrating what a different view, namely interpretive phenomenology reveals about clinical judgment, that is unaccounted for by the rational models. In the third part, I want to examine our educational practices in light of this new understanding of clinical judgment, and offer some alternative approaches to teaching nursing students.

REVIEW OF NURSING RESEARCH LITERATURE

The Language of Clinical Judgment Research

The language we use in the research literature is problematic from many perspectives. Several phrases are used interchangeably to refer to roughly similar aspects of nursing practice: nursing process, clinical problem solving, diagnostic reasoning, clinical decision making, and critical thinking. All of the terms imply certain meanings, both in the everyday language of our discipline, and to those conversant in the study of this phenomena; and in turn the language used shapes our understanding of the practice. All imply a deliberative rational process, and may be limiting in terms of capturing some important aspects of skilled nursing practice, not characterized by calculative reasoning. Nursing process, problem solving, and diagnostic reasoning all suggest a problem orientation. Despite our social policy statement and nurse practice acts in most states which define nursing as the diagnosis and treatment of human responses to actual or potential health problems, there is much, much more to the clinical judgment of nurses than is implied by this narrow orientation. Moreover, to those conversant in the broader research literature, the terms decision making and problem-solving are both theoretically laden; for example, decision making in the decision theory literature suggests that it is the rational selection of alternatives from a set of mutually exclusive possibilities; the selection is based on values associated with each possible outcome, and the probability of each outcome given the possible course of action. I don't think that this is what most nurse educators mean when they talk about decision making.

For lack of a better term, I use the term clinical judgment to refer to the ways in which nurses come to understand the problems, issues or concerns of clients/patients, to attend to salient information, and to respond in concerned and involved ways. This term is also problematic in that it creates the image of deliberative clinical reasoning and misses totally the skillful, fluid, and intuitive response of the experienced nurse.

Dreyfus and Dreyfus (1986) point out that the meaning of "judgment" changes depending on the skill level of the practitioner—which is partly why it is so difficult to come up with both a generalizable term to capture the performance, and a context-free definition. Here is what they say about acquisition of skills in addressing unstructured problem areas:

> . . . *areas in which the goal, what information is relevant and the effects of our decisions are unclear. Interpretation, whether conscious, as in the case of the competent performer, or nonconscious and based upon holistic discrimination, as for the more skilled, determines what is seen as important in a situation. That interpretive ability constitutes*

'judgment.' Thus according to our description of skill acquisition, the novice and advanced beginner exercise no judgment, the competent performer judges by means of conscious deliberation, and those who are proficient or expert make judgments based upon their prior concrete experiences in a manner that defines explanation. (p. 36).

Major Areas of Investigation

Since the mid-1960s, some 70 studies have appeared in the nursing research literature related to clinical judgment (Tanner, 1987; Fonteyn, 1991). I'd like to briefly review what has appeared in this literature. There are four broad categories of studies. In the first, correlates of clinical judgment, investigators have explored those variables associated with performance in clinical judgment. Clinical judgment performance is typically measured by use of simulation—wherein the subjects' responses to a simulated patient situation are compared with some standard—usually a well educated specialist in the area of practice. Critical thinking, usually as measured by the Watson-Glaser Critical Thinking Appraisal, shows no relationship to measures of clinical judgment. In several cross-sectional studies, both education and years of experience do relate to clinical judgment performance. The more education, the better the performance. Interestingly, in many studies, there is a curvilinear relationship between years of experience and performance, where performance increases for the first six-to-eight years, depending on the study, then declines after that. I suspect that this is a problem of measurement—in that neither what makes up expert performance and what is necessary for the person to perform as an expert can be captured through use of simulation.

The second category, teaching clinical judgment, has not been very promising. There have been only a handful of studies. They have shown that decision analysis is useful when nurses are provided with decision trees relevant to the problem at hand, but no study has demonstrated any teaching approach which actually improves general performance in clinical judgment. Interestingly, I have never been able to locate a single published study which examines the effectiveness of the nursing care plan as a teaching method.

The third category, measures of clinical judgment, has included principally studies reporting psychometric characteristics of various forms of simulations. While most are purportedly reliable, the studies which have examined the relationship between performance on simulation and performance in practice suggest that these measures have questionable validity. As we will later see, it may also be a basic problem in assumptions underlying these measures.

In the fourth category, the largest by far, are numerous studies describing how expert nurses make judgments, and/or how beginners differ from those experts, or develop in their clinical judgment skill. It is this last category of research in which I've done most of my work, and which obviously I think has the greatest potential for influencing our practice as educators. This research greatly influences our understanding of what clinical judgment is, how nurses ought to do it, and thereby clearly shapes all of our educational practices.

Two major approaches to this grouping of studies have been: (1) the rational or cognitive models, such as decision analysis or information processing theory, grouped together because of their shared assumptions; and (2) those rooted in a phenomenological perspective. These two approaches differ greatly in their underlying assumptions, questions, and methods, and understanding these differences will help us sort out our educational practices. Generally, the studies using cognitive models tell us that, for the most part, there are differences between beginner and expert, but that there is a huge problem of "task-specificity," i.e., that performance and approach vary greatly by the so-called "demands of the task-environment." (See for example, Corcoran, 1986; Tanner, Padrick, Westfall and Putzier, 1987). Using interpretive approaches, however, Benner has helped us understand the situational nature of expertise, and why these cognitive models attempting to capture a context-free set of strategies must inevitably fall short.

Assumptions of Cognitive Models

The approach to the study of clinical judgment in nursing, relying on the cognitive models, has emphasized the search for thinking strategies that are used and/or are useful regardless of the particular aspects of the patient situation. Studies on nursing clinical judgment using cognitive models focus almost exclusively on some context-free set of strategies that might characterize human performance when faced with a class of tasks. Cognitive models are firmly rooted in the Western philosophic tradition of rationalism, and these assumptions in turn are deeply embedded in our practice as educators, even if we don't accept their translation into some of the research methods and findings. In the rationalist view it is assumed that it is possible to make explicit all the important knowledge, beliefs, and assumptions that we bring to bear on any particular decision situation. Hence, research methods are directed toward making these aspects of decision making explicit; decision analysis models for example, require that probability statements be expressed regarding the value of particular outcomes, and the likelihood that those outcomes will be produced with different interventions.

The Western philosophical tradition is based on the assumption that detached theoretical knowledge is superior to the involved practical viewpoint. The scientist who devises theories is discovering how things really are, while ordinary people in everyday life have only a clouded idea. In clinical judgment, the clinician who stands outside the clinical situation in a detached objective way, collecting or at least sorting data into objective and subjective piles is likely to arrive at superior judgments compared to the clinician who gets involved in the situation.

The final assumption is that of mental representations as a way of perceiving the world. The common sense of our discipline and of the western tradition is that in order to perceive and relate to things, we have some content in our minds that corresponds to our knowledge of them. The assumption of representation shows up in much of our literature aimed toward theories and concepts as guides for action—assuming that underlying every human action, most notably expert human action is a theory in some form of mental representation.

The assumptions of rationalism show up in our understanding of nursing practice. In the diagnosis treatment model, nursing is the diagnosis and treatment of human responses to actual or potential health problems. On this view, nursing, like other professional practices is the instrumental application of theory and scientifically-based knowledge to the problems of practice (or the technical-rationality model of practice, Schon, 1983). Teaching is then directed toward acquisition of facts, principles, theory; clinical teaching emphasizes the application of theoretical knowledge to the particular patient. Emphasis is on the nursing process, planned care based upon a solid scientific rationale.

On this view there is little room for other than analytic approaches to narrowly defined patient problems. The role of the context, the nature of the situation, the importance of embodied know-how and emotion as aspects of clinical judgment simply cannot be accounted for on this view. As Gardner (1985) summarized:

*A feature of the cognitive science is the deliberate attempt to deempha-
size certain factors which may be important for cognitive functioning
but whose inclusion at this point would unnecessarily complicate the
cognitive-science enterprise. These factors include the influence of affective factors or emotion, the contribution of historical or cultural factors
and the role of the background context in which the particular actions or
thoughts occurred. (p. 6)*

The Interpretive Turn

Beginning in the early 80s Patricia Benner introduced Heideggerian
phenomenology to the study of nursing practice. Heidegger's philosophy stands in stark contrast to the rationalist tradition. While I would
never pretend to be a Heideggerian scholar, some of his writings, and
Dreyfus's and others' interpretations of them are particularly helpful
in extending our understanding of nursing as a practice (Heidegger,
1927/1962; Benner & Wrubel, 1989; Dreyfus, 1979; 1987; 1992; Dreyfus
& Dreyfus, 1986; Packer, 1988; Winograd & Flores, 1991).

The object of study in an interpretive phenomenological study is
the semantic structure of everyday practical activity—what people actually do when they are engaged in the everyday tasks of life. Heidegger (1927/1962) distinguished three modes of engagement: The *ready-to-
hand* mode is the most basic one. This is the mode of most practical
day-to-day activities, in which one's awareness is essentially holistic;
that is, a person's awareness of the situation in which she is engaged
cannot be broken down into discrete physical objects, but is understood as a network of interrelated projects. The *unready-to-hand* mode is
entered when the individual encounters some problem or breakdown
in the practical activity which interrupts the ready-to-hand mode. The
source of the breakdown becomes salient in a way that it was not in the
ready-to-hand mode. However, it is still seen as an aspect of the task,
rather than as an element which can be examined out of context. The
present-at-hand mode is entered only when the individual detaches her
self from ongoing practical activity and relies on use of rational calculative processes to deal with the breakdown. Here, the individual
analyzes the elements of the situation out of context.

The ready-to-hand mode is the starting place for interpretive inquiry. The study of nursing practice using this approach is the study of
what nurses actually do when they are engaged in the everyday practice of delivering nursing care. The interpretive approach seeks to

make explicit the practical understanding of human actions by providing an interpretation of them.

This aspect of Heidegger's work is central to our consideration of clinical judgment in nursing. The rational models which have dominated most of our research on clinical judgment as well as our teaching practices completely overlook the ready-to-hand way of engagement. In stark contrast to the tenets of rationalism, Heidegger argued that the ways in which we render the world and our lives understandable cannot be made completely explicit. There is no neutral viewpoint from which we can see our beliefs as objects, since we always operate within the background framework that our beliefs provide. The interpreter and the interpreted do not exist independently; existence is interpretation and interpretation is existence.

Heidegger reverses the value of practical vs. theoretical understanding, insisting that we have primary access to the world through involvement with the ready-to-hand. On this view, detached contemplation can be illuminating, but it can also obscure phenomena by isolating and categorizing them. To categorize human experiences with illness along the lines of nursing diagnosis often obscures rather than clarifies our understanding of and responses to people.

Connected to both of the preceding points is Heidegger's rejection of the primacy of mental representation. If we focus on concernful activity instead of on detached contemplation, the status of this representation is called into question. Using Heidegger's favorite illustration—in driving a nail with a hammer (as opposed to thinking about a hammer) one does not need to make use of any explicit conceptualization of the hammer or think about any of its properties or defining characteristics. One's ability to act comes from his familiarity with hammering, not his knowledge of a hammer. In Heidegger's view, it is possible to know and act without such conceptual guides to action.

Benner, in her widely acclaimed work (1984) applied the Dreyfus model of skill acquisition to the study of nursing expertise. The model, drawing on Heideggerian phenomenology, points to skilled performance as ready-to-hand, and reverses the western assumptions of what constitutes expertise. Benner found that as expertise develops practice changes in at least four major ways: (1) movement from reliance on abstract principles and rules to use of past, concrete experience; (2) shift from reliance on analytic, rule based thinking to intuition; (3) change in the nurses' perception of the situation from one in which it is viewed as a compilation of equally relevant bits to an increasingly complex whole in which certain aspects are salient; (4) passage from detached observer, standing outside the situation to a position of involvement, fully engaged in the situation. This is a departure from the rationalist views of expertise in at least two important ways: (1) the relative emphasis on practical vs. theoretical knowledge; (2) the importance of involved, situated understanding as opposed to disengaged reasoning.

AN INTERPRETIVE STUDY OF SKILLED CLINICAL JUDGMENT

Now, for the last seven years, I've had the opportunity to work with Patricia Benner; the last four have been a collaboration with many others on the study of expertise in critical care nursing.[1] Briefly, the purposes of that study were to: (1) describe clinical knowledge embedded in the practice of expert ICU nurses; (2) describe the nature of skill acquisition in critical care nursing; (3) identify institutional impediments and resources to expert practice; and (4) identify educational innovations that might help our students eventually become expert practitioners. We interviewed 130 nurses, mostly BS prepared and mostly practicing in ICUs, in eight hospitals in three metropolitan areas. They were grouped by level of experience and identified expertise as follows: (1) new graduate up to six months out of school; (2) intermediate with up to two years of ICU experience; (3) proficient with at least five years of experience; and (4) expert also with at least five years of experience and identified by co-workers as the outstanding nurses in the unit. These nurses were interviewed in groups (by level of experience) and 48 of them were also observed intensively and interviewed individually about how their practice developed. The narrative accounts provided by these nurses and the observations of them in their practice provided rich data for interpretation of skill development in clinical judgment.

In the following account, the nurse's central concern was her involvement with the family of a dying patient. In it we will see illustrated several dimensions of family care which Catherine Chesla has recently explicated in her analysis of our data (Chesla, 1990). The nurse

[1] *Clinical Expertise in Nursing*. Funded by the Helene Fuld Health Trust, Patricia Benner and Christine Tanner, Co-principal Investigators; Catherine Chesla, Project Director. With assistance from Stuart and Hubert Dreyfus, and Jane Rubin.

seeks out the family, is solicited by their story of H.'s illness and suffering, and recognizes their preeminent position in the patient's world. There is a shift in the nurse's focus of care from the patient to the family. She provides perspective for the family through her experience with similar patients, orienting the family to the patient's current status and possible outcomes, while being sensitive to the family's ability to hear and understand her explanations. Also significant in this account is the nurse's already understanding the severity of H.'s condition, setting up what would stand out in the situation as relevant.

Nurse: *We had a patient who had been in the OR having a CABG (coronary artery bypass graft). I'd gotten word that he had been hospitalized before, had a very poor heart, multiple MI's, poor ejection fraction. As I was coming to work that evening, I had also gotten word that his family was sitting and waiting in our waiting room. The patient wasn't back from surgery yet, and I heard they were there, so I thought I'll go out and meet them, which I try to do when it works out that way. They were stressed to the max; the minute I walked out they jumped off the chair, they knew I was coming to talk with them. I introduced myself, explained that we really don't hear much until they actually get up to the unit and just talked about what to expect and that they could come in after an hour or so. They proceeded to tell me this whole story about what this poor man had gone through and how it was so rough on him, and so on.*

So the patient returned from surgery, and sure enough, was sick as everything, on every drip known to man, ballooned, had had a real hard time coming off bypass, the whole thing. As I listened to report and I went into the room, looked at him, and it was clear that it's going to be a miracle if this man leaves this hospital alive. That was the sense I had. So I got settled. I went out and had the family come and just tried to give them a sense of what to expect . . . And we just hit it off or something. They needed—it was like they were just looking for this release valve and I gave it to them. At that point we just kind of clicked.

A few days went by and the patient was really sick, but eventually, amazingly he kind of turned the corner and we were able to start weaning drips. We got him de-ballooned. We got him extubated. And we were all astounded that this man was alive, he was extubated, he was lucid, and he was talking to me. His grandson came in and visited, and his grandson was his pride and joy. The two of them were going at it.

He told me how he got his nickname, what he did with his grandson, went to this ballgame, to that ballgame. But it was still obvious, even though he looked better, it was really obvious that he was very, very fragile and any little thing was going to tip him over the edge. And another day or so went by, and it came time to pull his chest tubes and unfortunately he got a pneumothorax and that was all he needed. I knew that any little thing was just going to be his demise, and sure enough he ended up having to get reintubated, chest tubes put in. It was decided at that point that what he needed was medical management and he was sent back to CCU.

A few days later, his family came up looking for me. H. had gotten to the point where he was in end-stage cardiac disease and there was nothing else they could do and they finally decided to make him a DNR. I said to the family, "do you mind if I just go in and see him?" At that point he was ventilated and sedated and paralyzed and he had the tropical IVAC forest behind the bed. I had seen him that sick but it bothered me to go down there and see him that sick again. He had gotten better and my last image of him was this man sitting up in bed raving about his grandson.

I went out to the family; they were obviously preparing themselves for his death, and I just felt awful 'cause here I see this man getting better then right back to being as sick as he could possibly be. They were beside themselves. I think they felt guilty about making him DNR and they had this insatiable need to know that they had done everything they could. They felt like, well, maybe there's more.

Interviewer: *Were they asking you that?*

Nurse: *Not in those words, but that was the sense I was getting from what they were saying. Finally, it hit me. I just got this image of him sitting up in bed talking to his grandson and I said, you did do everything. Look how sick he was when he first came into the unit. He got better. We helped get him as better as his heart would let him get. But his heart was too sick. They were kind of able to say, "Yeah, I guess we did." He did get better, but he was just too fragile.*

At that point, all of us are sitting in the room, tears are coming down the eyes and at that point they were able to just kind of loosen up and talk about him. And talk. It was like they were preparing themselves for his death. And you know it just seemed like someone sort of took them off the hook. You don't have to feel guilty anymore. At this point, mak-

ing him a DNR was the kindest thing you could do for him. I feel like in that situation, even though the outcome for the patient was bad, I was able to make a difference with them, because they were going through a lot. It was kind of hard for me, because its always stressful when someone dies and you have to go and tell the family. You know, it's always "What do I say," you know, where do the words come from? For him, I drew on the situation of him, being sick, getting better, look at these milestones he's gone through just in the past few weeks. It's especially hard in those situations where I have to tell the family. I don't mind so much if I know them, but if they don't know me and know what I've been through with their family member, I don't like that. Sometimes I feel like I really know them and that they would appreciate hearing it from someone they know and that someone they know cares and has worked really hard with them, and with the patient.

First, it should be apparent from this exemplar how little of the practice could be captured by a diagnosis-treatment model. The nurse was solicited by the patient and family, "just sort of clicked." She recognized the patient's fragility, saying it was "really obvious that any little thing might tip him over." She immediately understood how on edge the family was, and responded to their need for a "release valve." No theoretical label can capture the meaning of this experience for the family— labels characteristically used in the nursing diagnosis literature (such as ineffective family coping) simply do not convey sufficient meaning for this nurse to know how to respond to the family's concerns. What's transparent in the practice is the skill of managing rapidly changing situations—understanding the patient's fragile state, managing the ventilator, chest tubes, and drips—these simply do not show up as an issue for the nurse, although clearly she was responsible for this aspect of the patient's care. This non-conscious holistic discrimination of the patient's state and appropriate response with little evidence of deliberation is characteristic of expert clinical judgment. There is no evidence of analytical reasoning to discern either the patient's medical status, nor the family's concerns.

At least six aspects of clinical judgment are apparent in this narrative that tend to be overlooked, or simply not show up in studies framed by cognitive models: (1) the role of context and the situation; (2) the role of narrative; (3) the interplay of theoretical knowledge and practical know-how; (4) the role of intuition and reason; (5) the role of emotion; (6) the importance of knowing the patient.

The Role of the Situation

Cognitive models control for context by producing simulated situations that minimize possibilities for "extraneous" variables. According to cognitive models the private subject stands in opposition to an objective situation, controlling what data to collect, deciding what actions are relevant given the data. The subject stands outside the situation, touching it only through mental representations. In stark contrast is the view that judgment can only occur in the context of a particular situation, where meaningful aspects simply stand out as important and where the choice of responses is guided by the nurses' interpretation of the situation. Nurses inhabit their clinical world in an involved way, rather than in a subject-object way of the cognitive models.

Here, this nurse was solicited by the family's concerns. Standing outside of the situation was not even a possibility for her. She understood the past for this patient, had an immediate clinical grasp of the current, and could project the future. Because of this understanding, the nurse could project the future for the family. She gave the family a "sense of what to expect," drawing on their story of his past, and understanding of the current situation and a projection of the likely future. Families, of course, have great difficulty with this; everything is new to them, and they are unable to project or plan during this time.

In her narrative, this nurse, like many others in our study, refers to "getting settled." This may be interpreted as getting situated. It is getting to know the particularities of this patient situation—here, getting a sense of the patient—"I looked at him;" his medical management like the drips, IV sites, chest tubes, character of drainage, EKG, arterial lines, pulmonary artery line. Once she had gotten "settled," knew what was immediately needed by the patient, she could attend to the family's concerns. Nurses also talk about being "off," not having a grasp of the immediate, "working stupid," where they mean simply they are not situated. They aren't in the position of having the most salient aspects show up; instead they may resort to calculative reasoning, collecting elements of information to try to get a bigger picture. Until they get situated, they feel uneasy.

The Role of Narrative

This exemplar also illustrates the important role of narrative in clinical judgment. Early in the situation, the family gave the patient's story, a story of extreme illness and suffering. Throughout the nurse's account is a sense of her increasing involvement with both the patient and his family by understanding his story, how his illness has disrupted it and his relationships with family, particularly his grandson.

Kleinman and his associates have called attention to the narrative component of illness, claiming that patient narratives may help clinicians direct their attention not only to the biological world of disease but to the human world of meanings, values, and concerns (Kleinman, Eisenberg, & Good, 1978; Kleinman, 1988). Bruner (1986) claims that human motives, intents and meanings are understood through narrative thinking, which he contrasts with paradigmatic thinking that conforms to the rules of logic. It is clear in this exemplar that understanding the patient's situation and connecting with the family was made possible by hearing their account of the experience with the illness. Further, this understanding set up the nurse's ordering of priorities— seeing the patient first, then meeting again with the family. Ultimately this understanding also created the possibility for her to respond to the family's grief and feelings of guilt in an involved, meaningful way; this would not have been accomplished had she stood outside the situation, or not engaged in hearing the human dimensions of their experience. In short, narratives communicate aspects of the human experience with illness that cannot be conveyed through decontextualized abstract labels, or through disengaged, analytic reasoning.

The Importance of Knowing the Patient

This exemplar illustrates a pervasive, yet virtually invisible aspect of nursing practice referred to nearly universally as "knowing the patient." (Tanner, Benner, Chesla, & Gordon, in review). As in this exemplar nurses would simply comment "I really knew him" or "I was the only staff member who knew him." In cases of breakdown, it was not uncommon for nurses to explain as a source of breakdown, "I didn't know the patient." Embedded in the discourse of knowing the patient is meaning central to the nurses' practice: getting a grasp of the patient, getting situated, understanding the patient's circumstance in context with salience, nuances, and qualitative distinctions. Nurses use the phrase to refer to two distinct ways in which they know their patients: (1) knowing the patient's typical pattern of responses; and (2) knowing the patient as a person. Both are central to skilled clinical judgment. Here is an excerpt that illustrates the former. This is a nurse who works in newborn intensive care. The excerpt illustrates how knowing the patient's patterns of responses is the nurse's basis for particularizing care.

> *The baby I'm taking care of now is a twitty little preemie. She is the ultimate preemie. All you have to do is walk in front of her isolette and have a shadow fall across her face and she desaturates. She cannot stand knowing there is anyone else in the world, but I found that I was able to suction her by myself and keep her saturation in the 90's just by being slow and careful. This baby usually has terrible bradycardia and desaturations when she is suctioned. She developed a reputation for being a real little nerd, but I haven't had any problem with her for the first couple of hours.*

Knowing the preemie is personalized and particularistic even though this baby's responses are typical of premature babies, as the nurse notes, "she is the ultimate preemie." Knowing the particular baby and her responses is at the heart of clinical judgment about the source of the baby's oxygen desaturation and bradycardia and directs the nurse's care for the baby.

In the exemplar describing the nurse's care of H. and his family, several other aspects of knowing the patient stand out. Clearly, the nurse got to know H. and his experience with the illness through the family; then she was open to him, to the way in which he expressed his concerns, his caring for his family, his wishes regarding continuing life support. Through knowing H., the nurse's clinical judgements were based not on external interpretations, but on the meanings as constituted by the patient and his family.

The Role of Emotion

Also evident in this exemplar is the role of emotion. The nurse describes how it bothered her to see H. so sick. She referred to coming to understand his world as "My last image of him was this man sitting up in bed raving about his grandson." For this nurse, the patient is no longer a medical case, but a person with a life full of meaning. She is engaged emotionally in a part of his life world, and "feels awful." This emotional involvement made it possible for her to respond to the family in a sensitive and meaningful way.

Two other important aspects of emotional involvement are overlooked by cognitive models. First, we are learning from our study that learning how to be involved with patients and their families is a skill—learned through trial and error—instances range from being "over-involved" and feeling with the patient their pain and suffering, to a detached, uninvolved stance in which the practice becomes flat and meaningless. Through these experiences nurses get involvement right. Learning to cry with families, as the nurse did in this exemplar is one small aspect of learning the skill of involvement.

Another important role of emotion is its service to clinical judgment. The experienced nurse has finely attuned emotional responses that serve to alert her that something may be awry. They feel uneasy, anxious when the clinical situation doesn't match expectations, yet they still don't have a full clinical grasp. This vague feeling of disease signals the experienced nurse to explore further. In contrast, the new graduate is often overwhelmed by anxiety and fear of making a mistake, and to cope may simply have to dampen emotional responses (Benner, Tanner, & Chesla, 1992).

The Role of Intuition and Reason

In our prior studies, we have described the role of intuition in clinical judgment (Benner, 1984; Benner & Tanner, 1987), and this exemplar illustrates several aspects of intuition. We used the term intuition to refer to a judgment without a rationale. This is not to say that the judgment is irrational, only that it is not arrived at through rational, conscious, or calculative reasoning. It is a direct apprehension of the meaning of a situation.

In this exemplar, the nurse recognizes a pattern of likely demise. She says, "It was really obvious that he was very, very fragile and that any little thing was going to tip him over the edge." It is not clear from her description why it was obvious. However, it is likely that in the care she was providing she was seeing a pattern of responses characteristic of "fragileness"—noticing what happens when the patient is turned, coughs, eats, etc., noticing fluctuations that go beyond the expected range of responses.

I think what often troubles educators about the notion of intuition is that we cannot account for how the judgments are made; a logical argument may be constructed occasionally, but there is no apparent rationale. There is a tacit cultural assumption here that calculative reasoning based in scientific principles is always superior to direct and immediate apprehension. In the rational model, the proof in our conclusions lies largely in the way we reached them—through a logical sequence of thought. There is no such external proof for judgment by intuition. Dreyfus and Dreyfus (1985) describe one approach that is a safeguard to wildly wrong intuition, without recourse to calculative reasoning—that of deliberative rationality:

> *The conscious use of calculative rationality produces regression to the skill of the novice or at best, the competent performer. To think rationally in that sense is to forsake know-how and is not usually desirable. If decisions are important and time is available, a more basic form of rationality than that of the beginner is useful. This kind of deliberative rationality does not seek to analyze the situation into context-free elements, but seeks to test and improve whole intuitions. (p. 36)*

We have evidence in numerous other exemplars of experienced nurses employing this strategy. It is particularly apparent when they are preparing to make a case with a physician for different treatment options than those currently prescribed; they want to assure themselves that their grasp of the situation is the best one available, and they purposefully test out other possible understandings of the situation. Other approaches include (1) considering the relevance and adequacy of past experiences that may underlie a current intuition and (2) consideration of possible consequences if the intuition is wrong.

THE INTERPLAY OF THEORETICAL KNOWLEDGE AND PRACTICAL KNOW-HOW

The role of practical knowledge in skilled professional practice is increasingly claiming attention of scholars from diverse fields (e.g., Kuhn, 1968; Polanyi, 1962; Schon, 1983, Benner, 1984). Benner described several ways in which practical knowledge shows up in the practice of expert nurses. The above exemplar illustrates how this nurse's understanding, expectations, and sets from caring for many, many patients after CABG created the possibility for her grasp of H.'s likely prognosis. She knew from her experience what a patient should look like after CABG, she knew the likely course of recovery. When she looked at H., she knew that "it's going to be a miracle if this man leaves this hospital alive."

The narrative accounts provided by nurses in the study are rich with examples of practical knowledge and skilled know-how. Qualitative distinctions are common, such as knowing when a patient is comfortable, distinguishing between want and need, recognizing the color of diminished cardiac output, and seeing the subtle changes in color over time, all of which are only possible in the context of deep background of experience with similar situations. (Rubin, in progress)

In the tradition of cognitive modeling, the only knowledge that counts is that which can be formalized and rendered explicit. But it is becoming increasingly clear that we know more than we can say. Distinctions among knowing—that and knowing how (Benner, 1983), tacit knowledge, knowing-in-action, appear throughout nursing literature. As participants in the Western tradition, it is now tempting for us to reverse the hierarchy, placing supreme value of practical knowledge over theoretical knowledge. Dreyfus (1987) cautions us about this likelihood and points out the important interrelationship between practical and theoretical knowledge:

> *The relations between these important human capacities is much too complex to be captured in any hierarchy. Nursing is a special combination of theory and practice in which it is clear that theory guides practice and practice grounds theory in a way which undercuts any philosophical attempt to say which is superior to the other. Likewise, in cases of breakdown or in new areas where intuition is not developed, reasoning and theory are necessary guides, but reasoning always presupposes a background of intuitions which can never be replaced by rationality and the necessity of intuitively guided practice. Nursing is a skill which relies on theoretical understanding. Although the expert nurse will find that he or she relies on fewer and fewer rules in applying theory to practice, practice will be improved not just by experience, but by a deeper and deeper understanding of theory. (p. 9).*

EDUCATIONAL IMPLICATIONS FOR UNDERGRADUATE EDUCATION

The findings from our study challenge some of the basic assumptions which guide current educational practices in nursing and other health professions. Here I will outline some of the assumptions, highlight the evidence we have which challenges the assumptions, and suggest some general ways in which nursing educational experiences may be restructured. Then I will discuss one experimental approach which attempts to incorporate some of these ideas.

Assumptions Challenged by This Study

1. The Nature of Clinical Decision Making/Clinical Judgment. Our emphasis on classroom didactic teaching and the use of nursing process as a major instructional and evaluation strategy, may foster the development of analytic thinking. This emphasis carries with it the assumption that disengaged reasoning is always more reliable than involved practice. We have found in our work that disengaged, analytic thinking, standing back from a situation, is a useful strategy for the beginner who is flooded with anxiety or emotion. Our work also shows that with experience, nurses become more involved rather than more detached; they grasp the meaning of a situation directly rather than through analytic thinking; knowing the patient, his usual patterns of responses and knowing him as a person, in embodied direct ways figure prominently in their clinical judgments. Detached analytic reasoning is needed in cases of breakdown, where direct apprehension doesn't occur, or when the nurse notices that vague, uneasy feeling of not having the right grasp.

While we would expect that problem solving and analytic thinking will continue to be important in our educational practices, students also need experiences that will help them understand how their clinical thinking will develop. They also need experience in: (a) problem identification—practice with fuzzy underdetermined situations, which rely on recognition of changing relevance and historically based understanding, rather than solely theoretical predictions of anticipated problems; (b) experiences in overcoming secondary ignorance—knowing what they don't know; (c) experience in having direct apprehension of a complex clinical situation, reflecting on their newly acquired skilled know-how; (d) experience in hearing and interpreting narrative accounts of patients' stories, understanding the patient's concerns and ways of coping without having to analyze from a detached stance.

2. The Relation between Theory and Practice. In our traditional approaches to nursing education, we have assumed that practice is the instrumental application of research based theory to the solution of patient care problems. The direction between theory and practice is predominately one-way—theory guides practice. The students are taught theory in the classroom, then clinical experiences are sought which help them apply this theory to the care of their patients (sometimes with great difficulty since available practice situations seldom correspond directly with what is taught in "theory" classes).

Our research has pointed out that the relationship between theory and practice is far more complex than the traditional assumptions (educational practices) suggest. Theory is extremely important for guiding the beginning clinician to the right region—for example, to know *that* he or she should evaluate a patient for fluid in the lungs or crepitus. Theory is also important for helping nurses learn to expect certain kinds of responses when addressing illness, suffering and comfort issues—for example that a grieving family may show a range of emotions from rage to complete denial. Such theory however, by definition as an abstraction, falls short of the mark in describing the particular situation and in guiding even the beginning clinician's response. Practice must also be guided by attending to individual patient and family responses, how clinical problems are manifested in particular patients, compared to how theory would suggest their manifestation; practice must also be guided by attending to the human concerns of illness and suffering, by understanding the particular patient's and family's issues, concerns, and ways of coping. The know-how needed for skilled clinical practice is overlooked by the traditional view of the relationship between theory and practice.

Clinical experiences are essential for far more learning than the direct application of theory to practice. Students need experience to help fill out the theory, to learn to make qualitative distinctions, for example to recognize what crepitus is like in different situations. Moreover, students need experience in remaining open to clinical situations—rather than having responses all worked out in advance, as we often expect them to do, they also need experience in learning to attend to particular patient responses in particular situations. They need experience working side by side with an experienced nurse who can help point out salience, nuances and qualitative distinction, and who can guide them in clinical interpretive activities. They need experience and guidance in recognizing the limits of formal theory in describing, predicting, or responding to particular patients concerns. They need practice in reflection—the kind of reflection that stays true to the issues in the particular clinical situation.

From our study, we have identified a number of learning issues which show up repeatedly in the narratives of beginning and competent level nurses. These issues illustrate what must be learned *from* practice, areas which cannot be directed through traditional conceptions of the theory-practice relationship. Among these issues are: (1) gaining a sense of self as a nurse; (2) coping with technology and the technology/human interface; (3) developing a sense of future possibilities—learning about trajectories, and learning to keep open to the possibilities in the situation; (4) negotiating with physicians, moving from a stance of delegating responsibility "up" to assuming responsibility for making a case for what a patient needs in a particular situation; (5) facing suffering and death; (6) learning the skill of involvement; (7) learning to cope with their own anxieties, fears, and concerns; and (8) getting situated in the practice—learning timing, the sense of personal, patient and family space, learning the art of watchfulness, and learning the pace of the unit. These are clearly not issues guided by a theoretical account of the practice, but must be learned through experience.

3. The Separation of Thought from Emotion; Cognitive from Affective. In our traditional approaches to education, we have carried on with the Cartesian tradition of separating mind from body, of the objective, observable measurable from the subjective, inner experiencing. By the nearly universal adoption of the behavioral model of education in nursing, we have directed our teaching only toward those outcomes which could be expressed behaviorally and measured objectively. We have gone to great extremes to write "terminal," level and course, behavioral outcomes, carefully separating the cognitive from the affective from the psychomotor.

At issue from our work is that this educational model overlooks and in some ways covers over the possibility of embodied knowing, the role of emotion in skilled judgment, the skill of involvement, and the role of narrative in grasping a situation.

SOME SUGGESTED TEACHING APPROACHES

These assumptions are basic to our educational practices. Simply adding new strategies to our collection of teaching approaches is not what our study suggests, but rather it proposes fairly significant changes in the selection of content and experiences for the curriculum, in the relationship between theory and practice courses, in the approach to classroom teaching, and in the kind of clinical experiences offered to students.

Identified below are some particular areas in which teaching practices may be modified and which are supported by a different set of assumptions. It is important to note that the salience of any particular approach is dependent on the student's prior experience with similar situations, their grasp of the current situation, and their command of theoretical knowledge relevant to the situation.

1. Provide frequent opportunities for students to "fill out" the theory in clinical practice particularly in learning to make qualitative distinctions and in problem identification in fuzzy and underdetermined situations. These opportunities may be provided through (a) interactive video or other format for presentation of simulated or actual patients presenting with particular problems, issues or concerns; (b) teaming with competent or expert nurses, "rounding" on patients who have similar problems or concerns, where qualitative distinctions can be pointed out; (c) more experience with the same patient population over time. Much of our efforts now are directed toward providing students with diverse experiences, so they have a small dose of experiences with a variety of patients. It may be desirable to have experience with the same population (e.g., patients with selected chronic conditions, expectant or new mothers) throughout the upper division curriculum, with expert guidance in seeing the different issues and concerns of individuals and families and those that are shared among the population.

2. Particularly for experienced RN students, opportunities for students to reflect on past experiences in light of new theoretical or scientific information is important, as is the opportunity to challenge, test and refine theoretical knowledge in clinical practice.

3. Reduce reliance on the nursing care plan as the primary instructional and evaluation method. It may be useful in the early portions of the curriculum, to help provide students a broad framework for thinking like a nurse. But in virtually every clinical situation, the kind of decision making is much more dynamic than can be captured on a static plan of care.

The following alternatives may be used for teaching the kind of clinical thinking required in practice: (a) use guided reflective writing, helping students recall the specifics of a clinical situation, their thoughts, feelings and actions, comparing what they found with the expectations and sets developed from formal theoretical knowledge, from prior experience in nursing or from their personal knowledge; (b) use interaction with faculty and preceptors during clinical practice not solely for recall of factual information as it might apply in the particular situation, but for noticing and pointing out changes in the situation, coaching the student in considering how the plan of care may change.

4. Restore the narrative to the undergraduate curriculum. Illness has a narrative component. Illness interrupts a patient's and family's stories. Expert and competent nurses get to know the patient often through narrative accounts of their experiences. They know what matters to the patient and family in their illness and recovery. This way of knowing is covered over by the emphasis on theory and instrumentalization of formal assessment procedures—e.g., acquiring a formal medical and social history which objectifies the patient's experience. In clinical experiences or in other ways, students can be coached to learn the patient's story as well as their history.

An Educational Innovation

At Oregon Health Sciences University, an experimental course was developed for beginning students. It was an effort to test an alternative approach to instruction that challenged some of the basic assumptions of our traditional educational practices. This approach grew from our new understandings about the development of expertise in nursing practice, and relied extensively on the role of narrative and the use of writing as a way of learning (Allen, Bowers, & Diekelmann, 1989).

The course titled "Living with Chronic Illness" was structured to focus on patients' narrative accounts of their experiences with chronic illness. We chose three conditions which we thought would be representative of some of the issues of living with a chronic condition— COPD, HIV disease and Alzheimer's. Each of the three conditions were taken up by the class for a three week period. The first of the three weeks, at least one patient, and in the case of Alzheimer's, three families, talked about their experiences of living with the condition.

Prior to the discussion with the patient or family, students were given some basic reading—usually research about living with the condition and a brief, fairly simple reading outlining the pathology of the disease and its treatment. They were given a set of questions to guide their thinking and writing in preparation for hearing from the patient. The questions asked them to reflect on their own personal experiences, on what they knew formally about the condition, and what they expected to hear from the patient or family.

The second of the three weeks, an expert clinician presented exemplars and paradigm cases from his or her practice and responded to students' questions about nursing practices in caring for these particular patients. Prior to this class session, the students were given a set of questions to guide their writing about: (a) reflections on what they had heard from the patients, recalling, describing, and interpreting a particular instance reported by the patient, identifying the problems and central concerns, and suggesting in broad terms the nursing responsibilities and practices that might be responsive to these concerns; (b) how they felt in response to the patient; (c) to anticipate, again in broad ways the kind of nursing roles that the experts might describe; (d) posing one or more questions about facts, principles or theory that would be needed to provide care to the specific patient who presented in class.

The third of the three weeks was devoted to discussion of the students' reflections, questions and concerns. Prior to this class, they were encouraged to find ways to answer pressing questions that could be answered through textbooks or discussions with faculty and peers. They were also asked to write about their reflections on the clinicians' accounts of particular situations.

This course was set up to meet several aims, and in many instances achieved them. These were:

1. Learning to recognize what knowledge is needed to respond to patients concerns and to find ways to obtain that knowledge.

2. Hearing narrative accounts of patients' experiences in coping with illness, interpreting those accounts, and identifying the central concerns.

3. Capturing the beginning student's naive compassion, and showing how that may be focused on interpreting concerns of patients and in advocating for them.

4. Beginning to grasp aspects of nursing practice (e.g., coaching, teaching, monitoring and recognizing early problems) in the care of chronically ill patients.

5. Recognizing personal knowledge, biases and sets, and how this may impact nursing practice.

6. Working on the skill of involvement.

7. Beginning to understand the role of emotion in clinical judgment—tuning in to the anger when the system has failed to respond to a patient's or family's need; recognizing the feeling of discomfort when the knowledge needed is not there.

8. Beginning to understand the model of skill acquisition, and developing some comfort in being a novice.

Probably as much factual, theoretical content on the pathology and nursing care of patients with these conditions was "covered" in the class as would have been in a traditional lecture course. But it was particularized and students were helped to see the limits of formal theory in accounting for and describing a specific patient's experiences and in their particular manifestations of the disease.

This teaching approach was used for undergraduate students, with limited experience. There was one LPN student in the course, several graduate students interested in seeing how the teaching approach was working, and several faculty. I would venture to say that we all learned a great deal about coping with a chronic illness in general, and about these patients' experiences in particular. For all of us new questions were raised—from the pathology of the condition to the atrocities in the health care system in its lack of responsiveness and resources. My point is that I think it might be a useful approach for students with experience in nursing practice, though their learnings are likely to be quite different from the students not in practice.

SUMMARY

In this paper, I've attempted to explicate ways in which the cognitive models rooted in the rational tradition have dominated our thinking about clinical judgment in nursing—both in framing research into so-called "cognitive processes" and in shaping our educational practices. Using exemplars from a study of clinical expertise in nursing, I have described several aspects of clinical judgment which cannot be accounted for by the cognitive models. I've highlighted assumptions underlying our educational practices which are challenged by our new understanding of clinical judgment and offered one illustration of an alternative approach to teaching which may be relevant for RN education.

REFERENCES

Allen, D., Bowers, B., & Diekelmann, N. (1989). Writing to learn: a reconceptualization of thinking and writing in the nursing curriculum. *Journal of Nursing Education, 28*(1), 6–11.

Benner, P. (1983). Uncovering the knowledge embedded in practice. *Image: The Journal of Nursing Scholarship, 15*(2), 36–41.

Benner, P. (1984). *From novice to expert: Excellence and power in clinical nursing.* Menlo Park, CA: Addison-Wesley.

Benner, P., & Tanner, C. (1987). Clinical judgment: How expert nurses use intuition. *American Journal of Nursing, 87,* 23–31.

Benner, P., & Wrubel, J. (1989). *The primacy of caring.* Menlo Park, CA: Addison-Wesley.

Benner, P., Tanner, C., & Chesla, C. (1992). From beginner to expert: Gaining a differentiated clinical world in critical care nursing. *Advances in Nursing Sciences, 14*(3), 13–28.

Bruner, J. (1986). *Actual minds, possible worlds.* Cambridge, MA: Harvard University Press.

Chesla, C. (1990). Care of the family in the intensive care unit. Education Session, American Nurses Association Biennial Convention. Boston, MA.

Corcoran, S. (1986). Planning by expert and novice nurses in cases of varying complexity. *Research in Nursing and Health, 9,* 155–162.

Dreyfus, H. L. (1979). *What computers can't do: The limits of artificial intelligence.* Revised edition. New York: Harper and Row.

Dreyfus, H., & Dreyfus, S. (1986). *Mind over machine.* New York: Free Press.

Dreyfus, H. (1987). Theory in a practice discipline. Paper presented at the conference: Stress, Coping and Caring in Clinical Nursing Practice. Berkeley, CA, May, 1987.

Dreyfus, H. (1991). *Being in the world: A commentary on Heidegger's being and time, division I.* Cambridge, MA: MIT Press.

Dreyfus, H., & Dreyfus, S. (In progress) The relationship of theory and practice in the acquisition of skill. Helene Fuld Health Trust Study of Clinical Expertise in Intensive Care Nursing.

Fonteyn, M. E. (1991). Implications of clinical reasoning studies for critical care nursing. *Focus on Critical Care, 18*(4), 322–327.

Gardner, H. (1985). *The mind's new science: A history of the cognitive revolution.* New York: Basic Books.

Kleinman, A. (1988). *Illness narratives: Suffering, healing and the human condition.* New York: Basic Books.

Kleinman, A., Eisenberg, L., & Good, B. (1978). Culture, illness and care: Clinical lessons from anthropologic and cross-cultural research. *Annals of Internal Medicine, 88,* 251–260.

Polkinghorne, D. E. (1988). *Narrative knowing and the human sciences.* Albany, NY: SUNY Press.

Rubin, J. (In progress). The role of qualitative distinctions in expert practice. Helene Fuld Study of Clinical Expertise in Intensive Care Nursing.

Schon, D. A. (1983). *The reflective practitioner: How professionals think in action.* New York: Basic Books.

Tanner, C. (1987). Teaching clinical judgment. In Fitzpatrick, J., & Taunton, R. (Eds.) *Annual Review of Nursing Research, Volume 5.* New York: Wiley.

Tanner, C. (1989). Using knowledge in clinical judgment. In Tanner, C., & Lindeman, C. *Using Nursing Research.* New York: National League for Nursing Press.

Tanner, C. A. (1986). The nursing care plan as an instructional method: Ritual or reason? *Nurse Educator, 11*(4), 8–10.

Tanner, C., Benner, P., Chesla, C., & Gordon, D. (In press). The phenomenology of knowing a patient. *Image.*

Winograd, T., & Flores, F. (1986). *Understanding computers and cognition: A new foundation for design.* Norwood, NJ: Ablex Publishing Co.

3

Transforming RN Education: New Approaches to Innovation

Nancy L. Diekelmann

The explication of ideas, understandings, and practices that are the world of RN education offers us a future of new possibilities. Addressing innovation *as* innovative practicing, I will:

1. Explicate our current understanding of what constitutes "innovation" in RN education. Part of this explication is an attempt to reveal the need to rethink the meaning of innovation in our lives as teachers;

2. In demonstrating new approaches to innovation, I will describe possibilities for transforming RN education that are embedded in our narrative accounts of our lives as teachers;

3. Lastly, I will point to several issues in front of us to consider as we go about our lives of transforming RN education.

INNOVATION IN RN EDUCATION

Excellence in education, coupled with an eye "to innovation," is a commitment we share as nurse educators. I would like to discuss with you

Note: This research was funded by a grant from the Helene Fuld Health Trust as a part of the *Practice of Teaching in Nursing* study.

our interest, as teachers in nursing, in innovation and in creating changes in RN education. My research on the practice of nurse teachers, funded by the Helene Fuld Health Trust, is intended to reveal ways to help us to think differently about curriculum innovation. Who could be against innovation? Pure innovation as such does not exist since most innovation has what we have done before always already embedded in it (Gadamer, 1975; Heidegger, 1969; 1991). What I intend to evoke is an understanding of how transformations are characterized by an *explication of how we think.*

Heidegger has asserted that "we are still not thinking . . . although the state of the world is becoming constantly more thought-provoking." (Heidegger, 1954, p. 4). Thinking then about innovation in our particular practices as teachers, the question becomes:

How Would I know an Innovative Approach to Teaching, Learning or Curricula for RNs, if I Saw or Heard One?

Traditional View of Innovation: Understanding Comportment Toward Innovation as a Kind of "Fore-sight"*

Our tradition and our experience as teachers is to have a kind of fore-sight that considers innovation as having the characteristic of being new and unfamiliar to us (Heidegger, 1962). There is a tendency to reject something that we have tried before that has been unsuccessful. In addition, we discount approaches if we have heard about them before, or have successfully used them. Missing from this approach to thinking about innovation is that it may be in the familiar, and in the reflecting on what we currently do successfully, that innovative practicing will arise.

The view of innovation as coming from some other—a consultant, an expert, or a researcher—de-skills nurse educators and encourages us to believe we do not know what we are doing or how to create a future of innovation and new possibilities for RN students. This is certainly not a plea to turn a deaf ear to innovative practices that are not part of our experience. It is rather to acknowledge that to think of innovation only as something new from the outside rules out the possibility

---

Fore-sight: Interpretations are always already rooted in the viewpoints and perspectives we see in advance and press toward.

of the innovation as residing and arising from our collected lived experiences (fore-having*). It also covers over and reduces to marginal status innovations we may have currently embraced.

Traditionally, new approaches have been labeled as teaching or learning strategies that describe specific activities to be adapted by teachers for RN students. One group of strategies consists of tools such as audio-visual learning packages, computer-assisted instruction, or video technology. Other strategies are process oriented, such as critical thinking and problem solving activities, or group process approaches.

Innovations in curriculum strategies are traditionally recognized as new ways of organizing content or planning clinical experiences, or as new ways of describing the curriculum. The major curricular questions of selection and sequencing of content for RNs generate constant and frequent suggestions for new approaches, e.g., new ways of designing course work for RNs, RN to MS programs, or courses for RN students that are moderated by patients discussing their lived experiences. Another curricular question is the role of experience in nursing education. Here innovation is often recognized because it describes new kinds of practicums, or use of different agencies in the community for RN students.

To suggest that part of what may appear problematic is that the innovation that is suggested is not unrecognizable or of a fundamentally different nature is *not* to suggest that traditional approaches to innovation should not and will not continue. To suggest there are other paths to innovation is not to dismiss or devalue traditional approaches to changing our teaching strategies, the processes of education, or approaches to the curriculum for RN students. Rather I seek a new path that will extend and expand our understanding of innovation. By understanding I mean not a tool for consciousness, or some other faculty that humans possess; but rather understanding in the sense of Heideggerian phenomenology, that is, understanding as a fundamental mode of existing in the world. My emphasis will be on revealing the practices of teaching that are *innovating* and reveal and reflect the understanding of teachers as they practice (Palmer, 1969, pp. 227-231).

There is danger in advocating a return to the practice of teaching for new resolutions if the return is a thinking which is non-reflexive and uncritical about our day-to-day experiences. Rather I propose, a kind of

---

Fore-having: Interpretations are always already rooted in the taken for granted background of a "world" that we have been given.

thinking that recalls how we teach where our practice is always kept open and problematic. This is a kind of thinking that questions practices when they are successful *and* when they are a part of breakdown. Reflexive thinking holds current understandings as open and problematic to enable the possibility for anything to emerge. By holding open to critique all practices, a conservative return to the "tried and true" is avoided. Reflexive thinking moves to embrace critical and feminist critiques and deconstruction of the modes of thinking that contribute to current practices. *How* we return to practice is the kind of thinking that matters. Reflexive thinking that reveals shared practices and common meanings within the practices of teaching that are innovating are what we seek to make visible. This transformed relationship to the nature of the old is full of new possibilities for nursing education.

An Interpretative Approach to Innovation

Let us begin a journey that originates with a critique turning on the *Decentering of the Self as an Autonomous Entity.* Cartesianism* and the part of the modern occidental epoch that has its roots in continental Europe is at the core of practices which attempt to focus a will to power on the certainty of our knowledge of objects (Heidegger, 1979, 1982, 1984, 1987). To begin this journey I have embraced the work of philosophers like Martin Heidegger and others who write and think about our current condition. Heidegger (1962) shows how Descartes' explication of rationality and the ensuing rise of the scientific method gave rise to the possibility that everything in the world could be treated like an object (e.g., students, the teaching process, cognitive gain), or like a mental state (anxiety in RN students, denial, or motivation). While these two approaches were and are extremely helpful in our day-to-day lives, there is danger in them. The first is that as we attempt to reduce the world to objects or mental states and investigate them, we then begin to be required to control them (Heidegger, 1977a). Inherent in the scientific method as scientism is a commitment to control. That is, if "this" is the case, then "that" *will* or *must* happen. As we dwell increasingly in this kind of existence, we become ever more concerned about power and control for its own sake (Heidegger, 1979, 1982, 1984,

---

Cartesianism. Cognizing humans as seen as the ultimate ground for all that is directly observed. Rational certainty determines the link between the Knower and the Known.

1987, 1977b). Power does not "ek-sist,"* but rather, energy *as* force exists in the physical world. It is imperative that we work to differentiate between power, energy, and force.

This has great importance for considering innovation in education. Critical and feminist pedagogies are alternative forms of schooling which are committed to the unveiling of practices which are enslaving students and teachers (Apple & Christian-Smith, 1991; Aronowitz & Giroux, 1991; Ben-Peretz, 1990; Giroux, 1992; Kliebard, 1992; Miller, 1990; Stanley, 1992; Weiler, 1988; Welker, 1992). These forms of scholarship are committed to emancipation and an analysis of the power relationships and ideologies that are embedded within our schooling practices. Notice I do not talk here about intentional states. While intentionality is an important part of critical and feminist analyses, I do not imply that we as teachers consciously intend the outcomes that occur. For example, a teacher could work very hard on ways to reduce anxiety in RN students. Yet the students may experience the course as anxiety provoking, no matter what the intentions of the teacher, and respond with anger and hostility. Two paths that emerge that can help us with innovation in RN education come from critical social theorists and feminist scholarship. We can however, travel a third path. It takes advantage of both critical social theory and feminist scholarship but moves beyond to discuss what matters—not intentional states, but rather the comportment or behavior that accompanies these states. This path, rooted in Heideggerian phenomenology, proposes that another way to think about thinking is to consider what matters as *how* we comport ourselves toward objects. Objects exist as physical entities, and mental states as objects can be described, but rather than concentrate on these, Heidegger suggests we should concentrate on our comportment (Heidegger, 1971, "The Thing"). Comportment should be distinguished from behavior because behavior is usually considered something that is the object of analysis. I use comportment to describe those practices we engage in on a day-to-day basis. Thus, teaching becomes a practice with particular skills that exists in a particular community that shares practices and meanings. Teachers and students and clinicians make up a special nursing community, a world of shared practices and common meanings. RN students are a particular community within nursing education. Therefore, another path to innovation is

---

*Ek-sist: A term Heidegger used to clarify and differentiate the human way of being (*Dasein*) from physicalist or psychologistic determinations. See: On the Essence of Truth, p. 128, in *Basic Writings*.

to reflect on the lived experiences of teachers and RN students to unveil shared practices and common meanings.

The method I use to analyze the lived experiences of persons is Heideggerian hermeneutics. Hermeneutics is an approach to the interpretation of written or spoken texts (language) in order to make visible meanings embedded in the texts: via structures of fore-having, foresight, and fore-conception* (Heidegger, 1962). Hermeneutics as a path of thinking is an approach to understanding that unveils the common meanings and shared practices of persons within particular cultures. It can be transformative since, as a language experience, it both shapes and is shaped by the experience. Hermeneutical thinking is thinking as comportment. It is fluid, not final, and seeks a revealing understanding such that for every revealing there is a concealing (Heidegger, 1954).

NEW APPROACHES TO INNOVATION: THE NARRATIVE ACCOUNTS OF TEACHERS AND RN STUDENTS

Teaching Thinking in Nursing: Revealing Innovation in Our Narratives

In my study on *The Practice of Teaching in Nursing*, the narratives of nurse teachers revealed the fore-having (Heidegger, 1962, p. 191) of interpretive understandings that shape their practices (Diekelmann, 1992 a & b). Attending to the shared practices and common meanings, the themes and constitutive patterns that emerge from doing hermeneutical analyses of these stories shows teaching as a welcoming and staying. The consideration of *how* we as teachers participate in welcoming and staying in our practice gives us a new take on what we do with RN students. It can be a way to think differently about our practice as teachers. Listen to this teacher who describes how she welcomes students (fore-sight as, and encouraging foresight. Heidegger, 1962, p. 191, footnote 3):

"The teacher as the lighter of the lamp—not the filler of the bucket."

When I first went into teaching, I spent a lot of time with students getting to know each other. Names and stuff like that, and I still do but

---

Fore-conception: Interpretations are always already rooted in the claims that belief systems, theories, paradigms, and principles make on us.

now I know how to tell them about me in a way that they get to know each other. And early on in the course, I watch for talent and brilliance. In those early lectures, I put things out there and I see if anyone else is interested in them. And I see who takes up intellectual challenges with me. And sometimes no matter what, it's a long time into the course and then a student opens up and you see wonderful scholarship. And for those RN students I stay right with them and I say, more, more, it's OK to do this kind of thinking. Come let's think together.

Teachers as well as RN students bring situated thinking and practical knowledge with them as they return to school. The teaching strategies we use to develop their thinking as comportment may more closely resemble approaches we use with graduate students. It is easy to focus on content to the exclusion of the *how* of our thinking with students. Yet how we welcome RNs, not just back to school and into our classrooms, but into thinking comportment, is what matters. This lighting up is the gift of teaching. A student reflects on her recent experience of welcoming and staying:

As I think about it I visualize myself reading, walking along, reading . . . and as I move along and stop a woman moves with me and holds a light over my head, so I may see . . . and then it seems it is not one woman, but many who appear on the path, just as I need the light and they travel a distance with me until another joins me . . . and I move along with one then another. And while they hold the light, I read aloud and we talk, and move on . . . The path does not seem to end and there is some darkness ahead, but there is no tension in me as I look at that darkness. I have come to know that the light can always be found because the source is in me and comes to life when I open to another and we interact and find meanings together.

This is the sense of a learning that welcomes and stays. It is a connecting with students. One RN student describes her experience in a course in which she feels overwhelmed by the course content. In class she tells the teacher how she is feeling. She says:

I told him I didn't know where to start. He said, "You must start where you are standing." Then something hit me, there is no right way, it's my way that I am all about. So I read what caught my attention and soon I was filling in gaps and bringing together ideas and wow, new curiosities emerged.

A shared practice and common meaning of RN teachers is how they bring students to conceive their own knowledge and wisdom, their fore-conceptions. An experienced teacher of RN students says:

> *I used to spend all my time looking for what students don't know and can't do. Now, it's just the opposite. I spend all my time with them empowering and showing them what they do know and understand and the excellence in what they are doing. It's an important shift in my teaching and I didn't actually realize it until we were talking about it now.*

This teacher reflects in the context of telling her stories of teaching and moves toward narrative as releasement to transform teaching practices (Heidegger, 1966). It is in the telling of the stories, in the listening, and in the reflecting on them that new possibilities for our practice emerge.

A constitutive pattern of this study, the teacher-as-learner, shows how teachers dwell in the world through learning with RN students. Teachers have been viewed as information givers or as facilitators of learning. Both the transfer of power and attention to the concepts of empowerment require teachers to make issues of power central to their teaching.

This constitutive pattern offers a new perspective for us to consider. The teacher-as-learner is not a new role for the teacher, rather it has always existed, as fore-conception: a way of being with RN students. It is comportment in which teachers attune themselves to the creation and recreation of meaning among their students. Students do not teach the teacher information. It is teachers continually teaching in ways that maintain them as learners. Teachers-as-learners, sometimes learn how their RN students learn, and sometimes bring difficult questions that have meaning for them into their teaching. In this sense, learning occurs ontologically, as distinguished from epistemologically, viewing learning as accumulation of knowledge. The teacher becomes an explorer of meaning and significance with RN students; that is, they attain a hermeneutical, not solipsistic, understanding of their experiences (fore-conception). When teachers are learners they are in the world through the continual rebirth of their struggle to understand. The primordial state of teaching, that which comes before teaching as information telling, facilitating learning, or evaluating is teaching as learning; the how of moving into nearness with fore-having, fore-sight and fore-conception. Learners-as-teachers are always open to new possibilities, constantly transforming and being transformed in their relationship to the meanings of their Being-in-the-World (Heidegger, 1962). Teaching becomes learning. Learning is hearing. It is not merely listening but hearing in the sense of dialogue and meaning. Schooling is the struggle to understand. There is a fundamental difference in the commitment to learning that shapes the practice of teaching that is different from the practice of nursing.

This approach to learning is dwelling as a moving into nearness such that the conditions for the possibility for anything to show up become unveiled (Heidegger, 1971). Teaching is what we are always already so close to. It is seeking for and being in a way to understand that which is on the one hand close and so familiar and on the other hand an abyss of nearness. In this way, the interpretive study of the lived experiences of teachers with RN students is not the study of teaching but rather learning. This is the nature of teaching in nursing; teaching as disclosure.

Another pattern that emerged in this study is how teachers come to realize that "the less they teach" RN students the more learning can occur. In teaching less, teachers are situated to be learners side-by-side with their students. This relationship reconceptualizes the hierarchical relationship of students and teachers and begins to create a community of learners. The literature of critical, feminist, and postmodern pedagogy has the potential to provide us with rich insights into the transformation of our relationships with students and create a community of learners.

But there is a deeper sense of the learning *as* teaching. It is that there is no such thing as teaching; only learning. I would argue that teaching is a special kind of learning and research likewise is a special kind of learning. In this sense, then, teaching and research are co-founded in learning. This teacher points us to her understanding. She says:

> *For me teaching is a scholarly activity. I like something that makes me think and extends my thinking and I expect to get that out of any class I teach.*

Understanding that it is the community of teachers that matters in creating this kind of possibility for scholarship or learning, she says:

> *There is no scholarly work that's not done without others. One teacher does not make a difference; it is the collective community of scholars*

each sharing perspectives that enrich and educate our students and each other for life.

ISSUES IN TRANSFORMING RN EDUCATION

Teaching So Much That Learning Cannot Occur/ Creating Places for Learning and Only Learning to Occur

We are working too hard at teaching; too immersed in the labor of teaching. Indeed, out of the best of intentions to care for our students we are leaping in and teaching so much that there is no time for our own learning. I would argue that students can get so taken up with the "assignments" of our courses that there is no time for them to think; in what we are trying to teach, it is thinking that matters.

Our practice of teaching does not come to us "organizationally." Yet we put so much time into developing systems to manage our lives that there is no time to *live a life*. What I am pointing to is what matters greatly to us in the *how* of living our lives. Do we spend it always being guilty that we are unorganized, or do we begin to make our wanting to get organized problematic? Where does that come from and what is the meaning of organizing our practices as teachers (Dreyfus, 1984)? Living messy or in the open region of chaos, could create a place for us to be more available to our students for dialogue. It could provide time to talk to each other as teachers in unhurried ways that reveal new possibilities for thinking together. Living messy could transform our lives together, our relationships with each other and the nursing curriculum. If we were able to make how much time we spend on teaching-related activities problematic, and were successful in carving out time for a place for us to learn, we would be innovative.

As members of a predominantly female discipline, we could struggle with finding a way to return our personal lives to the center of what we do. A teaching career should be attached to, not take over our lives. It is dangerous when our teaching practice is the center of our lives. When faced with crisis, such as having a short time to live, what clearly emerges for most of us is that what matters is our lives with our beloved friends and families. Suzanne Gordon (1991) exhorts us to take care that we do not as women succeed by adopting the current model of success. It is one that encourages us to compete, become skilled to the exclusion of involvement, and to be at home in the pursuit of the chimera of power. This is neither a women's issue nor a one dimensional slogan of conservative politicians; a danger lurks for both men and women who labor so furiously. We must slow down the pace in our schools. Perhaps we can never organize the curriculum, clear our desks, or get our syllabi "perfect."

When was the last time any of us sat in on a course given in another department? When was the last time we had a full day to read—not course related materials, but the long overlooked books that we've been dying to read? When was the last time you went to the library and spent an afternoon looking at all the current periodicals—not just in your area of interest or our discipline, but of anything that catches your gaze? It is learning that grounds us as teachers, and we need to recall learning to our practice of teaching.

Our curricula are not "learning friendly." We spend enormous amounts of our time massaging our curricula, when we would much rather be learning or spending more time thinking together with students. If we could begin to call into question *how* we spend our time as teachers, and treat as problematic everything that seems tangential, such as "regular" committee meetings with small agendas, we will begin to know those activities of our community that are central to creating a *fair* and *respectful* community out of which to practice. Perhaps it should be staffing, teacher and teaching problems, the distribution of resources such as building and space, promotion, merit and retention that we should talk more about rather than less. These activities matter greatly to a fair and respectful community. Yet the institutions in which we work tend to treat personnel issues as confidential, teacher and teaching problems as individual, and the distribution of resources as administrative responsibilities. They are not so easily categorized. If we would struggle to overcome the problems current cultural practices create, we could develop new ones that both preserve thoughtful practices as well as provide the connecting conversations necessary to transform our teaching communities.

The most important understanding I have had with the teaching study came when I realized after I had read interviews of teachers from all levels of nursing education, from doctoral faculty to instructors in diploma programs, that not one of them mentioned anything about the meaning (Heidegger, 1962, p. 193) of the curriculum. It was as if the curriculum was invisible. Yet we make such a big deal of the nursing curriculum. We all have committees that monitor it and we look at it with a magnifying glass when we are accredited. And yet, on a day-to-day basis, it is absent from the conversations that shape our practices as teachers. Does that mean there is no such thing as a curriculum? Or that it doesn't matter? Ask teachers who are on curriculum committees preparing for an accreditation visit and they will answer that the curriculum is alive and well in our schools. Certainly the decisions of selection and sequencing of subject-matter (not just what we teach but also what we don't teach), the role of experience in our curriculum, and the relationship of evaluation to learning are central questions of what traditionally constitutes the curriculum. And these decisions can have profound effects on the lives of students and teachers. But what matters about these decisions is the centrality we give them in our day-to-day lives as teachers.

I am beginning to appreciate that we learn to bend these rules with students and each other, just as we bend rules for patients. When we are forced to use a particular theorist or framework, just like nurses who are forced to use a particular language, we do a "slow code." Eventually whoever is forcing us gives up. We are seeing the demise of nursing diagnoses as well as curriculum or conceptual frameworks. There was a time in our history when we were appropriated to behavioral education in order to create a place in higher education for the kind of scholarship that is now happening. There are important conversations that are generated when teachers come together to look across courses in our curricula. We are now different teachers, differently experienced and prepared, and it is timely to move our curriculum conversations to include the contributions of interpretive, critical, feminist, and postmodern pedagogy.

Recalling the Narrative to RN Education/ Overcoming the Deficit View of RN Education

The RN students come to us with a wealth of understandings about nursing practice. Traditionally, RN students are asked to "prove," "show," or "demonstrate" that they are able to accomplish course requirements. This can be accomplished by taking NLN PEP tests, developing a portfolio, and accumulating evidence and analyzing professional experiences in relation to course objectives and requirements. While there is often great flexibility and the best of faculty intentions, the RN student frequently experiences this process as having to "prove" herself, with the resulting curriculum designed to meet the "deficits" in her previous schooling and professional practice experiences.

However, by encouraging RN students to do a hermeneutic analysis of their practice as an entry experience we could begin to give them the language and way to reflect on their practice experiences as a central activity of returning to school (Rather, 1992). It would be both a celebration of their practice as well as a revealing of their various levels of expertise. Nurses with beginning experience can see what is in front of them. They can come to understand what returning to school can offer them as opposed to that offered to more experienced RN students who may be ready for graduate level courses. This is another way for us to overcome the current deficit approach to schooling RNs.

Currently we share a history of awareness that some RNs know a great deal of what is offered in baccalaureate education and others very little. How to give RNs credit for their knowledge, experience and expertise is often framed in a deficit view. That is, we look at what *they don't know or can't do*. And we view innovation as all the possible ways to prove what you know and can do. So portfolio, PEP tests, credit by exam, credit by experience are all viewed as innovative. And they are. But another possibility is to call into question this view. Though well intended, this approach makes it difficult to focus on what RNs *can do*. It eliminates the possibility of a rule that opens any course to an RN at whatever level and leaves the risks involved in this decision up to the RN. How will we ever know the transformation that practice does to learning if we limit the possibilities for seeing it? Can even inexperienced nurses take doctoral level courses and be successful? My concern is that as we become more experienced in nursing education and our curricula become more exacting, the danger is that this question will neither be answered nor even asked.

Learning AS Thinking:
The Meaning of Transforming

It is a truism that we all think and consequently think we think. Teachers are thinkers and they become skilled in responding to the call to thinking. It is a thinking that reveals and discloses new possibilities that shape and co-found our practice as teachers, and it is this kind of thinking that means so much to us. I speak now of writing as thinking, of reading as thinking, and dialogue as thinking. It is this kind of thinking in which we understand that we don't go to thoughts, they come to us (Heidegger, 1971). Yet we live in communities in schools and universities that make thinking that reveals and discloses, impossible. We have learned to secrete away times for us to think; often at night and on our week-ends. Yet it is thinking that shapes our practices as teachers and connects us with the possibilities of a new future.

We leave teaching or get stuck in practice when it is impossible for learning as thinking to occur.

Who better to help us in creating a place for thinking in the nursing curriculum than RN students? These practitioners who on a daily basis in their nursing practices understand the meaning and centrality of clinical thinking, suffer from the same danger. Yet we know how to recall thinking to our practice. Through narrative dialogue, a conversation that calls out the best in us, we begin to see the thinking that is embedded in our practices. RN students are at home in this clinical thinking and many are knowledgeable of *how*, just as are some teachers, to create a place and a community life that enhances thinking.

I do not refer to a thinking that is rarefied, objective, or removed from the social and political contexts in which we live. Rather I speak of a resolute, engaged, thinking that is deeply committed and involved. It is our comportment as thinking and our thinking comportment to which I point. Only by making problematic our community life and how it influences our teaching practice, our ability to care and be cared for, can we stand out into a unique kind of clearing.

Do I see transformative change going on? The answer to this lies in reflecting on our experiences here. Will you leave having a new idea that calls you to thinking? If so, then you understand the meaning of that experience and *how* a moving into nearness with those kinds of experiences can create a new future—through the transformation of our thinking and dwelling. It will be here that we keep open the possibility for anything to emerge and in so doing will create a future of new possibilities for ourselves and our students and for nursing. For me, this is the meaning of transforming RN education.

REFERENCES

Apple, M. W., & Christian-Smith, L. K. (Eds.). (1991). *The politics of the textbook*. New York: Routledge, Chapman and Hall, Inc.

Aronowitz, S., & Giroux, H. A. (1991). *Postmodern education: Politics, culture, and social criticism*. Minneapolis, MN: University of Minnesota Press.

Ben-Peretz, M. (1990). *The teacher-curriculum encounter: Freeing teachers from the tyranny of texts*. New York: State University of New York Press.

Diekelmann, N. (1988). Curriculum revolution: A theoretical and philosophical mandate for change. In *Curriculum revolution: Mandate for change* (pp. 137–157). New York: National League for Nursing Press.

Diekelmann, N. (1989). The nursing curriculum: Lived experiences of students. In *Curriculum revolution: Reconceptualizing nursing education* (pp. 25–41). New York: National League for Nursing Press.

Diekelmann, N. (1992a). Nursing education: Caring, dialogue and practice—A Heideggerian phenomenological approach. *Japanese Journal of Nursing Research, 24*(4).

Diekelmann, N. (1992b). Learning-as-testing: A Heideggerian hermeneutical analysis of the lived experiences of students and teachers in nursing. *Advances in Nursing Science, 14*(3): 72–83.

Diekelmann, N., Allen, D., & Tanner, C. (1989). *The NLN criteria for appraisal of baccalaureate programs: A critical hermeneutic analysis.* New York: The National League for Nursing Press.

Dreyfus, H. (1984). Knowledge and human values: A genealogy of nihilism. In Sloan, D. (Ed.). *Toward the recovery of wholeness: Knowledge, education, and human values.* New York: Teachers College Press.

Gadamer, H. G. (1975). *Truth and method.* New York: Crossroad Publishing Company.

Giroux, H. (1992). *Border crossings: Cultural workers and the politics of education.* New York: Routledge, Chapman and Hall, Inc.

Gordon, S. (1991). *Prisoners of men's dreams: Striking out for a new feminine future.* Boston, MA: Little, Brown and Company.

Heidegger, M. (1954). *What is called thinking?* (J. Gray, Trans.). New York: Harper & Row, Publishers.

Heidegger, M. (1962). *Being and time.* (J. Macquarrie & E. Robinson, Trans.). New York: Harper & Row, Publishers.

Heidegger, M. (1966). *Discourse on thinking.* (J. Anderson and E. Freund, Trans). New York: Harper & Row, Publishers.

Heidegger, M. (1969). *Identity and difference.* (J. Stambaugh, Trans.). NY: Harper & Row, Publishers.

Heidegger, M. (1971). *Poetry, language, thought.* (A. Hofstadter, Trans.). New York: Harper & Row, Publishers.

Heidegger, M. (1977a). *The question concerning technology and other essays.* (W. Lovitt, Trans.). New York: Harper & Row, Publishers.

Heidegger, M. (1977b). *Basic writings.* (D. Krell, Ed. & Trans.). New York: Harper & Row, Publishers.

Heidegger, M. (1979). *Nietzsche, Volume One: The will to power as art.* (D. Krell, Trans.). New York: Harper & Row, Publishers.

Heidegger, M. (1982). *Nietzsche, Volume Four: Nihilism.* (D. Krell, Trans.). New York: Harper & Row, Publishers.

Heidegger, M. (1984). *Nietzsche, Volume Two: The eternal recurrence of the same.* (D. Krell, Trans.). New York: Harper & Row, Publishers.

Heidegger, M. (1987). *Nietzsche, Volume Three: The will to power as knowledge and as metaphysics.* (J. Stambaugh, D. Krell, F. Capuzzi, Trans.). New York: Harper & Row, Publishers.

Heidegger, M. (1991). *The principle of reason.* (R. Lilly, Trans.). Bloomington, IN: Indiana University Press.

Kliebard, H. M. (1992). *Forging the American curriculum: Essays in curriculum history and theory.* New York: Routledge, Chapman and Hall, Inc.

Miller, J. L. (1990). *Creating spaces and finding voices: Teachers collaborating for empowerment.* New York: State University of New York Press.

Palmer, R. E. *Hermeneutics.* (1969). Evanston, IL: Northwestern University Press.

Rather, M. (1992). "Nursing as a way of thinking"—Heideggerian hermeneutical analysis of the lived experience of the returning RN. *Research in Nursing & Health, 15,* 47–55.

Stanley, W. B. (1992). *Curriculum for utopia: Social reconstructionism and critical pedagogy in the postmodern era.* New York: State University of New York Press.

Weiler, K. (1988). *Women teaching for change: Gender, class & power.* South Hadley, MA: Bergin & Garvey Publishers, Inc.

Welker, R. (1992). *The teacher as expert: A theoretical and historical examination.* New York: State University of New York Press.

Part II

Issues in RN Education

4

Ideological Barriers to Nursing Education for Returning RN Students

Christina D. Horne

Of the more than two million licensed registered nurses, only 27 percent have as their highest earned credential the baccalaureate degree (*Nursing Datasource*, 1991). Since the introduction of the "open curriculum" concept in 1970 by the National League for Nursing (NLN), there has been a burgeoning movement toward the establishment of educational mobility programs for registered nurses (RNs). Recent statistics from the NLN show a trend for larger numbers of RN students returning to baccalaureate education in nursing (*Nursing Datasource*, 1991). Although there is a positive enrollment trend, RN students are expressing frustration about arduous curricula fraught with duplication, barriers, and a denigration of their previous knowledge and experience (Beeman, 1990).

The purpose of this paper is to explore the historical and ideological factors which persist as barriers to returning RN (RRN) students. This discussion consists of two parts: (a) the identified barriers encountered by RRNs and (b) the ideological factors which have impeded the RRN's pursuit of advanced nursing education.

BARRIERS

Many registered nurse graduates of diploma and associate degree programs have been discriminated against in their pursuit of advanced

61

nursing education. In 1981, the Institute of Medicine's study of nursing and nursing education reported that "nurses who choose to upgrade their education may find confusing, often circuitous, and expensive pathways" (p. 6.17). As a result of such educational obstacles, RRN students have expressed a strong sense of frustration as shown through the following three quotations:

> *The system does little to facilitate the needs of RNs; I spend much energy challenging, arguing, petitioning, and running around in circles (Beeman, 1990, p. 43).*

> *[The advisor's] going through [the transcript]—this is too old—scratch those four credits—scratch those five credits—I felt violated by the time it was over, and it was done in a very cavalier manner. . . . [I asked her why all these classes must be taken over] and she said, "then we know you can do it" (Rather, 1990, p. 215).*

> *You [the RRN student] come away from there [the nursing courses] thinking I learned nothing about nursing, or the process of nursing, or the advancement of nursing . . . I'm suffering through my nursing courses. They're so dry and repetitious (Rather, 1990, p. 218).*

These statements convey a sense of the basic problems encountered by the RRN student. Specific barriers that hinder the pursuit of advanced nursing education are lack of flexibility, inconvenient scheduling, geographic inaccessibility, and duplication of nursing knowledge and experience in available programs (NLN, 1987). A more recent survey conducted by *RN* (Lippman, 1991) has shown that many of these same barriers persist. Of all these barriers, the duplication of nursing knowledge and experience was singled out by Beeman (1990) as being the most difficult obstacle.

The barriers encountered by RRNs for educational advancement have been identified in earlier studies (Allen, 1977; Lenburg, 1975; Stevens, 1981). A comparison of the barriers reported in these early studies with ones identified in more recent research indicates that the same obstacles have persisted over time. Based on these findings, educational mobility barriers for RNs continue despite the time and research that have been devoted to the issue since the early 1960s.

IDEOLOGICAL FACTORS

With the identification of the primary barriers to educational mobility for nurses, a groundwork has been laid to gain insight into the contemporary difficulties RRNs are encountering in their pursuit of recognition and advancement within the profession. The historical and ideological factors that shape American higher education and nursing education provide insight as to why RRNs experience continued obstacles and oppression in advancing their education.

Institutional Chauvinism

"Institutional chauvinism," a term coined by Parker (1979), focuses on access to and mobility within institutions of higher education. This factor is not unique to nursing students but applies to any learner who decides to proceed through a college or university in a nontraditional manner. Within higher education there exists a hierarchy of institutions in terms of quality and reputation. As a result of this hierarchy, educational institutions often take an arrogant or protectionist position when interacting with each other. Emphasis is placed on competition rather than on cooperation between institutions (Parker, 1979). Unfortunately, this leads to additional barriers for students seeking admission or transfer to academic programs because of a belief that these nontraditional students have deficits in their education and are not well prepared to meet the academic challenges of a four year college.

A form of institutional chauvinism occurs when universities complain that there is a great variation in the quality of community college programs. This has resulted in careful scrutiny of transfer records and the frequent denial of credit to students. On the other hand, community colleges frequently charge universities with academic snobbery when their credits are rejected by the universities (Parker, 1979).

Statute of limitations for a degree is another example of institutional chauvinism. Most institutions of higher education require at least the last 30 credit hours of degree coursework, including a certain number of credit hours in a major, to be taken within a specified time frame prior to the date the degree is to be granted, usually five to seven years (Lonborg, 1984). Along with this, is frequently a residency requirement for taking classes on campus (Greenleaf, 1990). Both of these policies present problems to students such as RRNs who are inaccessible to degree-granting institutions because of distance, or who have a conflict between work and school because of an overriding need to meet financial obligations.

A final example of institutional chauvinism is the variance in total number of units or credit hours required for graduation. In a survey of the California public education system, Hansen (1988) found that graduation from a BSN (generic) program required credit hours ranging from 123 to 144. From this same survey, a wide variation was found in the maximum possible number of credits that an RN could transfer from an associate degree program to a baccalaureate program, with as few as two or as many as 36 credit hours reported. This unevenness in the acceptance of transfer credit within only one state educational system is a prime example of institutional chauvinism.

Educational Philosophies of Teaching-Learning

The next group of ideological issues to be considered focuses on the educational philosophies of teaching-learning, such as andragogy versus pedagogy, the acquisition of skills by adults, and patriarchal pedagogy versus feminist andragogy.

Andragogy versus pedagogy. Kidd (1959) and Knowles (1980, 1984) have both documented the differences between andragogy (the art and science of helping adults learn) and pedagogy (the art and science of teaching children). Knowles has been credited for popularizing the theory of andragogy in American higher education. The theory Knowles (1980, 1984) developed rests on five main assumptions: (a) as an individual's self-concept matures, he or she moves from total dependence to self-directedness; (b) while maturing, the individual accumulates a broad range of experiences which help to bring definition to the adult as to who he or she is; (c) readiness to learn by an individual coincides with the developmental tasks required for the performance of social roles rather than what is biologically demanded; (d) adult learning is more problem oriented than subject oriented, along with a time perspective that focuses on the immediate application of knowledge rather than on future application, as occurs with children; and (e) internal factors rather than external factors are responsible for motivating the adult to learn.

Current enrollment demographics of RRN students demonstrate that practically all of these individuals are adults and nontraditional students (Baj, 1985b). The problem that has arisen is that many nurse educators continue to utilize the theories and principles of pedagogy in their teaching methodologies regardless of the type of learner (Baj, 1985a). Linares (1989) and Beeman (1990) have each documented the high levels of personal and professional stress and frustration RRN students have experienced while enrolled in baccalaureate programs. A possible reason cited by Baj (1985a) for these unacceptably high levels of stress and frustration may be conflict in the learning theories that traditional baccalaureate programs uphold.

When Linares (1989) considered individual learning styles with an emphasis on adult learning principles, more of the RN students' educational goals and learning needs were met. These results indicate that nurse educators must realize that RNs returning to school for advanced degrees should be evaluated in terms of their learning needs on an individual basis rather than be grouped with the traditional generic nursing students. If the RN student is provided with educational opportunities based on the principles expounded by Knowles, then personal and professional development will undoubtedly be enhanced (Beeman, 1988, 1990).

Skill acquisition by adults. Demographic data show RRN students have all undergone a "nurses' training program" and have been employed as nurses in a diversity of health care settings, but primarily in the role of a hospital staff nurse for six years or more (Green, 1987; Zorn, 1980). Furthermore, two frequent complaints voiced by RRN students have been the lack of respect from faculty for their previous knowledge and work experience, and the repetitiveness of content in many of the nursing courses (Beeman, 1990).

Traditionally, generic baccalaureate programs, even in the upper division, are geared to the novice learner. The RRN student, who is no longer a novice nurse and who decides to enroll in a generic baccalaureate program, might well encounter a conflict with the developmental level of skill acquisition being offered (Baj, 1986). As a result of this conflict, two unwelcome outcomes can occur according to Benner (1981): (a) students experience a loss of self-confidence because of their inability to verbalize their skills immediately, and (b) instructor credibility is lost because the experienced competent student can readily point out many exceptions to the context-free rules and guidelines often presented by the instructor.

Many RRNs perceive themselves as functioning at a level above novice, and at a competent level in some cases, particularly with regard to the technical skills of nursing (Baj, 1986). Thus, there may be a natural conflict in skill level performance between the level RRN students perceive themselves as functioning at and the level most generic baccalaureate nursing programs are designed for. This aggravates the already existing role stress and could well impede learning by the RRN, according to Baj (1986).

This conflict of skill performance has been observed by Benner (1981, 1984). When a learner has expertise beyond the novice level, he or she can have difficulty when asked to cite the context-free rules and aspects that he or she no longer depends on for problem solving. Further empirical data to support this observation were found by Dreyfus and Dreyfus (1980) when working with the instructors of Air Force pilots. The Air Force instructors' efficiency and accuracy in detecting errors on the instrument panel deteriorated when they were forced to follow the prescribed guidelines for scanning the instrument panel that had been taught to the novices.

.The complaints of previous experience being ignored along with reported high levels of stress by RRN students has been well documented in the literature (Baj, 1986; Beeman, 1990; Muzio & Ohashi, 1979; Nyquist, 1973; Woolley, 1978). A possible explanation for these problems may be the failure by nurse educators in generic baccalaureate programs to consider the RRNs' level of skill acquisition development. Additional research is needed to examine the relationship between RRN students, the skill acquisition model, and the baccalaureate nursing curriculum.

Patriarchal pedagogy versus feminist andragogy. Although the term "feminist pedagogy" is commonly used in the literature (for example, see *Getting Smart* by Lather, 1991), the term "feminist andragogy" is more appropriate in the context of adult learning by RRN students. Nursing education has historically relied on teaching and learning principles derived from patriarchal ideologies and world views (Muff, 1988). Most academic disciplines, methodologies, and theories have a masculine bias as their fundamental basis (Bernard, 1973; Gilligan, 1979, 1982; Keller, 1978, 1985). The content judged to be important, skills which are thought to be useful, and mental processes that are involved in considering the abstract and impersonal and, thus, labeled as "thinking" have all derived from a predominantly male experience of the world (Chinn, 1989).

Since the inception of nursing training programs, the teacher-student relationship has been one of deference (Reverby, 1989). The underlying notion has been that the teacher is the authority with all of the worldly knowledge and the student must absorb this knowledge without question. This perspective reinforces the context of a dominant-subservient relationship which has evolved from the patriarchal model. Freire (1985) criticizes authoritarian and elitist educators. Furthermore, Freire advocates that "the very practice of teaching involves learning on the part of those we are teaching as well as learning, or relearning, on the part of those who teach" (1985, p. 177). Thus, the teacher-student relationship functions most effectively based on egalitarian principles.

Language is an important tool that can be used to resist or oppress another person or group. Hooks (1990) states that one is "wedded in language, . . . [and has] being in words" (p. 146). Nursing unfortunately has succumbed to the usage of language and knowledge from the patriarchal system. This is particularly evident by nursings' reliance on the mechanistic, medical model when developing nursing theory and when conducting research. Thus, the usage and selection of words by nursing further demonstrates the acceptance of oppression and the devaluing of our occupation.

As for the basis of our body of knowledge in nursing, we have relied on many theories and methods that are blatantly sexist (Mulligan, 1980). Stereotypical views of female division of labor and anti-women bias in personality theories are just two examples of such sexism (Kravetz, 1976). The dispersion of this knowledge without critical explanation has undoubtedly pervaded the clinical practice of nursing. The use of language and knowledge has kept nursing confined within the traditional roles of society. Language and knowledge perpetuate how people behave and the occupations they pursue (Huebner, 1975).

Even though many nurse educators are female, nursing has clearly continued to promulgate a patriarchal perspective within its own socialization and education of students (Muff, 1988). As a result, RRN students have also fallen victim to the perpetuation of the dominant-subservient relationship in nursing and an oppressive pedagogy (Rather, 1990). This is evidenced by faculty attempts to "de-skill" the RRN by redefining nursing competence based on specialized knowledge only the teacher controls (Apple, 1982), and in their subscribing to a deficit view of RRNs' knowledge and experience (Rather, 1990). Specific examples of the oppressive pedagogy experienced by RRNs are: (a) the required writing of lengthy patient care plans (30 pages) by RNs who have practiced for 20 years; (b) the taking of attendance and use of designated seats in nursing classes; (c) the reifying of nursing theories and nursing diagnostic categories in measuring the professionalism of nursing to the neglect of practical nursing experience; and (d) the requiring of "educative" experiences that are repetitious (Rather, 1990).

Recently, nurse educators have begun to realize that there are problems in the education system and that an alienation of students from themselves and their work is occurring. Basically, some have concluded that "nurses are eating their young." This has led to a recent curriculum upheaval in nursing with a strong feminist perspective (Hedin, 1989).

> *Chinn (1989) clearly articulates feminist andragogy as: content that is viewed and experienced with women at the center. It draws on women's writings and other forms of women's accounts of their views and experience. . . . It draws on skills that are central to women's experience. It nurtures attitudes that are valued in terms of women's realities. It draws on women's ways of thinking. (p. 11)*

The underpinning of feminist andragogy is feminist praxis which is grounded in feminist ethics and ideas about the way the world could be for all people. "Feminist praxis incorporates thoughtful reflection and action that occur in synchrony toward the goal of transforming the world" (Chinn, 1989, p. 12). "Power over" others is rejected in favor of personal empowerment which is a central concept of this feminist perspective.

Nursing has begun to consider a major attitudinal shift and is reflecting on how it has continued to promulgate a patriarchal perspective. However, there continues to be a great deal of resistance from within and outside the profession. Nursing needs to become even more aware of how patriarchy, within the contexts of social, cultural, and economic thought, may impact the decisions of prospective RRN candidates for the baccalaureate degree in nursing as well as their treatment while within the academic setting.

Schism Between Technical and Professional Nursing

The next ideological factor focuses on the promulgation of an attitude of "professional elitism" which has intensified the schism between technical and professional practice in nursing. Historically, there has been a long-standing animosity toward the nonbaccalaureate nurse. Reverby (1989), in describing the efforts of nursing to develop its professional image and status at the turn of the 20th century, writes:

> *In organizing professional nursing associations, they sought, through voluntary and legislative means, to limit the numbers in nursing and to standardize and raise its educational requirements. . . . In doing so,*

they attacked the background, training, and ideology of the majority of working nurses. (p. 121)

This same attitude continues to plague the thinking of the nursing community today (Muff, 1988). As a result, RRN students may encounter roadblocks to gaining entry into baccalaureate nursing programs as discussed earlier in this chapter.

This controversy over educational mobility programs for registered nurses originates partly from the assumptions put forth by Montag when developing the associate degree programs of nursing in 1952. Montag (Montag & Gotkin, 1959) firmly believed that associate degree and baccalaureate programs could not and should not be articulated because the purposes, curricular content, and teaching methods of the two programs are so different. Furthermore, she stated that the "ladder concept of curriculum development was indefensible" (Montag & Gotkin, 1959, p. 25). Consequently, Montag stipulated that associate degree programs should offer only a terminal degree in nursing.

Montag's philosophical stance has been supported over the years by other educators who believed that it was impossible to build advanced nursing content into an education started at the community college level without completely resocializing these students (Anderson, 1972; Sorensen, 1976; Woolley, 1978). According to Waters (1989), "there is the belief that to sanction defined relationships between educational levels would be academically and professionally shoddy" (p. 93). Additional support for Montag's philosophy was amplified in the American Nurses Association (1965) position paper on nursing education which differentiated technical from professional nursing by assigning different functions to the two.

This notion that the associate degree in nursing is a terminal degree goes against some strongly entrenched democratic ideals. Educational mobility is seen as a right of every individual regardless of status or personal background (Rudolf, 1962/1990). As a result, two compelling forces—the force of maintaining quality education by controlling entry into the profession and the force of egalitarianism whereby an opportunity is provided for anyone desiring to advance   are in conflict. This conflict between excluding the nonelite and providing educational opportunities to the masses has led to many fierce battles within the nursing community (Lenburg, 1976). It has also continued the manifestation of various barriers to those who desire to pursue additional nursing education (Haase, 1982).

Nursing's attempts to enhance its prestige and occupational status

by raising educational requirements fits the sociological framework
of Weber (1978). In attempting to professionalize nursing, prominent
leaders and educators in nursing have asserted that the baccalaureate
degree will become the required credential for entry into the profession
(NLN, 1986). As a result, access to certain jobs in nursing is restricted
to people with a particular background or status by credential. For
those who attempt to become part of this status group, such as RRN
students, the road is fraught with numerous obstacles, such as denial
of credit for previous training and ignoring their individual learning
needs while enrolled in a baccalaureate nursing program (Beeman,
1988, 1990; Linares, 1989; NLN, 1987). These obstacles or barriers are
purposely imposed in order to limit the upward mobility of individuals
who are not part of the elite group (Hammack, 1990).

Fortunately, since the late 1960s, there have been nurse educators
who believe that nurses who are graduates from diploma and associate
degree programs should have the opportunity for upward educational
mobility (Greenleaf, 1990; Hart & Sharp, 1986; Lenburg, 1975; Matheney, 1975; Thomas & Thomas, 1988; Waters, 1989). As a result, a burgeoning growth of mobility programs for registered nurses has occurred. In some cases, a separate track within the four-year generic
program has been developed or an upper division degree program that
admits only licensed registered nurses has been established to meet
the needs of this special group of learners—the RRN student (*Nursing
Datasource*, 1991). However, even though there is a positive enrollment
trend, the barrier of "professional elitism" continues to persist and remains a nemesis to the nursing profession.

Class and Cultural Biases

The final ideological factors to be addressed are the issues of class elitism and ethnocentrism in nursing. In 1990, 18 percent of the total admissions to schools of nursing were minority students (*Nursing
Datasource*, 1991). Larger proportions of African-American, Asian, and
American Indian students are enrolled in baccalaureate programs (12%,
3.1%, and 0.6%, respectively) as compared to diploma (9.4%, 2.2%,
and 0.1%) and community college (9.4%, 2.3%, and 0.5%) programs.
Hispanics are represented almost identically among the different program types (*Nursing Data Review*, 1991). These data dispute the assumption that a majority of the minority students attend associate
degree and diploma nursing programs as compared to baccalaureate
programs of nursing.

However, if one examines the broader picture in terms of the percentage of all minorities enrolled in nursing as compared to the percentage of whites in nursing (18% and 82%, respectively, according to *Nursing Datasource*, 1991), the dominant culture in American society predominates in nursing as well. Nursing curricula teach the styles, values, and health concerns of the majority (the white culture), with minimal attention given to minority issues. As a result, the dominant culture's reality is perpetuated (Greenleaf, 1990).

Furthermore, minority college students enrolled in predominantly white schools experience a "culture clash" with the white educational milieu as well as experience feelings of loneliness and alienation because they perceive themselves as "not being wanted" by the institution (Allen, Nunley, & Scott-Warner, 1988; Claerbaut, 1976, 1978; Rodgers, 1990). Unfortunately, this can result in a loss of identity for minorities as well as lack of recognition for their cultural heritage. In order to survive in this ethnocentric system, most minorities subscribe to a strategy of moving from the "margin to the center" as described by Hooks (1984). The minority nurse learns the behavior that is expected of a nurse as mandated by the white dominant culture, but retains those aspects of the minority culture that make him or her unique from the majority.

Given Hodgkinson's (1985) demographic predictions that one of every three Americans will be nonwhite by the year 2000, extensive efforts must be taken to recruit greater numbers of minority members into nursing, especially to the baccalaureate level. What better source than returning minority RN students could we have in helping to meet our nation's future health care needs?

With the advent of the newly adopted NLN accreditation criteria for baccalaureate nursing programs (NLN, 1991), a commitment to a culturally, racially, and ethnically diverse community is mandated throughout the nursing curricula. As a result, nurse educators must review their curricula and evaluate them for culturally blind educational practices. In addition, baccalaureate nursing programs must begin to accelerate recruitment endeavors for minority students as well as improve their strategies to retain these students.

As for class elitism, most of the RRN students come from working class families where their mother's education did not continue beyond high school (Baj, 1985b). Community colleges have primarily served "blue collar" students and students from lower socioeconomic groups (Vaughn, 1979). A major criticism of community colleges is that they promote the economic and social status quo rather than true upward mobility. Karabel (1972) and Zwerling (1976) both maintain that community colleges perpetuate the existing social order by tracking students based on class into terminal vocational programs that limit graduates to the world of semiprofessionals and technicians. Furthermore, Dougherty (1987) showed that students entering a two-year college program with a desire to obtain a baccalaureate degree are significantly less likely to secure that degree than students of similar academic ability and motivation who go directly to a four-year college.

Based on this information, RRN students who desire to pursue a baccalaureate degree in nursing are already stigmatized because of the previous type of academic credential they have received. These disadvantaged students are burdened with additional difficulties in trying to transfer to a four-year program, as well as in successfully completing the baccalaureate program once accepted.

Conclusions

Returning RN students continue to encounter a number of barriers that impede their progress toward obtaining a baccalaureate degree in nursing. These barriers are the result of a pervasive number of historical and ideological factors.

As a first step to eliminating these barriers, nursing must take stock of its internal conflicts and recognize the importance of nontraditional students already engaged in the delivery of health care in meeting the needs of society. These sentiments are expressed in an article by Smullen (1982) about the "quiet revolution" of RNs returning to school:

> *Without minimizing at all the crucial role of generic baccalaureate education or of the profound effects of graduate education on clinical practice, I maintain that the education, resocialization, and ongoing professionalization of the already-licensed RN, whether she is actively practicing or seeking reentry, whether she is a fairly recent graduate or one with 20 years of experience, holds more promise for finding solutions to acute issues confronting nursing than any other facet of nursing education, and has been vastly underestimated in its importance. (p. 371)*

Additional remedies for overcoming these obstacles will require nursing to consider major attitudinal changes and shifts in philosophies. Some examples of needed changes are a broadening of nursing's view of learning to include alternative modes of instruction that go beyond the walls of the classroom, dispelling the perpetual beliefs that RRNs have "deficit" knowledge and are "second-class" citizens within the profession, and finally, a redefining of the teacher-student relationship which advances a "mutual connectiveness" or a collaborative relationship between the teacher and student.

Nursing's current curriculum revolution, with the adoption of the caring model, principles of adult learning, and a feminist perspective, provides an initial solution for breaking down some of the ideological barriers which continue to impact the decisions of all prospective nursing candidates, but particularly RRN students. Perhaps with this emerging thinking, nursing can become a profession rich in diversity and free of the forces of exploitation and oppression. Nursing can become a liberator for the educational advancement of RRN students.

REFERENCES

Allen, M. (1977). Yes, I have my degree, but. . . . *American Journal of Nursing, 77,* 468.

Allen, M. E., Nunley, J. C., & Scott-Warner, M. (1988). Recruitment and retention of black students in baccalaureate nursing programs. *Journal of Nursing Education, 27,* 107–116.

American Nurses Association. (1965). *Educational preparation for nurse practitioners and assistants to nurses: A position paper.* Kansas City: American Nurses Association.

Anderson, E. H. (1972, March). *The associate degree program—A step to the baccalaureate degree?* Paper presented at the National League for Nursing's Ninth Conference of the Council of Baccalaureate and Higher Degree Programs, New York.

Apple, M. (1982). *Education and power.* London: Routledge & Kegan Paul.

Baj, P. A. (1985a). Can the generic curriculum function for the returning RN student? *Journal of Nursing Education, 24,* 69–71.

Baj, P. A. (1985b). Demographic characteristics of RN and generic students: Implications for curriculum. *Journal of Nursing Education, 24,* 230–236.

Baj, P. A. (1986). Stress of the returning RN student. In W. L. Holzemer (Ed.), *Review of research in nursing education* (Vol. 1, pp. 107–124). New York: National League for Nursing Press.

Beeman, P. (1988). RNs' perceptions of their baccalaureate programs: Meeting their adult learning needs. *Journal of Nursing Education, 27,* 364–370.

Beeman, P. B. (1990). Brief: RN students in baccalaureate programs—faculty's role and responsibility. *The Journal of Continuing Education in Nursing, 21,* 42–45.

Benner, P. (1981). Characteristics of novice and expert performance: Implications for teaching the experienced nurse. In K. Jako (Ed.), *Researching second step nursing education: Vol. II. Proceedings of the second annual national second step conference* (pp. 103–119). Rohnert Park, CA: National Second Step Project, Dept. of Nursing, Sonoma State University.

Benner, P. (1984). *From novice to expert: Excellence and power in clinical nursing practice.* Menlo Park, CA: Addison-Wesley.

Bernard, J. (1973). My four revolutions: An autobiographical history of the American Sociological Society. *American Journal of Sociology, 78,* 773–791.

Chinn, P. (1989). Feminist pedagogy in nursing education. In National League for Nursing (Ed.), *Curriculum revolution: Reconceptualizing nursing education* (pp. 9–24). New York: National League for Nursing Press.

Claerbaut, D. (1976). The black nursing student at the liberal arts college: A study in alienation. *Nursing Forum, 15,* 211–218.

Claerbaut, D. (1978). Expansionist trends in health care and the role of minority students: A challenge for nursing education. *Journal of Nursing Education, 17,* 42–47.

Dougherty, K. (1987). The effects of community colleges: Aid or hindrance to socioeconomic attainment? *Sociology of Education, 60,* 86–103.

Dreyfus, S., & Dreyfus, H. (1980). *A five-stage model of mental activities involved in direct skill acquisition.* Berkeley: University of California Press.

Freire, P. (1985). *The politics of education: Culture, power and liberation* (trans. Donaldo Macedo). South Hadley, MA: Bergin & Garvey.

Gilligan, C. (1979). Women's place in man's life cycle. *Harvard Educational Review, 49,* 431–446.

Gilligan, C. (1982). *In a different voice: Psychological theory and women's development.* Cambridge, MA: Harvard University Press.

Green, C. P. (1987). Multiple role women: The real world of the mature RN learner. *Journal of Nursing Education, 26,* 266–271.

Greenleaf, N. P. (1990). Overcoming barriers to educational mobility in nursing. *Nursing Forum, 25,* 23–29.

Haase, P. T. (1982). *Pathways to practice. A series of final reports on the SREB nursing curriculum project.* Atlanta, GA: Southern Regional Education Board. (ERIC Document Reproduction Service No. ED 240 938).

Hammack, F. M. (1990). The changing relationship between education and occupation: The case of nursing. In K. J. Dougherty & F. M. Hammack (Eds.), *Education and society: A reader* (pp. 561–573). San Diego, CA: Harcourt Brace Jovanovich.

Hansen, H. A. (1988, May). *A study of baccalaureate degree nursing program curricula in California.* ADN-BSN Articulation Committee of the California Association of Colleges of Nursing and the Associate Degree Nursing Directors of California.

Hart, S. E., & Sharp, T. G. (1986). Mobility programs for students and faculty. In National League for Nursing (Ed.), *Looking beyond the entry issue: Implications for education and service* (pp. 53–66). New York: National League for Nursing Press.

Hedin, B. A. (1989). With eyes aglitter: Journey to the curriculum revolution. *Nurse Educator, 14,* 3–5.

Hodgkinson, H. L. (1985). *All one system: Demographics of education—kindergarten through graduate school.* Washington, DC: Institute for Educational Leadership.

Hooks, B. (1984). *Feminist theory: From the margin to center.* Boston: South End Press

Hooks, B. (1990). *Yearning: Race, gender, and cultural politics.* Boston: South End Press.

Huebner, D. (1975). Curricular language and classroom meanings. In W. Pinar (Ed.), *Curriculum theorizing: The reconceptualists* (pp. 217 236). Berkeley, CA: McCutchan.

Institute of Medicine. (1981). *Six-month interim report by the committee of the institute of medicine for a study of nursing and nursing education.* Washington, DC: National Academy Press.

Karabel, J. (1972). Community colleges and social stratification: Submerged class conflict in American higher education. *Harvard Educational Review, 42,* 521–562.

Keller, E. F. (1978). Gender and science. *Psychoanalysis and Contemporary Thought, 1,* 409–433.

Keller, E. F. (1985). *Reflections on gender and science.* New Haven, CT: Yale University Press.

Kidd, J. R. (1959). *How adults learn.* New York: Association.

Knowles, M. S. (1980). *The modern practice of adult education.* Chicago: Follett.

Knowles, M. S. (1984). *The adult learner: A neglected species* (3rd ed.). Houston: Gulf.

Kravetz, D. (1976). Sexism in a woman's profession. *Social Work, 21,* 421–426.

Lather, P. (1991). *Getting smart: Feminist research and pedagogy with/in the postmodern.* New York: Routledge.

Lenburg, C. B. (Ed.). (1975). *Open learning and career mobility in nursing.* St. Louis: Mosby.

Lenburg, C. B. (1976). Alternate educational patterns. In J. A. Williamson (Ed.), *Current perspectives in nursing education: The changing scene* (pp. 159–173). St. Louis: Mosby.

Linares, A. Z. (1989). A comparative study of learning characteristics of RN and generic students. *Journal of Nursing Education, 28,* 354–360.

Lippman, H. (1991, February). How hard will it be to get your BSN? *RN, 91,* 32–37.

Lonborg, R. E. (1984). RN to BSN: A degree of difficulty. *American Journal of Nursing, 84,* 1297–1300.

Matheney, R. V. (1975). Open curriculum—Yes! In C. B. Lenburg (Ed.), *Open learning and career mobility in nursing* (pp. 84–89). St. Louis: Mosby.

Montag, M. L. & Gotkin L. G. (1959). *Community college education for nursing*. New York: McGraw-Hill.

Muff, J. (1988). Of images and ideals: A look at socialization and sexism in nursing. In A. H. Jones (Ed.), *Images of nurses: Perspectives from history, art, and literature* (pp. 197–220). Philadelphia: University of Pennsylvania Press.

Mulligan, J. E. (1980). Together we go, separate we stay. In B. C. Flynn & M. H. Miller (Eds.), *Current perspectives in nursing: Social issues and trends* (Vol. 2, pp. 210–220). St. Louis: Mosby.

Muzio, L. G., & Ohashi, J. P. (1979). The RN student—unique characteristics, unique needs. *Nursing Outlook, 27,* 528–532.

National League for Nursing. (1986). *Looking beyond the entry issue: Implications for education and service.* New York: National League for Nursing Press.

National League for Nursing. (1987). *Report to the coordinating committee on education and practice, national league for nursing, on educational mobility for nurses.* New York: National League for Nursing Press.

National League for Nursing. (1991). *Council of baccalaureate and higher degree programs: Accreditation criteria.* New York: National League for Nursing Press.

Nursing data review. (1991). New York: National League for Nursing Press.

Nursing datasource 1991: A research report. Trends in contemporary nursing education (Vol. 1). New York: National League for Nursing Press.

Nyquist, E. B. (1973). The external degree program and nursing. *Nursing Outlook, 21,* 372–377.

Parker, P. C. (1979). Access and mobility in higher education: The search for a common currency and a gold standard. *Liberal Education, 65,* 120–134.

Rather, M. L. (1990). The lived experience of returning registered nurse students: A Heideggerian hermeneutical analysis. *Dissertation Abstracts International, 51,* 1747B. (University Microfilms No. 90-24783)

Reverby, S. M. (1989). *Ordered to care: The dilemma of American nursing, 1850–1945.* New York: Cambridge University Press.

Rodgers, S. G. (1990). Retention of minority nursing students on predominantly white campuses. *Nurse Educator, 15,* 36–39.

Rudolf, F. (1990). *The American college and university: A history.* Athens, GA: The University of Georgia Press. (Original work published 1962)

Smullen, B. B. (1982). Second-step education for RNs: The quiet revolution. *Nursing and Health Care, 3,* 369–373.

Sorenson, G. (1976). Sounding board . . . in support of the generic baccalaureate degree program. *Nursing Outlook, 24,* 384–385.

Stevens, B. (1981). Program articulation: What it is and what it is not. *Nursing Outlook, 29,* 700–706.

Thomas, K. J. & Thomas, H. K. (1988). Articulation of credits: Continuing education for career ladder upward mobility in nursing. *The Journal of Continuing Education in Nursing, 19,* 103–108.

Vaughan, G. B. (1979). The challenge of criticism. *Community and Junior College Journal, 50,* 8–11.

Waters, V. (1989). Transforming barriers in nursing education. In National League for Nursing (Ed.), *Curriculum revolution: Reconceptualizing nursing education* (pp. 91–99). New York: National League for Nursing Press.

Weber, M. (1978). *Economy and society* (2 vols.). Berkeley, CA: University of California Press.

Woolley, A. S. (1978). From RN to BSN: Faculty perceptions. *Nursing Outlook, 26,* 103–108.

Zorn, J. M. (1980). A research profile of today's baccalaureate nursing student. *The Journal of Continuing Education in Nursing, 11,* 7–9.

Zwerling, L. S. (1976). *Second best: The crisis of the junior college.* New York: McGraw-Hill.

5

Review of Research Related to Educational Re-entry for the Registered Nurse: 1985–1991*

Mary Lou VanCott
Cecile Lengacher

INTRODUCTION

The largest portion (66.5 percent) of nurses in the United States are prepared at either the diploma or the associate degree level (National League for Nursing [NLN], 1991). More RNs than ever are seeking an education beyond their basic associate degree or diploma in nursing. They are enrolling in programs because they are personally motivated to achieve a higher education level and reach their highest potential; they bring into the college mature learners who challenge faculty and administration. The need for nurses with additional educational credentials has dramatically increased within the health care system (USDHHS, 1988). Nurse educators are confronted with issues related to access to the baccalaureate in nursing for the RN student population, the need to develop curricular options which will enhance progression through the education process, and the need to provide nontraditional and flexible educational experiences while maintaining quality programs. In addition, these returning RN students have very different personal and professional histories, ranging from newly graduated to many years of nursing practice experience. In order to assist these stu-

*An extension of this study has been previously published in *Review of Research in Nursing Education*, Volume V.

dents, educational re-entry for RNs has become a focus for nursing research. The analysis of current research will assist educators to improve nursing education methodologies and curricula.

METHOD

This review of research related to educational re-entry of the registered nurse was limited to those studies appearing in the literature from 1985 through 1991. A computer search was completed to identify journals citing studies on research related to RN students. Studies were identified in the following journals: *The Canadian Nurse, Journal of Continuing Education in Nursing, Journal of Nursing Education, Journal of Professional Nursing, Nurse Educator, Nursing Research, Image*, and *Western Journal of Nursing Research*. Following the computer search, a manual search was then conducted of the journals. Only published articles that described a scientific research approach that systematically assessed curricular issues or personal characteristics of RN students re-entering the education system to seek a baccalaureate degree were included in the study. The majority of the 31 studies that were identified as meeting study criteria were found in the *Journal of Nursing Education*. No research articles on this topic were found upon a manual search of *Nursing Research*. Each study in the sample was reviewed related to variables studied, use of conceptual frameworks, research design, sampling procedures, data analysis, and research outcomes.

OVERVIEW OF THE RESEARCH STUDIES

Before discussing the analysis of the studies, it is interesting to note the characteristics of the researchers who have conducted these studies. Of the authors identified through the review of literature, 16 held a PhD, 12 held an EdD, 3 held a DNSc, 6 held an MS, 1 held a Master's degree in Education, and 2 held baccalaureate degrees in nursing. All but two of the studies were conducted by authors who were faculty members in university schools of nursing. Primary authors' ranks or positions were identified as: professors (N=2), associate professors (N=9), assistant professors (N=12), and other ranks and positions (N=7). A conclusion that can be drawn from this review is that this area has not been perceived as a priority for research investigation by senior faculty members in institutions of higher education.

Of the studies reviewed, the most frequently employed research design (58 percent) was descriptive/exploratory in nature. Only three of the investigators utilized an experimental method and six used a quasi-experimental design. Only two of the studies had a longitudinal element; there was limited use of time series and no evidence of repeated measures design. Few studies used qualitative research methods, such as phenomenology, ethnography, or grounded theory. There was limited use of multisites for data collection. Few of the studies reviewed were designed to test a theory and there was no evidence of commonality in use of theoretical models. There was evidence of linking of theoretical frameworks to the investigation, however, most studies were based upon limited general frameworks of previous research in the area.

CATEGORIES OF RESEARCH CONCERN

The empirical studies included in the research were divided into six categories for critique and discussion: personal characteristics, developmental patterns, and motivational dimensions of RN students; studies related to types of programs, innovative teaching/learning strategies specifically for use with RN students; and role socialization/professionalism of the RN student. Of these categories, most ($N = 15$) of the research concerned the description of the characteristics of RN students (48.4 percent). Eleven studies (35.5 percent) related to curricular or programmatic issues, and the remaining five studies (16.1 percent) examined the role socialization/professionalism of the RN student.

Characteristics of the RN Student

The demographic differences between RN students and generic students have been studied by numerous investigators. Topics relevant to student characteristics have included analyses of demographic differences, personality and learning characteristics.

Demographic Differences   Raj (1985) studied demographic differences among 251 RN and generic students enrolled in a single program. This study offered a unique perspective by including students from only colleges and universities that admit RNs to NLN accredited generic baccalaureate programs. Only 39.6 percent of senior RN students as compared to 81 percent of senior generic students were students on a full-time basis. There were more married or divorced RN (56.8 percent) than generic students (34.5 percent). RNs (13.8 percent) received less financial aid than generic students (41.5 percent). Generic students had a higher percentage of marriage or engagements (22.7 percent) than RN students (11.3 percent) but fewer childbirths (0.9 percent) compared to RNs (9.2 percent). The RN student also had a higher incidence of family illness (14.2 percent) than the generic student (7.3 percent). An unexpected finding was that subjects in both groups had one or more dependents, which is an important issue in nursing education regarding academic advising and progression. RN students were older (M = 32 years) than generic students (M = 23 years) and were employed more hours in a nursing role (27 hours per week compared to 11.49 hours), resulting in a monthly household income for RN students of $2,150 compared to $1,630 for generic students. A specific question, concerning RNs only, showed that 51 percent had been registered nurses for six or more years.

Two groups of RN students (N = 72) were compared on demographic characteristics and academic performance in a study by McClelland and Daly (1991). Differences between the RN student enrolled in an on-campus program and the RN student enrolled in a satellite campus program revealed that students at satellite centers were older, employed, worked more hours per week, traveled farther to class, had more children, and planned a longer time to complete their studies than RNs on the main campus. Satellite campus RNs had higher ACT/PEP mean scores and transfer GPAs than RNs in on-campus programs. Using an analysis of covariance, significant differences were found on grades in two courses RNs received on campus and in the satellite area. Grades for satellite campus students were lower, but these RNs worked more, had more children and drove further to class.

MacLean, Knoll, and Kinney (1985) examined the graduates (N = 198) of an RN/BSN program in an eight year longitudinal study. Data were descriptive in nature and identified demographic variables, type of programs originally graduated from, length of program, and effectiveness of the program. Findings indicated that in 1972, 9 percent of the students were single as compared to 70 percent in 1978. In addition, length of time in the program decreased from an average of 6.6 years in 1971 to 4.3 years in 1979. The amount of professional related activity increased after graduation to 59 percent as compared to 47 percent prior to enrollment in the program.

A study which has significant implications for recruitment and advisement of registered nurse students was conducted by Lange (1986).

This study surveyed 965 RNs for the purpose of identifying the level of interest and plans to enroll in baccalaureate nursing education, in order to obtain data for recruiting, advising, and program planning for RN/ BSN students. Findings of this study indicated that those who planned to enroll were younger, less likely to be married, more likely to hold associate degrees, and to have graduated more recently. Lange recommended advisement conferences be held to discuss strategies for facilitating adjustment to the new role of student.

Dugas (1985) conducted a similar study, using a random sample of 364 Canadian registered nurses in order to identify the characteristics of the students, interest in returning for a baccalaureate degree, and needs related to desired courses and scheduling/location of courses. The primary focus of the study was evaluation of delivery of courses over a teleconference mode which, in Canada, has proven to be successful. Seventy-five percent of the sample graduated from a diploma program in nursing. One-third of the diploma graduates indicated they had taken some university courses in the past ten years and were interested in continuing their education. Ninety-three percent indicated an interest in credit courses in the areas of administration, public health, and teaching. The preferred scheduling of classes was evening (70.5 percent). The preferred method of instruction was identified as classroom teaching (97.3 percent), followed by correspondence courses (36.2 percent), and televised courses (19.5 percent). Findings also indicated the nurses desired continuing education courses which carried credit toward a baccalaureate degree. The primary barrier to further education was identified as family responsibilities.

Personality Characteristics.   A longitudinal study to identify specific personality characteristics of RNs returning for their baccalaureate degree was conducted by Everett (1988). The intent of the evaluation was to use the data to individualize the baccalaureate program to the special needs of the RN student. The sample consisted of two groups for comparison: 31 RN baccalaureate degree students and 20 diploma school students. The study assessed differences in personality characteristics as measured by the California Psychological Inventory. Results indicated that although many RN students had graduated from a diploma program, they demonstrated the qualities and values of individuals from generic baccalaureate programs, and the diploma students demonstrated more traditional characteristics. Results indicated that RN students were characterized as mature, forceful, aggressive, and independent with leadership potential. Furthermore, RNs appeared more respectful and accepting of others, appreciative, helpful, conscientious, and sympathetic than the diploma school students. Despite the small sample size, Everett's study does suggest that curricula should focus on developing characteristics consistent with the behaviors expected in the profession: leadership, accountability, responsibility, and scholarly inquiry.

Learning Characteristics. Differences in learning characteristics (constructs of locus of control, self-directed learning readiness, and learning style preference) between 170 RNs and 175 generic students were examined by Linares (1989). Three instruments were used to assess the constructs: the Adult Nowicki-Strickland Internal-External Scale, the Learning Preference Inventory, and the Self-Directed Learning Readiness Scale. The sample for this quasiexperimental study was attained by volunteers in the first nursing course of the program. Results suggested that nursing students had an internal locus of control and that nursing students were self-directed in their learning. Linares reported, however, that statistically significant differences were found among ethnic groups for locus of control. For example, caucasian students were more internal in their locus of control than black or Hispanic students. Hispanic students scored lower than black or caucasian students on the Self-Directed Learning Readiness Scale and hispanic and black students indicated a greater preference for the concrete learning mode than caucasian students. Age appeared to influence readiness as older students indicated a greater readiness than younger students. Although a large sample size was used in the study, caution should be taken in interpretation of the results due to the lack of information reported on reliability and validity of the instruments used for data collection.

Developmental Patterns

As identified from the previously reviewed studies, RN students come into the educational system with multiple roles and responsibilities. Their level of developmental maturity may have impact on their educational experience.

A descriptive comparative study designed to identify developmental differences in life stages, ego development, and learning styles was conducted by King (1986). King used a conceptual framework by Weathersby which incorporates the life stages defined by Levinson (1978), ego development defined by Loevinger (1976), and learning styles defined by Kolb (1974). The sample consisted of 49 RN and 30 generic senior students in one nursing program. Three instruments were used to assess developmental patterns: ego development was measured through the Washington University Sentence Completion Test (WUSC) (Loevinger & Wessler, 1970); learning styles (divergers, convergers, assimilators, or accommodators) were measured through the Kolb Learning Style Inventory (Kolb, 1974); and Tarule's Education Experience Inventory by Weathersby (1977) measured life phases and the impact of education on adult development. Results indicated that RN and generic students differed on the demographic variables of age, number of semesters completed in school, previous attendance at other institutions, previous degrees, and marital status. Results showed significant differences among the groups in relationship to life stage and ego development. The majority of generic students (83.3 percent) were in Early Adult Transition, in which they were beginning to form adult identities with an emphasis on self-discovery. The majority (36.5 percent) of RNs were in Age 30 Transition or Mid-Life Transition (18.3 percent). This finding supports the assumption that the RN student had already made choices about life. Early Adult Transition for generic students meant they were beginning to form adult identities with an emphasis on self-discovery. RNs scored significantly higher than generic students when comparing ego development. While generic students perceived their education primarily as a future investment, RN students perceived their education as a life-long process as well as an investment for the future. There were no significant differences between RN and generic students regarding assessment of learning styles.

In a follow-up study by King (1988), 49 RN students were compared to 30 generic students on adult development, student development, and valuing of program characteristics and their impact on the educational process. Findings showed that RNs and traditional students differed significantly in ego development and life stage but not on learning styles. RNs scored significantly higher in ego development than generic students and had more advanced perceptions and interpretations of life events than generic students. Differences also were found in the two groups related to perception of program characteristics. RNs reported greater flexibility, autonomy, and independent goal setting than generic students. This finding lends support for the dual track curriculum model as a more effective strategy to help facilitate adult developmental needs of RN students.

Lee (1988) used Lazarus' model as a basis for a study on coping methods used by returning RNs. The sample consisted of 111 students: 71 enrolled in a specially designed program for RNs and 40 in a generic program. A critical incident technique was used for data collection. Students were asked to describe how they coped with a stressful situation in classroom and clinical situations. Coping strategies were categorized as direct action (verbal response, social networking, preparation against harm, avoidance, attack and inaction, or as palliation, such as intrapsychic coping) or somatic coping. Findings revealed coping methods for students in each program were similar. Eighty-two percent of the respondents used direct action. Preparation against harm and social networking were reported by 58 percent of the respondents.

Mattson (1990) also examined developmental maturity and coping strategies among RN students. The research was an exploratory, descriptive study involving 138 students in one BSN completion program. Two predictors of coping effectiveness were identified: developmental maturity and past successful coping. Although there was no correlation between age and developmental maturity, a strong link was found between developmental maturity and perceived coping effectiveness. Findings suggested that older, female RN students may adjust better to their academic environment than younger students. Use of support systems to encourage ventilation of feelings and development of problem-solving skills was recommended to assist RN students when dealing with the stressors related to continuation of their education.

Motivational Dimensions

Fotos (1987) surveyed 57 RN students to identify motivational dimensions that precipitate returning to college. A modified Education Participation Scale (EPS) and a personal data form were used to assess the reasons for returning to school. Findings indicated that nurses enrolled in the program were primarily motivated by a "desire for professional advancement" (p. 121). Pressures by society and personal reasons were indicated to be of less importance. Fotos' demographic results indicated that a high percentage of registered nurses are working many hours and going to school either part-time or full-time, have expenses, children, and household responsibilities. While the small sample size limits generalizability of the findings, Fotos provides support for the assumption that orientation programs for RN students are essential to provide information necessary for the RN to survive in school.

Similar to Fotos, Lethbridge (1989) examined the motivational dimensions underlying the reasons for RNs in rural New England to return to school. This descriptive, correlational study of 132 RN students utilized the Educational Participation Scale, as modified by Carmody (1982), for data collection. Three motivational factors were related to the decision to return to school: professional advancement, knowledge, and improvement in social welfare skills.

Perceptions and attitudes of 233 registered nurses upon entrance and exit in two types of programs, generic and second step baccalaureate completion, was studied by Thurber (1988). Data collected from multiple sites revealed factors motivating the student to return to school. Motivating factors for returning to school were enjoyment of learning (87.6 percent) and career advancement (88 percent). The need to improve job performance was indicated by two-thirds of the sample. Findings indicated that more students chose second step programs (61.8 percent) than generic RN programs (38.2 percent). Significant differences in perceptions were found in the sample upon entering into the two types of programs, however, exit perceptions were found to be more alike between programs.

Types of Programs

Another area of research related to program development. Several studies compared and evaluated various types of programs and curricula for RN students.

Stressful clinical and didactic experiences of the RN returning to school were examined by Lee (1987). The highest stress in clinical courses related to scheduling, inadequate instruction, and relations with staff. Findings indicated that papers, recitations, and relationships with instructors or peers evoked the most stress in the classroom setting. Didactic stressful experiences were more frequently reported than clinical experiences. RNs in specifically designed programs identified inadequate instruction as the principle area for stress in comparison with RN students enrolled in generic programs. RN students in generic programs identified examinations (specifically grades and schedule pressures) as the predominant stressor.

Blatchley and Stephen (1985) investigated the RN student within generic programs. The sample consisted of 57 National League for Nursing (NLN) approved generic programs that were randomly selected. Specific questions related to admission policies for RNs, basic

nursing credits, and special courses required. The process of RN socialization was also addressed. Thirty schools required a GPA range from
2.0 to 2.7 with 2.5 the most common. Most schools required prerequisite credits to be met prior to admission. The number of basic nursing
credits that could be earned by challenge varied from 14 to 47 with a
mean of 30. The types of examinations utilized varied from national
examinations, such as ACT/PEP, to teacher-made examinations. Seven-
teen schools developed special bridge courses for RNs to assist transition from technical to professional status and were the major processes
through which socialization occurred.

Arlton and Miller (1987) conducted a national survey of 328 programs to identify advanced placement policies for awarding nursing
and general education credit to RN students. Results indicated that the
majority of the programs (85 percent) were generic baccalaureate that
admitted RNs, while only 15 percent (N = 49) were RN only. Three-
fourths (N = 238) of the generic programs indicated that 25 percent of
their enrollment consisted of RN students; 34 schools reported a 25–50
percent RN enrollment. The number of credit hours required in the
RN-only programs ranged from 60 to 69. In the generic programs,
there were generally between 40 to 69 credit hours required. Ninety-
five percent of all schools provided the opportunity for RNs to obtain
academic credit prior to the nursing major. Results showed that associate degree nurses were allowed to transfer credits from one academic
institution to another, but diploma RNs were required to take some
form of challenge examination. The most frequent types of examination
used in generic programs were teacher-prepared (70 percent) in comparison with the ACT/PEP exams (53 percent) used predominately in
RN programs. The majority of programs allowed approximately one
half of the nursing major to be challenged. The most frequently used
clinical challenge examinations were the NLN and ACT/PEP tests,
along with preparation of a care plan when enrolled in a course. Actual
clinical examinations were required by 19 percent of the generic and 4
percent of the RN only programs. Many programs were generous with
their challenge policies, but prohibited challenge in specific content
areas (for example, research, leadership/management, professional
practice, community health, and advanced practice). Programs reported using other challenge mechanisms for general education and
support credit awards from sociology (32 percent) to anatomy and
physiology (8 percent).

Beeman (1988) conducted a descriptive study to examine differences between RN and generic students in their perceptions of their academic programs. Subjects included 284 undergraduate students from 12 programs including 188 RN students in generic BSN programs, 129 in RN-only programs, and 96 non-RN students. Results indicated that RN students in generic programs felt that some areas of their program inhibited learning. RN students in RN-only programs indicated their program promoted learning and fostered self-direction/learning. Results of qualitative analysis indicated the need for greater flexibility in scheduling, more credit for previous experiences, and different requirements for entry for RN students. Beeman provided evidence that RNs returning to school identified the importance of the structure of the educational environment to promote development.

Since 1978, extension sites for RN/BSN programs have become prominent however, minimal data are available on development and implementation of programming at these sites. Tiffany and Burson (1986) examined how extension sites were implemented by baccalaureate programs in 30 schools. These investigators identified through their analysis three innovative curriculum models. One model shifted instruction sites depending upon where most of the students lived. Another had outreach sites in a 700-mile radius with a single faculty member traveling to each site. A third model modularized courses in the program and allowed students to do independent study to meet course requirements.

Professional resocialization was examined by Cragg (1991) in a qualitative study of 24 RN students who had taken distance courses in nursing. Telephone interviews were conducted with students in four universities. Results indicated that students knew about professional issues and attitudes even though the distance education provided limited contact with faculty from the main campus.

Outcomes of one locally-based outreach RN/BSN program located 70 miles from its parent institution were evaluated in a study conducted by Borst and Walker (1986). The 16 graduates included in the sample indicated an increase in their perception of self-esteem (N = 13) and earned promotion in their place of work following graduation (N = 9).

Innovative Teaching/Learning Strategies

Published research regarding the development of innovative strategies for teaching RN students has been limited. Typically, studies were conducted at single institutions limiting generalizability. Several diverse topics have been examined. Farley and Baker (1987) conducted an experimental study that examined the effect of training on selected self-management procedures related to interpersonal skills among 24 RN students. Sullivan (1987) examined critical thinking, creativity, and clinical performance at the beginning and upon exit of a single program. DuFault (1985) investigated locus of control among 32 RN students enrolled in a one-credit semester course. The course focused on values clarification and commitment to the future of nursing practice. Finally, Daniels, Denny and Andrews (1988), in an experimental study on empathy in communication, taught 53 RN students through the use of a microcounseling technique. Findings indicated that this approach significantly improved empathy scores and reflection of feeling on the Carkuff Indices of Communication.

Role Socialization and Professionalism

Because of the increasingly changing roles of women today and changes in the profession, role socialization grows more important as an area of research interest. Several studies focused on role socialization and potential multiple role conflict experienced by the RN student returning into the academic setting.

Role Socialization. The degree of congruence between the interpersonal orientation of the RN seeking a baccalaureate degree in nursing and the student's perception of the student role was examined by Rendon (1988). The role relationships of 167 registered nurse students in five baccalaureate programs were examined in this correlational study. The two instruments used were the Rendon PSR Scale (the student's perception of own role as student) and the Cohen CAD Scale on interpersonal orientation. Results on the PSR scale revealed a strong commitment of the RN student toward the student role. Over one-half of the students, however, did not feel respected by their faculty because they were treated as novices and perceived themselves as more clinically competent than their faculty. Findings revealed that full-time students had a greater congruence with their student role than part-time students. The perception that the curriculum was less appropriate for the RN student increased with the registered nurse's years of experience. Rendon concluded that assertive RN students need to be viewed less critically by educators and considered more as individuals who cope better.

The effects of multiple roles for RNs entering the academic setting were examined by Campaniello (1988). The most important single variable explaining role conflict was motherhood, and the variable most directly influencing well-being was conflict. Women who had multiple roles experienced greater well-being than those with fewer roles.

Lynn, McCain, and Boss (1989) also studied professional socialization in 30 RN/BSN students and 193 generic/BSN students in a longitudinal study. Through use of ANCOVA, RN/BSN students did not demonstrate significant differences from entry to exit on the Nurses' Professional Orientation Scale (NPOS) compared to generic students. The Six-Dimension scale of Nursing Performance (Six-D) was used to supplement the NPOS data. RN/BSN students exhibited higher scores at graduation on the teaching/collaboration, interpersonal/communication, and planning/evaluation scales of the Six-D scale.

Professionalism. The concept of professionalism was studied by Lawler and Rose (1987). The sample for this study consisted of 25 senior generic baccalaureate students, 18 senior RN students and 36 senior associate degree students. Ex-post facto design was used to compare the differences in professionalism. Two instruments were used to assess the dimension of professionalism: Stone's Health Care Professional Attitude Inventory (modified by Lawler) and the professional subscale from Corwin's Nursing Role Conception Scale. Results confirmed that there was a difference in nursing graduates prepared at different educational levels with the RN/BSN graduate consistently showing more professional orientation than the generic/BSN or ADN graduate. Lawler and Rose demonstrated that working as an RN could have possibly socialized the nurse to a greater extent.

In a descriptive study by Swanson (1987), similarities and differences were explored between 194 generic and RN students in total role investment, quality of effort, and nursing performance. Nine nursing programs were used for data collection. The instruments utilized were the Total Role Investment Scale; the Pace College Questionnaire which measured quality of effort and the Six Dimension Scale of Nursing Performance modified by Lubno (1984). In comparison to the two groups of students, generic students had college educated parents, were younger, predominantly caucasian, and unmarried. In assessment of total role involvement, RNs (both RNs in a generic program and RNs in an RN completion program) scored significantly higher as compared to generic students; however, there were no significant differences between RNs in a generic program and RN completion students. There were no significant differences among the two groups of students on total quality of effort, however total nursing performance was significantly higher for RN completion students than for generic BSN students.

CONCLUSIONS AND SUGGESTIONS FOR FUTURE RESEARCH

The areas of investigation and knowledge generated by the studies found in this review indicate research efforts that have been fragmented and nongeneralizable. There have been few attempts to replicate previous research or to build upon any existing research in the area. This finding is similar to the findings of Stember (1984) who reviewed curricular research in nursing and found that studies did not build upon each other either conceptually or methodologically.

As nursing moves toward greater autonomy and independence, educational programs must enhance learning experiences for the RN student so that autonomy and independence are rewarded rather than discouraged. Based on this review, the following directions for future research are suggested:

1. Research on curricular issues for RNs who represent a diverse population should be addressed with consideration given to personal and academic factors affecting progression. Didactic and clinical instruction should be evaluated as well as desired outcomes at the professional level.

2. Multiple roles held by adult male as well as female learners need to be explored as males are becoming a larger part of the nursing student population.

3. Research on parental support services, such as child-care programs and individual/group counseling supports in academic settings needs to be conducted.

4. Considerations need to be explored related to integration of the RN into the student role, role socialization, and professionalism of the RN student. In addition, examination of working versus nonworking nurses is needed, to determine effects of working on role conflict and well-being. Longitudi-

nal studies could evaluate the direction of the effects of multiple roles upon the RN student.

5. Future studies focusing on development of characteristics consistent with professional behaviors need to be conducted.

6. Examination of motivational dimensions within large RN populations and refinement of an instrument to assess these dimensions in the RN returning to school need to be explored.

7. Research evaluating the development and implementation of programming at extension sites needs to be further explored.

8. The development of innovative, tested strategies for teaching/ learning related to such diverse topics as empathy, professional role, and improvement of interpersonal and critical thinking skills in RN students would enhance the educational experience of the RN student.

9. Replication, in multiple sites, of research that has been conducted related to educational re-entry of RN/BSN students needs to be done to enhance the credibility of research findings. Repeated measures and larger sized samples would also assist in validation of findings.

REFERENCES

Arlton, D. M., & Miller, M. E. (1987). RN to BSN: Advanced placement policies. *Nurse Educator, 12*(6), 11–14.

Baj, P. (1985). Demographic characteristics of RN and generic students: Implications for curriculum. *Journal of Nursing Education, 24*, 230–236.

Beeman, P. (1988). RNs' perceptions of their baccalaureate programs: Meeting their adult learning needs. *Journal of Nursing Education, 27*, 364–370.

Blatchley, M. E., & Stephan, E. (1985). RN students in generic programs: What do we do with them? *Journal of Nursing Education, 24*, 306–308.

Borst, B. B., & Walker, W. J. (1986). A locally-based baccalaureate nursing program for registered nurses. *Journal of Nursing Education, 25*, 168 169.

Campaniello, J. (1988). When professional nurses return to school: A study of role conflict and well-being in multiple-role women. *Journal of Professional Nursing, 4,* 136–140.

Carmody, C. E. (1982). Motivational orientations of registered nurse baccalaureate students. (Doctoral dissertation, Columbia University).

Cragg, C. (1991). Professional resocialization of post-RN baccalaureate students by distance education. *Journal of Nursing Education, 30,* 256–260.

Daniels, T. G., Denny, A., & Andrews, D. (1988). Using microcounseling to teach RN nursing students skills of therapeutic communication. *Journal of Nursing Education, 27,* 246–252.

DuFault, M. (1985). Changing locus of control of registered nurse students with a futuristic-oriented course. *Journal of Nursing Education, 24,* 314–319.

Dugas, B. W. (1985, May). Baccalaureate for entry to practice: A challenge that universities must meet. *The Canadian Nurse,* 17–19.

Everett, H. (1988). Personality characteristic of registered nurses in baccalaureate education. *Nurse Educator, 13*(5), 27–36.

Farley, R., & Baker, A. J. (1987). Training on selected self-management techniques and the generalization and maintenance of interpersonal skills for registered nurse students. *Journal of Nursing Education, 26,* 99–102.

Fotos, J. C. (1987). Characteristics of RN students continuing their education in a BS program. *The Journal of Continuing Education in Nursing, 18,* 118–122.

King, J. (1986). A comparative study of adult developmental patterns of RNs and generic students in a baccalaureate nursing program. *Journal of Nursing Education, 25,* 366–371.

King, J. (1988). Differences between RN and generic students and the impact on the educational process. *Journal of Nursing Education, 27,* 131–135.

Kolb, D. (1974). *Building a learning community.* Washington, DC: National Training and Development Service Press.

Lange, L. L. (1986). Recruiting, advising, and program planning for RN/BSN students. *Western Journal of Nursing Research, 8,* 414–430.

Lawler, T., & Rose, M. (1987). Professionalization: A comparison among generic baccalaureate, ADN and RN/BSN nurses. *Nurse Educator, 12*(3), 19–22.

Lee, J. (1988). Analysis of coping methods by returning RNs. *Journal of Nursing Education, 27*, 309–313.

Lee, J. (1987). Analysis of stressful clinical and didactic incidents reported by returning registered nurses. *Journal of Nursing Education, 26*, 372–379.

Lethbridge, D. J. (1989). Motivational orientations of registered nurse baccalaureate students in rural New England. *Journal of Nursing Education, 28*, 203–209.

Levinson, D. (1978). *The seasons of a man's life.* New York: Ballentine Books.

Linares, A. Z. (1989). A comparative study of learning characteristics of RN and generic students. *Journal of Nursing Education, 28*, 354–360.

Loevinger, J. (1976). *Ego development.* San Francisco: Jossey-Bass.

Loevinger, J., & Wessler, R. (1970). *Measuring ego development: Construction and use of a sentence completion test.* San Francisco: Jossey-Bass.

Lubno, M. (1984). Cost effectiveness analysis of selected baccalaureate and associate degree nursing education programs in Texas. Unpublished doctoral dissertation, The University of Texas at Austin.

Lynn, M., McCain, N., and Boss, B. (1989). Socialization of RN to BSN. *Image, 21*, 232-237.

Mattson, S. (1990). Coping and developmental maturity of RN baccalaureate students. *Western Journal of Nursing Research, 12*, 514–524.

MacLean, T. B., Knoll, G. H., & Kinney, C. K. (1985). The evolution of a baccalaureate program for registered nurses. *Journal of Nursing Education, 24*, 53–57.

McClelland, H., & Daly, J. (1991) A comparison of selected demographic characteristics and academic performance of on-campus and satellite-center RNs: Implications for the curriculum. *Journal of Nursing Education, 30*, 261–266.

NLN, 1991. *Nursing data review.* New York: National League for Nursing Press.

Rendon, D. (1988). The registered nurse student: A role congruence perspective. *Journal of Nursing Education, 27*, 172–177.

Stember, M. L. (1984). Curricular research in nursing. In Werley, H. H. & Fitzpatrick, J. J. (Eds.). *Annual review of nursing research, Volume 2.* New York: Springer.

Sullivan, E. (1987). Critical thinking, creativity, clinical performance, and achievement in RN students. *Nurse Educator, 12*, 12–16.

Swanson, M. J. (1987). Baccalaureate nursing education: Students' perceptions of roles, effort, and performance. *Journal of Nursing Education, 26*, 380–383.

Thurber, F. (1988). A comparison of RN students in two types of baccalaureate completion programs. *Journal of Nursing Education, 27*, 266–273.

Tiffany, J. C., & Burson, J. Z. (1986). Baccalaureate nursing education at extension sites: A survey. *Journal of Nursing Education, 25*, 124–126.

United States Department of Health and Human Services. (1988). Secretary's Commission on Nursing, Final Report Volume I. Washington, DC.

Weathersby, R. (1977). A developmental perspective on adult's use of formal education (Doctoral dissertation. Howard University). Dissertation Abstracts International, 38A.7085-A-7086A (University microfilms No. 7808621).

6

"Harbingers of Entry into Practice": the Lived Experience of Returning RN Students

Marsha L. Rather

In the United States today there is a demand for better educated nurses which is urgent and growing. By the year 2000, the U. S. Department of Health and Human Services projects that there will be twice as many jobs for nurses with master's and doctoral degrees as nurses available to fill the positions, and a 30 percent shortfall of baccalaureate prepared nurses to fill BSN required positions (Bureau of Health Professions, U. S. Department of Health and Human Services, as cited in Lass, 1990). By contrast, the same study predicted that there will be 75 percent more nurses prepared at the hospital diploma or associate degree level than positions which require them. A continuing question is how can nursing education meet projected demands for BSN and advanced degree nurses?

An important source of potential BSN nurses is the large population of Registered Nurses (RNs) currently prepared at the hospital diploma and/or associate degree (ADN) level. Baccalaureate programs are moving to recruit these nurses to return for the BSN, hence the label "returning RNs" (RRNs), and there has been a steady increase in their enrollment (National League for Nursing [NLN], 1989). Although the movement to differentiate credentials and work roles for ADN and BSN graduates has achieved little progress, the "entry into practice" issue is another factor encouraging RRN enrollment. However, attrition of RRNs is also an acknowledged problem, and research indicates that many RRNs are displeased with their experiences in baccalaureate curricula (Beeman, 1988; Hillsmith, 1978; Ipock, 1982; MacLean, Knoll, & Kinney, 1985; Murdock, 1986; Portnoy et al., 1980; Rendon, 1983). Curricula which challenge and extend the nursing knowledge of RRNs need to be devised in order to discourage attrition and encourage more RNs to return to baccalaureate education.

The current "curriculum revolution" is a call for major reform in nursing education. There is a growing recognition that innovative curricular and instructional strategies must be explored in order to better prepare nurses to address the changing health care needs of our nation (and world). NLN resolutions call for curricular innovations that enhance caring practices, promote community, recognize diversity, and critique beliefs and assumptions inherent in the current health care system (NLN 1989 Resolutions, as cited in Tanner, 1990). As practicing nurses, RNs return to school ready for the kind of educational experience that will help them make a difference in health care today and in the future. Research in RRN education is timely in that it might reveal strategies for innovation which would enhance nursing education in general, and RRN education in particular.

There has been little research from the RRN's points of view as to what they find meaningful about their experience of baccalaureate education. Most research has investigated only selected aspects of the return to school situation from the researchers' points of view, for example, program characteristics (Blatchley & Stephan, 1985; MacLean, Knoll, & Kinney, 1985), barriers and motivators to participation (Hillsmith, 1978; Inman, 1982; Murdock, 1986), resocialization and role theory (Blicharz, 1985; Campaniello, 1988; Little & Brian, 1982; Smullen, 1983), stress and coping theory (Kausch, 1988; Lee, 1987, 1988; McBride, 1985), and adult learning frameworks (Beeman, 1988; King, 1988; Presz, 1988; Sullivan, 1987). Because of a lack of interpretive studies, we know little about the meaning of returning to school from the perspective of those who actually live the experience. Inquiry into the meaning of the phenomenon of returning to school might reveal new possibilities for innovation in curriculum and instruction which would enhance the learning of students as well as teachers. This phenomenological study was developed to reveal the common meanings embedded in the experience of returning to school as it is lived by RNs.

METHOD

After granting their informed consent, fifteen RRN volunteers from three baccalaureate nursing programs participated in private, extended

(90 minutes), unstructured, audio-recorded interviews. Participants were asked to talk about anything that really stood out in their minds about what it is like to be a RRN student. Subsequent interview probes depended upon individual responses, and were used only to clarify statements made by participants. Verbatim transcripts of the interviews were analyzed hermeneutically by a team of researchers using Heideggerian phenomenology as the philosophical background.

Heideggerian phenomenology (Heidegger, 1927/1962) is a particular tradition of philosophy that is specifically concerned with explicating the meanings embedded in lived experience. Hermeneutics is a systematic approach to textual interpretation (Polkinghorne, 1983). Heidegger described the hermeneutical process as a continual, circular movement from parts to the whole, and back again (Heidegger, 1953/1959). Analysis seeks the meanings of a particular text, then links common meanings from multiple texts into themes, and finally expresses the relationship between several themes as a constitutive pattern. Thus, an understanding of the whole is grounded in the parts, and vice versa. This method of data analysis was introduced into nursing research by Patricia Benner (1984), and has been described elsewhere in detail (Diekelmann, Allen, & Tanner, 1989; Rather, 1990, 1992).

Nine themes and one constitutive pattern emerged from the data of this study (Rather, 1990); this paper describes one of the themes, "Harbingers of Entry into Practice." When this theme emerged from a Heideggerian hermeneutical analysis of the data, additional analysis in the form of critical hermeneutics was conducted. This secondary analysis was necessary as the theme reflected issues of power and oppression; critical hermeneutics seeks to uncover hidden power relationships embedded in meanings (Diekelmann, Allen, & Tanner, 1989; Thompson, 1990). Nursing and educational texts which embrace critical theory (Allen, 1986; Apple, 1979, 1982, 1986; Freire, 1968/1970; Giroux, 1983, 1988; Hedin, 1986, 1987; Melosh, 1982; Mezirow, 1985) were utilized to explicate issues of power and control.

FRAMEWORK FOR DATA ANALYSIS

The issue of "entry into practice" immediately emerged as an important concern for RRNs interviewed in this study. This refers to the position by many nursing leaders that a baccalaureate degree should be the minimum education required for entry into "professional" nursing practice, as opposed to "technical" nursing practice which would require an associate degree or hospital diploma (ANA 1978 Resolutions, as cited in Riffle, Lamberth, Moine, & Fielding, 1985, p. 199). Painful and divisive debates over entry into practice, titling, and licensing have ensued as practicing AD and diploma nurses and their educators fear disenfranchisement.

Nearly every participant in this study made it plain that the issue of "entry into practice" was at least an item for consideration as they made their decision to return to school. Further, the "entry" issue remained significant for many of them, resurfacing both during and after their BSN schooling experience. Clearly, the meaning of "entry into practice" changed for some of them through involvement in baccalaureate education. As these new meanings were appropriated, their view of nursing education also changed. The theme which emerged from the data describes my understanding that today's returning RNs are harbingers of how this issue will be played out in the nursing culture in the future. That is, much as the robin is the harbinger of spring, foretelling or foreshadowing the warm weather which is on the way, the RRNs of the early 1990's are the harbingers who foreshadow the ultimate success or failure of the entry into practice initiative in encouraging more nurses to obtain the baccalaureate degree.

HISTORICAL BACKGROUND TO THE ENTRY ISSUE

The basic educational preparation required for entry into practice has been an issue for nursing since its inception. When the first three training schools for nurses opened in the United States in 1873, there were no standards and even domestic workers could present themselves as nurses for hire without having any formal education in nursing (Melosh, 1982). Largely drawn from the lower socioeconomic class, such "practical or domestic nurses" utilized common sense knowledge to care for the sick, as women traditionally have through the ages. "Domestic nurses" outnumbered "trained nurses" by a ratio of 14:1 in 1900 (Christy, 1980). "Trained nurses" could be graduates from one-, two-, or three-year hospital programs. Any hospital could open its own nurse training program, and one in four did (Melosh, 1982). "Hospitals" could consist of facilities small enough to be run by just one physician.

Early nursing leaders addressed the entry issue by persuading state legislatures to pass nurse practice acts (Ashley, 1976; Christy, 1980;

Melosh, 1982). Statutes varied widely and often failed to specify the minimum length of nursing education (Christy, 1980). Nursing leaders necessarily came up against the hegemonic control of physicians over the education and practice standards of nursing. Physicians were concerned that nurses not be "overly" educated, or educated in institutions outside of their control (such as universities), because nurses might then begin to question the physician's authority and/or patient care decisions (Ashley, 1976; Melosh, 1982).

Although the concept of baccalaureate education as the minimum standard for entry into "professional" nursing practice was discussed in two separate national reports in 1948 (Anderson, 1981), the idea did not receive any widespread publicity until it was published as a position paper by the American Nurses Association (ANA) in 1965 (Christy, 1980). Support for the baccalaureate degree for entry into professional practice was based primarily on three arguments (Riffle et al., 1985). First, it would bring order to a very disorderly educational system. Second, the explosion of scientific knowledge and increasingly complex technology in the health care system demand a more sophisticated educational base for nursing practice. Lastly, collegiate education would facilitate the professionalization of nursing, enhancing its status and leading to increased autonomy in patient care decisions.

CRITIQUE OF PROFESSIONALISM

One thrust of the entry into practice issue is grounded in the ideology of professionalism. Nurses are not alone in seeking "professional" status. We live in an era of "professional" bartenders, hairstylists, truck drivers, and blackjack dealers, as well as "professional" nurses. In seeking the label of "professional," workers are actually seeking the power and prestige associated with a label which was first attached to the elite professions of law and medicine. Our everyday understanding is that professionals are experts in the task to be performed, someone with specialized knowledge that can be trusted to assess and act on a problem autonomously, who keeps the best interests of the client always in the forefront. The combination of specialized knowledge with altruistic service seems to justify the broad autonomy and special privileges enjoyed by professionals in their work (Allen, 1986).

However, revisionists' analyses (Allen, 1986; Apple, 1986; Melosh, 1982) dispute the claim to altruism, and argue it merely serves to legitimate (not define) professional prerogatives to determine the scope and application of their expertise post hoc. Professions such as law and medicine are actually very interested in maintaining their dominance and its monetary rewards, and do so by carefully controlling standards of education and certification. In this view, the professions are monopolies.

Allen (1986) has further noted that professionalization is being used by nurse leaders and educators to perform an ideological function; ideology is a system of ideas, values, or beliefs about social reality which serves to legitimate the vested interests of powerful groups through a special rhetoric (Apple, 1979). Thus, leaders seek to locate the occupation of nursing within the professional social structure in hopes of garnering prestige, autonomy, and higher salaries, but also misrepresent this placement as "natural," or "obvious."

Professionalization in nursing has continuously been played out as the controversy over entry into practice. Although the goal of early nursing leaders in adopting the rhetoric of professionalism was to empower nurses, nurses have never gained the measure of control over their work which defines professional autonomy because of the hegemonic control of physicians who designed the apprenticeship educational system and practice standards for nursing (Anderson, 1981; Ashley, 1976; Melosh, 1982; Moloney, 1986). In addition, the rhetoric of professionalism is exclusionary and elitist; it has been used to secure the privileges of a few at the expense of many, thereby perpetuating socioeconomic class divisions (Allen, 1986; Melosh, 1982). Thus, nurse leaders from Nightingale on sought to exclude lower-class women from nursing through admission and retention standards couched in terms of "respectability." The issue of standards for licensure forced smaller nursing schools out of the educational market, and excluded self-styled nurses such as midwives from the occupation of "trained" nursing.

Today's debate over "technical" vs. "professional" nursing has resulted in the closure of hundreds of good diploma schools of nursing. There exist today only 209 diploma programs in the United States (as compared to 721 in 1968), but 789 associate degree programs (as compared to 324 in 1968) (NLN, 1989). In this manner, much of nursing education has been reduced from a three-year to a two-year program. Although there are 467 BSN programs (as compared to 233 in 1968) (NLN, 1989), if you are poor, or live in a rural area you are less likely to attend a BSN program, no matter what your abilities and talents. Baccalaureate nurses are more apt to be drawn from the new "petty bourgeoisie," as Apple (1979) calls it. As a result, the entry into professional practice initiative has disenfranchised many poor and working class persons, as well as stigmatized the 70 percent of practicing nurses who are AD and diploma school graduates (Moses, 1989), nurses who will have to be "grandfathered" into "professional" licensure.

Divisive social class distinctions are further perpetuated through the competencies outlined for both roles, in that elite "professional" nurses are designated for middle-management roles, responsible for patient care but directing others (i.e., "technical" nurses and auxiliaries) to do it (Kramer, 1981; Primm, 1986). This 1948 letter to the editor of *Trained Nurse* might just as easily have been written yesterday:

> *Those with degrees get the bossing jobs. Those without degrees roll up their sleeves. I think there is a distinct class consciousness between the haves and the have-nots. Is this what we want? (quoted in Melosh, 1982, p. 68)*

Finally, the entry into practice initiative encourages discrimination and competition between BSN and non-BSN nurses by purporting to set up two categories of nurses who can be distinguished by their level of functioning. What actually occurs is labeling based on educational preparation. The problem is that neither nursing studies nor the studies of industrial efficiency experts have been able to produce a reliable measure to define nursing skills, much less break them down into two levels of functioning, i.e., "technical" versus "professional" (Melosh, 1982). In contrast, Benner's research (Benner, 1981, 1984; Benner & Tanner, 1987; Benner, Tanner, & Chesla, 1992; Benner & Wrubel, 1989) has shown that the skilled practice of nursing is contextual, and develops *with experience* over time, along a continuum of levels from novice to expert.

Presentation of the Theme: "Harbingers of Entry into Practice"

My first participant, Tracy, spoke about the issue of entry into practice as follows:

> *It seems that . . . every [few] years . . . it was surfacing—this issue about entry into practice was coming up . . . and it just buzzes through the hospital—now what are we going to do? Here we are a lot of us with our associate or diploma and we only had but one BSN working in*

*this small hospital. So I think we all got worried. They said, you don't
have to worry; you're going to get grandfathered in. Well, I'm the type
where to get grandfathered in just isn't enough, and I didn't want to
just be given something. I wanted to earn it, so I thought well, maybe I
should go back at this time.*

Clearly the concept of "grandfathering" carried negative meanings for
these RRNs, as if it were merely some consolation prize given to those
who could not compete in the educational race. Further, there was a
sense of mistrust, because "we all got worried." Kim speaks of this
mistrust as a need to insure her future:

*I was insuring my future . . . we did not want to be classified as
technicians. And that's why we went. To insure ourselves that that
would not happen. . . . You do what you think you have to do to insure
your own safety in the profession.*

The idea of being grandfathered into professional (versus technical)
nursing status was also repugnant to participants because they already
considered themselves to be *professional* nurses. Part of what it means
to be a nurse is to be professional; because they were already nurses,
they were already professional. The RRNs found this common understanding that nursing was among the "professions" was shared by
their non-nursing collegiate classmates. Dana told me,

*They couldn't understand what that meant for me to be in a [freshman-
level liberal arts course] . . . they had a hard time understanding why
someone like me who's 30 years old, and who's already a practicing RN
professional was in this low level class; they couldn't figure that out.*

Because the RRNs believed that they were already practicing professional nurses, it was difficult for them to understand why the nursing
hierarchy deemed it necessary for them to acquire a bachelor's degree,
in addition to their basic nursing certificate, to be labeled "professional" nurses and be treated accordingly. As Robin succinctly stated,
"I had to go back to be a nurse when I was a nurse."

The RRNs also lived the issue of entry into practice daily in the
workplace. Again, it was Robin who summed up their dilemma:

*You knew that in order to have advancement you needed to go get your
bachelor's because that's what the hierarchy said, but . . . I was already*

in a position of leadership [as a nurse manager], so I wouldn't be doing anything different—all I needed was a piece of paper just saying I could do the same thing I did . . . [There was] a resentment because of how we were sub-nurses, even though we were doing the same work, had the same responsibilities, made the same decisions, and in most cases were in charge of those people who had bachelor's. . . . I'd been a nurse so long, and now I'm going to have to go back to get a piece of paper to say I'm a nurse. And I already am one.

Returning RNs received mixed messages when they were made to feel they were "sub-nurses" yet were given positions on the ward or in nursing management where their responsibilities were the same as or more elevated than those of BSN nurses. These RRNs viewed the bachelor's degree as a credential, "a piece of paper," which would merely certify their existent level of knowledge and expertise.

The entry into practice issue was also experienced as being intimately wed with the RRNs' sense of personhood, as Pat told me:

I always felt that it was really unfair that I had to go back to school and I have felt that for many years, and I thought that [given the] level of education that I had that I could do what I wanted to do. If I wanted to be a head nurse, I could be it if I wanted to be, because I had worked for that . . . Forget all that entry into practice—they don't know what they're talking about. I'm a good person even though they don't think I am. You think of it in those terms, even though it has nothing to do with what kind of person you are—your professional things are threatened, and I think a lot of people feel like that.

The RRNs' lived experience with members of the nursing hierarchy and BSN graduates in the workplace was thus interpreted as demonstrating the disrespect these persons had for diploma and ADN educational programs. I also learned how baccalaureate nursing faculty contributed to the RRNs' feelings of resentment. Kelly told me,

But there was such a fundamental lack of respect for my diploma pro gram which I found rather offensive also. I invested three years of my life in that program. I had practiced for 13 years as an RN out of that program. I had the same [RN] licensure that [the teachers] had. The same that all of their baccalaureate nurses have, and I thought, again, to be judgmental about it . . . There was definitely an air—and I'm sure there was a sense of what in the [heck] are these diploma nurses doing running Alzheimer's centers, directing the Bone Marrow Procurement Program for this whole area—three states or whatever—and the fact is that there are some very competent nurses that graduated from all kinds of programs.

One nurse manager spoke of her interactions with the nursing faculty as follows:

I think maybe once you've gone up the ladder [of the hierarchy] a couple of times, and all of a sudden you're back on the bottom rung [at school]. . . . [It's like you] got taken down off the ladder from where you were . . . now you're back down here again, and you really don't know how to act, and some of the instructors didn't give you credit for what you already knew. . . . They're preparing you for the job you already have . . . because [they said] "the BSNs are at [management] level and you're going to have these kinds of jobs" [but] we were already up there. . . . So all of a sudden you felt like you were explaining yourself. You know, it was almost like you had to explain [how you got] . . . to be in that position that you were [in].

These RRNs felt their practical knowledge and skills as well as their existent theoretical knowledge of nursing were being devalued. Yet as Benner's research (1984) so well illustrates, both practical ("knowing-how") and theoretical ("knowing-that") knowledge are refined in actual practice situations. Experience is a requisite for expertise. Rather than denigrating the RRNs' nursing knowledge, faculty should assist them to uncover and describe some of the assumptions, expectations, and graded qualitative distinctions which underlie expert practice. This is the manner in which knowledge in an applied discipline advances.

Rather than being used to structure an argument for the baccalaureate degree as a means of extending basic nursing education, the entry into practice issue has traditionally been used by nursing leaders and baccalaureate educators to promulgate a view of the BSN as a means of making up the deficits in diploma and ADN education. Participants in this study perceived this view was held by their teachers. As Gail derisively noted,

A lot of times the instructor would say, "you'll be just so glad to get your degree; you just wouldn't believe what a difference it will make."

*And we'd all say, "why is it going to make such a difference when we're
already practicing? It's not going to make any difference."*

One participant spoke of her almost adversarial encounter with an advisor:

*She looked at my transcripts, and she said, "Well, don't expect grades
like these. School's much harder now than it was before when you
went." . . . she went on to say they had these [certifying] exams that
you could take, or you could retake all of these classes. . . . She said,
"Well, don't worry—at this point in time we have no limit on the
number of times you can take these exams. [You can take them] Over
and over again." . . . Also, she's going through [the transcript], "This
is too old—scratch those four credits. Scratch those five credits." I felt
violated by the time it was over, and it was done in a very cavalier
manner. . . . [I asked her why all these classes must be taken over] and
she said, "Then we know you can do it." I said, "I have passed all of my
licensure exams. I have worked as an RN [for 10 years]. . . . Do you
really think I'm less intelligent than generic students because I have a
diploma?"*

The deficit view of education arises directly out of Tylerian/behavioral
notions of education as job preparation and education as additive (accumulation of "facts"), notions which contribute to a results-oriented
view of education which requires one to *prove* what one knows (Apple,
1979; Giroux, 1988; Kliebard, 1970). If the purpose of baccalaureate education is merely job preparation, then the curriculum must assure
both uniform factual content and clinical practicums for all participants.
The curriculum which is "prescribed" in order to remedy deficits then
requires that RRNs take a basic course in nursing management even
though they already work as nurse managers, or a practicum in community nursing even though they manage a community health center,
etc. As Diekelmann, Allen, and Tanner (1989) have shown, the status
quo was further reinforced in that, until recently, NLN criteria for accreditation of nursing schools were also grounded in Tyler's (Tyler,
1949) rationale.

These RRNs disclosed common meanings embedded in the entry
into practice issue which were significant for them. Dialogue in the
nursing culture about how much education nurses should have has
been heard and, for whatever reasons, RNs are beginning to return to

school in record numbers. The question remains what will these har-bingers tell other RNs about their return to school experience that will ultimately affect and reconstitute the entry issue? For as they share their experiences of baccalaureate education with non-BSN nurses in the workplace, the current cohort of RRNs changes the constellation of shared meanings in the nursing culture regarding nursing education. Nursing education will then be viewed through this new lens of shared meanings.

Many RRNs will go back to the workplace carrying the message that baccalaureate education, in spite of all the publicized changes, con-tinues to fail to live up to their expectations. As Terry said, "it didn't feel like an educational experience should feel." Although the nursing faculty seemed to think they were making up for deficits in the RNs' basic education, many RRNs viewed nursing coursework as boring and redundant. Erin was frankly resentful.

> *I don't know that the experience was all—I mean, it wasn't all bad . . . I love the liberal arts part of going back; I just loved it, but the RN stuff—and I was going through some old notes and stuff that I hadn't thrown away, and I thought I didn't really learn anything in the RN classes. They went over some mandatory stuff, but I had been a nurse for five or six years when I started going back to school, and it was stuff that wasn't new to me. A lot of it, I felt, was a waste of time. Just busy work that they had to fill in, probably because they had to make us take some nursing classes.*

Behavioral education and its concomitant view of deficit learning, in which we are all steeped as members of this culture, had led Erin to believe that baccalaureate education would give her new information, information that her basic nursing program did not provide. Instead, many RRNs found that the nursing knowledge being presented was the basic, "common sense" nursing they already knew. Sandy, for in-stance, told me:

> *I love to learn. But I look at those nursing classes and I don't feel like I've learned that much in nursing. I really haven't. It's been a joke. . . . I'm just amazed that I'm not learning. And it's not that I'm not study-ing. . . . [but] it's common sense. . . . We have played a game. I'll do this, but it's ridiculous. . . . I haven't learned anything in nursing really that I can say that I'm that much better a nurse because I have my degree.*

A major problem with behavioral education is that when course content and learning objectives/outcomes are prescribed in advance, it is more difficult for teachers to change the content based on their students' interest or expertise.

These RRN students wanted to move beyond the basics to advanced learning in nursing. Lee said:

> *Sometimes I feel like I should be at a different level. I feel like I should be in graduate school. I feel like I should be doing all of these other things. I'm doing basic level classes, and it's very hard to try to keep perspective on that, and it's hard not to get angry. . . . [I tell myself] you'll be done in a year, and then you can go on to what you want to do. . . . I have to take classes I feel like I've already had . . . when I was a student [nurse] before. Now it's to the point where I'm just like, well, I just have to get it done, and that's that. This is what they want me to do in order to get this. I just have to do it.*

These RRNs are plainly seeking the kind of advanced content that the master's degree has been designed to provide. Returning RNs commonly saw themselves more as graduate students than as basic degree students.

Other RRNs found their baccalaureate experience to be profoundly meaningful as they experienced powerful transformations in their thinking about nursing, learning, and themselves; this pattern, "Nursing As A Way of Thinking," has been described in detail elsewhere (Rather, 1992). Harbingers such as Pat will be likely to promote baccalaureate education. She said:

> *I learned so much about other things. . . . it really opened up new roads . . . or new horizons or expanded horizons . . . that whole thinking process of all the other classes coming into nursing and to my idea of nursing, and I guess . . . I just feel that I'm a more well-rounded practitioner, and so I guess that's why I say it's positive.*

Pat experienced a transformation in how she thinks as a nurse, which has changed the way she practices nursing. As a result of her baccalaureate schooling experience she sees new possibilities for nursing, and for her own way of being.

Clearly the BSN was also meaningful for some RRNs as "a means to an end," that end being the master's degree. Some RNs entered baccalaureate education already knowing that they would go on for the master's degree. One such participant spoke of the baccalaureate degree as the "foundation for the house; you need it to build on." Other RRNs established the master's degree as their goal as a result of their baccalaureate education. Dana demonstrated this change in her thinking:

> *I've told people lately—the more knowledge I gain, the less I feel like I know. There's such a wealth of knowledge that the more you learn, it makes you realize where you stand. You just don't know very much, and there's so much to be gained, and it makes one hungry and thirsty for more. I think that's what the important thing about education is. The more you get, the more you want. . . . People that are not in school—they're amazed—they talk to me and ask what do you want to do? And I'll say go to graduate school, and then I'm thinking about going to law school.*

Where an advanced degree is, or becomes the RRN's goal, baccalaureate education will likely be promoted.

Some of the participants also discussed how the meaning of entry into practice had been transformed by their return to school experience. These new proponents of baccalaureate education told me:

> *And now I feel totally different. I really feel now that everyone should have a bachelor's degree for family practice and to be a nurse—starting whenever they want to start that . . . I'm talking about the future, because if we look at our other professions, all those people have undergraduate degrees, and they are getting the credibility that they need, so I think nurses need to step up and say, yes, so do we.*

Those harbingers who were very positive about baccalaureate education told me they now overtly and/or covertly try to recruit their colleagues to come back to school, or at least try to "sort of spark more of their interest in learning." Jean spoke at length about sharing what she had learned in hopes of "making nursing a better place."

> *I just like to talk to [the nurses at work] about things. Like things that I did in my [BSN] program . . . and just get them to start thinking . . . not [with] that narrow focus, but thinking beyond that. Doing beyond that. . . . But the people that I see a lot of potential in . . . I try to always be looking out for them and if I see a big seminar I'll be sure they get a flyer—and I say, "I'm going to do this really fun thing—do you*

want to do it?" . . . Whether it's doing a disaster inservice for the Red Cross or something like this . . . I guess I work at that all the time to show by example. . . . That's what I feel like I'm doing now that I'm through the [BSN] program . . . at least that way I feel like there is some hope . . . more people have to take the push and make the move or something to make nursing a better place. So I just try to do my part, but not that I think that I can change everybody, but people that just need somebody who's interested in their growth. I think I can make a difference.

Jean seeks to empower her co-workers through sharing her engaged, open, and reverent way of learning. Here is an example of how the whole community of nursing benefits from the advanced learning of one of its members.

SUMMARY AND IMPLICATIONS

Common meanings embedded in the entry into practice issue were often interpreted by RRNs in this study as a personal attack. They mistrusted the promise of "grandfathering" and chose not to be associated with it; they believed they needed to take independent action to insure their future in nursing practice. They believed themselves to be "professional" nurses already, and their lived experience of the workplace told them that their level of practice was at least as good as that of a baccalaureate nurse. Although they understood themselves to already be professional nurses, they were exposed to co-workers, administrators, and teachers who denigrated their educational preparation. They were confused as they tried to demonstrate the competence of their previous education and their knowledge of nursing practice. Thus common meanings embedded in the "entry" issue constituted an important aspect of their return to school experience.

How the RRNs interpreted their return to school experience affected their understanding of the entry into practice issue. Those who experienced transformative education, education which transformed their thinking, their nursing practice, and their selves, changed their views of the entry issue. These harbingers will likely carry the message to their colleagues that baccalaureate education is meaningful. RRNs who experienced baccalaureate education as boring, repetitious, and oppressive will likely dissuade their colleagues from "making the same mistake."

If the pain and struggle over "entry into practice" is not to have been in vain, nurse educators need to insure that these harbingers leave baccalaureate education having been challenged to realize new possibilities for themselves. We need to encourage dialogue among teachers, students, administrators, and practitioners to create innovative new approaches to RN education.

What is needed are innovative RRN curricula informed by phenomenological, critical, and feminist pedagogies (Allen, 1990; Bevis & Murray, 1990; Diekelmann, 1990; 1992; in press; Hedin & Donovan, 1989; Pagano, 1988; Van Manen, 1991; Wheeler & Chinn, 1989). For instance, numerous authors have attested to the empowerment experienced by students who study the oppression of nurses in school and in the workplace (Chinn, 1989; Cohen, 1992; Hedin & Donovan, 1989). Dialogue about the history of nursing and nursing education using critical and feminist perspectives makes visible hidden patriarchal assumptions values which contribute to oppressive practices. RRNs could use this new lens to examine and critique many issues of importance to health care in this country, connecting their learning with their practice.

I have found in my own experience teaching RRNs that the groundbreaking phenomenological research of Benner (1984) is an excellent framework for structuring RRN courses. Through Benner's work, RRNs come to understand the importance of practical knowledge, which is acquired through experience. They become eager to share their own paradigm cases (an experience you never forget because it teaches you something about what it means to be a nurse); discussing paradigm cases in class makes visible the practical knowledge and expertise of the RRNs and validates what they already know about nursing. In this manner, their prior learning and practical experience are publicly shown to be accessible and valuable. Ensuing dialogue in the classroom brings forward possible alternative views of the clinical situation described in the paradigm, as well as theoretical understandings which the situation may confirm or challenge, thereby enhancing the learning of all participants. The conversation naturally turns to what *more* can be learned, i.e., how to extend, or move toward an increased understanding of what is already known versus how to make up for deficiencies in the knowledge base. Phenomenological inquiry thereby empowers the returning RN.

RRN curricula should also move beyond basic nursing knowledge and challenge students to look at the most difficult clinical problems we have. Many, though not all, RRNs have rich experiential backgrounds which move them well beyond beginning nursing practice, and so are ready to grapple with situations which exhaust their current understanding and repertoire of approaches. The use of case studies and paradigms which would present these clinical situations as contextual wholes supports and encourages the manner in which proficient and expert nurses think and learn (Benner, 1981, 1984; Urden, 1989).

Paradigm cases can also be used to demonstrate prior learning and award degree credits to RRNs. Although the concept of a portfolio for awarding RNs baccalaureate degree credits is not new (Marsh & Lasky, 1984), an innovative practice at the University of Wisconsin-Madison is to have RNs write their paradigm cases and then analyze them for the nursing knowledge embedded in them. Rather than having to "prove" their knowledge in pre-specified categories (e.g., nursing theory, pathophysiology, pharmacology) by an acontextual listing of theories, facts, and figures, the narrative portfolio allows RRNs to demonstrate to faculty their clinical judgment—how they select and use relevant information in specific contexts, using both analytic and intuitive processes (Corcoran & Tanner, 1988). Degree credits are awarded when faculty deem that the thinking the RRN demonstrates in his or her portfolio corresponds to the achievement of learning outcomes for beginning level nursing courses. In addition, the narrative portfolio is used to link RRN students who are applying to the RN-MS program with graduate faculty advisors to facilitate program planning (see RN to MS Dual Degree Option, below).

This study has revealed that RRNs do not consider baccalaureate education to be remedial. Rather, they expect advanced learning. Many RRNs seek the master's degree as their educational goal. Unlike their "generic" counterparts, RRNs enter BSN education with an understanding of nursing practice and what it means to be a nurse. For these reasons, RRNs are more like master's than baccalaureate students in nursing, and their movement into graduate studies needs to be expedited. In recognition of this fact, "RN to MS" programs are being developed rapidly in this country. One example is the University of Wisconsin-Madison's RN to MS Dual Degree Option. This option allows RNs to devise individualized curricula which build upon prior learning by allowing the substitution of selected master's level courses for baccalaureate courses; although courses cannot count toward both degrees, the learning that has taken place can be credited. The MS degree credit requirements for the School of Nursing (36 credits), which far exceed the minimal MS degree requirements of the Graduate School

(18 credits), are simply reduced to reflect courses already taken to meet BSN requirements. In this manner, the length of the nursing master's program can be reduced by up to two semesters.

I would also propose that the issue of "entry into practice" could be reconstituted in a manner which eschews our legacy of elitism and divisiveness. I believe professional nursing cannot be separated from technical nursing, in that nursing does not exist along such a continuum. This research has unveiled nursing as a way of thinking, thinking that is the questioning of all that is (Rather, 1992). Such thinking is not given to us with the baccalaureate credential. We come to know this kind of thinking by reflecting on experience, and each person must learn to practice this thinking for him or herself (Heidegger, 1954/1968). In addition, nursing is a craft which is developed to varying degrees in practice (Benner, 1984). As with any skilled practice, nursing can be recognized along a continuum of ability which is dependent upon context (skilled baseball pitchers may not be skilled batters). The theoretical information ("knowing-that") one learns about nursing is only one aspect to skilled performance; one must also learn the practical knowledge ("knowing-how") of nursing through experience. Thus, the issue of how much formal education in what type of educational setting should be mandated for nurses could be reconstituted as a matter of "every nurse should obtain as much formal education as he or she possibly can." What matters is the quality and accessibility of nursing education rather than organizing a hierarchy of entry level degrees.

In the language of possibilities, more education is a positive thing in and of itself; there is no need to degrade and devalue ADN and diploma education in order to increase the value of baccalaureate education. In this new view, what matters about baccalaureate education in nursing is that new understandings and new possibilities for our being (as persons who are also nurses) may be opened up as we participate in the different meaning worlds of a rich variety of other persons. In this sense, more education is "better" for all of us, and it is better for the whole nursing community when one RN returns to school. Baccalaureate education explicitly sets up a situation in which such possibilities may emerge, but it is not the only path to thinking.

REFERENCES

Allen, D. (1986). Professionalism, occupational segregation by gender, and control of nursing. *Women & Politics,,* 6, 1–24.

Allen, D. (1990). The curriculum revolution: Radical re-visioning of nursing education. *Journal of Nursing Education, 29*, 312–316.

Anderson, N. (1981). The historical development of American nursing education. *Journal of Nursing Education, 20*, 18–36.

Apple, M. (1979). *Ideology and curriculum*. London: Routledge & Kegan Paul.

Apple, M. (1982). *Education and power*. London: Routledge & Kegan Paul.

Apple, M. (1986). *Teachers and texts: A political economy of class and gender relations in education*. London: Routledge & Kegan Paul.

Ashley, J. (1976). *Hospitals, paternalism, and the role of the nurse*. New York: Teachers College Press, Columbia University.

Beeman, P. (1988). RNs' perceptions of their baccalaureate programs: Meeting their adult learning needs. *Journal of Nursing Education, 27*, 364–370.

Benner, P. (1981). Characteristics of novice and expert performance: Implications for teaching the experienced nurse. In K. Jako (Ed.), *Researching second step nursing education: Vol. II. Proceedings of the second annual national second step conference* (pp. 103–119). Rohnert Park, CA: National Second Step Project, Dept. of Nursing, Sonoma State University.

Benner, P. (1984). *From novice to expert: Excellence and power in clinical nursing practice*. Menlo Park, CA: Addison-Wesley.

Benner, P., & Tanner, C. (1987). Clinical judgment: How expert nurses use intuition. *American Journal of Nursing, 87*, 23–31.

Benner, P., Tanner, C., & Chesla, C. (1992). From beginner to expert: Gaining a differentiated clinical world in critical care nursing. *Advances in Nursing Science, 14*(3), 13–28.

Benner, P., & Wrubel, J. (1989). *The primacy of caring: Stress and coping in health and illness*. Menlo Park, CA: Addison-Wesley.

Bevis, E., & Murray, J. (1990). The essence of the curriculum revolution: Emancipatory teaching. *Journal of Nursing Education, 29*, 326–331.

Blatchley, M., & Stephan, E. (1985). RN students in generic programs: What do we do with them? *Journal of Nursing Education, 24*, 306–308.

Blicharz, M. (1985). Nursing role conception of registered nurses returning to school for a bachelor's degree in nursing. *Dissertation Abstracts International, 46,* 3003B.

Campaniello, J. (1988). When professional nurses return to school: A study of role conflict and well-being in multiple-role women. *Journal of Professional Nursing, 4,* 136–140.

Chinn, P. (1989). Feminist pedagogy in nursing education. In *Curriculum revolution: Reconceptualizing nursing care.* New York: National League for Nursing Press.

Christy, T. (1980). Entry into practice: A recurring issue in nursing history. *American Journal of Nursing, 80,* 485–488.

Cohen, L. (1992). Power and change in health care: Challenge for nursing. *Journal of Nursing Education, 31,* 113–116.

Corcoran, S., & Tanner, C. (1988). Implications of clinical judgment research for teaching. In *Curriculum revolution: Mandate for change* (pp. 159-176). New York: National League for Nursing Press.

Diekelmann, N. (1990). Nursing education: Caring, dialogue, and practice. *Journal of Nursing Education, 29,* 300–305.

Diekelmann, N. (1992). Learning-as-testing: A Heideggerian hermeneutical analysis of the lived experiences of students and teachers in nursing. *Advances in Nursing Science, 14*(3), 72–83.

Diekelmann, N. (in press). Behavioral pedagogy: A Heideggerian hermeneutical analysis of the lived experiences of students and teachers in baccalaureate nursing education. *Journal of Nursing Education.*

Diekelmann, N., Allen, D., & Tanner, C. (1989). *The NLN criteria for appraisal of baccalaureate programs: A critical hermeneutic analysis.* New York: National League for Nursing Press.

Freire, P. (1970). *Pedagogy of the oppressed* (M. Ramos, Trans.). New York: The Continuum Publishing Corp. (Original work published 1968.)

Giroux, H. (1983). *Theory and resistance in education: A pedagogy for the opposition.* South Hadley, MA: Bergin & Garvey Publishers.

Giroux, H. (1988). *Teachers as intellectuals: Toward a critical pedagogy of learning.* South Hadley, MA: Bergin & Garvey Publishers.

Hedin, B. (1986). A case study of oppressed group behavior in nurses. *Image: Journal of Nursing Scholarship, 18,* 53–57.

Hedin, B. (1987). Nursing education and social constraints: An indepth analysis. *International Journal of Nursing Studies, 24,* 261–270.

Hedin, B., & Donovan, J. (1989). A feminist perspective on nursing education. *Nurse Educator, 14*(4), 8–13.

Heidegger, M. (1959). *An introduction to metaphysics* (R. Manheim, Trans.). New Haven: Yale University Press. (Original work published 1953.)

Heidegger, M. (1962). *Being and time* (J. Macquarrie & E. Robinson, Trans.). New York: Harper & Row. (Original work published 1927.)

Heidegger, M. (1968). *What is called thinking?* (J. Gray, Trans.). New York: Harper & Row. (Original work published 1954.)

Hillsmith, K. (1978). From RN to BSN: Student perceptions. *Nursing Outlook, 26,* 98–102.

Inman, C. (1982). Factors influencing registered nurses to participate in educational programs leading to a baccalaureate or higher degree. *Dissertation Abstracts International, 43,* 627A.

Ipock, B. (1982). Anger in the returning student: A descriptive survey. *Dissertation Abstracts International, 43,* 3186A.

Kausch, M. (1988). A profile of the RN returning to school for a BSN degree: Health promotion behaviors, role strain, self-esteem, family stress level, marital adjustment, spousal support and coping mechanisms (Doctoral dissertation, University of Wisconsin-Madison, 1988). *Dissertation Abstracts International, 50,* 1179A.

King, J. (1988). Differences between RN and generic students and the impact on the educational process. *Journal of Nursing Education, 27,* 131–135.

Kliebard, H. (1970). The Tyler rationale. *School Review, 78*(2), 259–272.

Kramer, M. (1981). Philosophical foundations of baccalaureate nursing education. *Nursing Outlook, 29,* 224–228.

Lass, L. (1990, January 25). Today's nurses: Better educated, better paid, more opportunities. *USA Today,* p. 5D.

Lee, J. (1987). Analysis of stressful clinical and didactic incidents reported by returning registered nurses. *Journal of Nursing Education, 26,* 372–379.

Lee, J. (1988). Analysis of coping methods reported by returning RNs. *Journal of Nursing Education, 27,* 309–313.

Little, M., & Brian, S. (1982). The challengers, interactors and mainstreamers: Second step education and nursing roles. *Nursing Research, 31,* 239–245.

MacLean, T., Knoll, G., & Kinney, C. (1985). The evolution of a baccalaureate program for registered nurses. *Journal of Nursing Education, 24,* 53–57.

Marsh, H., & Lasky, P. (1984). The professional portfolio: Documentation of prior learning. *Nursing Outlook, 32,* 264–267.

McBride, V. (1985). Social networks among returning women students enrolled in an urban community college nursing program. *Dissertation Abstracts International, 46,* 1809A.

Melosh, B. (1982). *The physician's hand: Work culture and conflict in American nursing.* Philadelphia: Temple University Press.

Mezirow, J. (1985). Concept and action in adult education. *Adult Education Quarterly, 35,* 142–151.

Moloney, M. (1986). *Professionalization of nursing: Current issues and trends.* Philadelphia: J. B. Lippincott.

Moses, E. (1989, June). [Selected findings from the 1988 sample survey of Registered Nurses]. Unpublished raw data, U. S. Department of Health and Human Services, Health Resources and Services Administration, Bureau of Health Professions, Division of Nursing.

Murdock, J. (1986). Characteristics of registered nurse students and their returning to school experiences: Toward creating more responsive educational environments. *Dissertation Abstracts International, 47,* 2469A.

National League for Nursing. (1989). *Nursing student census with policy implications, 1988* (NLN Publication No. 19-2239). New York: National League for Nursing Press.

Pagano, J. (1988). Teaching women. *Educational Theory, 38,* 321–339.

Polkinghorne, D. (1983). *Methodology for the human sciences.* Albany, NY: State University of New York Press.

Portnoy, F., Balogh, E., Chasan, P., Devito, J., Dolloff, J., Flynn, J., Frazier, B., Okraska, C., Pemberton, J., Polito, M., Turnell, A., Walker, A., & Wyer, W. (1980). RN students analyze their experiences. *Nursing Outlook, 28,* 112–115.

Presz, H. (1988). Assessment of beliefs about conditions affecting adult learning in baccalaureate nursing programs. *Dissertation Abstracts International, 49,* 1036A.

Primm, P. (1986). Entry into practice: Competency statements for BSNs and ADNs. *Nursing Outlook, 34,* 135–137.

Rather, M. (1990). The lived experience of returning registered nurse students: A Heideggerian hermeneutical analysis (Doctoral dissertation, University of Wisconsin-Madison, 1990). *Dissertation Abstracts International, 51,* 1747B. (University Microfilms No. 90-24783)

Rather, M. (1992). "Nursing as a way of thinking"—Heideggerian hermeneutical analysis of the lived experience of the returning RN. *Research in Nursing Health, 15,* 47–55.

Rendon, D. (1983). Self-role congruence in the registered nurse student in baccalaureate nursing programs. *Dissertation Abstracts International, 44,* 1413B.

Riffle, K., Lamberth, F., Moine, G., & Fielding, J. (1985). Entry into practice: The continuing debate. In J. McCloskey & H. Grace (Eds.), *Current issues in nursing* (2nd ed.) (pp. 197–218). Boston: Blackwell Scientific Publications.

Smullen, B. (1983). Role change and the RN student: A process described (Doctoral dissertation, The University of Rochester, 1983). *Dissertation Abstracts International, 44,* 1414B. (University Microfilms No. 83-21715)

Sullivan, E. (1987). Critical thinking, creativity, clinical performance, and achievement in RN students. *Nurse Educator, 12*(2), 12–17.

Tanner, C. (1990). Reflections on the curriculum revolution *Journal of Nursing Education, 29,* 295–299.

Thompson, J. (1990). Hermeneutics and nursing research. In L. Moody (Ed.), *Advancing nursing science through research* (Vol. 2). Newbury Park, CA: Sage Publications.

Tyler, R. (1949). *Basic principles of curriculum and instruction.* Chicago: University of Chicago Press.

Urden, L. (1989). Knowledge development in clinical practice. *The Journal of Continuing Education in Nursing, 20,* 18–22.

Van Manen, M. (1991). *The tact of teaching: The meaning of pedagogical thoughtfulness.* Albany: State University of New York Press.

Wheeler, C., & Chinn, P. (1989). *Peace and power: A handbook of feminist process* (2nd ed.). New York: National League for Nursing Press.

7

The Discursive Constitution of Nursing Education: Exploring the Discursive Context of Problem-Solving

Nina Bruni

Objects are constituted in particular epistemes and these have first to be understood (Marshall, 1990, p.18).

THE NATURE OF NURSING AND NURSES

The past three decades in Australia have seen many changes in nursing education. Perhaps the most visible and the most controversial was the commencement in 1974 of the first college-based basic nursing program (MacKay, Brooke, & Bruni, 1981). This was heralded as a radical departure from the prevailing system of education for general nurses— a hospital-based apprenticeship in the care of the ill.

The relocation of basic nursing programs to the higher education sector, which encompasses colleges and universities, was accompanied by various changes in the understanding of nursing and nurses, and in the intent and process of nursing education. For example, the neophyte nurse was to be *educated* rather than trained. She, or indeed he, was understood to be a *student of the profession* of nursing not an apprentice of the trade of nursing. Initiation into the profession was to involve the student's introduction to *the discipline of nursing*. Curricula were reworked; new areas of nursing knowledge were developed and/ or traditional areas revised or deleted. During the period of relocation new categories of people were created: the academic nurse educator, the student of nursing, the nurse researcher, the nurse practitioner, and the client.

The new system of education was presented by its advocates as both a cause and an effect of change (Bruni, 1990). The graduates were charged, for example, with being the forerunners and instigators of *positive* change in the health care system. It was argued that their new knowledge would equip them to provide a better quality of care, in a variety of settings, to all groups within the Australian community. They would be able to provide holistic, individualized client care.

The tertiary, or higher education, system was hence posited as a progressive development and one which would equitably serve the interests of all parties—lecturers, students, and clients.

Notions of progress and equity are implicit in much of the contemporary literature and research on nursing education and are variously adopted by nurse educators as "factual" descriptors of the present system. The study from which this paper is drawn offers a challenge to these commonsense assumptions.

FOCUS OF THE PAPER

The study is concerned with the role of power in contemporary nursing education. It focuses on the way power is invested in the knowledge and the activities of nurse educators, and on the power of their practices to shape the knowledge and practices of students. It explores the way in which notions of progress and rational neutrality are shaped or constituted.

In questioning the purported neutrality of the daily activities of the nurse educator and of her "ways of knowing" the study asks:

What shapes the nurse educator and what does she, in turn, shape?

This paper discusses one area of the study—an analysis of a unit on clinical decision-making for client care (CDM). This section of a larger study aimed to unravel the knowledge which shaped the practices of educators who taught the unit and to explore the implications of their practices for students. It asked: What relations were set up between the educators and the students; and what practices did the students engage in? Did these practices suggest that the unit would help students to develop the skills of analysis and critical reflection, skills which are currently highly valued in tertiary students and in the graduate nurse? Indeed the "concrete thinker," the student who is perceived to be unable to think abstractly or "critically," is the bane of educators who maintain that such cognitive skills underpin professional nursing practice (Allen, 1990). This paper provides some insight into the construction, or constitution, of this "problem student."

THEORETICAL UNDERPINNINGS

In working through the research questions the study employs the concepts of *power and knowledge*, articulated by Foucault (1977) as the power/knowledge relation—a notion which argues for their mutual interdependence. Within this relation power is understood to be a productive, positive force rather than an essentially oppressive, negative force. It is also, however, seen as limiting or constraining (Ball, 1990a). It is exercised at all levels of activity, often unconsciously.

Power is not the perogative of a few who occupy positions of authority nor of specific institutions. It is identifiable in its exercise as "technologies of power" (Foucault, 1977), that is, as *discourses* or knowledge, and the *practices* these entail, which shape the objects of the discourse—for example, the "good student." Discourses specify who can speak, when, and with what authority (Ball, 1990a).

The concept of *subjectivity* is also central to the study. It refers to an individual's identity, or self-consciousness, understood as the product of that person's location in a particular network of power/knowledge relations. Exploration of the subjectivities of nurse educators illuminates the field of power/knowledge relations which constitute them, and which they in turn constitute or challenge.

THE RESEARCH PROCESS—CRITICAL ETHNOGRAPHY

The methodology of the study was shaped by a poststructural understanding of ethnography (Hammersley, 1992; Lather, 1991). Hence, in addition to the adoption of a critical theoretical perspective within which to locate the data, the research field was recognized as a social and political arena of which the researcher is an integral part (Angus, 1986; Tyler, 1985). Relations set up between researcher and participants encouraged open, reciprocal dialogue. Analysis was informed by the notion of deconstruction, the central focus of which ". . . becomes the way in which texts construct meanings and subject positions for the reader, the contradictions inherent in this process and its political implications, both in its historical context and in the present" (Weedon, 1987, p. 16).

The study was located at a School of Nursing within an Institute of Higher Education in Australia. The data relevant to CDM were gathered through informal discussion with all staff involved in teaching the nursing program and subsequent observation of the teaching sessions of two educators, Barbara and Susan, who conducted the CDM unit. Written texts, including the curriculum, lecture notes, overhead transparencies, a student guideline text and "class handouts," also provided insight into the construction of CDM.

ORGANIZATION OF THE CDM UNIT

The unit was one of four which made up a first year nursing subject. This subject focused on those processes deemed relevant to the achievement and maintenance of a client's level of well-being.

The CDM unit consisted of 11 hours of lectures (two one-hour sessions and three three-hour sessions), and eight hours of tutorials (four two-hour small group discussion sessions), conducted over a four week period. One lecture and one tutorial were conducted each week. Lectures and tutorials were differentiated by the lecturers in terms of their educative function. Lectures were understood as forums in which the theoretical aspects of CDM were presented to students, while tutorials were posited as classes in which emergent issues would be explored through discussion.

The First Year student body was divided into two groups, Group A and Group B, each of which consisted of approximately 195 students. One CDM lecturer conducted the lectures for Group A, the other for Group B. However, this division was not maintained for the tutorial sessions; these were composed of approximately 95 students drawn from Group A and Group B.

DISCOURSES OF CDM—
A RATIONAL PROCESS OF CARE

The course accreditation document stated that ". . . problem-solving processes are used in order to reach the goal of nursing i.e., promotion, attainment, maintenance and restoration of health." Stated functions of the graduate, as a first-level practitioner, included "utilizing the problem-solving approach in the provision of care, working with clients/patients in a goal directed way to facilitate the fulfillment of basic needs in order to achieve maximum potential for daily living." In other words, problem-solving was posited as theoretical knowledge, knowledge which functions to control and guide practice. As Cherryholmes (1988) puts it, such knowledge is "generalized, articulated, systematic, scientific, objective and disinterested" (p.80). Without this knowledge, practice is understood to be informed by practical knowledge which is "idiographic, tacit, less systematic, nonscientific, subjective, politically committed" (Cherryholmes, 1988, p.80) and inferior. This interpretation of the theory/practice dichotomy clearly informed the program.

Both lecturers endorsed the program's rationale, relating the importance of CDM, as a form of problem-solving, to its implications for clinical practice. CDM was charged with enabling students to structure their daily clinical work by providing them with a framework for their clinical practice.

CDM was consistently talked of as being a logical and rational process, both in its internal coherence and in its application to the process of caring for clients. Deviations from this delineated, sequential process constituted unsound, illogical practice.

The appropriateness of CDM for structuring care within any care setting, and for any type of client group, was not questioned. It was understood to be a culture-free process. Its purported universal applicability was implied in the student "Guideline" text. Hence, while a client's perceptions, in particular her/his cultural needs, were to be acknowledged in working through the process, these, in no way, compromised the integrity of the process.

The unit was also seen to assist students to develop their capacity for critical reflection. In this sense it was seen by Barbara to constitute the difference between training and education.

"Well, I believe that education is that you're encouraging students to critically reflect on events that they can analyze, they can . . . um . . . adapt their practice as a result of what they're thinking rather than being spoon-fed something and having predigested facts and ideas, and just knowing how to do something rather than knowing why for instance. That's training."

The importance of the unit was also explained by reference to its integration with other units in the program. Susan indicated that the theme of problem-solving ran through the program.

In summary, CDM was posited as a neutral, objective, and rational process or tool which, if correctly applied, would ensure that client needs were met. Its understanding was devoid of any notions relative to the social construction of knowledge, reasoning, or of interaction.

EXPLORING THE SUBJECTIVITY OF THE CDM LECTURERS

Within the context of the School of Nursing the subjectivity of the CDM lecturers was shaped by the various subject positions they occupied. Both lecturers perceived themselves to be policy implementers and transmitters of knowledge; one lecturer adopted the subject position of facilitator of the students' progression through the program. Discourses of compliance, commitment, coping, and concern informed their daily activities—discourses shaped by notions of efficiency and effectiveness.

The Educator as Policy Implementer

CDM lecturers stated that they were aware that "policy" directed that student admission numbers increase annually, although a recession climate pervaded the institute and the school. They perceived themselves and other lecturers as implementers of institute and school policy.

Reduced funding and increased student numbers were identified as having a negative impact on the quality of their work. However, they did not contest existing policies, nor did they express great concern with their powerlessness to determine or effect policy. Rather, they saw themselves as having to accommodate to its dictates. Of major concern was their heavy workload.

Lecturers clearly felt a pressure being exerted "on" them to be efficient. In addition to carrying a formal student contact time of approximately 20 hours per week, lecturers stated that they were requested to undertake research, to upgrade their academic qualifications and to assist in various ongoing school activities. "Working at home" was adopted as a practice of coping with the workload—indeed, coping was seen as an issue of an individual's organizational ability (Ball, 1990b).

The Educator as Transmitter of Knowledge

Both CDM lecturers also adopted the subject position of transmitter of knowledge. They saw teaching as an activity which involved "getting across" specific areas of knowledge—as detailed in the curriculum. They engaged in various practices to achieve that end. Clearly, in this context both lecturers positioned the student as "content internalizer."

Effective transmission was, however, perceived as somewhat problematic. Both lecturers asserted that the timing of the sessions (such as tutorials on Friday afternoon), and the absence of student study time during the weekdays (students had classes from 8 a.m. to 6 p.m. most days with an hour lunch break), prompted them to ensure that all the "necessary" information was provided by them during session time. The large class size also generated some concern about possible classroom management problems and the identification of individual students' learning needs. They also stated that the teaching resources, such as tutorial rooms, were inadequate, and that they would therefore be under additional pressure to "motivate" the students.

The Educator as Facilitator

One lecturer adopted an additional subject position—that of facilitator. This encompassed various practices which involved being "an equal" with students, being a role model and being caring—to be achieved by relating to students "naturally," with honesty and concern.

The Student as Learner and Neophyte Nurse—Motivated and Caring

Lecturers differentiated between students on the basis of students' motivation to enter the career of nursing. Motivation was linked to age. "Mature-age students" were identified as the most highly motivated students; they were seen as eager to adopt the subject position of learner. The "good" student was also presented as one who was interested in the area of health and who was intrinsically "caring and giving." The "bad" student lacked these qualities.

In summary, the lecturers positioned themselves as neutral entities relative to the difficulties they encountered as nurse educators. Problems were located within the machinations of the institute or the school, or within the student. They did not problematize the program nor suggest that the practices in which they engaged helped both to shape the context in which they worked and to generate the objects of their concern—such as the poor student.

This discursive context thus set up relations between lecturer, as knower and perhaps helper, and student as learner of transmitted knowledge and neophyte nurse. In the next section the teaching practices by which CDM was produced in the classroom, rather than passively transmitted, are explored. The analysis also reveals some of the practices by which the lecturers established, and confirmed, the authority of their voice and the "truth" of their knowledge.

THE DISCURSIVE PRACTICES OF CDM LECTURERS

Integrating Lectures and Tutorials

The focus of lectures and their integration with tutorials emphasized the "use" of CDM content for the assignment task. This task constituted a simulated nursing situation to which students were to apply the CDM framework. The priority placed on the assignment in CDM sessions was evident in the practices of both lecturers.

Barbara explained the integration of the sessions in the following way: "They [students] get the theory, then they do a practice [in class], then do it [their assignment task]." A three hour lecture on Assessment, for example, consisted of theory, a "break" of fifteen minutes, followed by a practice session which involved students working through assessment data to generate a nursing diagnosis. This session was followed by a tutorial in which students worked through the assessment stage of their assignment. Clearly a discourse of knowledge application informed this understanding of tutorials, as distinct from a discourse of learning through reflection, which they had articulated in the initial interview.

Prioritizing the Assignment Task

Emphasis on "doing" the assignment was also evident in the lecturers' practices of orienting the content of the lectures to the assignment task. This was achieved in several ways: first, by raising the issue of the task with the students by pointing out the relevance of introduced theory, by doing exercises in class, and/or discussing the assignment submission details; second, by stressing the need for students to internalize and apply the frameworks of their texts; and third, by affirming the need for students' attendance at tutorials.

The use of texts, in particular the student guideline, was predicated on the notion that these offered the "correct" interpretation of CDM. Students were not asked to critique the proffered discourse of CDM in order to develop their own discourse. Rather, they were to follow the text in class as directed, use it as a resource for terminology which they should employ, and use it as a guide for the structure and content of the assignment. The students' voice was not to be heard. As Cherryholmes (1988, p. 63) argues: "The only way to exclude readers from making meaning is to assume that a text has one 'correct' interpretation, that it is univocal . . ." Indeed, the texts employed in the sessions offered a consistent reading of CDM and the lecturers' teaching practices assumed a stability of meaning. By focusing on what the texts said as against what they omitted to say, each text appeared to speak with one voice—a voice shared by all the texts cited by the lecturers. Students were not informed that critiques of its constitutive discourses, such as that offered by Benner (1984) which privileges practical knowledge, were available in the nursing literature.

The Practices of Knowledge Transmission

In adopting the subject position of neutral knowledge transmitter, premised on the existence of an accepted body of knowledge, lecturers focused on the development of strategies to ensure that the content was made available to students, effectively and efficiently, and that the learning objectives, encapsulated in the assignment, were achieved. As indicated earlier, these imperatives were also shaped by the large class sizes, the teaching venues, and the heavy workloads of both staff and students.

The Practices of Sharing and Mixing. Lecturers were concerned that students in both groups be exposed to the same material. Strategies aimed at that end included the "mix" of Group A and B students for tutorials and the sharing of overhead transparencies.

The Practice of Overhead-Transcription. The prescribed content of each lecture was consistently presented to students on numerous overhead transparencies. Material was introduced to students on the screen. The lecturer then worked through its content by reading it to students and/or explaining it, and continually paraphrasing it. Definitions of core concepts were also presented on overheads. Overheads were also used to indicate the importance of material. Comments such as: "You need to know this" and "Why is documentation essential?" preceded the display of the relevant material.

Lecturers' use of overheads constituted students' practices as learners of the displayed material. Moreover, they read the text in ways which invited the students to transcribe it. It was repeated, perhaps several times; definitions in particular, were repeated slowly as if the students were in a dictation class.

A rule of transcription emerged. At the sight of an overhead the students began writing.

Acceptance by lecturers that the dominant student practice during the sessions was "overhead transcription" was implicit in some of their comments; for example, after displaying an overhead of a "sample" assignment, Barbara asked her group: "Which is subjective data? Come on, you've got to think . . . you're not writing down so you must be doing *something*." On another occasion she told students: "You don't have to write this down . . . this is a thinking exercise." Evidently overhead transcription and thinking were understood to be mutually exclusive activities.

Susan told her group in their last session that the exam for CDM would be ". . . on essentially the overheads you've had in this series." She had assumed they knew the rules: that overhead material had to be transcribed and learned.

Students indeed appeared to have internalized the rules. A norm of transcription prevailed in the classrooms. The content of the overheads constituted the material to be learned. As one student told the researcher: "I just take notes . . . to learn later. I don't bother listening . . . as long as I take some notes." Indeed, two students seated in the middle section of the lecture theater were observed to wear headphones throughout one session and to transcribe the content of each overhead. Evidently the need to transcribe overhead material overruled the need to listen to the lecturer. Another student supported the notion that such class notes were adequate, saying: "I don't use the library. I don't have to."

In order to "get through" their prepared material, lecturers attempted to "hurry along" the students. Students were encouraged to transcribe quickly with comments such as: "We're running short of time," "We're almost finished" and "Just one more (overhead)." Students learned another rule: to write quickly.

The practice of overhead transcription generated problems for both lecturers and students. As indicated above, the perceived need to function efficiently resulted in the practice of working quickly through the material. Those students who could not "get it all down" before the transparency was removed either interrupted their neighbors or simply "gave up." Indeed, students gave no more than monosyllabic responses, usually "Yes," to the questions that lecturers posed regarding the displayed material. They were too busy writing.

The overhead material was hence uncontested and presented as uncontestable. The practices of questioning employed by lecturers within this context also affirmed the truth of CDM.

The Practice of Confirmation: Questioning. The questioning strategies denied the possibility that students would contest the knowledge and hence devalued their voice. Such confirmation was achieved in several, mutually supportive, ways.

The possibility of students questioning, or commenting upon, the content presented by the lecturer was minimized by her frequent reminders of the need to move quickly through the content. Students learned that input into the session was not a norm of attendance. Lecturers also established a norm of student silence throughout lectures by responding to student chatter with a "Sh . . . Sh!." Other students often pre-empted the formal reprimand as they sought to hear the lecturer.

Lecturers' use of questioning also minimized student input. Questioning was linked to the use of overheads or texts in terms of the timing and nature of the questions asked. Prior to showing an overhead which concerned a new item or area of knowledge, students were frequently asked a question which pre-empted its content, for example: "Why is documentation necessary?" Only rarely did students offer an answer. After a few seconds the overhead was displayed. It "showed" students the correct answer. The rules that the "lecturer knows the answer," "the answer will be on the overhead," and "transcribe overheads" constituted a fourth rule of student activity: "don't bother to answer questions."

The rhetorical nature of questions asked as the lecturer reviewed the presented material, such as "Does it all make sense?," also reinforced the notion that "teacher knows best."

Students were asked questions which affirmed the truth of the material presented by the lecturers; lecturers' questions also presumed an acceptance of the CDM framework. They created no space in which it could be contested; for example, "Any questions about evaluation—what it entails and what is expected of you [in the assignment]?" Students' responses indicated their involvement in working through the material, unquestioningly accepting its logic. The same approach was evident in the group work sessions. Students were asked to "fit" data into pre-existing categories; for example, "Are there any [NANDA] labels that relate to these problems? Tell me." "Do you think that's a good one?" "What data supports that? . . . What else?"

Although lecturers did not actively create a space in which oppositional discourses to those they "owned" could be developed, one student did attempt a challenge. This occurred in the first lecture. Her attempt was thwarted, however, as her concern was transformed and located within the discourse of the lecturer. In this initial lecture the student pointed to the reductionism implicit in the conception of the "scientific" problem-solving method being described. The lecturer had outlined the second step, that of data collection, and offered the following "case" as an example of the type of data to be obtained: "If a client has a respiratory problem, we are not really interested in if he can walk well!" The student raised her hand and asked: "But we learned to look [at clients] holistically?" The lecturer effectively dismissed the query by saying: "But we must prioritize problems." Discussion of the nature of holistic care as non-reductive was hence denied; the issue raised by the student was countered by an appeal to "common sense" in terms of the need to save a life and the "reality" of the complexity and amount of nursing work. The lecturer subsequently discussed "prioritizing" as an aspect of the decision-making process. As Davies argues:

> The absence of an appropriate alternative discourse leads the teacher, unwittingly, to knit back up the fabric [of the prevailing social order]. . . . He [the teacher] uses his rights to ask questions and to determine meanings, and thus to set his interpretation up, not as one that lies in opposition to hers [the student], but as one that stems directly from hers (1989, p. 233).

SITES OF RESISTANCE

Various sites of resistance were, however, evident. For example, when asked by the researcher about CDM, students indicated some concerns. They expressed disinterest in the unit, stated that they were bored and that they could not see the relevance of CDM to nursing. When asked which units were important they cited anatomy and physiology and those concerned with client needs. Clearly, their evaluation was informed by conceptions of nursing which differed from those which informed their lecturers.

The restlessness, personal chatter, and "illicit" reading observed among some students in class, and their departure at session breaks, indicated their opposition to the positions made available to them within the lecturers' discourses. Students who engaged in such activities were likely to be categorized negatively—as lazy or lacking in motivation.

Like their lecturers, the students were shaped by a network of power/knowledge relations which disciplined them through various modes of classification, control and containment (Ball, 1990a). And while they developed oppositional discourses, these remained marginal and virtually unheard. As Ball (1990b, p.157) has argued for the discourse of management: ". . . it eschews or marginalizes the problems, concerns, difficulties, and fears of 'the subject'—the managed." Clearly, the students constituted "the managed."

DISCUSSION

The analysis of the discursive context of CDM outlined in this paper has contested the notion that the tertiary system of nursing education is neutral in its operation; that is, devoid of relations of power. It has revealed the network of technologies of power by which lecturers and students were constituted, and which they, in turn, constituted or challenged.

Discourses of rationality, efficiency, effectiveness, and coping were revealed to be dominant. These excluded discourses which address the socially constituted nature of the context in which the lecturers and students were located. Lecturers, for example, did not contest institute or school policy; they embraced its imperatives as they sought to be competent knowledge transmitters. Nor did they explore or challenge the meanings and values which informed their teaching practices and the teaching materials they employed. Indeed, they were unaware of the relations they set up between themselves and students and of the implications of the practices subsequently adopted by students. In essence, their educative practices were not informed by discourses which critically explored the social and political dimensions of the context which shaped them and which they, in turn, helped shape.

Further, it is argued that the various practices which shaped students, and the discourses of CDM which were presented to them, and within which they had to work, helped to produce a category of student who was not asked to engage in analysis, critical reflection, or abstract thinking: the "concrete thinker." Lecturers, hence, unwittingly shaped the "problem" they were seeking to resolve. As Davies (1989, p. 232) puts it: ". . . it is possible to see teachers setting out to teach equitably and failing to do so because their discourse constitutes the pupils in exactly the ways that they are saying is no longer appropriate."

The analysis presented in this paper is not intended as an evaluative exercise. It has not revealed an array of "good, acceptable, and poor" traits of teacher performance. Rather, the analysis points to the complexity of the educative process—a process in which relations of power are fundamentally implicated. It contests the notion that change in any one dimension of this process will necessarily be transformative, that is, will fundamentally alter the process "for the better." Such an assumption is clearly unwarranted.

The belief, for example, that the introduction of a humanistic curriculum will, per se, generate an environment in which students are free to develop their own ideas and practices ignores the network of power/ knowledge relations within which they, and their lecturers, are shaped. Moreover, rather than constitute an environment in which less power is exercised, the innovation merely constitutes a new form of student subjection or discipline. It presents a different pattern of control. However, this assertion does not imply that change should not be sought, for teaching practices which create possibilities for the formulation of new knowledge are sorely needed in nursing education. Rather, it argues that the pattern of relations generated by the intended innovation needs careful consideration before change is implemented.

As Lather (1991) maintains, liberatory pedagogies too often fail to probe the degree to which "empowerment" becomes unproductive and perpetuates relations of dominance. The creation of empowering discourses, hence, implies that educators engage in critical self-reflection before they "develop, implement and evaluate."

Indeed, Marshall (1990, p. 26) says: "The problem [of change] is to recognize when modern power is being exercised and whether resistance is the appropriate response." Hence, planned change should involve exploration of the discursive constitution of the object of concern and of the posited strategy of change, for ". . . objects are constituted in particular epistemes and these have first to be understood" (Marshall, 1990, p.18). The construction of empowering discourses is a challenge open to all in nursing education, whatever their level of teaching.

REFERENCES

Allen, D. G. (1990). The curriculum revolution: Radical revisioning of nursing education. *Journal of Nursing Education, 29,* 312–316.

Angus, L. (1986). Research traditions, ideology and critical ethnography. *Discourse, 7*(1), 59–77.

Ball, S. (1990a). Introducing Monsieur Foucault. In S. Ball, (Ed). *Foucault and education: Disciplines and knowledge.* New York: Routledge, Chapman & Hall.

Ball, S. (1990b). Management as moral technology: A Luddite analysis. In S. Ball, (Ed). *Foucault and Education: Disciplines and Knowledge.* New York: Routledge, Chapman & Hall.

Benner, P. (1984). *From novice to expert: Excellence and power in clinical nursing practice.* Menlo Park, CA: Addison-Wesley.

Bruni, N. (1990). Holistic nursing curricula: Towards a reconstruction of health and nursing. *Unicorn, 16,* 100–108.

Cherryholmes, C. H. (1988). *Power and criticism: Poststructural investigations in education.* New York: Teachers College, Columbia University.

Davies, B. (1989). The discursive production of the male/female dualism in school settings. *Oxford Review of Education, 15,* 299–241.

Foucault, M. (1977). *Discipline and punish: The birth of the prison.* London: Penguin.

Hammersley, M. (1992). *What's wrong with ethnography?* London: Routledge.

Lather, P. (1991). *Feminist research in education: within/against.* Geelong, Victoria: Deakin University.

MacKay, L., Brooke, A., & Bruni, N. (1981). *An evaluation of a college-based basic course in nursing.* Canberra: Australian Government Publishing Service.

Marshall, J. D. (1990). Foucault and educational research. In S. Ball, (Ed). *Foucault and education: Disciplines and knowledge.* New York: Routledge.

Tyler, S. (1985). Ethnography, intertextuality and the end of description. *American Journal of Semiotics, 3,* 83–98.

Weedon, C. (1987). *Feminist practice and poststructuralist theory.* Oxford: Blackwell.

8

Diverse Thinking Styles of Nurses

Pat Hayes
Alice Kienholz
Joyce Engel
Rama K. Mishra

A concern for optimizing the problem solving and decision making ability of nurses was translated into a need to determine whether profile characteristics that typify nurses' thinking style preferences could be identified. Nurses need to be able to act in a way that is situationally responsive to the demands that are placed on them in the work setting. Every nurse brings to patient care a repertoire of knowledge and skills that is the basis of clinical judgment and action. This process of care occurs in a multidimensional environment that can exert considerable stress and strain on both the cognitive appraisal and psycho-motor abilities of the nurse. There is only a rudimentary understanding of the way in which such a complex repertoire of knowledge and skills is sustained, honed, expanded and/or modified over time. Although learning theory and instructional theory have provided insight into the process of acquiring new knowledge, how knowledge is used in problem solving and decision-making is currently the focus of increased attention.

An emerging body of research has focused on the components of clinical judgment in terms of cognitive strategies (Tanner, Padrick, Westfall, & Putzier, 1987), how professionals think (Powell, 1989; Schon, 1983), and the process of intuition (Benner & Tanner, 1987). From these themes there emerges a notion that some form of interaction occurs among three major entities: empirical information about the activity being undertaken, the cognitive ability and kinaesthetic skill necessary to carry out the activity, and intuitive ways of knowing that merge the apparently unknown with the particular and the general. The interaction has at its core the "indeterminate zones of practice—uncertainty, uniqueness, and value conflict [that] escape the canons of technical rationality" (Schon, 1987, p.6). This core is central to many of the problems of clinical practice and could have some influence on how problems are addressed by the practicing nurse.

The foundation of any nursing activity is what is known about a problem; the crucial information necessary to act or refrain from acting. One question that has not been completely explored is whether each individual registered nurse (RN) has a style of thinking that directs and drives the process of gathering and organizing knowledge, and thus influences clinical judgment. The longtime use of the nursing process as a method of identifying problems and planning care uses an analytical, logical style of reasoning. Are RN students expected to use this linear method when they attempt to process information that is best approached through using holistic patterns? Can different styles of thinking be the basis for conflicts between RN students and their instructors? Might such conflicts be present in clinical settings where diverse thinking styles result in different nursing care plans?

To answer these questions we must first establish whether we can identify thinking styles in individuals and groups. Identifying inquiry modes would enable the styles of thinking used by nurses to be identified and throw new light on how individuals use different approaches to deal with the same problem. "Inquiry modes serve to orient the inquirer to a problematic situation in some fashion, lending a differential 'spin' to the inquirer's definition of the problem" (Franceschini & Butler, 1989, p. 3). What are the inquiry modes that RN students bring into the adacemic setting? Do nurses have an identifiable thinking style that could be used to enhance instructional processes?

A study was conducted to obtain a profile of the thinking styles of nurses and to test the proposition that nurses have identifiable thinking style preferences. The Inquiry Mode Questionnaire [Revised] (InQ[R]) (Harrison and Bramson, 1988) was chosen to identify nurses' thinking styles.

REVIEW OF THE LITERATURE

Churchman (1971) proposed that systems of inquiry begin with elementary units of evidence, and that rules exist for insuring the validity of the conceptual whole that is built from these elementary units. Each system of inquiry has a differential basis of evidence and rules resulting in a different construction of the problem. Churchman (1971) identified five modes of inquiry derived from the five main traditions of inquiry ascribed to Hegel, Kant, Singer, Leibniz, and Locke. These were subsequently operationalized by Mitroff and Pondy (1974) when they looked at agency preferences in public policy analysis and decision making.

In psychology, theory organizing and knowledge use is the domain of cognitive style. Harrison and Bramson (1982) integrated various approaches to cognitive styles with Churchman and Mitroff and Pondy's work on inquiry systems in the process of developing the Inquiry Mode Questionnaire (InQ). It "builds upon current social psychological theory and social science metatheory to give us insight into the nature of human inquiry" (Franceschini & Butler, 1989). The InQ measures the relative preference among the five modes of inquiry. Preferences for particular modes of inquiry have come to be called thinking styles by Harrison and Bramson (1982) who have used the terms Synthesist, Idealist, Pragmatist, Analyst, and Realist to label the five styles.

According to Harrison and Bramson (1982) thinking styles can be associated with characteristic behaviors that accompany each style although there is no claim that stylistic preference is linked to cognitive ability. They propose that Synthesist and Idealist styles are substantive, value-oriented ways of thinking and Analyst and Realist styles are functional and fact-oriented. The Pragmatist draws from both sides of the spectrum to serve the needs of the moment.

The lack of demonstrated links between the InQ and cognitive ability was supported in a study of math anxiety, math achievement, and styles of thinking by Reece and Todd (1989). They found that although high scores on the preferences of Synthesist and Analyst were significantly associated with low scores on math anxiety there was no significant finding related to ability on an in class statistic test.

Age and experience may also have an influence on thinking style, but when the cognitive styles of teachers were studied it was found that there were no differences that related to experience. There was however a difference attributed to the size of the room in which teaching took place and the Pragmatist style of thinking (Cervetti, Franceschini, & Sojourner, 1989). The difference was not found in the larger classroom.

Harrison and Bramson (1982) defined the Synthesist as challenging and idea oriented. The Idealist is receptive and need oriented. The Pragmatist is adaptive and "pay-off" oriented. The Analyst is prescriptive and method oriented. The Realist is empirical and task oriented. It is proposed that Synthesist and Idealist styles are substantive, value-oriented ways of thinking and the Analyst and Realist styles are functional and fact-oriented. The Pragmatist spontaneously draws from both ends of the spectrum to serve the needs of the moment. It has been shown (Harrison and Bramson, 1982) that about 50 percent of people prefer a single style of thinking, 35 percent have a preference for two styles of thinking in combination, and 2 percent prefer three styles of thinking in combination. About 13 percent have an even preference among at least four of the styles, and will use each style in a calculated way, depending on the situation.

The seminal work of Harrison and Bramson has generated a number of other studies that consistently support the model. Construct validity has been identified by Kagan and Tixier y Vigil (1987) and Hughes and Franceschini (1989). The model has been found to discriminate between the thinking styles of students in architecture and medicine (Kienholz & Hritzuk, 1986). The measurement tool has also been used as a variable in studies in education related to teacher effectiveness (Kagan, & Tixier y Vigil, 1987), aspects of cognitive style (Cervetti, Franceschini, & Sojourner, 1989; Hughes, & Franceschini, 1989) and math anxiety (Reece, & Todd, 1989).

Based upon Harrison and Bramson's (1982) experience with gathering data on the InQ from a small number of nurses, they proposed that nurses would fall into the Idealist/Realist categories. They also claim that thinking styles can be identified through the characteristic behaviors that accompany each style.

In recent years there have been a number of studies that have examined how nurses process information in order to become expert practitioners (Benner & Tanner, 1987; Tanner, Padrick, Westfall, & Putzier, 1987). These studies have provided insight into nurses' thinking through the examination of various approaches to cognitive styles. In contrast, the InQ model of thinking styles approaches the problem through an examination of the five main ways people have thought throughout history.

METHOD

A survey was conducted of RNs seeking continuing education. Volunteers were solicited from among three groups of practicing RNs: those who were attending a nursing conference (N = 45); those who were taking classes toward a post-RN baccalaureate degree (University A, N =

94; University B, N = 77). All subjects volunteered (and had the opportunity to withdraw at any time without penalty) in order to generate the convenience sample of 216. As there was no intention to make group comparisons the groups were not kept separate for analysis.

Instrument

The InQ (Harrison & Bramson, 1982) is a forced choice, self-rating measure consisting of eighteen statements, each of which is related to five response options. Each response option represents one of the five thinking styles that are to be ranked in order of preference. A scaling procedure is used on the ranked responses to attain a score for each of the styles of thinking. A score of 60 or more indicates a marked preference for a style of thinking, and with scores of 72 or more, the preference tends to become a commitment. Scores of 48 or less indicate a marked disinclination for that style and 36 or less show a virtual disregard for that style. Scores between 49 and 59 on at least four styles indicate an even preference.

Reliability and validity of the InQ was initially established by Bruvold, Parlette, Bramson, and Bramson (1983). Internal consistency was identified when eighty-five of ninety items correlated with their denoted sub-test at $p = 0.001$, and only eight of the 90 items did not discriminate between highest and lowest scores on each sub-test at $p = 0.001$ level of significance. A further test of reliability demonstrated that test/retest stability of scores had a correlation coefficient of $r = 0.75$. Construct validity was established through factor analysis of item data ($n = 495$) using a Quartimax rotation. A five-dimensional factorial structure was identified that matched the typologies and demonstrated differential measurement. A one-way ANOVA (Analysis of Variance) repeated measures, using thinking styles as the repeated factor, has also demonstrated significant findings (Cervetti et al., 1989). Concurrent validity has been established with the "Human Information Processing Survey" that measures right- and left-brain and integrated styles (Kienholz & Hritzuk, 1986), and parts of the Myers-Briggs Type Indicator (MBTI) that measures personality types (Hughes & Franceschini, 1989). Although in the latter test there was no significant relationship with introversion-extroversion, a moderate to somewhat weak correlation was found when the InQ scores were run against the remaining three dimensions of the MBTI.

Reliability and validity studies for the original InQ were first reported as acceptable for profile interpretation, at both the group and individual level, by Bruvold, Parlette, Bramson, and Bramson (1983). Results were obtained from an item analysis and factor analysis conducted on 460 questionnaires, completed by a cross-section of occupational groups in the Western United States. Reliability was established based on the results from 60 university students who completed the questionnaire with a six week test-retest interval between testing. Further studies evaluating concurrent validity have been reported by Kagan and Tixier y Vigil (1987) and Kienholz and Hritzuk (1986).

The InQ[R] version of the instrument, used in this study, has recently been developed to correct minor language problems and strengthen nine items that were identified in item analysis as requiring improvement. A test-retest reliability assessment of the InQ(R) was conducted on a sample of senior and graduate students in education and architecture at a Canadian University (N = 88) (Bramson, 1987). The reliability of the InQ(R) was found to be comparable to the original version. The tool is considered to be able to identify different thinking styles.

Procedure

The InQ(R) was administered to each of the three groups that comprised the sample of 216 subjects. The questionnaire took 20 to 30 minutes to complete. Subjects were provided with an interpretation of their results, which served as an incentive to participate.

RESULTS

InQ(R) scores were obtained from every subject. Choices on the five ranked responses to the eighteen items were added to obtain a score

Table 8.1   Range of Dominant Thinking Style Preferences

| Scales | SCALES | | | | |
	Synthesist	Idealist	Pragmatist	Analyst	Realist
Synthesist	(0)	5	0	4	1
Idealist	5	(36)	9	18	13
Pragmatist	0	9	(8)	5	20
Analyst	4	18	5	(25)	15
Realist	1	13	20	15	(29)

( ) Indicates number of subjects having a single preferred style.

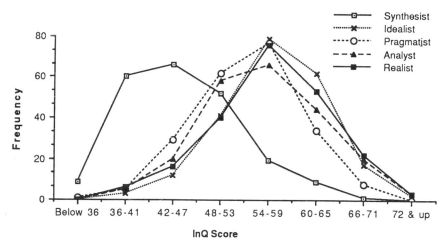

Figure 8.1   Frequency distribution of the InQ(R) Scales.

on each of the five styles of thinking for every subject. Table 8.1 depicts the range of dominant preferences and the relative combinations from all 216 subjects for the five dominant styles of thinking.

Preferences for single and combined styles can be seen in Table 8.1. No subjects preferred the Synthesist style alone. Whenever the synthesist style was preferred it was in combination with either the Idealist, Analyst and/or Realist styles. The frequency distribution of each preferred style is presented in Figure 8.1 and Table 8.2. The number of three-way thinkers was 5 (2.32 percent), and those with a level profile were 23 (10.65 percent). These included those with four scores in the fifties and one at 48 or below.

A single preferred style of thinking was identified by 98 (45.4 percent) of the subjects. The Idealist and Realist styles were clearly preferred by most subjects with 81 (37.5 percent) receiving scores of 60 or more on the Idealist, and 78 (36.11 percent) preferring the Realist. The Analyst style was preferred by 67 (31.02 percent). This contrasts with the Pragmatist style that was preferred by 42 (19.44 percent) subjects, while the Synthesist style was preferred by 10 (4.63 percent).

The polygon of the frequency distribution (Figure 8.1) among the thinking styles, portrays a similar dispersion of scores across the different styles except for the Synthesist mode. The frequency distribution in Table 8.2 and the polygon in Figure 8.1 can also be interpreted in light of the level of preference above the score of 60 (preferred style) and

Table 8.2 **Frequency Distribution For the InQ(R) Scales***

Range	Synthesist	Idealist	Pragmatist	Analyst	Realist
Below 36	9	0	1	0	0
36–41	60	3	5	5	6
42–47	66	12	29	20	16
48–53	52	41	62	58	40
54–59	19	79	77	66	76
60–65	9	62	34	44	53
66–71	1	17	8	20	22
72 and Up	0	2	0	3	3

*n = 216

below the score of 47 (disinclined style). The range of dominant thinking styles and the frequency distribution have to be contrasted and compared to appreciate that many subjects had a combination of more than one thinking style.

Subscale intercorrelations using Pearson's product moment test were in the directions expected except for the fact-oriented Realist and Analyst styles that were found to be negatively correlated ($r = -0.25$, $p<.01$). The value-oriented Synthesist and Idealist styles of thinking were positively correlated although not at a level of statistical significance. The remaining correlations, however, were statistically significant at $p = 0.05$ level or better. The Synthesist was negatively correlated with the fact-oriented Realist ($r = -0.45$, $p<.01$) and Analyst ($r = -0.17$, $p<.01$) styles of thinking. The action-oriented, adaptive Pragmatist style was negatively correlated with the more reflective Synthesist ($r = -0.4$, $p<.01$), Idealist ($r = -0.26$, $p<.01$), and Analyst ($r = -0.51$, $p<.01$) styles, but positively correlated with the action-oriented Realist ($r = 0.2$, $p<.01$) style of thinking. The Idealist and Analyst styles of thinking were negatively correlated ($r = -0.15$, $p<.05$). As predicted the Idealist and Realist styles of thinking were negatively correlated ($r = -0.53$, $p<.01$).

A one-way ANOVA repeated measures, using thinking styles as the repeated factor, demonstrated that the Pragmatist, the Idealist, and the Synthesist modes were each found to be significantly different from one or more of the other thinking styles ($F = 84.87$, $df = 4,860$ $p = <.000$). Significant differences were found ($p<.05$) between the Synthesist style of thinking and all four other styles (P < S [$F = 8.22$]; A < S

[F = 10.28]; R < S [F = 11.24]; I < S [F = 11.57]). Significant differences were also found (p = <.05) between the Pragmatist and the Realist (R < P [F = 3.02]) and the Pragmatist and Idealist (I < P [F = 3.35]) styles of thinking.

DISCUSSION

The findings provide evidence to support the contention of Harrison and Bramson (1982) that nurses prefer the Idealist and Realist styles of thinking. Results from the frequency scores, for nurses preferring the Idealist and Realist styles (scores of 60 and above), hold true. The three-way style of thinking matched the findings of previous studies, and the level profile was 10.65 percent versus the 13 percent established as the population norm.

Pearson subscale intercorrelations showed correlations in the expected directions for the five styles of thinking. Yet, the negative correlation of the fact-oriented Analyst and Realist styles merits further discussion. Both styles are fact-oriented, consequently, one might expect that they would be positively correlated. The key to understanding their difference, however, lies in the approach each takes to that factual orientation. The Analyst uses a reflective and methodical approach, whereas the Realist uses an impulsive and efficient approach. The Analyst focuses on plans and methods to achieve goals and the Realist focuses on immediately perceived facts and results. The Synthesist and Idealist styles were positively correlated although not statistically significant at p = 0.05 level. One would expect these value-oriented, substantive ways of thinking to be positively correlated, but, the lack of statistical significance in the correlation suggests unique qualities exist within these two value-oriented styles. While both have a high tolerance for ambiguity and a tendency to conceptualize, the Synthesist is best in controversial situations and is interested in change, whereas the Idealist is best in unstructured value-laden situations and is interested in harmony.

The InQ(R) preferences for the Idealist style of thinking (N = 81) indicate that nurses will probably respond to situations and problems in a way that is holistic, caring, and concerned with high standards. On the other hand, those who prefer the Realist style of thinking (N = 78) are results-oriented, empirical, and efficient. It is of interest to note that only 13 of the 216 subjects preferred the Idealist/Realist styles in combination. Consequently, as Harrison and Bramson (1982) point out, the potential for compatibility problems between those who prefer the Idealist, and those who prefer the Realist styles of thinking, is high. Furthermore, due to the preferences for the Idealist and Realist styles of thinking, nurses might negate or disregard the possibility of creative solutions or innovative responses, associated with the less preferred Synthesist and Pragmatist styles.

Since it is the Analyst style that epitomizes the nursing process and this is the style that lays the foundation for much of the thinking processes in basic nursing education programs, we are left with the question as to what happens to the creative thinkers? There have not been sufficient studies in this area to identify whether thinking styles modify and change over time, or whether initial preferences are maintained throughout life. In conjunction with these speculations, one might also question whether or not methods of instruction can alter thinking styles. Certainly nurses can be made aware of their thinking styles and the strengths and liabilities of those styles. Each of the five styles could be available as an alternative approach when problems are complex, and diversity of approach is a recognized need (Harrison & Bramson, 1982).

Harrison and Bramson's (1982) initial observations were based upon a sample of nurses from the United States of America while the subjects in the current study lived in Canada. The question arises as to whether there are differences in thinking style preferences based upon culture, geographic regions, or educational systems. Demographic variables were not addressed in the original studies, but it would be of interest to know whether there is any change in styles of thinking, or patterns among the styles, as one matures. Current cross-sectional studies are inappropriate for analyzing whether the even preference profile is a product of maturation.

There are limitations in that the sample subjects for this study were volunteers seeking some type of continuing education. The question of bias could also be raised as the subjects may not represent the general population of RNs.

A potential area for future study might involve the blending or integration of the models of thinking styles with theory being advanced for reflective practice (Schon, 1983; 1987; Powell, 1989). Facility in the use of a variety of thinking styles and their appropriate application, could serve to enhance reflective practice in nursing and provide a vehicle for its implementation. Opportunities for RN students to understand the potentials for conflict and cooperation among the different styles could facilitate reflective practice.

Using the theory that individuals think differently, Engel and Kienholz (1989) have discussed how different thinking styles may affect nursing students. For instance, the individual who struggles with patient care plans and becomes flustered when making decisions, may have a preference for a thinking style that is different from the analytical style that typifies the reasoning associated with the nursing process. They further question what happens to the creative thinkers among nursing students. Rather than the creative styles of the Synthesist and Pragmatist, it is the Analyst style that is typified in the nursing process. Nursing educators need to know the thinking style of today's students in order to guide them in capitalizing on strengths and developing areas of potential liability. Can the strengths inherent in different thinking styles be capitalized on in making clinical judgments? Is it possible to tailor problem solving exercises and decision making activities to fit the individual thinking styles of nurses?

Understanding and becoming aware of personal thinking styles provides each nurse with a framework for learning new approaches to differentiating their own strengths and liabilities. The framework will also enable the nurse to better grasp the reality of differences that exist in people's thinking, which could facilitate interpersonal communication with colleagues and clients.

CONCLUSION

Considerable implications exist for nurse-educators concerning the present findings that RNs think as Idealists and Realists. There is a potential for dialectic confrontations associated with these different approaches to problem solving both in the classroom and the clinical setting. The ability to identify styles of thinking, so as to assist students in capitalizing on their strengths and minimizing liabilities, provides an added dimension for instructional planning. The diversity of nurses' thinking might be considered a liability if it becomes the basis for poor communication and conflict. Indeed, inappropriate or excessive use of one's preferred style of thinking may even be detrimental to certain aspects of clinical judgment. Nevertheless, the strength of nursing lies in the very diversity of thinking styles brought to the profession by every nurse, and that diversity needs to be fostered through recognition of the quality of our differences and the strength that comes with the appropriate mixture of styles and skills.

REFERENCES

Benner, P., & Tanner, C. (1987). Clinical judgment: How expert nurses use intuition. *American Journal of Nursing, 87*, 23–31.

Bramson, R. M. (1987). Addendum I. In *InQ styles of thinking: Administration and interpretation manual.* Berkeley, CA: Bramson, Parlette, Harrison & Associates.

Bruvold, W. H., Parlette, N., Bramson, R. M., & Bramson, S. J. (1983). An investigation of the item characteristics, reliability and validity of the Inquiry Mode Questionnaire. *Educational and Psychological Measurement, 43*, 483–493.

Cervetti, M. J., Franceschini, L. A., & Sojourner, D. S. (1989). Cognitive styles among teachers of elementary "at risk" children. Unpublished paper presented at the Annual Meeting of the Mid-South Educational Research Association, Little Rock, AR.

Churchman, C. W. (1971). *The design of inquiring systems.* New York: Basic Books.

Engel, J., & Kienholz, A. (1989). Diversification in problem solving: Implications and educational strategies. In *Clinical decision making in nursing* (pp. 22–24). Papers from the annual meeting of the Western Region Canadian Association of University Schools of Nursing.

Franceschini, L. A., & Butler, E. D. (1989). Of epistomologies and inquiry modes. Paper presented at the Annual Meeting of the Mid-South Educational Research Association. Little Rock, AR.

Harrison, A. F., & Bramson, R. M. (1982). *Styles of thinking.* New York: Doubleday. (In paperback retitled as *The art of thinking*, New York: Berkley Books, 1983.)

Harrison, A. F., & Bramson, R. M. (1988). *InQ Inquiry Mode Questionnaire: A measure of how you think and make decisions.* Berkeley, CA: Bramson, Parlette, Harrison & Associates.

Hughes, T. H., & Franceschini, L. A. (Nov. 1989). A comparison of the Myers-Briggs Type Indicator with the Bramson-Harrison Inquiry

Mode Questionnaire. Paper presented at the Annual Meeting of the Mid-South Educational Research Association. Little Rock, AR.

Kagan, D. M., & Tixier y Vigil, Y. (1987). Student's cognitive style and their ratings of their teacher's effectiveness. *Educational Considerations, 14*(1), 2–6.

Kienholz, A., & Hritzuk, J. (1986). Comparing students in architecture and medicine: Findings from two new measures of cognitive style. *Psychological Reports, 58,* 823–830.

Mitroff, I. I., & Pondy, L. R. (1974). On the organization of inquiry. *Public Administration Review, 34,* 471–479.

Powell, J. N. (1989). The reflective practitioner in nursing. *Journal of Advanced Nursing, 14,* 824–832.

Reece, C. C., & Todd, R. F. (Nov., 1989). Math anxiety, math achievement and the analyst style of thinking. Paper presented at the Annual Meeting of the Mid-South Educational Research Association, Little Rock, AR.

Schon, D. A. (1983). *The reflective practitioner: How professionals think in action.* New York: Basic Books.

Schon, D. A. (1987). *Educating the reflective practitioner.* San Francisco: Jossey-Bass.

Tanner, C. A., Padrick, K. P., Westfall, U. E., & Putzier, D. J. (1987). Diagnostic reasoning in nursing: An analysis of cognitive strategies. *Nursing Research, 36,* 358–363.

Part III

Innovative Approaches to Curriculum, Classroom, and Clinical Instruction in RN Education

9

RN-BSN Curriculum Development: A Dynamic, Student-Centered Approach

Mary Lou Rusin

INTRODUCTION

Designing and implementing a baccalaureate curriculum for the returning RN adult learner (RRN) is a challenge to nursing faculty. The learning styles and needs of the adult learner are different than those of traditional college-age students and require special attention.

This paper will examine the curriculum of one RN to BSN program which is based on a philosophy of facilitating the RRNs' achievement of a baccalaureate degree, while at the same time, promoting the emergence of a professional nurse who is empowered to assume a nursing leadership role of change agent and client advocate, and thus move the profession forward. Centering the curriculum process on a holistic approach, and understanding and planning for the assessed needs of the RRN population has resulted in a dramatic change in enrollment in the nursing department of this particular college.

PHILOSOPHY OF A STUDENT-CENTERED CURRICULUM

Increasing the educational credentials of registered nurses will enable nursing to achieve a more broadly recognized professional status in the health care delivery system. The academic setting should establish clear, well-articulated, noncumbersome pathways, or educational ladders to allow registered nurses prepared at various levels, the opportunity to improve their educational status. This philosophy of improved educational access provides the foundation for establishing the nursing curriculum.

Unfortunately, colleges and universities have not been as responsive to the needs of their RRN clientele as possible. A "pecking order" continues to exist in nursing education which devalues "technical education" as compared to learning at the "professional" level. This bias thwarts nursing's efforts to unify and gain professional strength since a majority of nurses are prepared at the technical level (Fralic, 1989). Nurses must have the opportunity to build upon, rather than repeat, their nursing knowledge and previous education, and to move from a technical orientation to more theory-based practice—preparation better equipped to deal with the nursing practice demands of today as well as the future.

Nurses often cite reasons such as distance, scheduling conflicts among work, home, and school, financial problems, and lack of credit for previous learning as constraints which prevent their return to school (Lange, 1986). These barriers become roadblocks to even the most interested and motivated students. The student-centered curriculum recognizes these barriers, and by applying the processes of flexibility, negotiation, and compromise, provides a quality nursing curriculum which accesses registered nurses to the baccalaureate degree.

Adult Learning

Adult learning principles are well documented in the literature. Malcolm Knowles (1980) traces the development of andragogy—the art and science of helping adults learn, as compared to pedagogy—the art and science of teaching children. Knowles views these models of assumptions about learners as being not mutually exclusive, but rather as two ends of a spectrum. The major differences are in the individual's perspectives regarding self-concept, prior experience, learning orientation, and time. Most adult learning theorists and researchers agree with Knowles that motivation as a component of learning is self-directed and internally stimulated in the adult learner. This high motivation brings the element of self-direction into play in the adult learning process. In the andragogical model, the teacher facilitates the process of learning and change for the student (Knowles, 1970). Designing the curriculum to capitalize on these specific positive traits of the adult learner allows maximum learning to occur.

Looking at characteristics of the learner to provide a theoretical basis for curriculum development is a key ingredient of many classic curriculum models. Ralph Tyler's (1950) model refers to the learner as being the source of educational objectives; the Knowles (1980) model includes diagnosing the needs and interests of the individual; and, Cyril Houle (1989) makes direct reference to the concept of individualization. When developing a curriculum for adult learners, the educator needs to consider the students' important attributes of self-direction and motivation. The faculty must capitalize on these elements to create an optimal learning atmosphere and maximize potential learning capability for the students. The way in which the adult learner perceives the educational activity directly impacts the amount of learning that takes place.

As an adult learner, the RRN student has unique characteristics and needs. Traditionally-based baccalaureate programs need to re-examine their underlying philosophies and conceptual frameworks as a beginning step to better serving these students. In fact, generic programs may be inappropriate for the RRN based on differences in prior knowledge and patterns of thinking, experiential knowledge, age and life stage, and career goals and aspirations between the RRN and her "traditional" student counterpart (Muzio and Ohashi, 1979; Rather, 1992).

Lifelong Learning

Lifelong learning is a necessity in today's world of knowledge explosion and rapid change. Information is changing over at a rate of every 18 months. Knowles (1980) views lifelong learning as the organizing principle for all education. Knowles describes "learning how to learn" as a coping mechanism for adults facing the challenge of fast-moving ideas and technology.

Cross (1981) examines the growth of the "learning society" as being initiated by change, demographic change—the fact that the American population as a whole is shifting toward a middle age, or adult concentration; social change—rising educational attainment, changing career patterns, changing roles for women and equal opportunity; and, technological change—the knowledge explosion.

CURRICULUM

Curriculum is defined in its broadest and most classic sense as encompassing all of the learning experiences provided by the school (Saylor & Alexander, 1966). The learner, the teacher, the environment as well as the content are all integral parts of the curriculum. For the student-centered curriculum approach to be successful, each of these elements must be considered in terms of the adult learner's differing strengths and weaknesses.

The Learner

The need for lifelong learning has become evident in the nursing profession and is due to a number of factors, including the changing role of nursing and the health care delivery system, the technologic revolution and computer technocracy, and the knowledge explosion in general. Basic nursing education programs can no longer be considered to be the end point of formal knowledge aquisition for the nurse. Statistics show more and more nurses returning to the academic environment to pursue advanced credentials in nursing, most notably the baccalaureate degree.

Changing economic times have forced many nurses to look at methods of developing a "mobility package" for themselves in the event of job dissolution, dissatisfaction, or spousal career relocation. In order to translate work skills into new employment or career opportunities, it is increasingly clear that a bachelor's degree in nursing is required. There is general consensus that the baccalaureate degree is the desired preparation for entry into nursing practice (Stevens, 1981). Preferences in actual hiring practices are obvious by simply scanning the want-ads. Statements such as "BS required" and "BS preferred" are the rule rather than the exception.

Lange (1986) found that there was a set of motivating factors which RNs cited as being reasons for obtaining a baccalaureate degree. Work-related motivators and personal rewards were cited by more than 50 percent of the nurse respondents in this study.

As the nurse returns to school, a new and additional role must be assumed—that of learner. The RRN is a multidimensional person, and must adapt to the various roles he or she occupies. Campaniello (1988) states that the act of returning to school enhances the well-being of the nurse, since additional benefits, the personal rewards, can be perceived by the student which counteract the negative impact of role overload and role conflict. "The nurses in this study . . . evidence greater well-being as they increase the multiplicity of their roles" (p. 139). Taking action on a long term goal of achieving the baccalaureate degree can be therapeutic for the nurse who has procrastinated moving on this educational objective for some time.

For many RRNs, school becomes an important part of their lives, as they enjoy the personal as well as professional impact of the academic setting. Nurses who may have become complacent about their lack of power in the employment setting, often "recommit" to nursing as they re-examine the issues plaguing the profession from a new perspective. The sense of accomplishment and boost in self-confidence which comes from successfully completing coursework in nursing and the liberal arts and sciences is an intrinsic reward for the learner, and one which the RRN may not have anticipated. Students remark that school essentially becomes like a hobby to them, and in the words of one RRN ". . . it sure beats bowling!" Rather (1992) documents the development of clinical performance improvement as the RRN moves to the level of expert in the academic setting.

The personality characteristics of the adult learner can be grouped into positives and negatives when applied in the context of the academic environment. Adults who seek a college degree are a motivated and educationally mobile group. Generally, RRNs are mature, forceful, strong, aggressive, and independent with leadership potential and superior intellectual ability (Krouse, 1988). However, adult students also face many conflicts in their quest for higher education. Academic skills may have deteriorated due to non-use, especially in the area of grammar and composition, and time conflicts create a situation in which education cannot be the learner's top priority. These students also demand a more egalitarian teaching/learning atmosphere, and assertive behaviors can border dangerously on aggression. In order to capture the "teachable moments," the curriculum must be designed so that it challenges the learner, and amplifies those personality characteristics which are hallmarks of leadership behavior.

Even the most self-confident RRN may suffer anxiety and self-doubt when entering the "ivory tower" of academia. For the nurse who is able to skillfully negotiate the bureaucratic tangle of the health care system, charting the new and unfamiliar waters of the college setting may be stressful. A naive approach to academic education may compound this anxiety and self-doubt (Lange, 1986).

Faculty

The faculty role in teaching adult learners is multidimensional and based on supporting the student's strengths and providing guidance in the learning environment. This role can be incongruent with the traditional or generic program faculty expectation, and requires faculty to develop specialized skills and philosophical orientation. To establish an optimal teacher-student relationship, the faculty need to be "seasoned"—to learn through guided experience about the special needs and capabilities of the RRN population. Faculty must also recognize and validate their own perceptions about the teacher and student roles. Faculty must understand the adult learners' assets and liabilities, and be prepared to proactively support the access of RRNs to education.

Faculty who teach in RN to BSN programs need to develop more collegial relationships with the RRNs, and actually expect to learn from the students' experiences. Diekelmann (1989) refers to this phenomenon as "teacher as learner—the learner as teacher." The resulting learning atmosphere created by this interchange of learning roles is an exciting one for both students and faculty.

In the world of adult learning, the classroom is not seen as the one mystical place where learning must take place, but rather, as one alternative for learning. Faculty must be comfortable with the notion that there are multiple methods and environments which facilitate learning, and the teacher does not necessarily need to be physically present to operationalize the curriculum. The key words for the faculty to remember are flexibility, negotiation and compromise. These approaches support the RRNs' needs, and relate to the high levels of motivation and self-direction which are characteristic of these learners.

The advisement role for faculty who deal with RRNs also varies from that of the traditional academic advisor. Since the RRNs are occupying a myriad of roles, it is the job of the academic advisor to "pave the way"—to help the students anticipate problems or barriers to their educational goals, whether the barriers emanate from the home and/or academic setting. Developing a library of reading materials to more fully explore such issues as "academic shock," the uniqueness of adult learners, role transition, reactions to returning to school, and support system development can be a vehicle to provide RRNs a smoother transition into the academic environment. Advisors can also share tips for "academic survival" including topics such as word processing skills, writing, note taking, preparation for classes and other course requirements, test taking, structuring study areas at home, and accessing day-care resources. Since peer support is an invaluable resource to the adult learner, the faculty advisor can also emphasize the importance of networking and facilitate it among the RRNs. Nurses returning to school find comfort in the knowledge that they are not alone in their situation. The old adages "misery loves company," and "we're all in the same boat" have important meaning for the RRN. "Sharing concerns and methods of coping also builds a sense of community and mutual support, which is 'empowering'" (Rather, 1992, p. 53). However, even in light of the finest academic advisement and anticipatory guidance, faculty should anticipate some amount of "acting out" behavior by the RRNs. Frequent disphoric episodes, confusion, and expressed dissatisfaction are signs of stress which are typical in the adult learner (Rendon, 1988). Such "academic shock behavior" should be dealt with in a sensitive, non-defensive manner by the faculty (Green, 1987). The path to academic satisfaction and achievement is never a smooth one when dealing with adult learners.

An important source of support for the RRN learner is found in the family. Spousal or significant other support as well as support from the work environment contribute to decreased role conflict and enhance learning experiences for the RRN (Campaniello, 1988).

Since needs of the adult learner differ from those of traditional students, the faculty advisement role must be tailored to provide optimal benefit. The perception that less advisement is necessary for RRNs since they are already motivated, persistent, and responsible learners is incorrect. Adult learners actually may require more advisement hours since their problems and concerns tend to be very complex and cross-cut many important role functions. The student-advisor ratio should be kept low in order to account for the vast diversity of the student population and assure that advisement services are accessible to the RRN. "Feeling like a number, not a person" detracts from the advisement relationship; the faculty advisor needs to have the time to know both the student's professional and personal situations, and needs to convey a genuine interest in supporting the student's success in the academic environment.

Teaching adult learners requires the faculty to master a vast repertoire of teaching methodologies—creativity is the password. Activities which strengthen the positive attributes of adult learners such as discussion groups, seminars, debates, student presentation, and small group activities challenge this population of learners and permit them to take an active, empowered role in the learning process. The faculty member also needs to realize that the concepts of flexibility, compromise and negotiation can be applied without endangering quality. Rather, these concepts further develop the climate of respect which enables learning to take place. In this climate, both faculty and students recognize each others' expertise and learn from it rather than being threatened by it.

Content

The content component of the curriculum at this small, private college is also based on knowledge and support of the specific needs of adult learners. A 45 credit hour liberal arts core, a 30 credit hour related course requirement, and the 45 credit hour nursing major compose the 120 credit baccalaureate degree nursing program. Within each of these credit components, there is a great deal of flexibility which allows the individual student to select courses and structure course content to meet her own personal, professional, and/or career goals.

The liberal arts core area assures that each student at the college is exposed to a broad range of educational topics, such as history and government, philosophy and religion, literature, and fine arts, as well as sociology, psychology, mathematics, and science. A liberal, college-wide transfer credit policy allows RRNs with coursework already completed in any or all of these areas to transfer credit as long as a minimum grade of "C" was earned in each course. Transfer credit can also be obtained through approved independent study programs such as the Regents College Examination Program, and the College Level Examination Program (CLEP). The only required courses for RRNs in the core curriculum are statistics (mathematics core) and general chemistry (science core). The remaining courses can be selected from a wide range of offerings which may or may not directly relate to the practice of nursing. For example, to meet the philosophy/religion requirement, the RRN can choose any two courses ranging from such topics as Medical Ethics, to Question of the Human, to The Meaning of Care in a Technological Society. In their first semesters at the college, many RRNs select courses with very direct, obvious relationships to health care practice. As the RRNs become increasingly aware of the impact of all educational experience on their lives and practice, it is typical for them to make course selections more broadly as they progress toward degree completion.

There are four requirements in the related required course area: anatomy and physiology, microbiology, and pathophysiology. Typical RRNs transfer in all of these requirements except pathophysiology. The remaining 16 credits can be used by the student to select an array of elective courses which can be arranged to meet their own personal or professional educational goals. By judiciously selecting courses to fulfill this requirement, the RRN has the opportunity to develop a minor area of study in either the liberal arts, business, or science divisions of the college. Many RRNs are choosing to develop minors, since it is viewed as a way of maximizing the educational experience, and adding dimension to one's baccalaureate degree.

The 45 credit nursing major is divided into two sections: lower division (freshman and sophomore level coursework), and upper division (junior and senior level coursework). All nurses transfer the 15 credits of lower division coursework. Associate degree graduates directly transfer this credit. Since diploma program nursing courses are completed in hospital rather than college settings, and therefore have no academic credit attached to them, diploma graduates must "validate" their knowledge of basic fundamentals of nursing practice. Successful completion of a three-part, teacher-made, paper and pencil clinical validation exam allows the diploma graduate to transfer the lower division nursing credits also. In order to make this validation process more acceptable and less threatening to the diploma-prepared nurse, there is no charge to take the exam or to transfer the credit, and the exam can be completed by the student by simply arranging a mutually agreeable time with the department secretary. The clinical validation exam must be completed before enrolling in any upper division nursing courses.

The upper division nursing coursework is developed to promote resocialization into the professional role and fosters the self-direction and independence of the learner. Learning strategies that are geared toward advantaging the adult learner include: contract assignments, guided independent study experiences, using students as content experts, and promotion of open discussion among students regarding all aspects of the curriculum and educational process (Green, 1987). The first three nursing courses are theory-based, and no clinical experience is attached to these courses. All of these courses are prerequisite to three clinical courses which move in client-focus from care of the individual, to care of the family, to care of the community. Immersing the RRNs in theory in the beginning of their nursing coursework provides them with a broader theoretical basis for nursing practice, and divorces them (in the academic setting) from the traditional, technically based roles in nursing with which the majority of RRNs are intimately familiar. Showing RRNs that there is a broad and autonomous scope of nursing outside of institutional settings is exciting, enlightening, and readies them to participate in clinical placements.

There are three options for clinical experiences: traditional, flexible-time, and student-designed. Traditional clinical experiences are offered on one day per week and placements are selected and arranged by the nursing faculty. Establishing a particular day for all clinical experiences enables the RRNs to arrange their work schedules far in advance, and causes fewer work-related scheduling conflicts. Flexible-time clinicals are also arranged by the faculty, but are designed to meet the scheduling needs of nurses who cannot arrange their work schedule to meet the traditional clinical timeframe. Typically, these clinicals take place in the evenings or on weekends. Finally, the student-designed clinical option allows qualified students to pursue their own interests and to "try on" expanded roles in nursing in a non-threatening atmosphere. In order to set up this type of clinical, the RRN must identify a master's prepared nurse preceptor and develop clinical objectives congruent with the course objectives. All arrangements must meet with the approval of the nursing faculty (Cresia, 1989).

The final, or capstone course revolves around professional issues and gives the RRN a chance to re-examine the profession from a baccalaureate perspective as well as to formulate action plans. Teaching strategies such as debates and "reaction papers"—responding to controversial issues using research based rationale in a short (four page) format—develop the RRNs' abilities in communication and also empower them to assume the role of change agents for the profession.

Environment

The learning environment is an important component of the curriculum since the RRN must interface with a multitude of unfamiliar offices, policies, and people in the educational bureaucracy. The coordination and support of this component is essential to providing a smooth transition for the RRN into the academic setting.

The small campus environment provides an atmosphere of support for the adult learner. For many of the multidimensional adult learners, time is a valuable commodity, and services across the campus are structured to conserve both time and energy. Admission and registration are completed in a one-step process and can be accomplished in a one hour meeting with a nursing faculty advisor. Not standing in lines is a real enticement to the RRN. Centralized academic services including the library, bookstore, computer center, business office, financial aid office, and registrar, further streamline access to the learning environment.

Lange (1986) found that RRNs were more likely to use personal or family finances to pay for school expenses, and were reluctant to use school loans to finance their education. Since registered nurses "fall through the cracks" of need-based financial aid programs, the college provides funds to offset tuition costs through a "Tuition Grant" program for registered nurses which can underwrite up to 50% of tuition and fees. These grants are not need-based and every RRN automatically qualifies for this program. The grant program covers both full-time and part-time students and is guaranteed to remain in place for each student through completion of the program. Thus, financial considerations do not impact on the RRN's ability to determine a flexible courseload. There is no change in the tuition grant program for nurses who receive tuition reimbursement monies from their employer; in fact, reimbursement funds are deducted from the student's bill at the beginning of the semester—the college waits for the reimbursement check to be issued rather than having the student pay the money out of pocket. These arrangements diminish the RRN's anxiety and stress related to returning to school in a very tangible way.

Scheduling with the RRNs' needs in mind also improves their access to higher education and helps to conserve their time. All nursing courses are offered in three-hour time blocks each semester in both the day and evening. Students can arrange their schedules to take as many as 12 credit hours (full time status) on one day per week. While some students do set up their schedule in this way, the more common approach is to take two courses (six credits) on one day or evening each week. This type of scheduling is done campus-wide and makes education available to all RRNs regardless of their work schedule and other commitments.

Faculty across the college have had the opportunity to meet the RRNs in their classes and provide much support for their endeavors. Frequent communication and outreach efforts by the nursing faculty further enhance other faculty's understanding of the special needs of the nursing student population.

A three hour nursing orientation program for all new RRNs is scheduled each fall prior to the start of classes. The program helps to put together the educational jigsaw puzzle and untangle the red tape of the ivory tower of academia. RRNs also have the opportunity to meet other nurses, faculty, and current and past students, all of which supports their goal aquisition and decreases stress.

Recruitment efforts are specifically targeted at working RNs and are ongoing throughout the year. Outreach to hospitals, and other employing agencies is a primary method of recruitment. Nursing faculty are often involved in agency visitations, and also provide inservice programs on a limited basis for area health care institutions. On-campus open house programs for RNs are scheduled three times a year. All recruitment efforts are focused on articulating the personal and professional value which the baccalaureate experience can provide.

Recruitment efforts across the Western New York State area resulted in the development of off-campus programs in geographically remote locations of the state. These off-site programs are located in four areas ranging in distance between 30 to 75 miles from the home campus. All nursing courses are cycled to these off-campus sites, and are taught by faculty who have taught on the home campus. These off-campus programs operationalize the philosophy of the Nursing Department and its commitment to accessing registered nurses to higher education.

SUMMARY

A student-centered curriculum is possible to design which does not compromise quality. However, the mechanics of creating and operationalizing such a program are a complex matter and require the ongoing support, assistance, and involved commitment of everyone involved under the broad umbrella of curriculum. Given the highly specific learning needs of RRNs, a student-centered curriculum is most easily implemented in an RN only program, where each element of the curriculum can be tailored expressly to match learning style. RRNs describing the attributes of RN only designed programs cite the support of independence that is the hallmark of such programs. For these reasons, RN only programs best address the needs of adult learners (Beeman, 1988).

The rewards of success are significant for all involved. The institution garners increased enrollments of academically qualified, excellent students. The faculty have a wide variety of students in their classes, thus providing a cosmopolitan, enriching, experience-related atmosphere. Finally, RRNs reap the benefit of a quality nursing education program which can facilitate achievement of career and personal goals, and help them to establish a new set of life goals and perspectives as well. In fact, research on baccalaureate completion programs shows that this second step education option may actually benefit the nursing profession as a whole since second step entrants (RRNs) have significantly more professional attitudes (Thurber, 1988). By supporting the leadership behaviors such as motivation, self-directedness, and assertiveness that the RRN possesses, empowerment of the nurse occurs. These behaviors are specific to the RRN and set her apart from the generic baccalaureate student. These personality and learning characteristics can be enablers for RRNs to move the profession ahead, and can be valuable assets to equip them for the nursing profession's future (Rendon, 1988). The results of one study indicated that the associate degree RRN was a more professional product upon completion of the baccalaureate degree than either the generic BSN or ADN graduate (Lawler, 1987).

Development of additional curriculum strategies to further hone the student-centered nursing curriculum should be investigated and implemented, for ". . . those programs which attempt to be more flexible and adapt to the needs of this student population will be the ones that survive to produce our future nursing leaders" (Thurber, 1988, p. 272).

REFERENCES

Beeman, P. (1988). RNs' perceptions of their baccalaureate programs: Meeting their adult learning needs. *Journal of Nursing Education, 27,* 364–370.

Campaniello, J. A. (1988). When professional nurses return to school: A study of role conflict and well-being in multiple-role women. *Journal of Professional Nursing, 4,* 136–140.

Cresia, J. L. (1989). Reducing barriers to RN educational mobility. *Nurse Educator, 14,* 29–33.

Cross, K. P. (1981). *Adults as Learners.* San Francisco: Jossey-Bass Publishers.

Diekelmann, N. (1989). The nursing curriculum: Lived experiences of students. In *Curriculum revolution: Reconceptualizing nursing education* (pp. 25–41). New York: National League for Nursing Press.

Fralic, M. F. (1989). Issues surrounding RN/BSN education: A view from nursing service. *Journal of Professional Nursing, 5,* 64–113.

Green, C. P. (1987). Multiple role women: The real world of the mature RN learner. *Journal of Nursing Education, 26,* 266–271.

Houle, C. O. (1989). *The Design of Education.* San Francisco: Jossey-Bass Publishers.

Knowles, M. S. (1970). *The adult learner: A neglected species.* Houston: Gulf Publishing Co.

Knowles, M. S. (1980). *The modern practice of adult education–from pedagogy to andragogy.* Chicago: Association Press.

Krouse, H. J. (1988). Personality characteristics of registered nurses in baccalaureate education. *Nurse Educator, 13,* pp. 27, 36, 39.

Lange, L. L. (1986). Recruiting, advising, and program planning for RN/BSN students. *Western Journal of Nursing Research, 8,* 414–430.

Lawler, T. G. (1987). Professionalization: A comparison among generic baccalaureate, ADN, and RN/BSN nurses. *Nurse Educator, 12,* 19–22.

Muzio, L. G., & Ohashi, J. P. (1979). The RN student–unique characteristics, unique needs. *Nursing Outlook, 27,* 528–32.

Rather, M. L. (1992). "Nursing as a way of thinking"–Heideggerian hermeneutical analysis of the lived experience of the returning RN. *Research in Nursing and Health, 15,* 47–56.

Rendon, D. (1988). The registered nurse student: A role congruence perspective. *Journal of Nursing Education, 27,* 172–177.

Saylor, J. G., & Alexander, W. M. (1966). *Curriculum planning for modern schools.* New York: Holt, Rinehart & Winston, Inc.

Stevens, B. (1981). Program articulation: What it is and what it is not. *Nursing Outlook, 29,* 700–706.

Thurber, F. W. (1988). A comparison of RN students in two types of baccalaureate completion programs. *Journal of Nursing Education, 27,* 266–273.

Tyler, R. (1950). *Basic Principles of Curriculum Development.* Chicago: University of Chicago Press.

10

Twenty Years of Success and Still Growing

Elisabeth Pennington, Ann Kruszewski,
Theresa Allor, Janet Barnfather,
Claudia Moore, Carol Zenas,
Mary Hoenecke, and Elaine Van Doren

INTRODUCTION

Nineteen ninety-two marked the 40th anniversary of Associate Degree education in the United States. Thus, this conference on "RN Education" is timely and takes on unique importance as we reflect how far nursing has come over these forty years. We acknowledge that for many years diploma school graduates sought additional education, the baccalaureate degree in nursing. Associate degree education programs provided graduates who increased the demand for baccalaureate education at the very time that baccalaureate programs were undergoing transformation and growth. During this same forty year period the nursing profession identified and clarified its definition, its theory and knowledge base, and its contribution to the health care needs of the country. Within this context of change, education for the Registered Nurse (RN) student has not only been legitimized, it has become an expected part of all basic nursing programs.

In this chapter, the University of Michigan School of Nursing, shares its history, current approach to RN education, and planning and thinking for the future.

HISTORY

In 1970 the University of Michigan School of Nursing began to explore an educational track for RN students. Prior to this time, the School had few RN students. The University of Michigan was, and is, a major research university with a fairly traditional approach to undergraduate education. To acknowledge and design a program for community college transfer students took courage and persistence. The university considered such an undertaking as strange and suspect of quality and rigor.

Fortunately, there were visionary and committed individuals on the nursing faculty. They were aided in their work by a consultant from the National League for Nursing, Dr. Mary Dineen (Dr. Dineen went on to become the Dean of the School of Nursing at Boston College and recently retired from that position) and were guided by a commitment to an Open Curriculum approach to RN education (Dineen, 1970).

A sub-committee of the curriculum committee developed a program in which the RN student would transfer courses from other two- and four-year colleges, utilize a "credit-by-exam" approach for some courses, enroll in two matrix courses, and enroll in a fairly typical senior year sequence. While many schools had programs whereby they admitted the RN student into the basic program, or gave some advanced standing (and there were still some schools who awarded "blanket credits" for diploma education), this program was among the first specifically designed to acknowledge the student's previous education and incorporate those learnings into the degree requirements. The first students were admitted in 1971 and the first two students graduated in 1973.

Once the program for RNs was established on the Ann Arbor campus, the faculty of the School of Nursing recognized the need in Michigan for advanced education for RNs who were geographically distant from existing BSN programs. A training grant was submitted to the Department of Health Education and Welfare requesting funding for the development and implementation of *Community-Based BSN Programs*.

This project was funded and began in November, 1974. At that time there were only three publicly supported institutions offering baccalaureate degrees for RNs in Michigan and they were concentrated in the southeastern area of the state. More than 20,000 RNs resided outside this area. An off-campus program to serve the needs of this RN population at a reasonable cost was developed by the School of Nursing in collaboration with the University of Michigan Extension Service and the Office of Educational Resources and Research (Davis, 1978). The design of this special project established programs at Flint, Kalamazoo, and Traverse City. The location of these programs greatly extended the nursing community being served.

Among the goals of the community-based program was the implementation of an examination system whereby RNs could receive course credit for knowledge gained in prior educational programs and clinical settings. Specific courses were determined appropriate to be designated for Credit By Exam (CBE). Support materials were identified and study guides were developed and published. Through the use of these materials, individual RNs could evaluate their knowledge and, where necessary, augment it through additional study prior to writing the examination for credit. These program materials were acknowledged in the profession as excellent and were displayed by invitation at the American Nurses Association Convention in Atlantic City in June, 1976. This program was well received in the community and detailed evaluation indicated that the quality of the program and student satisfaction was high (Lusk & Davis, 1980).

It took time, commitment, and resources to keep these CBEs current and pertinent, along with revising the accompanying study guides. Over the years revisions were made, but knowledge was exploding rapidly, faculty were changing, and resources were needed for other projects. Many of the original CBE exams have now been replaced with standardized examinations from ACT/PEP and NLN.

An additional change has been made in the Flint program for RNs. It was first housed at the University of Michigan in Flint, which was originally a small extension of the Ann Arbor campus, but over time became a full multi-purpose college with a mission focused on teaching and local and regional needs. Today, it is fully accredited by Middle-States Accrediting Association as a branch of the University, as is the University of Michigan Dearborn campus. The RN study program at Flint continued to operate under the aegis of the School of Nursing during this period of growth. In 1986 a review of program status was conducted which determined that the nursing program at Flint could become an independent nursing program. Separate faculty, policies, and curriculum were developed and approved by the Board of Regents. This past March (1992) Flint received NLN accreditation for its RN studies program.

Thus, what started in 1970 has evolved to encompass two off-campus sites at Kalamazoo and Traverse City, has sustained an on-campus program, and has given birth to a new program for the State of Michigan. To date the RN studies program has graduated over 1500 professional nurses whose influence has been felt all over the midwest.

CURRENT PROGRAM

Nothing ever stands still, and certainly not nursing curricula. The School of Nursing undertook a major revision of the undergraduate curriculum in 1987. Changes in the basic program prompted changes in the RN studies curriculum. The faculty of RN studies also took this opportunity to reaffirm a belief statement about RN studies education.

First, we believe that professional nursing is characterized by caring for clients within a nursing conceptual framework. The Registered Nurse Curriculum focuses on those skills, knowledges, and experiences needed to function within such a framework and to make the transition from technical to professional practice. Secondly, we believe RN students are adult learners. Thus, they are autonomous, self-directed learners who are highly committed to the nursing profession. In this aspect they are more like graduate students than traditional undergraduate students. Finally, the focus of the program is on integrating, synthesizing, and reframing prior knowledge into a conceptual model of nursing. Thus, we do not ignore previous nursing education, but use it.

Reflective of the original design, we continue to use a variety of approaches to completing program requirements. Figure 10.1 provides an overview of the RN studies program. It mirrors the basic undergraduate program, but still provides for a number of options—transfer credit, use of standardized examinations, use of credit-by-exam, as well as course enrollments.

The RN studies program is built upon the framework of the undergraduate curriculum with its four major organizing concepts of humankind, health, nursing, and environment. The challenge in building RN studies curricula is to plan for students with varying backgrounds in nursing education and practice who are balancing multiple personal roles. The RN studies faculty used its knowledge of curricula of the various technical nursing education programs in the State of Michigan and its beliefs about the differences between technical and professional nursing education in developing the RN curriculum.

The University of Michigan School of Nursing
BSN Curriculum for RN's

Level I

Fall Term	Credits	Winter Term	Credits
% English Composition	3	% Culture Selective	3
% + Sociology	3	% + General Psychology	3
% Liberal Arts Selective	3	% Biochemistry	4
% Elective	3	% Environmental Selective	3
	12		13

Level II

Fall Term	Credits	Winter Term	Credits	Spring/Summer Term	Credits
% @ 210 Anatomy/Physiology	6	% * 245 Pathophysiology	5	222 Health Assessment	4
% * 217 Growth & Development	3	% @ 210 Pharmacology	3		
# 265 Basic Essentials	7	% * 215 Research	3		
285 Dimensions of		287 Issues of			
Professional Nursing	4	Professional Nursing	4		
	20		15		4

Level III

Fall Term	Credits	Winter Term	Credits
# 345 Theory of Care of the Ill	6	# 426 Mental Illness	6
# 346 Nursing Care of the Ill	6	# 384 Maternity	6
% @ 317 Nutrition	3	% Statistics	3
% Elective	3	* 313 Family Concepts	2
	18		17

Level IV

(All Level I-III credits except electives and statistics must be completed prior to enrollment in Level IV courses)

Fall Term	Credits	Winter Term	Credits	Spring/Summer Term	Credits
388 Theory & Practice of		484 Comprehensive Community		428 Management	5
Professional Nursing	8	Health Nursing	8	423 Professional Development	
403 Societal Health Issues	2			for RN's	2
	10		8		7

Minimum Requirement for Graduation: 124 Credits

% = may transfer credit   # = may earn credit through NLN Mobility Profile II Exams
+ = may earn credit through CLEP   @ = may earn credit through NLN achievement tests
* = may earn credit through examination

Figure 10.1 Overview of RN Studies Program.

The basic undergraduate program is designed in four levels. The typical RN student enters the program somewhere between levels II and III. Students are required to have completed the culture selective, English composition, psychology, sociology, and one other required course from the undergraduate program to be eligible for admission. Students are also required to earn an acceptable score in equivalency examinations in the areas of medical-surgical, pediatric, obstetrical, and psychiatric nursing prior to admission. These are tested through the use of the NLN Mobility Profile II examinations. These examinations enable students to earn credit for Beginning Concepts in Nursing, Maternity Nursing, Care of the Ill, and Mental Illness courses in the basic curriculum for a total of 31 credits. A typical Associate Degree graduate in Michigan will transfer course work in anatomy and physiology, psychology, sociology, English composition, and several selectives from their first nursing program. Thus, the typical student will have earned 50 credits or more prior to admission, placing them at or very near junior status in the university.

The RN studies course work is designed to address the pervasive and progressive subconcepts of the undergraduate curriculum. The RN student is a technically prepared nurse who is competent in caring for the physical and psychological aspects of individuals in situations of illness and in the context of the client's immediate physical environment (usually in an acute care setting). Thus, the first learning experiences for the RN student still focus on the care of the individual, but with an emphasis on all dimensions of clients, not just the physical. The earliest course work also focuses on aspects of the nursing role which are not part of a typical technical nursing education, particularly judgment, inquiry, leadership, and the professional dimensions of knowledge and caring. Issues of role transition often are a source of internal conflict for the newly matriculated RN student and, therefore, are addressed early in the educational program. Skills such as health assessment, teaching and communication, which are not addressed in depth in the students' earlier nursing education, are included in early course work in the RN studies program. Attention is also given to how the professional nurse defines the environment and health.

Two bridge courses, *N285 Client Centered Dimensions of Professional Nursing* and *N287 Issues in Professional Nursing and Health Care Delivery*, were developed to address the previous aspects of professional role transition. Students may begin the RN studies program by enrolling in either of these courses (most students will choose this pattern) or the

Health Assessment course. The Research course is also taken early in the student's program in order to further develop the knowledge and inquiry components of the professional nursing role.

During the first three terms of enrollment, students also complete support and core course requirements from Levels I, II, and III of the program. These requirements may be met by enrolling in University of Michigan courses, by transferring an equivalent course or by taking an equivalency examination. The curriculum outline shows available options for each course. These options have been utilized for many years and work well to provide a flexible, high quality educational program.

When all course requirements from Levels I, II, and III are met, students move into Level IV of the program which begins with a clinical course, *N388 Theory and Practice of Professional Nursing*. Because this course is built on clinically-focused level objectives from Levels III and IV and provides a transition between the upper and lower divisions of the program, it is required to be completed prior to the Management or Community Health Nursing courses. N388 embraces content from the Nursing Therapies and Clinical Integration courses which is not covered in ACT or NLN equivalency exams and is designed to meet the unique learning needs of RN students within the curriculum concepts of humankind (focus on families as well as individuals), environment (with a focus on the contextual environment), health (with a focus on wellness and health promotion), and nursing (with a focus on the clinical application of the six dimensions of professional nursing).

Following N388, students enroll in the *Community Health Nursing and Management* clinical courses. A separate clinical section of the Management course is offered for RNs in order to accommodate their abilities, and for professional development needs, which are quite different than those of basic students at this level. Students also enroll in two core courses at this level, *Societal Health Issues* and *Professional Development for RNs*, which addresses the unique career development needs of RN students.

In summary, then, the current curriculum combines previous nursing education with professional level courses in order to achieve the overall course objectives, and the credit requirement of 124 credits. RN studies students take two courses (N285 and N287) for transition into professional practice, a clinical course N388, in which students have an opportunity to incorporate new learnings into their practice, *Community Health Nursing, Management*, and a variety of core courses meant to transmit specific and essential content. This is a rigorous and complete program. Students take some courses with basic students, and some courses separately. Acknowledgment of their learning needs as well as their skills and talents guide the learning activities. Students do not repeat any previous learning (this is often their concern) but learn to incorporate their technical education into a new professional paradigm which informs their practice.

The RN studies program does endorse the achievement of the same objectives as the basic program, since it is the baccalaureate degree which is the goal. However, this does not, in our estimation, mean that the outcome is exactly the same. We have stated earlier that in many respects the RN students returning to an educational program have some of the attributes of a graduate student. Specifically, they are more mature than basic students, they have experience with post-secondary education, they have experience in nursing practice, they have specifically chosen an educational program, they are motivated, and they have a variety of life experiences and current responsibilities which both contribute to and detract from the educational experience. This acknowledgment has led to two endeavors for the future.

THE FUTURE

The first endeavor is actually more in the present because it is in place. In May, 1991 the faculty of the School of Nursing approved an RN-MSN track (Table 10.1). In this program students earn both a baccalaureate degree and a master's degree in a clinical specialty. They substitute fifteen (15) credits of graduate study for undergraduate requirements. In a two-step admission process students begin taking the usual RN studies requirements while they prepare for and take the GREs, take six hours of graduate credit, and complete the application for the graduate program. At the end of the first year, successful students are admitted to the graduate program of interest. They will complete undergraduate course work and continue with graduate core courses in the second year. The third year focuses on requirements for the specialty.

The second endeavor is more exploratory in nature. As stated before, the faculty is committed to the acknowledgment of the student as an individual and an adult learner. Faculty invest a great deal of energy, concern, and time in providing for student learning needs. We do believe that the student leaves the program changed both person-

Table 10.1 The University of Michigan School of Nursing—RN-MS Suggested Curriculum Sequence

First Year—Stage I*

FALL**		WINTER		SPRING***	
285	Dimen. Prof Nursg 4 Cr	287	Issues of Prof Nrsg 4 Cr	222	Health Assess 4 Cr
543	History & Politics		Graduate cognate		Graduate
	of Nursing or other		or Statistics 3		cognate or
	Graduate cograte 3		—		Statistics 3
	7 Cr		7 Cr		7 Cr

*Students must also complete CBE's (e.g. Growth & Development, Patho, Pharm, Family, Nutrition) and any outstanding coursework from BSN Levels I, II or III during the first year.

**Students are strongly advised to take GRE's during Fall to allow time for possible retake.

***Students will be admitted to Graduate Program during Spring/Summer (paperwork, including GRE scores, must be submitted to Rackham by July 1).

Second Year—Stage II

531	Theory Dev. 3 Cr	484	Community Health 8 Cr	428	Management 5 Cr
482	Prof. Nrsg. Pr 5	403	Societal Health 2	631	Research or 3
630	Research 3		Issues		grad cognate
	—		—		or
	11 Cr		10 Cr	543	Hist & Politics
					of Nursing —
					8 Cr

Third Year

670	Leadership 3 Cr

and remaining graduate core, cognate and specialty requirements.

ally and professionally. What we do not know is the extent of the change and the process of that change. We believe that there may be critical development points for all students which could be facilitated by faculty in order to ease the experience for students. We also believe these critical points are different for basic students and RN studies students.

In order to identify these points, and the support needed at these times, the RN studies faculty has undertaken study of this phenomenon. A review of the literature revealed a great many studies related to stress, the student-role, and role transition. These studies infer an interaction between the individual and the educational program but are not specific about educational process. Initially Benner's work, *From Novice to Expert* (1984), helped inform our thinking. Acknowledging that this work focuses on the acquisition of skills, we attempted to transform clinical skill progression to professional "skills" progression. However, we found it difficult to progress the acquisition and proficient use of these "new" skills. We had to acknowledge that not all RN-BSN students were at the same starting point vis-a-vis professional skills. Finally, we had to admit that the Benner model was not sufficient for our work.

There is variety in the students entering the program and variety in students exiting the program. While all students meet the program objectives, not all students are truly affected by the educational process. So, we need to distinguish those who are affected by the process, as the major study group, in order to understand the process. We have identified three types of students:

1. Those who enter with nursing conceptualized as a job, and who leave with that same orientation. Despite receiving content related to professionalization and opportunities to review nursing as a life-long career, their thinking does not change. These are labelled Job-Job.

2. The second group enters the program already understanding that nursing is a life-long career and are eager to learn and experience professional activities. They are eager to acquire a repertoire of professional skills. This group is labelled Career-Career.

3. The third group, the major study group, are those we label Job-Career. These individuals enter the program thinking of

nursing as a job. Frequently they are not able to articulate their educational goals, but are open to the experience. At some point during the program they develop a career perspective and attitude. They are truly affected by the educational experience. We are in the process of developing tools to identify jobs vs. career orientation which will be administered as students enter and exit the program. Thus, we will only know our study population in retrospect.

We also are attempting to categorize our entry students. These categories need to be further refined and validated, but, we believe we have identified four "types" of students entering the RN-BSN program.

1. **Brand New:**   New graduate from AD or diploma program.
Little practice experience.
Little life experience.
Unsure about motivation to acquire degree.
Open to learning.

2. **Ready:**   Active practitioner.
At least two years of practice experience.
Some life experience.
May have a vision about nursing.
Internally motivated to acquire degree.
Open to learning.

3. **Seasoned:**   Four or more years of practice experience.
Substantive life experience.
Has a vision about nursing.
Internally motivated to acquire a degree.
Eager to move ahead with program.

4. **Rooted:**   Ten or more years of practice experience.
Substantial life experience.
No vision about nursing.
Externally motivated to acquire degree.
Not open to learning opportunities.

As of this writing (Summer 1992) we are testing these categories and classifications with our current students. We will then proceed with a formal study focused on student identification of the important events/ learnings that they consider turning points. We believe that if these turning points for RN students can be identified, they can be facilitated, and supported by faculty. Our ultimate goal is to increase the number of graduates with Job-Career orientation. This change in orientation would not only demonstrate program effectiveness, it would truly impact on nursing practice and the profession.

With the enhanced ability to document outcomes of professional education, we believe our future will be even brighter than our past.

REFERENCES

Benner, P. (1984). *From novice to expert: Excellence and power in clinical nursing practice.* Menlo Park, CA: Addison-Wesley.

Davis, W. K., Hitch, E. J., & Lechcitner, S. L. (1978). Developing a community-based BSN program. *Biomedical Communications, 6,* 15–18.

Dineen, M. (1970). Consultation Report. New York: National League for Nursing Press.

Lusk, S. L., & Davis, W. K. (1980). A community-based BSN program: A self-instructional approach. In S. K. Mirim (Ed.) *Teaching tomorrow's nurse: A nurse educator reader.* Wakefield, MA: Nursing Resources, Inc.

11

Factors Influencing the Retention and Progression of Students in an RN-MS Program

Darlene O'Callaghan
Joan M. Hau
Mary M. Lebold

INTRODUCTION

According to multiple regional and national studies, it is clear that there is a critical shortage of registered nurses (RNs) prepared with baccalaureate and higher degrees in nursing. Currently, the majority of RNs are prepared with associate and diploma degrees. The Report on Nursing (U.S. Department of Health and Human Services, 1986) states, ". . . projected requirements for full time equivalent registered nurses with baccalaureate degrees are about twice the projected supply for 1990 and 2000. For nurses with graduate degrees, the requirements are about three times higher than the projected supply" (p. 10). Development and delivery of innovative and flexible programs by which RNs can earn baccalaureate and graduate degrees in nursing are crucial to addressing and meeting the health care needs of this nation.

During the past 10 years, a variety of programs have been created for the returning RN seeking a baccalaureate degree in nursing. Redman and Cassells (1990) reported the existence of over 600 baccalaureate programs offering BSN education for RNs. Other accelerated programs, RN to Master's options, by which RNs can earn a master's degree in nursing have also been developed.

Most of the current literature on RNs returning to school focuses on the characteristics of RN-BS students and their personal change and/or

179

professional growth. Lytle (1989) noted in her review of the literature that a major portion of professional nursing articles related to the socialization and resocialization of the RN-BS student and the multiple roles that they carry. According to Witt (1992) there have been many studies done comparing the competencies of RN students to generic nursing students, predicting the success of RN students, and studying the attitudes of the RN students. Little has been written about RN-MS students and programs. This paper will describe the RN-MS option, and RN students and their experiences in the program at Saint Xavier University. The data presented in this paper are the results of a recent evaluation study of the RN-MS option.

OVERVIEW OF THE PROGRAM

In 1985, an articulated RN-MS option was developed in the School of Nursing at Saint Xavier University in Chicago. This program enables RN students to earn both a baccalaureate and master's degree in a condensed time frame. At the time the RN-MS option was developed, the School of Nursing had a well established BSN completion option. With an awareness of Cross' (1981) work in the area of adult learning and institutional barriers which hampered adult participation in continuing education, the BSN completion option was designed so that the RN student could complete the program in the day, evening, or weekend time frame. Faculty were aware that the majority of the RN students were employed full-time and would be attending school on a part-time basis. In developing the RN-MS option, faculty sought to continue program flexibility and establish a curriculum design that would facilitate RNs with associate and diploma degrees to obtain a graduate degree in nursing.

The idea for the RN-MS articulated option came from two sources: first, from reports of other institutions' development of RN-MS programs, and second from feedback obtained from our own RN-BS students. It was noted that the graduates of the RN completion option frequently went on to enroll in our graduate program. A survey of alumnae was conducted and it was found that 78 percent of the graduates from the RN-BS option were enrolled in or had completed a master's degree in nursing; of these, 50 percent had chosen Saint Xavier's graduate nursing program. These findings are consistent with Chornick (1992) who noted that RN completion students are more likely to continue their professional education than graduates of the traditional baccalaureate program. They also correlate with findings from the AACN report (Redman & Cassells, 1990) which notes that 72 percent of RN students indicated an interest in obtaining a graduate degree.

Based on the findings of a feasibility study, funding was sought and obtained from a private foundation and an RN-MS option was developed and initiated in 1985. This innovative option was created specifically to facilitate and support educational mobility and to strengthen the leadership abilities of nurses who already had a foundation in the profession. It was the first such program in Illinois.

There are many unique features of the Saint Xavier RN-MS option to insure program consistency. The RN-MS option is based on and flows from the existing undergraduate and graduate curricula. The student earns both a baccalaureate and a master's degree. The decision to award both degrees was based on research which shows that adult learners often start and stop their education (Cross, 1981). If a student decided not to continue into the graduate program, they could be awarded the baccalaureate degree. The program is designed for part-time study, although full-time study is possible. The RN completion student can earn credit through transfer of non-nursing courses (science credits have a 15 year time limit on transferability); CLEP, ACT/PEP, and departmental challenge examinations; and through portfolio preparation. The program contains an articulation level in which students may enroll in both undergraduate and graduate courses simultaneously.

Candidates for the program must meet the same admission criteria as candidates for the master's program, which differ from the requirement for admission to the BSN completion option. The following criteria must be met for admission to the RN-MS option: (a) two letters of recommendation, (b) a grade point average (GPA) of 3.0, (c) completion of the Miller Analogy Test, (d) an on-site interview with a faculty member, and (e) evaluation of writing skills. When students are admitted to the RN-MS option, they enter the nursing program directly and are ensured placement in the graduate program. Newly admitted RN students are classified as freshmen, sophomore, or junior students depending on the number of transfer credits. There are no prerequisite courses for admission; general education requirements and courses supportive to the nursing major may be taken after the student is admitted to Saint Xavier University. Registered nurses can complete the RN-MS option in 3 ½ years, taking 9 hours a semester. However, most take longer due to part-time study and the need to take the required liberal arts and support courses.

Academic advising is recognized by the School of Nursing faculty as a critical component to assure student satisfaction and retention. To ensure that they are progressing satisfactorily, each RN student is assigned a nursing faculty member as an advisor. This advisor assists the student with course planning and reviews the student's academic progress as she or he continues throughout the program. To provide consistency for the RN-MS student, three faculty members have served as advisors since the inception of the program. It was noted by advisors and administrators that students were not progressing in the manner that had been originally predicted. At the time, only three students had completed the program. As a result, an evaluation study was conducted to identify factors influencing student progression and retention in the program.

METHODOLOGY

Data were collected through retrospective analysis of the academic records of all RN-MS students admitted to the program between 1985 and January 1992 ($N = 63$). The data collected included those related to demographic variables, previous education, admission testing data, grades, grade point averages, transfer credit, and the information related to stop-out and drop-out. From these data, a profile of the RN-MS students enrolled in the last seven years was developed.

The mean age of the students was 34.9 years, with a range of 23–56 years. Seventy-seven percent were Caucasian and 23 percent were African-American. There were no other minorities represented. All the students were female. Marital status at the time of admission included 43 percent married, 27 percent single. No data were available for the remaining 22 percent of the population. These data were similar to the data in the study by Redman and Cassells (1990) of RN-BS students. Age, marital status, and gender were about the same. However this study had a higher population of minority students (23 percent versus 9 percent). The 23 percent figure is consistent with the other nursing programs at Saint Xavier which is located in a large midwestern city.

The majority of the students (58 percent) received their basic nursing education from diploma schools. The remaining number had graduated from associate degree programs. At the time of admission, 70 percent were employed as staff nurses. Twenty-six percent held middle management positions such as head nurse. The remaining 4 percent were in top nursing management positions such as Vice-President or Director of Nursing.

The mean score on the Miller Analogy Test was 40. This test was being used for admission by most of the Saint Xavier University graduate programs. Ninety-three percent of the population pursued their studies on a part-time basis; only one student (2 percent) studied full-time and three students (5 percent) combined part-time and full-time study.

The RN-MS student transferred into the program an average of 11.49 credit hours for the courses supportive to nursing, such as the sciences, psychology, and sociology. The range of credit hours transferred was 0–48. Twenty-one percent transferred no credit hours for support courses and one student transferred 48 hours. The range for all others was 3–27 credit hours. This did not represent a total of transfer credits. For the purposes of the study, the researchers gathered data only for the support course transfer hours.

The data revealed that 47 percent of this student population "stopped out," meaning that they took a hiatus from their education for one or more semesters. Of those who stopped out, 58 percent did so once, 35 percent stopped out twice, and 4 percent left three or more times during their course of study. Only three students had completed the entire program at the time of the study. These three students took 15, 14, and 12 semesters respectively to complete the program. This figure did not include the periods during which these students were stopped out. This time period was considerably greater than the designers of the program had predicted. The students' choice of part time study (six or less credit hours per semester) accounted for this discrepancy. The fact that this program seems longer than others can be attributed to the fact that students are admitted without prerequisite requirements. Requirements for general education and support courses may be fulfilled after admission to the program.

Using the data from the analysis of records, the population was divided into five groups to study their progression through the program. The groups were: (a) graduates of the RN-MS option, n = 3 (5 percent); (b) students currently enrolled in the graduate level, n = 8 (13 percent); (c) students currently enrolled in the baccalaureate level, n = 12 (19 percent); (d) students who dropped out of the program after receiving the baccalaureate degree, n = 16 (25 percent); and (e) students who attrited during the baccalaureate level, n = 21 (33 percent). No students dropped out after beginning the graduate level. Three students were on stop-out status and were not included in the study. Comparison of the means of the five groups showed that they were similar in age, ethnic group, marital status, admission test scores, basic nursing education, part-time status, transfer credit, grade point averages, and employment position.

A convenience sample of three students from each of the above five groups was selected to be interviewed about their experiences and progression in the RN-MS program. Fourteen of the 15 students were subsequently interviewed using a semi-structured interview guide. Interviews were conducted by faculty members familiar with the students. While familiarity with faculty might bias the stories, it was felt that this was balanced by the previously established rapport. Written permission was obtained from each interviewee and anonymity of the responses was assured. The questions were designed to elicit information relating to personal and professional goals, reasons for selecting and entering the program, progression in the undergraduate and graduate levels, factors helping and hindering their progression, and recommendations for program improvement. The interviews were audiotaped and transcribed verbatim. The data were organized and coded by category and ultimately grouped into four major themes (Merriam, 1988).

The major themes explored in the interviews were reasons for the return to school, a time of change and transition, factors influencing progression into and through the program, and patterns of progression in the RN-MS option. However, the interviewees' responses and their stories about their experiences in the program were frequently multidimensional and interconnected, and therefore, difficult to separate and categorize.

Reasons for Returning to School

One purpose of the interview process was to identify why some students chose the RN-MS option rather than the RN-BS option and to elicit their experiences about continuing their education. The reasons for returning to school to earn a master's degree were similar to findings of research on RNs seeking advanced degrees and for adults returning to education (Darkenwald & Merriam, 1982; Thompson, 1992). Adults engage in educational opportunities for multiple reasons. The

RN students interviewed in the study related that they thought they could achieve their professional goals faster by entering the RN-MS option. A current student said:

> *I knew I wanted to get my master's degree. But I also had to come back for my bachelor's degree. I thought I could get into it right now and have it all in place. I would get done sooner and achieve my goal faster.*

This supports findings of the AACN report (Redman & Cassells, 1990) which indicated that "greater than 56 percent of RN students identified the master's degree as a significant pre-enrollment motivator for acquiring the bachelor's degree" (p. 91).

The RNs also spoke of the need for credentials for career advancement, to obtain a position that required a master's degree or for job security. A current student responded to the question asking why she decided on the RN-MS option in this way: "I see that in the nursing field, if you want to advance or move forward you do have to have your master's degree." A similar thought is also contained in this response from an RN who stated:

> *At the time I decided to go into the program, I really felt that the writing was on the wall in terms of being master's prepared if I wanted to go beyond the position I was in, or for that matter, stay in a nurse manager position. So, I decided to get into the RN-MS because I already was an RN and practicing for many years, and I thought this seemed like the best option.*

Another student decided to become master's prepared, ". . . so that I could stay in [my] management position or if I wanted to go further in relation to a [nursing] directorship." A student who worked as a Director of Inservice Education notes:

> *I was very much involved with the reality of having the opportunity of having a position in administration and yet, not having the credentials. Finally, I thought I was at the point in nursing that I had to bite the bullet in terms of school.*

These comments reflect similar responses presented by Thompson (1992) in her study on the persistence of RN students: "The participants often mentioned career transition as reasons for entering a BSN program" (p. 103). Cervero (1988) and Darkenwald and Merriam (1982) reported that adults mainly continued their education because of job security and work-related motives. Many of the RN students interviewed revealed that job opportunities were a primary motivating factor in the decision to pursue the RN-MS option.

A few of the RNs spoke of returning to school for the pursuit of learning for learning's sake. One relates why she chose to return to school. "I guess because I found that it means a lot to me. It's very important to me. I think it's beneficial and I think I could really love it." An RN currently progressing through the master's program recalls that "I guess I was just eager to do something. To take some special interest courses just to get back in school again."

A Time of Change and Transition

The return to school, for many adults, is a time of change and transition. The students and graduates who were interviewed had been participating in school for several semesters; for some, it had been several years. Interviewees reported changing their jobs and rearranging lives to balance personal, family, and work responsibilities in order to meet the demands of school.

One student in her last year in the graduate program described her fear about returning to school:

I think it's the initial part—the fear of how much I would have to do in order to get into school. Looking ahead at how much time it would consume as well as just the fear of returning to school. [Yet] it was a requirement so I would have the credentials.

This student then continued to describe how the return to school became more than seeking a credential. She speaks of the impact of returning to school on her own personal change and growth:

Now I realize that I have developed. I am more critical in my thinking. I can see what a research focused program can do for me in practical experience. Continued quality improvement has been occurring. So from a pragmatic position I can see the advantages that I have. My writing skills have definitely improved. I'm more confident in that I'm working from not only an experiential base, but from more of an intellectual base. All the research articles we had to go through and all of the read-

*ing has given me legitimate ground for my opinions as well as my
thoughts. It is simply not my gut. . . . It also gives me the foundation
as to why you make the decisions and the judgments you do. In that
way, I think I've grown. I've softened. I also think I'm not as critical as
far as my own activities, that I'm more realistic in my practice.*

Lawler and Rose (1987) proposed that the RN returning for a baccalaureate degree may be different from the generic student to begin
with—more mature, committed, self-directed, and wiser in the ways of
the world (p. 22). Change was a significant part of the students' lives.
Several students spoke to acquiring new ideas and skills: "Lots of times
you don't even realize you're learning so many different things until
you're actually done with the process." Others reported learning more
about themselves: "You got an in-depth look at yourself, where you
were and where you were going." They reported changes in the way
they approached problems, communicated with others, and viewed
the world.

Many of the interviewees experienced a number of personal
changes due to life events such as marriage, divorce, birth of a child,
loss of a parent or spouse, a change in a job. In response to the question, "How do you think your life would have been different if you had
not chosen the RN-MS option?", one of the graduates responded:

*I probably would still have been married. I am divorced now. There are
times I think about that. There was just a lot going on that I had committed to at the same time. Within a year of starting school, I left an
organization I had been with for 14 years. So I left a lot of my support
systems. And I also could see there wouldn't be a future for me that I
would have here. I would have been Director of Nursing there and the
people in the organization would have supported me without a degree.
But I know that I could not have gone on . . . and I know that I needed
that; I also know that I've met a lot of different people. I've become a lot
more open minded. I don't know if it was school or if it is being open to
new ideas. Also other ways of seeing things as expert nurse in this time
of my life, looking back at novice nurses. So if anything, I think I've
been stimulated to learn more.*

Personal and family events impacted on their lives and on their commitment to school. Like other returning students, they managed multiple roles and the return to school added a new role for them to "jug-

gle." If the roles became too overwhelming, they would stop out of school to bring their lives back into balance. Thompson (1992) reported similar findings. The RN students in her study analyzed and manipulated external conditions so that they could return to school. Thompson described this process of reorganizing their roles and responsibilities as "reslicing the pie" (p. 100).

Some RN-MS students were able to balance their multiple roles by adjusting their work and life to accommodate the return to school. However, for some students accommodation was not possible. One student who withdrew from the RN-MS program described her conflict between work and school in the following manner:

> *I just didn't have time . . . it was too much. The job was too demanding to be able to keep up with the course for myself. I mean my personal life was going down the tubes and I just did not want to give that up. Then I kind of struggled with what I needed to do. When they hired me, they knew I was in this program . . . So I talked to my director at that time about it. . . . She made it clear to me—I won't lose my job. They'd make an exception because of my experience and the kind of work I did. . . . I always felt like—gee—I should be in school. But at the same time, the job I'm at became more and more demanding. . . . And I think that in the last half year, that I have come to the conclusion that most probably I will never get my master's. Unless I should win the Lotto and have nothing to do and want to occupy my time. Then I can to go to school.*

Factors Influencing Progression Into and Through the Program

The third theme was that of factors influencing students' progression into and through the program. Students related numerous factors that helped them as they progressed toward their degrees as well as those things that made their studying more difficult. The data were grouped into three sub-themes: program strengths, facilitators, and barriers to progression.

Program strengths were related to the perceived quality of the program, including the faculty and the structure of the program. Specific things cited by the students included the weekend college program, program flexibility, testing and portfolio credit options, attention to the needs of adult learners, flexible scheduling, off campus courses, reputation of the program, the advising system (including peer advisors), small sized classes and classes for RNs only. One of the graduates of the program commented:

> *Another reason I chose this program is because of the hours. I was able to come and finish at, I thought, a pretty decent time. Of course, I didn't finish as early as I had hoped to finish, but with the classes being offered in the evening time, early evening, like 5:00 . . . I thought it was real good and I liked that a lot about the program—able to get in and get out when you needed to. And the campus is good to get to and there's a lot of parking.*

Another student said:

> *It's all contained here. The agencies, as far as I'm aware, are very good learning agencies and that's real important. By the time you're at the master's level you have to have good resources like that. The instructors, the ones that I knew anyway, were excellent. And I feel that going straight through like that, there's a vision of the nurse that will come out of this program. And I think that it's a very good nurse who has very good credentials, a very good solid background both clinically and academically. And that is the best thing I could possibly think of—this whole program.*

The second category under the theme of factors influencing students' progression was that of facilitators—those factors that the students identified as aiding or helping their progression in the program. Some of the facilitators identified by students included an available, supporting faculty, tuition reimbursement, a non-threatening environment, family support, and peer networking. One student related how the program helped her.

> *It caters to the RN and the working individual. The instructors are really flexible and go out of their way to try and accommodate the student's needs. I can't think of any who don't. And it is done in a timely manner. That you can challenge all of the courses. And it builds. I can't say that I had any courses that were a repeat of knowledge except for one, the Leadership course, and I probably should have tried to challenge that.*

A new student at the baccalaureate level talked about the school's atmosphere, when asked what kinds of things were helping her in her progression.

Well, actually I guess it's this friendly, a new type of atmosphere that there is here. In my fall semester I had to have surgery. I missed a lot of classes. But during that time I had a lot of support from both my instructors and fellow classmates. In one class they taped classes. So that I could keep up. They sent cards. The instructors, they were very good at trying to put me at ease, so I didn't have to worry about school too. It just shows that atmosphere here. Kind of a caring environment. That I liked.

Location and ease of travel were identified as stimulators to continuing education in the study by Redman and Cassells (1990). The students in the present study also identified convenience and location of campus and off campus courses as facilitators.

Barriers to progression, the third subcategory, related mostly to personal, family and job roles and responsibilities, as well as the lack of articulation with their previous educational experience. The students spoke of the lack of acceptance of credit for previous education and repetition of content learned earlier. This in part related to the fact that many of the students were diploma graduates with little academic credit for their previous nursing education. The following student described her frustration relating to transfer credit.

It's just about having to take the ACT-PEPs. To have my nursing credits transferred. I know that is not just here. It is a lot of places. I felt insulted especially since I passed my state boards and I went to an accredited school. I shouldn't have to do that. It should just transfer.

The frustration expressed by this student is a common one in RN education. Thompson (1992) identified lack of transferability of courses and little or no credit for prior learning as barriers to participation. Some of the other barriers identified by Thompson that do not exist at Saint Xavier University were in fact seen as program strengths by the students in this study. Part-time study options and flexible scheduling were two examples.

Cross (1981) summarized numerous studies of barriers to participation in adult education. She classified them under three headings: situational, institutional and dispositional barriers (p. 98). Situational barriers included job and family responsibilities, lack of money, and child care. These barriers have also been cited in studies of RNs returning to school (Hagemaster, 1990; Perry, 1986; Thompson, 1992). The participants of this study named similar barriers. For some, these barriers had forced them to discontinue their education. Even those who had completed or were currently enrolled cited these as factors that made their education more difficult.

A student who had graduated with her MS just three weeks before the interview spoke of the difficulties she experienced in completing her education.

Once you're out working, it's hard to try to work part-time if you've got a family and children, it's hard to try to work part-time and go to school. So you end up working full-time and going to school. And then you have to worry about where you're going to get the money from.

The interviewer asked her, "How do you work full-time, take care of a family, and go to school?" And she replied,

Oh, it was so difficult. In fact, my husband told me when I was all done, "I guess now you can clean up the house a little bit." And actually he was being very nice. And I said, "No, I think I need to clean up a BIG bit." It was real hard at times. Now, my husband worked in the afternoons, but he was always off on Mondays. Most of my classes were on Monday, which was real good. But a couple of semesters I had a class, I think on Wednesday, and then last semester I had one on Thursday, which means I had to get someone to take care of the kids. And then a lot of times you want to spend time with your family. You know you can't, because you've got to get this paper done. And that part of it was very hard. In fact, my son told me a little bit before, "Mom, do you have to go to school? Can't you just drop out?" And I said, "Please don't say that to me, because I'm almost there." So if I had to recommend it to anyone, in fact if I had known myself, I would say get all you can get before you start having children because it does make it difficult. Sometimes I feel like you're cheating them out of something that you shouldn't be cheating them out of. As far as time is concerned, and being able to go places and do things, and you know you can't do it. If you do go, then you feel guilty because you know you've got that work to do and you've got to be up all night getting it done. And if you stay and do your work, then you feel guilty because you didn't take the kids or you didn't go with your husband. You know, it's really guilt no matter what you do. I thought that part was really hard. And a lot of times I was— late at night I was saying, "Lord, what am I going to do?" But I knew I would make it. It was just a matter of time, making it through. But if I had to do it again, I know I would do it before I even got married, let alone had children. If anybody wants to know, I'll tell them.

Patterns of Progression

The RNs' patterns of progression through the program was the fourth theme examined. The data showed that RN students had varied patterns of progression for multiple reasons. Rarely did a student take nine credit hours a semester as was proposed in the curriculum plan. A recent graduate of the RN-MS program spoke of her progression:

It was easy because we were given the program. I was lucky in that I always took two courses at a time and kept plodding away. There was always a course for me to take and it always fell in line with what I needed to do to complete the degree.

Another student noted, "Part of my goal was to try to take at least two courses per term and something during the interim [January term] and I've been able to do that." Periods of stop-out contributed to the variance in their progression through the program. One student related, "It took me almost 10 years to get my bachelor's. What would happen was, I was very much involved with work and would take a course and then drop." Employment responsibilities considerably slowed her progress through the program, a common occurrence for many of the students.

Some of the RNs attrited early in the program, others left after completing the baccalaureate level. These interviews revealed that often students had to overcome many obstacles to continue their education. After completing the baccalaureate degree the RNs spoke of needing time off for a break.

I felt like I wanted to finish something because if I got hit by a truck and didn't have the energy to go to school, at least I would have had a bachelor's degree. That was important to me, to finish something I was afraid I wouldn't finish.

A number of students spoke of personal situational crises occurring in their lives that affected their progression. One student dropped out for a short time. "I broke my ankle and I couldn't drive, so that slowed me down." Another student related how family responsibilities prevented her entrance into the graduate program after completion of the baccalaureate degree.

I wasn't able to go through with it. There were a lot of times I wished I had, but then a lot of other times I realized because of things, you know, at home and also with my parents and my husband's parents that I couldn't have done it even though I wanted to so much.

As was noted in the discussion of the profile of the students, many of them were married and had to deal with the added responsibilities of this role. A student recalled:

Well, as I was finishing up the bachelor's part of the requirement and heading into or towards the master's, things changed at home and my children began to need more of my time. Emotionally, they were going into their teen years and I realized that they needed more time than the master's program would allow me to spend.

Some of these RN students became pregnant during their progression through the program. One student related:

I wouldn't say it was real difficult, just staying with the program to get through. I had some personal things going on in my life at the time that kind of hindered me a little bit. I got pregnant and my daughter was born in May. So, I felt like I needed a year off.

Another student shared:

I had a stillborn baby girl and for the next year my life was really upside down emotionally and I just felt at that time that dealing with school was totally out of the question.

Yet another recalled, "I took one semester off because of having a baby. But then I started back up the next semester."

While some students had periods of stop-outs during their educational experience, and others dropped out after the baccalaureate degree, there were those who persisted through the master's level. The demands of their jobs and employers played an important role in the students' progression. One student was in a middle management position in an acute care setting when she entered the program and was expected to complete the master's degree in order to retain her current position. "I signed a contract that said I would finish this degree in this period of time."

DISCUSSION

The purpose of the evaluation study was to identify factors influencing student progression and retention in the program. The demographic data indicated that there were no differences among those groups of students who had completed the program, those enrolled in the program, and those who attrited from the program. Fourteen interviews were conducted with individuals from the five groups identified from the analysis of the academic records.

Examination of the data shows that the reasons for return to school, the need to balance multiple roles, the need for part-time study, and the impact of life events on commitment to or enrollment in school were similar to the findings of other studies conducted on returning women, RN-BS students and graduate nursing students (Bednash, Redman, Barhyte, & Wulff, 1990; Cervero, 1988; Lytle, 1989; Redman & Cassells, 1990; Thompson, 1992). Thompson (1992) described development of commitment to learning by the RN students in her study. A similar commitment was also noted in the interviewed students who had persisted in the program.

Since there is little known and written about RN-MS programs and students enrolled in these programs, this is an area in need of further study. Meta-analysis of the curriculum and policies related to RN-MS programs could provide a better understanding of the programs and their impact on students. A comparison of RN-BS to RN-MS students to graduate students could clarify the similarities and differences among and between these groups and help in the development of policy and support systems.

In developing an RN-MS program, there are several important considerations. A major finding of this study is that RN-MS students, due to part time enrollment and periods of stop-out, took a longer time than had been anticipated to complete the program. Educators who are planning and implementing RN-MS options need to take this into account as they design programs. There needs to be careful evaluation of existing courses and content to determine strategies to decrease the time needed for completion of the program. One solution is to examine courses, such as nursing research and professional issues courses, that could be counted toward the requirements for both degrees.

Courses need to be scheduled and offered in time frames and locations convenient for the students. This provides for more flexibility for the student and facilitates the return to school by decreasing barriers of travel, time, and distance.

Recognition of prior learning remains a challenge for program designers. The problems are similar to those that the RN-BS student experiences. Carefully designed articulation agreements with ADN programs is one way to facilitate the transfer of credit. Policies relating to the transfer of science credit and other credits need to be carefully evaluated in order to prevent needless repetition of content and other barriers to ongoing education. The development of clear guidelines and policies for both faculty and students aids the transition. One mechanism, other than examination, that recognizes prior learning is portfolio development; however, both students and faculty need support in learning how to prepare a portfolio and judge performance using this method.

Specific policies need to be developed for admission and progression into the RN-MS program. Admission criteria similar to that of the graduate program should be established because the RN-MS student is admitted into the graduate program. The data showed that a high percentage of our students stopped out at least once during the program due to life situations and changes not directly connected to the academic program or the students' academic performance. It is important that students earn both the baccalaureate and the master's degrees. This policy provides students with a degree, a feeling of accomplishment, and an exit point if life events alter their educational progress. In addition, if both are not offered, it may impact negatively on financial aid.

Little data exists on this population of students. As one begins an RN-MS program, collection of data should begin with the admission of the first student. Inclusion of a summary data profile sheet in each student's advising folder assists with advising and the tracking of students' progression. As most RN students progress at their own pace if permitted by the educational and employment systems, a good tracking system is essential for the monitoring of academic performance, stop-out periods and progression.

Establishment of support systems is an essential dimension of program development. Advisor, peer and/or family support were seen as critical factors by the students in this study. Students also cited faculty availability and support as an essential factor to their remaining in the program. For some students, faculty served as role models and students frequently stated that it was the quality of the faculty that drew them into the program.

Finances remained an important consideration for program retention. Students who were not receiving tuition reimbursement, stated that this was a major barrier to progression. Tuition reimbursement and scholarships are a definite assistance in retaining the RN-MS students.

Finally, the RN-MS program is one means to develop registered nurses with advanced degrees to meet the country's current and future health care needs. As RN-MS programs develop across the country, we as educators need to be open to dialogue and sharing our experiences with one another. More importantly we need to listen to the voices of our students and try to respond to their needs in constructive, creative ways.

REFERENCES

Bednash, P., Redman, B., Barhyte, D., & Wulff, L. (1990). *A data base for graduate education in nursing: Summary report.* Washington, DC: AACN.

Cervero, R. M. (1988). *Effective continuing education for professionals.* San Francisco: Jossey-Bass.

Chornick, N. L. (1992). A comparison of RN to BSN completion graduates to generic BSN graduates: Is there a difference? *Journal of Professional Education, 31,* 203–209.

Cross, K. P. (1981). *Adults as learners: Increasing participation and facilitating learning.* San Francisco: Jossey-Bass.

Darkenwald, G. G., & Merriam, S. B. (1982). *Adult education: Foundations of practice.* San Francisco: Harper & Row.

Hagemaster, J. N. (1990). RN education: Beyond the baccalaureate degree. *Nurse Educator, 15*(5), 33–35.

Lawler, T., & Rose, M. A. (1987). Professionalization: A comparison among generic baccalaureate, ADN, and RN/BSN nurses. *Nurse Educator, 12*(3), 19–22.

Lytle, J. E. (1989). *The process of perspective transformation experienced by the registered nurse returning for baccalaureate study.* Unpublished doctoral dissertation, Northern Illinois University, DeKalb, IL.

Merriam, S. B. (1988). *Case study research in education.* San Francisco: Jossey-Bass.

Perry, A. E. (1986). Reentry women: Nursing's challenge. *Nurse Educator, 11*(3), 13–15.

Redman, B. K., & Cassells, J. M. (1990). *Educating RNs for the baccalaureate: Programs and issues.* New York: Springer.

Thompson, D. (1992). Beyond motivation: A model of registered nurses' participation and persistence in baccalaureate nursing programs. *Adult Education Quarterly, 42,* 94–105.

U.S. Department of Health & Human Services, Public Health Service, Health Resources and Services Administration. (1986). *Report on Nursing: Fifth Report to the President and Congress on the Status of Health Personnel in the United States.* Washington, DC: U.S. Government Printing Office.

Witt, B. (1992). The liberating effects of RN to BSN education. *Journal of Nursing Education, 31,* 149–157.

12

Evaluating the Academic Experience for Returning Registered Nurses

Anne Loustau

BACKGROUND

The decade of the 1980s was a period of time during which Registered Nurses (RNs) returned to school to complete Bachelor's degrees in unprecedented numbers (NLN, 1990). Legislation supporting entry into practice, state plans supporting program articulation, and declining numbers of students applying to generic Baccalaureate programs served as stimuli to create programs which were specifically tailored to meet the needs of these students. The purpose of the study described within these pages is to present the findings from an initial evaluation of a program designed to facilitate the returning RN's efficient completion of the Bachelor's degree and an orderly transition into graduate study.

In 1988 faculty at the University of Washington School of Nursing began offering the RN/Master's program for returning RNs. The program is designed for nurses with Associate degrees or Diplomas in nursing who plan to complete a Baccalaureate degree and continue on to a Master's degree in nursing. Students may transfer up to 90 quarter credits of previous college work toward their Baccalaureate degree. They test out of junior level course work in medical-surgical, pediatric, maternity, and psychiatric nursing through ACT-PEP validation exams. They then complete the senior year of the program which includes a "bridge" series of courses, and core professional course work in research, the ethical and legal bases for practice, cultural diversity, family theory, social system dynamics, leadership, and community health nursing. The students may complete the senior year as part-time or full-time students. Once 180 quarter credits are completed and university and professional requirements are met, students receive the Bachelor of Science in Nursing.

REVIEW OF THE LITERATURE

Studies directed specifically at the RN student returning to school provided important clues about their unique characteristics, needs, and preferences. Baj (1985) in a comparison study of generic and RN students reported that the RN student was older than the generic student (mean age 31 years), and more likely to be married with responsibilities for dependent children. In addition to attending school the RN students worked an average of twenty to thirty hours each week, usually in medical-surgical settings, and attended school part time rather than full time. The majority had been RNs for at least six years. Linares (1989) confirmed some of these demographic findings. The mean age of her RN sample was 34 years with the majority having worked for five years in an acute care setting.

These students fulfill multiple roles in addition to being students, including homemaker, partner, mother/parent and paid worker (Green, 1987). One might expect stress to increase with the added demands and expectations of each role. However, Campaniello (1988) found that occupying multiple roles did not necessarily lead to role conflict and stress for these students. The benefits of returning to school and the anticipation of accomplishment of professional goals engendered a sense of well-being which outweighed the stress of fulfilling several roles. This was particularly true if there was support to pursue the academic degree from a partner in the form of assistance with household responsibilities and recognition in the work environment in relation to flexible work scheduling. Motherhood was the one exception to this finding with childcare responsibilities creating role conflict and the potential for stress. Rendon (1988) also reported that disruptions in family life which accompany the return to school are viewed as a major stress for these students. Along this same theme Dugas (1985) and Lange (1986) found that family responsibilities were identified by these students as the primary barrier to returning to school for the Bachelor's degree.

Lee (1987) identified specific stresses related to the student role for the RN student. These included meeting deadlines, receiving an unexpectedly low grade, clinical placement in an unfamiliar clinical setting such as the community, and didactic classroom instruction from an unprepared instructor. Specific coping strategies that these students utilized to deal with the stress they experienced in the academic setting included direct actions such as extra preparation for classroom and clinical work, seeking support from peers and family, and seeking faculty assistance if they were experiencing academic difficulty (Lee, 1988). Similarly, Mattson (1990) found that more mature students were better copers, taking action against stressors and using the support of others to find a solution to solve a problem.

Several researchers have identified factors that motivate these students to return to school for Bachelor's degrees including career advancement (Fotos, 1987; King, 1986; Thurber, 1988), increased knowledge and skills to improve job performance (Lethbridge, 1989; Thurber, 1988) professional development (Fotos, 1987; Lethbridge, 1989), and the anticipation of continuing on to graduate school (MacLean, Knoll, & Kinney, 1985; Thurber, 1988). These students view themselves as professional (Beeman, 1988), score higher on professional values than generic BSN students (Lawler and Rose, 1987), and are determined and committed to completing their programs (Rendon, 1988). As educators we have not always recognized that work experience has contributed to the professional development of the returning RN. Over one-half of the RNs in Rendon's (1988) study reported that they did not feel faculty respected their prior knowledge and accomplishments. Educational approaches which place these students with generic students do not always recognize the unique abilities and needs of the RN student and the learning that has occurred through work and life experience. King (1986) found that generic and RN students were significantly different in their adult developmental tasks with the generic students focused on starting their careers and the RNs, with careers launched, focused on issues of advancement and decisions about future career trajectories. The RN students in Rendon's (1988) study who were high on aggressive traits reported enjoying their academic experience but also felt that the curriculum was not appropriate for their needs and they were not as comfortable in the student role.

With the exception of Beeman (1988) and Lee (1987, 1988) the majority of the studies regarding returning RNs have relied heavily on quantitative information. Beeman (1988) used open ended questions and telephone interviews to ascertain program satisfaction and suggestions for change. Lee (1987, 1988) used open ended questions to collect information about stressful incidents and coping strategies. While quantitative information can provide specific information about these students, interview data can heighten our understanding of their experiences while they are enrolled in a program.

METHODOLOGY

The present study used a fourth generation approach to evaluation in the style proposed by Guba and Lincoln (1985). Fourth generation evaluation approaches redefine evaluation as a sociopolitical process in which evaluators and stakeholders, those individuals with vested interests in an academic program, collaborate with one another to describe issues and concerns. The process is interactive and educative for evaluators and respondents with both sides reaching common understandings of the educational experience. Expected outcomes include mutually defined strengths, problems, and recommendations for change. In this study the students were considered primary stakeholders and their perspectives about expectations, claims, concerns, and issues were sought. To this end, quantitative demographic data and information from a sample of interviews were combined to provide information about the characteristics and academic patterns of this group of returning RNs as well as their views of their experiences in the program. The goal was to use the information to modify the curriculum and to assist faculty in doing a better job of teaching these students.

Demographic data and academic patterns were collected from the RNs enrolled in the RN/Master's program between the years 1988 and 1992 (N = 96). Nine students were randomly selected from the graduating class of 1991 and agreed to be interviewed. Students responded to the following questions:

> What has it been like to be in the program?
> What stands out for you?
> What had you hoped/wished for?
> What have you learned about yourself?
> How do you think you have changed?

Interviews were tape recorded and transcribed. Transcriptions of the interviews were read and analyzed for information about the experience of being a returning student and ways the curriculum could be modified. The student comments clustered into four main themes: The Balancing Act, "Walking the fine line of being happily busy or over the edge;" The Peer Group, "A source of safety as students embark on an educational journey;" Finding a Faculty Role Model, "Putting an end to the mystique of academia;" and People Building, "Toward a new view of self."

FINDINGS

Demographics.   A total of 96 students entered the program between 1988 and 1992. They were older than the students described by Baj (1985) and similar to the students described by Linares (1989) with a mean age of 34.5 and a range of 21–51 years. Like the students described by Baj and Green (1987) they were multiple role individuals; partners, parents/caretakers, homemakers, and workers. They added the student role to this array of responsibilities. In spite of these commitments and in contrast to Baj (1985), seventy-eight (81%) were enrolled as full-time students. Sixteen (17%) were enrolled as part-time students. Two students (2%) withdrew from the program. Several studies (Fotos, 1987; King, 1986; Lawler & Rose, 1987; Lethbridge, 1989; MacLean, Knoll, & Kinney, 1985; Rendon, 1988; Thurber, 1988) suggest that returning RNs are highly motivated and academically able students and the data from this group of students supports these findings. The mean GPA for students entering the Bachelor's portion of the program has been 3.43. As of June 1992, eighty-seven (91%) of these students have completed the Bachelor's degree. Forty-three students (45%) continued on into the Master's program. The mean GPA for students entering the Master's program has been 3.54. Ten students have completed their Master's degrees and four students have enrolled in the PhD program.

Interviews.   The interviews provided important information about students' perceptions of their experiences in the program. Students talked about the stress that school added to their lives. The theme of a Balancing Act, "Walking the fine line of being happily busy or over the edge," emerged.

> *I've given a lot of thought to why it has seemed so stressful to me and to the other students, and I think because we're adults and we're already*

working and our time is already committed to other things before we ever get here that it is difficult. My life gets too pushed, and there is this fine line between being happily busy or over the edge in my life.

I think what I found hard was trying to make my work schedule and my other life schedule work with school. Each quarter was a little different so you always had to know ahead of time for scheduling and you had to say that you couldn't work on these days or nights because of school and family responsibilities.

Deadlines in particular add pressure to lives that are already filled with work and home responsibilities. One student said, "I don't like deadlines and I don't like to be rushed, and I've settled into that in my 40s, and the biggest drag in going back to school is the deadlines." Another added, "I think we've become accustomed to directing our own time and it is very uncomfortable to have others doing it for us."

In spite of the fact that these students add school to lives that are already filled with responsibilities, the majority choose to complete the Bachelor's degree as full-time students. They see the efficiency of being able to complete this degree quickly and they negotiate for the time to do this. A typical comment was, "A real advantage to this program is once all the prerequisites are done, you can finish your Baccalaureate in a year." One student said, "I said to my family, well if you will put up with some difficulty and having some things on hold for a while, I can finish this degree in a year." And another student spoke to the issue of time and resources, "A really big pull factor for this program is that you can get through relatively quickly and that makes it reasonable cost-wise."

During the initial quarter in the program students enroll in two bridge courses that are designed to support the transition into the professional core of course work. This time together also serves as an opportunity for networking and establishing a group identity. The Peer Group, "A source of safety as they embark on an educational journey" was a repeated theme.

At first I felt really apprehensive but then as I looked around and we all started talking I realized what a wonderful group of people this was and I felt really safe.

There was this incredible camaraderie among us. I never saw it develop so rapidly in a group. I had to leave school for a quarter and people wrote to me. It was incredible. I'd only known these people 12 weeks and they were writing me cards and calling—all the way to California!

We are RNs with work experience and people with life experiences, and we are more mature; and that consolidated us into the tightest little group you've ever seen.

This is a very elite group, they are incredible people, the cream of the crop, they are articulate, bright, enthusiastic, and very realistic.

The strength of this group identity, which provides security as they begin the academic program, becomes problematic in the second quarter when these students begin to take course work with the generic senior students. Integration with the generic students is difficult and the RNs express frustration with an educational environment that they perceive as contrary to their needs.

So then when you try to put us in with seniors, it just doesn't work. I was amazed at how vehemently opposed to belonging and being absorbed we were. And within our group there were people who just hated it and in class would make superior sounding comments like, "Well, we with our greater life experience." . . . And there are people sitting in class that are as old as we are.

We needed something beyond the basics, and to be with students that hadn't had the basics was frustrating, because we had to listen to all of their comments, and they were worthwhile to them as a group, they needed to be able to say those things, but they were too basic for us. So that was one of our really big frustrations.

I don't mind being with the undergraduates, but I do mind being with them if the idea is that I am going to learn less. I've gotten very selfish about that. Not that I don't mind sharing experiences, but I'm not here to teach them. I'm paying tuition just like they are, and I'm here to learn. I'm not here to teach them.

For many of these students returning to school is a big step. They spoke graphically of their initial image of the university as one of anonymity and impersonality.

I'd heard if I came to the university I would be in a huge classroom with millions of other people, the teacher would be way down in front if I got a real teacher at all, and it would probably be a TA who wouldn't care about me or the rest of the class.

They talked of the anxieties that they experienced as they began to negotiate their way through the completion of prerequisites and the application and admission process.

A really big block for me was the prerequisites, I had been out of school 20 years so it was the Math and Chemistry thing for me.

It was difficult for me to register the first time. It took me weeks to get my courage up to do this. I had never looked at a university catalog and I had to use the "Star" telephone system. It turned out I ended up in a master's course by mistake.

While the majority of our students tell us that they apply to this program with the hope of continuing on into graduate study, initially the thought of this is a bit frightening. One student said, "I read the brochure five times, and I finally called the school personally and I asked 'Do I really have to go to graduate school?'"

Time in the program and contact with students and faculty play an important part in lessening their fears of academia. Students described a process of Finding a Faculty Role Model, "Putting an end to the mystique of academia."

I found a faculty person to work with in an independent study and that has been a real growing experience for me. She helped me realize I could write a thesis.

I spent some time talking with. . . . And she helped me clarify how we are starting to use our strengths as women and invest them in our careers and profession and that was very validating. And once you are validated then you can begin to grow, because you can see those parts of yourself that other people may have laughed at since the time you were a little girl [are] suddenly okay. And once they are okay you can start to use them and you can move on. That, for me was a big step.

I've lost my fear of academia. I feel that I can go on. I'm actually beginning to feel that I can complete a Master's program, and I can complete a PhD program too. I'm getting over that fear. I've seen that other people accomplish these things and I'm beginning to believe that I can too.

To get my BSN was something that I thought, gosh, maybe I can do that. Graduate school didn't even seem within my reach, and now not only does it seem within my reach, it's probable.

While the experience of being in the program involved some stress, it was also very growth producing. Students described this process in terms of People Building, "Toward a new view of self." They spoke with pride of their accomplishments and feelings of confidence. They spoke of their newly developed cognitive skills and their newly found voice.

What I have this year besides a BSN, is not a whole lot of factual anatomy and physiology or whatever, but a different way of thinking, or clarifying my values . . . that sort of thing . . . I speak up more than I did and have really found out what I think about a lot of things and not what either my fellow students think or an instructor . . . I'm much more willing to disagree more and less likely to be part of the pack. The other day I said to one of my classmates, "No, that's not right in my opinion, that's your opinion; speak for yourself."

What stands out for me is how I feel about myself presently as a nurse. I have a lot more self-confidence than I did a year ago. I have the theory and the knowledge to back up the intuition that I started out with.

I feel capable of managing people. Whereas, before this year I was very fearful of that, often times an associate degree nurse with experience will be put into management positions just because of her experience, not necessarily because she has the knowledge to be a leader, and I feel really good about the classes that I've taken. They have been helpful to me. I feel ready now.

You know I really didn't know how to read a research article. I didn't understand research. I knew it was really important, it's vital to our field, and I wanted to be a good nurse, but I'd never really admitted to anyone or said to anyone that I really didn't understand the articles. I can read an article now. I can decide whether or not I agree with it. I have the freedom and the knowledge to do that. It's wonderful! I can say, well I think this study was silly or I think this is a wonderful study, and I might even be wrong, but I have the freedom to do that and the knowledge to make that judgment.

One student told the following story:

> *I was born in the same small town I live in, and I went to nursing school in that same small town, and I work in the hospital in that town, and I'm 36 years old, so just coming to the city was a big deal. I felt a little like a fraud. My friends who work at the University gave me a tour, and they wanted to take my picture in front of the school of nursing, and the rhododendrons were out and I remember while they were taking my picture feeling so bad because they were going to get these pictures developed and I was never going to get accepted (at least this is what I thought then) and it was going to be all for naught. . . . and here I am getting ready to graduate in two weeks. To be two weeks away from graduation is unbelievable. It's a dream come true for me.*

SUMMARY AND RECOMMENDATIONS

The quantitative data from this study informed us that the students in our program were similar to other groups of RNs described in the literature. RN students tend to be older and add the role of student to otherwise complex lives. They are academically able students with high GPAs and are highly motivated to achieve. Unlike the students described in the literature, our students tended to enroll in the Bachelor's completion portion of the program as full-time students. They saw the opportunity to complete the Bachelor's degree in one year of full-time study as a positive feature of the program.

The interviews provided additional information about the actual experience of being a returning RN. Students told us about their busy lives and the pressure that the student role added. They told us of the application and admission process, the myth of impersonality of the University, and the anxiety they experienced because of this. They talked with pride of their new found reasoning skills, their self confidence, and their ability to speak their opinions. They talked about the importance of the peer group and contacts with faculty and their sense that they had grown and accomplished a great deal during their time in the program.

In addition to giving a descriptive picture of the experience of being RN students, the interviews provided important clues regarding the curriculum. Opportunities for connectedness with one another and with faculty are important. An experience where these students are grouped together seems essential. Initially, this grouping provides an opportunity to bond with one another and serves as a haven of safety for these students at a time when they are anxious and uncertain. Creating an environment which helps them feel unique and which recognizes their skills and expertness as clinicians helps to build self-confidence and opens them to new ideas and learning. The opportunity to work with faculty is important in helping them realize their potential for further study. Linkages with faculty are transition steps to graduate study.

While much of their academic experience was eventually viewed very positively, the experience of being placed in large lecture classes with the basic students was seen negatively. Students told us about the resentment that they felt when they were mixed in with the generic students. These RN students saw themselves as special students with unique needs. Trying to integrate them into the main group of students was problematic. We are in the process of holding discussions in our school about ways to better manage this experience for these students.

Bridge courses have traditionally been utilized to socialize students into the professional portion of the Bachelor's curriculum and to give them the particular conceptual perspective of the program in which they are enrolled. Students let us know that these courses helped them to see the vision of where they were headed, that this program was not just about more information and technology but a new way of thinking and approaching problems and issues. Strategies that encouraged reflection and writing supported this vision. Bridge courses were also a means to introduce these students to skills of scholarship: writing, reasoning, thinking, and speaking.

The demographic data from these students informed us of the overall success of our program. Students complete the Bachelor's degree quickly and a large number of them successfully enter the Master's program. Additional time with the program will provide the opportunity to further assess these students' success with graduate study and their contributions to the practice community. The interviews allowed these students to tell us their stories and let us know them and the experience of being a returning student in today's world in a very personal way.

REFERENCES

Beeman, P. (1988). RNs' perceptions of their baccalaureate programs: Meeting their adult learning needs. *Journal of Nursing Education, 27,* 364–370.

Baj, P. (1985). Demographic characteristics of RN and generic students: Implications for curriculum. *Journal of Nursing Education, 24*, 230–236.

Campaniello, J. (1988). When professional nurses return to school: A study of role conflict and well-being in multiple-role women. *Journal of Professional Nursing, 4*, 136–140.

Dugas, B. (1985). Baccalaureate for entry to practice: A challenge that universities must meet. *The Canadian Nurse, 81*(5), 17–19.

Fotos, J. (1987). Characteristics of RN students continuing their education in a BS program. *Journal of Continuing Education in Nursing, 18*, 118–122.

Green, C. (1987). Multiple role women: The real world of the mature learner. *Journal of Nursing Education, 26*, 266–271.

Guba, E., & Lincoln, Y. (1985). Fourth generation evaluation as an alternative. *Educational Horizons, 3*, 139–141.

King, J. (1986). A comparative study of adult developmental patterns of RN and generic students in a baccalaureate nursing program. *Journal of Nursing Education, 25*, 366–371.

Lange, L. (1986). Recruiting, advising, and program planning for RN/BSN students. *Western Journal of Nursing Research, 8*, 414–430.

Lawler, T., & Rose M. A. (1987). Professionalization: A comparison among generic baccalaureate, ADN and RN/BSN nurses. *Nurse Educator, 12*(3), 19–22.

Lee, J. (1987). Analysis of stressful clinical and didactic incidents reported by returning registered nurses. *Journal of Nursing Education, 26*, 372–379.

Lee, J. (1988). Analysis of coping methods reported by returning RNs. *Journal of Nursing Education, 27*, 309–313.

Lethbridge, D. (1989). Motivational orientations of registered nurse baccalaureate students in rural New England. *Journal of Nursing Education, 28*, 203–209.

Linares, A. (1989). A comparative study of learning characteristics of RN and generic students. *Journal of Nursing Education, 28*, 354–360.

MacLean, T., Knoll, G., & Kinney, C. (1985). The evolution of a baccalaureate program for registered nurses. *Journal of Nursing Education, 24*, 53–57.

Mattson, S. (1990). Coping and developmental maturity of RN baccalaureate students. *Western Journal of Nursing Research, 12,* 514–524.

Rendon, D. (1988). The registered nurse student: A role congruence perspective. *Journal of Nursing Education, 27,* 172–177.

Thurber, F. (1988). A comparison of RN students in two types of baccalaureate completion programs. *Journal of Nursing Education, 27,* 266–273.

13

Women's Ways of Knowing and Teaching RN Students

Sandra J. Eyres

*Look at a classroom: look at the many kinds of women's faces, pos-
tures, expressions. Listen to the women's voices. Listen to the silences,
the unasked questions, the blanks. Listen to the small, soft voices,
often courageously trying to speak up, voices of women taught early
that tones of confidence, challenge, anger, or assertiveness are strident
and unfeminine. . . . Listen to a woman groping for language in
which to express what is on her mind, . . . deprecating her own work
by a reflex prejudgment: I do not deserve to take up time and space!**
—Adrienne Rich

This paper is about trying to understand the silence and the soft
voices in the RN classroom and how they can be made stronger. I will
present major concepts from *Women's Ways of Knowing* (Belenky,
Clinchy, Goldberger, & Tarule, 1986), discuss what I believe is their
applicability to RN education, and then give some examples of application in the classroom that I have found useful.

When we talk about advanced education for RNs we are talking

Several colleagues have played important parts in the evolution of the ideas presented
here: Sharon Fought, Melissa Gallison, Kathleen Shannon-Dorcy, and Joyce Zerwekh
from our teaching together, Mary Ersek and Anne Loustau from our research together,
and Faith Gabelnick from her consultation to our school.
*See *On lies, secrets, and silence: Selected prose 1966–1978,* © 1979, pp. 243-244.

about educating women for the most part. It is critical that we acknowledge that fact. This is not to imply less importance to men in our RN programs, but to recognize the special challenges and strengths of nurses who are women going back to college for a baccalaureate degree. Some of the dynamics I will discuss are gender related but none are gender specific (Clinchy, 1989; Clinchy & Zimmerman, 1982).

For the past five years I have taught one of the first courses that RNs take in our RN completion program. It is a course to help students "think nursing." It focuses on reasoning and other aspects of critical thinking. There is also an emphasis on helping students with some basic academic activities such as writing and understanding what they read. As an example, one of the assignments which has given me most insight into these students I call an "issue paper." They are asked to pick something in nursing or health about which reasonable people disagree, that cannot be resolved through simple fact finding. The more relevant it is to their work world, the better. They research at least two perspectives on this issue, identify and analyze the supporting arguments, draw their own reasoned conclusion, and compare their reasoned conclusion with their more intuitive ones. I ask them also to write about their response to doing the paper.

Critical thinking is currently a buzz word and universally accepted as a necessary component of nursing education. When one looks closely at different models for analyzing and evaluating arguments and the related cognitive tasks, they seem like a set up for feeling like a failure. When I went through the arduous task of learning formal reasoning, becoming at least passably facile, long after my formal schooling, it was a very puzzling and frustrating task. As a teacher of this course then, my quest was to find ways of teaching critical thinking and the related skills which would spare students the negative discouragement I had felt.

Over the years I have kept journal-like notes of what goes on in the classroom and about my contacts with students. This helps me think and helps me understand the students' voices through my own. I am also a hoarder of examples of their reflective writing. These have served as texts worthy of repeated attention in working toward understanding these complex, fascinating people. I will draw on both types of texts in this paper.

A FRAMEWORK FOR UNDERSTANDING VOICE

I had the good fortune to become familiar with Belenky, Clinchy, Goldberger and Tarule's work *Women's Ways of Knowing: The Development of*

Self, Voice, and Mind (1986) as I became more involved with the adventure of teaching RN students. I began seeing my students through this work and trying things in my teaching consistent with these authors' analyses of optimal teaching environments for women.

Their book begins:

> We do not think of the ordinary person as preoccupied with such diffi-
> cult and profound questions as: What is truth? What is authority? To
> whom do I listen? What counts for me as evidence? How do I know
> what I know? Yet, . . . They affect our definitions of ourselves, the way
> we interact with others, our public and private personae, our sense of
> control over life events, our views of teaching and learning, and our
> conceptions of morality (Belenky et al., 1986, p. 3).

The work of Belenky et al. (1986) was prompted in part by the earlier studies of Perry (1981) on the cognitive and moral development of young men at Harvard in the 1950s. Perry observed patterns of cognitive development which resulted from the initial exposure to the pluralism of people and opinions in a college setting. He and his colleagues validated these patterns through extensive interviews and inter-rater reliability testing.

Belenky et al. (1986) wanted to see whether Perry's results could be replicated for women. They did in-depth interviews of 135 women who were recent graduates, or were currently students in college, or were receiving services from human service agencies. Using the interview texts they inductively developed a descriptive scheme of these women's cognitive and ethical development. Their findings showed both similarities and differences with the Perry (1981) scheme developed on men. One of the important differences for women was expressed in terms of "voice." As used in the *Women's Ways of Knowing* work, voice means not only the ability to articulate one's own thoughts; it also includes the sense of self and considering what you say as a valid expression of knowing. The other difference in the findings, "connected and separate knowing," refers to the relationship of the knower to the known. These two themes in Belenky et al.'s work carried forward the thinking of others who were making important observations about female images of self, connectedness and morality, such as Gilligan (1982).

In *Women's Ways of Knowing* five major epistemological perspectives are presented based on women's views of knowledge, truth and authority.

Table 13.1. Women's Ways of Knowing Perspectives

Category	Descriptive Characteristics
Silence	Unable to trust own experience as knowledge. Authority seen as all-powerful. Unable to express opinions; without a voice.
Received Knowing	Information interpreted literally. There is always one right answer. Learn by being told and listening. Learning is receiving, retaining and returning the words of authorities. Thinking the same way as peers is important. Quiet own voices to listen to others.
Subjective Knowing	There are still "right answers," but truth is now within the person. Have begun to value own voices and experience as sources of knowledge. Multiple personal truths are viewed as the norm. Everyone can have own opinion and they are all equally valid. Can fear making conflicting opinions overt and losing connectedness with others. External authority is associated with power and mistrust.
Procedural Knowing	Procedure focused. How you decide more important than what you decide. Speak with voice of reason and look to voices of discipline as authoritative. Some truths are truer than others, truth can be shared.
Separate Knowing	Detached, critical, adversarial in approach with others. Believe in impersonal justice and procedures for establishing truth. Essentially autonomous, suspicious, assume anyone and everyone may be wrong. Critical thinking.
Connected Knowing	Operate in relationship with reciprocity. Work to accept others and remain connected even when there is disagreement. Use procedures for evaluating others' knowledge such as empathy and intimacy. Enjoy collaborative learning.
Constructed Knowing	Listen to own voices as well as others. Integrate separate as well as connected approaches to interaction. Can be analytical as well as connected. Respect own opinions as well as others' opinions. Knowledge is tentative. What is right in any situation is shaped by environment and individuals. Integrate internally and externally gained knowledge and have historical sense of self. Understanding comes from considering in context.

Adapted from Belenky, Clinchy, Goldberger, & Tarule, (1986) *Women's Ways of Knowing: The Development of Self, Voice, and Mind*, New York: Basic Books.

In **Silence** women are voiceless. They perceive that they can't "know" on their own, they are told what is so and what to do by unfriendly authority voices. We do not see much of this perspective by the time women get into nursing classes.

In the **Received Knowing** perspective women's own voice is still kept fairly quiet. They learn through listening to the words of others, of authorities like teachers and textbook authors. They are preoccupied with finding the right answer and they want to know exactly what will be on the test so they can memorize, store, and feed it back. Unfortunately, it's easy to perpetuate this perspective through the types of student evaluation used.

In **Subjective Knowing** women look inwardly to their own voices to find the answer. They begin to value and listen to their own voices. They expect their peers to have opinions different from their own, but expect them not to be argued because doing so causes disruptions in relationships.

In **Procedural Knowing** they are again looking outward and listening to the voices of others, focusing on *how* one learns, *how* one knows, the *process* of deciding what is so. They are busy trying to integrate the decision-making strategies and principles of the discipline. They are more able to separate the evaluation of their work from evaluation of self.

Belenky et al. (1986) noted different approaches in how women listen to others to carry out the thinking strategies of the discipline. Those they called **Separate Knowers** have successfully internalized the traditional academic perspective of trying to prove, disprove or convince. They take a basically adversarial, doubting approach as they are taught to challenge before accepting. This is the antithesis of most women's epistemology.

Connected Knowing is much more natural for women. From this perspective they believe; they try to get into the shoes of the author or speaker; they establish truth through understanding and being understood. They think *with* each other.

The goal of education is both connected and separate knowing (Belenky et al., 1986; Elbow, 1986). Naive belief and narrow egotistical doubt are equally debilitating.

In **Constructed Knowing** women listen to both their own voices and the voices of others. They can synthesize separate and connected knowing skills. They recognize that what is considered true or right can be shaped by context and that they participate fully in constructing it.

For nursing educators the work of Belenky et al. (1986) is a step forward in providing a potential structure for describing student beliefs about knowledge in a profession composed mainly of women. How can this typology inform us about RN students? First, where do these students tend to distribute among the perspectives of knowing? Which of these characteristics describe this special group of students?

In earlier work (Eyres, Loustau, & Ersek, 1992) replicating the *Women's Ways of Knowing* typology on entering generic nursing students, my colleagues and I found that almost all of the younger students fit in the received and subjective categories of knowing; most were a combination of these two. The older women students (over 23 years of age and thus older than the typical college sophomore) showed broader combinations of perspectives including procedural knowing and constructed knowing. But, procedural knowing and constructed knowing were, for those not having earlier college degrees, gained through experiences typical for the lives of women. For example, decision making and thinking carefully about options took place in the practical context of child rearing. These older women in the generic nursing program working toward their first college degree did not yet have the skills of critical thinking for reasoning with abstract ideas. Based on their life experiences, they fully realized that circumstances could influence what was true or right, and that they had to take the initiative in constructing a best decision. Yet, typical of adult students returning to school, they reverted to received knowing for learning in their nursing classes where the subject matter was new to them. The fact that older women students in the basic baccalaureate program showed a more mixed pattern of perspectives on ways of knowing and did not as neatly fit the categories is understandable in part when one considers the samples from which the Belenky et al. (1986) typology was derived. Few of the women interviewed by Belenky et al. were older and returning to school.

For RN students we see yet another permutation. Often these women are not novices in their profession and can be considered experts with extensive experience in nursing. In addition to the practical schooling of life experiences, they have their earlier formal education in nursing and their nursing experience. So, they are not about to go back to received knowing for nursing content.

There is diversity among RN students on characteristics relevant to this discussion. They vary in ways that influence ideas about self, voice, and authority for knowing. These include such things as amount of responsibility of their work roles, experience in taking responsibility for others in their personal social situations, and patterns of beliefs and communication in their families of origin. So one does see variations in perspectives on knowing in any single class of students.

CLASSROOM OBSERVATIONS

There are a few RN students who have so little voice that they have many characteristics of silent knowers. Their earlier education and social contexts have not promoted their sense of self worth or ability to know. This is an excerpt from a student's reflective writing about self.

> *As I read through the syllabus for each of my classes at the beginning of this quarter and saw phrases like "class participation" and "analytical" thinking, my doubts about my ability to succeed in this program were confirmed. I have struggled with low self-esteem and self doubt for a very long time. Meeting new people, facing new situations and sharing my thoughts with large groups causes definite feelings of discomfort. I absolutely detest drawing attention to myself! Knowing that I am a concrete learner makes me shudder at the thought of having to think analytically and abstractly! I struggled through several assignments before getting up enough nerve to call and ask for help or clarification.*

RN students with the least sense of voice and needing the most help have the most difficult time talking with the authority figure, the teacher, to ask for help. I suspect authority has, for them, not been approachable or helpful before, so why should expectations be different now?

Some RN students, especially those recently graduated from their basic programs, evidence the received knowing perspective. From another student's reflective writing:

> *In very small groups I interact fairly well, but I do not like to participate in classroom discussion. I learn best absorbing lecture material that is practical and allows me to take the role of an observer.*

In contrast, RNs with more experience become frustrated if they are treated as observers or empty vessels for knowledge about nursing, however, they more closely resemble received knowers for those aspects of formal education they have not experienced before. They depend on clear teachers' voices to help with academic skills like recognizing and working with abstract concepts or recognizing structure in a published article.

RNs certainly show signs of subjective knowing, that is, the notion that multiple views exist with an inability to find a best or better one. This is an excerpt from my notes:

> *Today I talked with a student about her issue paper because she was avoiding drawing a conclusion about whether her work setting should offer a new service. She said she couldn't decide. I asked, "What if you were an administrator and you had to come to a conclusion?" She replied, "That's why I can never be an administrator, because I can see both sides."*

Procedural knowing, thinking through options, weighing them, working toward a best decision, comes through as they talk about their child care arrangements and other family matters and their extensive practical work in their clinical arenas. Other aspects of this way of knowing such as the ability to suspend personal judgement to examine multiple perspectives and interpretations, and the deliberate and systematic use of reason are not as well developed. But, I find that nurses tend strongly toward connected knowing and are, by the nature of our work, empathic. So, it is fairly easy for us to see other points of view and make the transition to seeing the rationale behind these views. Here is an excerpt from a student's reflective writing at the end of a class period. We had just finished working with a case study where different small groups of students took the point of view of different players in the case. This student had been part of the group that constructed the point of view of the mother of the sick child called Susie.

> *This is a day of connections. It is vital to me as a person, as a nurse, as a student, to feel some connection with other people. . . . I appreciate the contact with new ideas, new ways of approaching familiar ideas, and new people that this class has made possible. It is easy to get stuck in a mindset of "I'm a small town nurse, at a small hospital, with a small mind." Through this class I feel a connection with the larger world of ideas and the nurses who generate these ideas. The connection or relationship to others is what makes it worthwhile for me. It's exciting to hear other people's different ideas and feelings. Sometimes something is*

said and it clarifies what I've already thought about in a murky sort of way. An example of this today was when we were discussing nursing diagnosis . . . It took me a while to get the connection between nursing diagnosis, labeling, and my practice as a nurse. Looking at the label of "non-compliance" suddenly seemed so obviously shallow and inadequate. While this is not a totally new idea, it became clear and relevant, instead of complicated and theoretical. As Susie's mother, the last thing I want is to be considered non-compliant—obviously an ignorant, uncaring, incompetent failure as a mother, and hence as a woman and person.

RN students show some characteristics of constructed knowing. They have made many life commitments. They do see themselves as authorities in their profession, but they see self as subordinate rather than collaborative with other types of authorities in their setting. They do not listen to the voices of self and others in full two-way dialogues and have not integrated both connected and separate knowing.

Analyzing what I know experientially from working with RN students against the *Women's Ways of Knowing* perspectives has been very helpful for me. It helps keep me from making erroneous assumptions about their strengths and expertise and where they are more dependent learners. It is easy to make unwarranted assumptions about their ability for conceptualization and analysis because they are so talented in their clinical knowledge. Conversely, it is too easy to discount their nursing knowledge when they do not speak in the voices we are used to in academic settings.

CONNECTED TEACHING ENVIRONMENTS

One cannot work long with the Belenky et al. (1986) framework before being firmly convinced that all students, especially women, should have the benefit of what they call connected teaching environments. To understand connected teaching we need to look more closely at some other central ideas.

Voice and Self

Voice is a major theme through *Women's Ways of Knowing*. Belenky et al. (1986) explained that phrases used by the informants such as speaking up, being silenced, or not being heard were used frequently giving a "sense of mind, self-worth, and feelings of isolation from or connection with others" (p. 18). Through this metaphor "voice," these authors learned that "the development of a sense of voice, mind, and self were intricately intertwined" (p. 18). Other writers about women help us understand this point.

In her stirring essay about women's transition to adolescence, Gilligan (1990) described this as a time of crisis in connections. At this juncture of adolescence girls face the dilemma of whether to be good, that is abandoning oneself in preference for caring for others, or to be considered selfish. During this period of development girls' understanding of reality is silenced and pushed underground. Our culture does not want to hear their questions—they are too disruptive.

In her discussion of the psychological limits and boundaries of women, Kaschak (1988) described women as being "driven to relatedness by the messages of the culture" (p. 10). In our society individuality is valued, but not for women. Women are to get their identity through relationships with others, particularly men. These alliances, at least potentially, offer psychological and physical protection. Outside of relationships women are largely invisible, so connectedness is survival. But this type of connectedness, for identity and protection, is not a kind which promotes self-esteem. Kaschak describes another kind of relatedness "that occurs . . . for the sake of affiliation and is qualitatively and experientially different" (p. 122). It involves not only meeting the needs of partner or children; it also includes "meeting one's own needs for non-driven caring and closeness. Relatedness in the name of safety or subordination is qualitatively and experientially different from relatedness in the name of caring and humanity" (p. 122).

In my experience RN students are surprised to encounter this second type of connectedness in the school setting. They express some amazement and great pleasure at finding it and bond very closely to their classmates. As one RN student said at the end of her program:

> We connected with each other and formed a very tightly knit group. We tend to speak in one voice. Then individuals have to be courageous to say "wait a minute. I don't necessarily go along with that view."

A word of clarification is in order for the various uses of the term "connected." I spoke of connected knowing: an empathic relationship between the knower and the person, work, or thing to be known. Then a

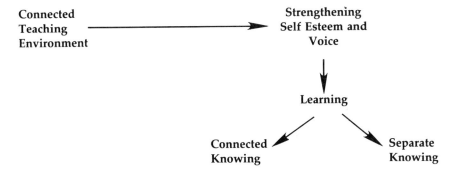

Figure 13.1   Relationship between connected teaching and learning.

caring type of connectedness was described for relationships between and among people. We move on to talking about connected teaching, which is caring connectedness in the promotion of learning.

Let us consider the relationships shown in Figure 13.1. While simplistic, they depict the essential notions for our purpose. We see connected teaching facilitating self-esteem and use of voice which enables both connected and separate knowing.

It is important not to equate the affiliative nature of entering RN students and their lack of argumentation with mature, connected knowing. When using case studies for applying nursing diagnosis they do not, without encouragement, recognize the perspectives of other important players in the case scenario. Clinchy and Zimmerman (1985) offer a rationale for this phenomenon. Until women can stand apart from self and reflect on self, they cannot draw on abstractions from their experience from which to empathize. They can only know through connecting if their own experience has been quite similar to the other person's. The stronger the voice and sense of self, the more women can generalize from their experience for connected empathic knowing. And, I believe, the stronger the voice and sense of self, the more separate knowing, or critical thinking, is also facilitated. They are able, through the connected safety of the classroom, to question and analyze, realizing that such dialogues are about abstractions and are not attacks on the self. Gilligan (1990) proposed that women's questions are more likely to be raised in secure relationships, where "no one will leave and someone will listen" (p. 27).

We are all familiar with RN students as they come to our educational setting. Many have felt the stirring of their still small voices and are excited by the prospect of self development although they have only vague expectations of what this will involve. They only know it's scary. This is one student's recollection upon hearing of the issue paper assignment:

> *I felt intimidated by the knowledge that I would be required to think deeply about something and then analyze what I thought. I was concerned that my opinions were not derived from intelligent thought. I didn't know if I was a critical thinker and what I would do if I found that I wasn't.*

A few will have more confidence in speaking up but many will continue their invisible ways until they feel safety and Kaschak's (1988) different kind of connectedness.

After assimilating the basic premises in *Women's Ways of Knowing*, my quest changed to "how can I help expand the knowing perspectives of these students? How can I help them strengthen their voices, feel empowered, and gain confidence in both connected and separate types of knowing?"

Connected Teaching and Learning As a Way of Being

In any teaching environment students can feel connected or alone. Feeling connected means feeling someone cares, feeling affirmed for what they know and for the potential they have for strong voice and knowing, feeling part of a learning community with empathy for understanding the perspectives of its members.

Connected teachers give off messages like: "You are a special person just as you are. You are complete without anything we can add. You have what it takes to accomplish your goals. Share your goals with me so we can figure out together how to meet them." Connected teachers are open to the questions that might disrupt the nursing culture, to a noisy classroom where voices can venture with increasing volume with assurance of safety.

In contrast, a separate learning environment gives off messages like: "You are an independent learner. You have to prove yourself worthy of not failing. You will be evaluated by those who know the answers using standards of success they have chosen." Silence results for those not sure of their voices and afraid of showing the inadequacy which they are sure exists.

We can either empower or disempower students. In the words of Belenky et al. (1986) "A woman, like any other human being, does need to know that the mind makes mistakes; but our interviews have convinced us that every woman, regardless of age, social class, ethnicity, and academic achievement, needs to know that she is capable of intelligent thought, and she needs to know it right away" (p. 193).

In applying the principles of connected teaching, I have found that many of the strategies most helpful are those recommended for modern teaching in general such as active engagement in the classroom, collaborative learning, and writing as a process. I was using these approaches before, but I would say the difference for me now, post *Women's Ways of Knowing*, is that I have changed in *why* I do what I do. The basic motivation of people-building through strengthening of voice and self leads to a different orchestration, a different mood, a different feeling between me and the students. There is a different background of relationship against which learning strategies take place. These classroom activities are merely tools to assist with *a way of being* with the students.

Some of the principles and strategies I have found useful are summarized in Table 13.2.

Establish Connectedness with Teacher and Among Pupils

To create a connected classroom there has to be two-way disclosure. I tell students at the beginning of the first class how frustrating and difficult it was for me to learn critical thinking, how it felt like I must be "dumber" than everyone else or I would have learned it more quickly. They need to know that teachers are human and have come through some of the same fires by which they feel tested. They need to know about our personhood to connect. Students say things like, "I was relieved to hear you had trouble with critical thinking."

Having students talk to each other during class time to become acquainted legitimizes the importance of who they are as people and the importance of our knowing about each other for the learning enterprise. I have them talk with each other about their concerns so they know they are not unique in feeling vulnerable. It breaks the silence, establishes some commonality to build upon, and lets them know they are not alone in the stressors with which they are coping.

Connectedness is promoted by helping them focus on the group as a learning community. One approach is to find as many dimensions of

Table 13.2   Connected Teaching Principles and Strategies

Establish Connectedness with Teacher and Among Students
Disclose about self (teacher).
Use class time for students to learn about each other.
Validate that fears are not unique.
Talk about and examine the learning community together.
Spend individual time with each student.

Promote Self Knowledge and Self Esteem
Use available tools for examining learning styles, information processing, etc.
Have them do a self analysis about strengths and challenges.
Do reflective writing in class to keep in touch with responses and feelings.
Stretch them with metacognitive exercises.
Maximize their control through choices.

Facilitate Success
Provide structure and clear expectations.
Model and practice before graded evaluation.
Have them work together and help each other.
Use work with peers as a stepping stone to more independent work.

Promote Voice
Use small groups or dyads for class exercises.
Do lots of free writing (as opposed to the formal, edited kind).
Dialogue with them on their in-class writing.
Have them read articles which help put into words their strong feelings.

Confirm Self as Knower
Use every opportunity to show them what they already know.
Acknowledge their expertise.
Maximize use of their expertise.
Enter abstractions through their experiential world.
Go for depth of thinking rather than "covering" more content.

Encourage Growth in Different Knowing Perspectives
Role play different perspectives.
Have them construct arguments for different positions.
Expose them to different frameworks for thinking about the same thing.

diversity as possible in the class. This not only legitimizes differences; it can bring to light an advantageous breadth of perspectives and skills of individuals.

Nothing helps my connecting as much as meeting individually with each student. Even though it may take a few weeks to accomplish, I make it an expectation that each RN student will make an appointment with me for 30 minutes early in the term. I lay out a sign-up sheet with available times so they don't have to do the scary part of contacting me to negotiate a time. When we get together I ask what led them to come for their degree, what their goals are, and what their concerns are. Students are always surprised that such conversations take place and are grateful for my "taking the time." This is another symptom of what Rich (1979) called the presupposition that "I do not deserve to take up time and space" (p. 244). These individual meetings are the quickest and most pleasant way for me to learn about the composition of my learning community, to plan for special needs and goals, and to learn their names.

Promote Self-Knowledge and Self-Esteem

There are a variety of instruments which students can fill out and score in class that inform them about their temperaments, how they process information, and their learning styles. The chances are good that they will never have looked at themselves this closely in such a systematic way. I find them fascinated by it. But, the bigger value comes when I have them write a synthesis of their strengths and challenges as a student based on the data, including their opinion of whether they believe the data accurately reflect their tendencies. There is no way to avoid thinking about yourself from "outside your self" when doing such exercises.

A similar thing is accomplished by on-going reflective writing in the classroom and metacognitive exercises about what it was like to work on some specific task. I try hard not to let the content of our deliberations take them far afield from keeping in touch with self. I try to get across that learning is an interaction between the self and what they are encountering.

Self-esteem is also enhanced by exhibiting faith in their judgment by giving them control over such things as use of classroom time and choices of assignments. In the last offering of the course I had them choose whether they wanted to do the issue paper alone or with someone. Those who teamed up worked in the same place and chose issues about which they had been having professional confrontations. They learned that they could reason together and come to a better understanding of the issue and a good solution.

Facilitate Success

Students are more likely to succeed if we don't underestimate the need for structure, specificity of instructions, and clarity of what we expect. In structure and clarity there is freedom.

I have found that what facilitates learning the most is working together. For example, I try to give them a running start on their issue paper by using class time to talk about potential topics and to brainstorm in dyads about the reasons supporting different views. It is in formal reasoning or separate knowing where the supportive connections mean the most in getting started. After they have worked up a first draft I ask them to present it to their classmates orally without being graded. The presenter is helping the class by providing an example from which to learn reasoning and analysis of arguments together, and the class helps the presenter by offering suggestions for how to improve the work for the next draft. It is in these interactive sessions where I see the real learning occur. They question and think out loud with relish. In a subsequent ungraded draft I write questions and make suggestions for additional refinements on the next and final graded draft. In a "separate" type of classroom this would be looked upon as spoon feeding or cheating when students help each other. In a connected classroom these types of activity logically follow because the goal is learning and empowerment rather than independent achievement at any cost.

Promote Voice

There are only a hand full of students at the beginning who will talk in the large class. Usually in dyadic or small group work the more timid voices can be heard. One of the things that I find most dramatic in its effect on getting them to express themselves is free writing. Even the most timid are quite open with their thinking when they don't have to talk out loud, and adding my comments to their writing offers a wonderful chance for dialogue with them.

One can anticipate many of the things they feel most strongly about. One always seems to be nursing diagnosis. I ask them to read an article in which the author complains about how using a nursing taxonomy gets in the way of real nursing. They practically cheer for the author and say things like, "That's what I thought all the time, but she has found the words to say it!" Having given voice to their feelings of frustration through someone else's writing we are then able to consider views of others on the need for a taxonomy and potential ways of improving its application. From a freer consideration of multiple views they can weigh the issue in more breadth as they come to a more informed conclusion of their own about the uses and misuses of nursing diagnostic labels.

I was a little shocked to receive the following note from one of the quietest students after we read an article on the sources of stress for nurses:

> *I want to thank you for assigning Chapter 68. I'm photocopying page 493 and thumbtacking it to my boss' forehead. All of the frustrations that have accumulated in me over the past 20 years are summarized there. I showed it to my husband and said, "See! I'm not just a whining bitch—there are other people who feel the same way!"*

Confirming Self as Knower

This strategy is based on Belenky et al.'s (1986) admonition that women need to know they are capable of intelligent thought and they need to know it right away. If one has students do a task the first session where the knowledge they bring is relevant, it helps them see that they do "know" and are capable of going on to more difficult tasks. For example, one can have them identify supporting evidence for a conclusion by deriving a diagnosis for a case study, something familiar from their work world.

As Rather (1992) has so clearly pointed out, RNs make meaning of the world through their clinical experience. In this course almost anything about critical thinking can be taught or at least started with the clinical context in mind. For example, it is easy to disempower in learning reasoning by picking topics that students have relatively little familiarity with, such as an international relations controversy. If one asks for examples of something that is currently a hot issue for them in their clinical or personal world, they will have knowledge of the circumstantial background which is an important first step in analytically thinking about an issue.

Encourage Growth in Different Knowing Perspectives

As noted earlier, these students benefit from being nudged into examining different viewpoints. They will not be successful connected or separate knowers unless they can imagine alternatives. As one student wrote in response to doing this in the issue paper, "I have learned that every hot issue really *does* have two sides." In courses which do not focus as much on analyzing arguments and on reasoning, the same push toward *multiplistic thinking*, as Perry (1981) would call it, is accomplished by using different conceptual frameworks or models.

I know that these principles and strategies are on the right track when students write at the end of the course things like the following:

> *"I've learned that it's OK to raise questions, that others having opinions different from mine doesn't mean I'm wrong."*

> *"It made me look at different views on the same problem rather than just accepting what is told to me."*

> *"I've learned a lot about myself. I have restructured my dialogue in my personal life both with my kids and husband."*

> *"I'm learning so much as a person. I appreciate the knowledge and ideas that are becoming a part of me. I appreciate being treated as a worthwhile person, with ideas worth listening to. It seems that we students are no longer thought of simply as empty vessels to be filled by the 'experts,' but as active participants in our own education and self growth. It's exciting and I'm growing and becoming a better person because of it."*

This is not to say all evaluations have been positive. During the struggle to find ways to apply the principles there have been less positive comments, such as "I still haven't figured out what this course is about."

CONCLUSIONS

Strategies grounded in principles for connected teaching derived from *Women's Ways of Knowing* and other bodies of literature have been briefly discussed. The examples given here are admittedly for a first course in the RN program and one focusing on critical thinking. The expectation is that, when tried, they will be found generalizable in other types of courses.

Two needs for caution exist. The first concerns pushing students to think analytically and form their opinions based on reasoning. It would be easy to infer that other ways of thinking and decision making central to nursing, such as the esthetic, practical, and intuitive (Benner & Tanner, 1987; Carper, 1978; Eisner, 1985; Jacobs-Kramer & Chinn, 1988), are inferior to critical thinking or are unnecessary. In so doing we would be doing the profession and students a disservice and repeating the common fallacy of not letting women engage with their whole person as they add additional perspectives and skills. Nurses need to be able to use their voices and to take a thoughtful position on issues, but not all thinking can take the form of verbal reasoning.

Secondly, while the strategies discussed here can be viewed as tangible procedures we may choose to adopt, they are not sufficient in and of themselves to make a connected learning environment in which RN students can grow. I have come to believe that the life blood of teacher-student interactions is largely a function of the beliefs and values of the teacher. Students know whether our behavior comes from deep within or from a prescription for classroom activities. They can tell whether we truly value them, which can make an interactive classroom an unfriendly stage for actors (teachers) who depend on memorized lines.

These students offer us the opportunity for a personal metamorphosis in which we open ourselves to really seeing them as we encourage them to look at themselves. Once we make personal connections with them we can learn from them as we help them learn. Which is, after all, what teaching is about.

REFERENCES

Belenky, M., Clinchy, B., Goldberger, N., & Tarule, J. (1986). *Women's ways of knowing: The development of self, voice, and mind.* New York: Basic Books

Benner, P., & Tanner, C. (1987). How expert nurses use intuition. *American Journal of Nursing, 87*, 23–31.

Carper, B. (1978). Fundamental patterns of knowing in nursing. *Advances in Nursing Science, 1*(1), 13–23.

Clinchy, B. (1989). On critical thinking and connected knowing. *Liberal Education, 15*(5), 14–19.

Clinchy, B., & Zimmerman, C. (1982). Epistemology and agency in the development of undergraduate women. In P. Perun (Ed.), *The Undergraduate Woman: Issues in Educational Equity*. Lexington, MA: Lexington Books.

Clinchy, B., & Zimmerman, C. (1985). Growing up intellectually: Issues for college women. *Work in progress*. No. 19, Wellesley, MA: Wellesley College.

Eisner, E. (Ed.). (1985). *Learning and teaching the ways of knowing*. Chicago: University of Chicago Press.

Elbow, P. (1986). *Embracing contraries: Explorations in learning and teaching*. New York: Oxford.

Eyres, S., Loustau, A., & Ersek, M. (1992). Ways of knowing among beginning students in nursing. *Journal of Nursing Education, 31*, 175–181.

Gilligan, C. (1982). *In a different voice: Psychological theory and women's development*. Cambridge: Harvard University Press.

Gilligan, C. (1990). Teaching Shakespeare's sister: Notes from the underground of female adolescence. In C. Gilligan, N. Lyons, & T. Hammer (Eds.), *Making connections: The relational worlds of adolescent girls at Emma Willard School*. Cambridge: Harvard University Press.

Jacobs-Kramer, M., & Chinn, P. (1988). Perspectives on knowing: A model of nursing knowledge. *Scholarly Inquiry for Nursing Practice: An International Journal, 2*, 129–139.

Kaschak, E. (1988). Limits and boundaries: Toward a complex psychology of women. *Women & Therapy, 7*(4), 109–123.

Perry, W. (1981). Cognitive and ethical growth: The making of meaning. In A. Chickering (Ed.), *The Modern American College*. San Francisco: Jossey-Bass.

Rather, M. (1992). "Nursing as a way of thinking"—Heideggerian hermeneutical analysis of the lived experience of the returning RN. *Research in Nursing and Health, 15*, 47–55.

Rich, A. (1979). *On lies, secrets, and silence: Selected prose 1966–1978*. New York: W. W. Norton & Co.

14

Innovations in Registered Nurse Education: From Oppression to Empowerment

Marianne Rodgers
Sallie Nealand

It was a class fairly near the end of their RN Transition course. Susan came to class looking disheveled compared to her usual appearance. She had worked on an oncology unit in a tertiary care center for about five years. In previous classes, she demonstrated undeniable pride in the flexibility her unit had developed. For example, she described adjusting a patient's daily hospital routine to meet that woman's need to meditate with her crystals. Her love of nursing was obvious, but her commitment to advanced nursing education remained tenuous because work, hobbies, and social life claimed so much of her energy. Another student, Phyllis, was leading a class discussion on stress and went around the room eliciting normal coping mechanisms. Susan sat quietly until asked for her response. The words burst out of her like bullets. "That's why I'm here! I've been home in bed for 24 hours! I just couldn't stand it! Four patients died this week—four patients who weren't supposed to die! I wasn't coming! I couldn't do anything! Then I thought 'I've got to go! They'll understand me! They'll know what I'm going through! They'll listen to me!'"

They did listen, exposing feelings and relating experiences. They did not make Susan's pain disappear, but in their connectedness, they shared it. This exemplar demonstrates the type of classroom climate we had hoped to create for returning RN students taking their first course in the school of nursing. As teachers, we had succeeded. A climate of mutual respect and trust, collaborativeness, supportiveness, openness, authenticity, and compassion existed in this classroom. Knowles (cited in Tennant, 1991) claims these as the essential attitudes and actions to set an appropriate climate for adult learning. Students in nursing need to have "a sense of being cared for as they are learning to care for others; a feeling of support and guidance when they are grappling with clinical experiences" (Benoliel, 1988, p. 341). How had we developed this atmosphere in which students and teachers could care for one another?

When planning the course, we relied more on our intuition as experienced teachers than on theories of teaching and learning. Our plans were not totally uninformed. Between us we had 30 years of teaching experience, and we were both doctoral students in higher education. We considered the concepts of adult education, feminist theory, and professionalism. In 1988, the educational concepts of equity, caring, empowerment, and transformation existed in the literature but were not yet part of our repertoire. However, the transformation from oppression to empowerment was taking place in our students. We recognized change in them beyond the concept of the self-directed adult learner. We saw a process in their interactions more powerful than autonomy. Through the construct of empowerment, we gained a new perspective from which to view our students' growth and to understand the strength of their connectedness.

Diekelmann (1992) explains that we must reflect on what we do successfully in order to transform our practice as teachers. Benner, in the video *Nursing Theory: A Circle of Knowledge* (Moss, 1987), describes the relationship between practice and theory. She states that practice and theory can transform each other, with new knowledge creating a continuous circle or feedback system. In this paper, we will describe our transformation as learners and teachers acquiring new lenses with which to view students as learners, teachers, and colleagues.

Mason, Backer, and Georges (1991) define empowerment "as the enabling of individuals and groups to participate in actions and decision-making within a context that supports an equitable distribution of power. . . . It is a process of confirming one's self and/or one's group" (pp. 72–73). Empowered nurses perceive the injustices in their work environment, have positive self-esteem, and believe they can effect change in the power structures of the health care delivery system. Lazzari (1991) and Belenky, Clinchy, Goldberger, and Tarule (1986) define student empowerment as an outcome of a student-teacher relationship of alliance where roles are shared. Indeed, de Tornyay (1990) proclaims that "the curriculum revolution is about teacher-student partnerships. It is about flexibility and individual differences in how and what one learns" (p. 293).

As educators, we understood flexibility as perceiving each student as an individual. Empowering students is a difficult enough task if all students begin at the same point, but they do not. RN students arrive in our classrooms with diverse life experiences as nurses, individuals, and prior students. Frequently their past educational experiences have been oppressive. The behavioral theory and objectives that nurse educators until recently proclaimed as the only acceptable theoretical approach to teaching set a power imbalance between students and teachers. The teacher as the authority decides the content students need to learn and measures all learning by breaking it into separate behaviors. This system, driven until recently by the NLN accreditation process, does not encourage or allow self-directedness, discovery, challenge, or recognition that at times students may have equal or greater knowledge than their teachers. It does not encourage connectedness between students. Intuitively neither of us had ever totally embraced this theory of education, but open rebellion against it came only after others brought our tacit discomfort to a level of propositional knowing (Allen, 1990; Bevis and Murray, 1990; Moccia, 1990). Although a paradigm shift is occurring in nursing education, most nursing educators have been thoroughly indoctrinated in behavioral theory both during their own educational preparation and in work experiences in schools of nursing. While new goals for education are emerging, it will take years to break away totally from Ralph Tyler's behavioral education model. Skeptics of its value existed long before the curriculum revolution, however. As early as 1975, Styles proclaimed she had:

> *a nagging feeling that when educators, including those of us who are nurses, speak in awesome tones about instructional objectives, we are worshipping at a monotheistic shrine. . . . behavioral objectives will save neither the world nor the nursing profession and, when pursued with singularity, may even retard the full flowering of both (p. 311).*

We proceeded to develop this course by discarding the behavioral objectives and focusing on engaging students in an educational dialogue that would make learning an exciting experience and empower them to become change agents. We dreamed of students who would develop a truly professional level of nursing practice. We needed only to define this professional practice and how to teach it. Our own transformation has led us to appreciate that student empowerment and assisting students to identify the knowledge in their practice is the desired outcome of the course.

THE COURSE DESIGN

Our work in this course at the University of Southern Maine School of Nursing (USMSON) did not arise in isolation as an innovative approach to RN education. Like many schools of nursing during the mid 1980s, USMSON experienced a sharp decline in nursing student enrollments, an increase in adult learners in all nursing courses, and a faculty transition from master's prepared to doctorally prepared. This precipitated an attitude change toward all nursing students and a heightened valuing of the RN student. The previous philosophy of challenging students to prove they possessed knowledge of basic nursing changed to a commitment to acknowledge their prior learning. In response, structural changes occurred. The school initiated an RN to MSN program. It established an articulation agreement with the University of Maine associate degree (AD) program and later added articulation for students graduated from any NLN accredited AD nursing program. Graduates from diploma nursing programs and graduates of AD programs not accredited by the NLN were offered two assessment options. They could sit for the NLN's Adult, Child, and Maternal Nursing Mobility Profile II exams, or they could develop a portfolio.

Innovations in process also occurred. The authors developed a community health practicuum for RNs in which students self-designed their learning experiences. At the same time, we were assigned to teach the five credit RN bridge course. The SON curriculum committee dictated the course's broad content areas. The committee selected content it believed was not covered in most diploma and associate degree programs which included: (a) professional roles and accountability; (b) nursing history, theory, and research; (c) health promotion; (d) family as client; (e) the environment as context; and (f) nursing process. Previously all courses had been taught using what Freire (1970) termed the banking concept. His analysis finds that in this style of teaching, "knowledge is a gift bestowed by those who consider themselves knowledgeable upon those who they consider know nothing. Projecting an absolute ignorance onto others, a characteristic of the ideology of oppression, negates education and knowledge as processes of inquiry" (Freire, 1970, p. 58). This occurred based on USMSON's adherence to the behavioral model which attempts to measure all learning. We focused our efforts on developing the learning experiences. We wanted this RN bridge course to have an innovative process that would promote self-esteem and autonomy, and trusted that with such a broad content outline, the class dialogue would dictate the specific content rather than the reverse of having content dictate process.

STRATEGIES TO PROMOTE DIALOGUE

Silence prevails as any first class begins. McKeachie (1986) suggests that students frequently refrain from talking in class for fear of being embarrassed speaking before strangers who may be critical. Knowing this, we start by giving our own life histories. These narratives speak to our roles as women, mothers, students, nurses, and teachers. This strategy of self-disclosure demonstrates that it will be safe in this class to be vulnerable. After we speak, students receive encouragement to share whatever they want about themselves. Lively dialogue often emerges from this very first class.

The first content introduced for discussion is the USMSON mission, philosophy, and conceptual framework. This content places students in context and begins a dialogue about what they consider the essence of nursing. Other strategies to place students in the framework of their nursing history include reading and discussing Melosh's *The Physician's Hand* (1982) and viewing in class a less than romantic depiction of nursing's history, *Sentimental Women Need Not Apply* (Hott & Garey, 1988). Students dialogue about philosophies of nursing at the beginning of each class until they have identified concepts important to their personal philosophy. Eventually they submit in writing their own philosophy.

Three practical benefits have grown out of this process. Discussions of nursing philosophy assist students to uncover their motivation for returning to school. Secondly, students report most job interviewers pose the question of personal philosophy of nursing. Finally, this dialogue helps students identify the specific knowledge bases they must describe when completing their portfolio. During the discussions of philosophy, connections begin to form between students.

Another assignment involves both process and content. Discussion of the content outline results in students selecting areas in which they will lead the discussion. Some students choose to work in a group while others decide to prepare alone. We suggest areas for students to address, but relinquish our own topics if students request them. Topics are broad. For example, one group may interpret nursing roles as teacher, advocate and collaborator, while another may choose to lead discussion of roles around the issues of codependency, horizontal violence, and oppression. The goal of process dictating content becomes a reality as students initiate dialogue based on their interpretation of the content. This process for promoting autonomy offers flexibility and adapts to the student's ability to perceive complexities in the context of nursing practice.

The evaluation process of these student led classes continues the partnership between student and teacher. Before students even select their topic, they negotiate a process of evaluation. As a group, students determine whether the teacher will act as a peer or have a weighted role in assigning a grade. The discussions include issues of anonymity, peer review, trust, self-assessment, the expected role of the teacher, and positive feedback. Every group has contributed to the grading process but how they have incorporated teacher input has varied widely.

Providing tools of learning can also contribute to student empowerment. During the early part of the course, students receive an orientation to the library, the nursing resource laboratory, the computer laboratory, and the *Publication Manual of the American Psychological Association* (American Psychological Association, 1983). To date, the vast majority of students taking this course have never used a computer for word processing, written a paper following a writer's manual, or accessed computer linked library resources. All of these learning tools assist students to develop written communication skills and self-confidence as learners who can access knowledge. Recently the students have been asked to write a term paper using these tools. They may select any topic of interest to them. Many choose to explore questions that have arisen in their practice. The assignment involves exploring the literature, presenting the information clearly and concisely, and using APA format accurately. In discussions on the assignment, we dialogue about the knowledge they have as practitioners which we hope they will learn to share through the communication method of publication. This assignment arose after students came back and told us that the RN bridge course would be a safe place to learn writing skills, whereas in later courses they felt threatened trying to master them.

The role learning tools and the term paper can play in empowering students became clear when one of us had the following experience with a student who is a caring young nurse working in newborn intensive care.

Janet was an attractive and vivacious young woman. She started work- ing in newborn intensive care (NICU) immediately after graduating from her basic program. When she moved to Maine the previous year, her new employment required her to accept a night shift assignment in NICU. She described becoming possessive of "her babies" because she had so little contact with their families. Her inability to relieve the pain of premature infants following surgery surfaced in discussions in sev- eral classes. She expressed frustration and anger related to interactions with one particular surgeon who did more surgery on preemies than any other doctor. His unwillingness to allow nursing to give these tiny babies pain medication distressed her enormously. You could see her pain as she talked about watching the babies suffer when she did not have access to adequate methods to comfort them. The surgeon, a perfec- tionist, was highly regarded for his knowledge, surgical skill, and genu- ine caring for his patients and their families. Yet he seemed able to ignore the pain of these tiny babies whom he so obviously cared about. She was unable to reconcile these inconsistencies, but she respected him deeply and felt powerless to talk to him about her concerns. How could she address "God"?

At one class, I asked her how other nurses she worked with felt about medicating these babies. I suggested that the term paper assignment might give her the opportunity to examine literature and research the problem. After a couple of weeks, we talked again about her concerns. She had gone to the nursing literature, and the research agreed with her discomfort. She obviously had developed more confidence in the indisputable truth of her knowing that these babies were suffering.

I suggested that it might be time to talk with the surgeon. She knew these babies, and she knew what other nurses believed. She needed to know what he believed. She met with the surgeon and came away empowered. They exchanged research findings, he explained his con- cerns of potentially harming the infants with medication, of depressing their vital functions, and she explained the pain she witnessed and could not ease. In their dialogue, they found a compromise. Both un- derstood that the other wanted the best for these tiny helpless patients.

She told me she believed that learning how to put her personal know-ing as a nurse with the collective knowing of the profession had given her a new way to confront barriers to her practice. The tools of learning had helped to empower her.

OUTCOMES

Student connectedness has been one of the most consistent outcomes of this bridge course. Every class spontaneously decides to share names, addresses, and phone numbers. One class went beyond the usual promise of "we must get together sometime." They have met regularly for two years. The last invitation to join them was to an over-night "girls" party at one of their homes.

Examining their experience of practice in depth also forms a com-mon thread for every class. Students often share that their work places do not provide enough time for this type of dialogue. Students fre-quently observe that listening to nurses from different practice areas helps them identify common strengths and barriers to nursing practice. The dialogue builds self-esteem and empowers them to examine nurs-ing practice critically and develop strategies for change.

A number of students have told us that this course provided a new type of learning experience for them. For the first time, they felt their knowledge was respected, and they were treated as adults. At gradua-tion this year, two students recounted that starting in a course with an adult-learning focus helped give them the courage to continue. Cross (1981), in pulling together theories of adult motivation, learning, and development in her Chain-of-Response (COR) model, notes that each educational encounter affects motivation to engage in another learning situation. The bridge course provides a positive educational experience and encourages students to become life-long learners.

Has the course been successful in promoting dialogue for all stu-dents? Certainly not! Recently a faculty member came to us about a student in her graduate seminar who, she knew, had been in one of our first transition courses. "How did you keep Ellen from monopoliz-ing the discussions," she asked? We had to confess that we never did. We used all our skills; avoiding eye contact, calling on others, even taking her aside. Other students tried to challenge her without success. Yet today, after five years, our colleague reports the same behavior with which we struggled. She does not dialogue, she commands. Verduin and Clark (1991) describe learning as change in attitudes, habits, values, skills or knowledge. Interaction with people, ideas, or objects mediates the process. We cannot be sure that Ellen has experienced these changes.

CONCLUSIONS

Acknowledgment of less-than-perfection in teaching methods and outcomes can encourage an openness to new constructs and unlock new perspectives on learning and students. Discussing how nursing education institutionalized the behavioral model as the only correct method of teaching, Tanner (1990) states that one "aspect of the curriculum revolution is emancipation from singular and narrow views of what constitutes education" (p. 297). Today the concepts of empowerment, equity, caring, and connectedness provide nurse educators with new approaches. Cross (1991) reviews the paradigm shift occurring in all of higher education toward a more emancipatory style of teaching and learning. With this growing acceptance of a new world view, danger exists that the stamp of approval will be conferred on a new "perfect" teaching method. The commonality of all these constructs is respect for the students and the partnership between learner and teacher. "The cycle is one of confirmation—evocation—confirmation" (Belenky et al., 1986, p. 219). The essence of emancipatory teaching comes from the teacher's profound respect for the individual, a collective knowledge of students, and a dedication to assist them in realizing their potential.

REFERENCES

Allen, D. G. (1990). The curriculum revolution: Radical revisioning of nursing education. *Journal of Nursing Education, 29,* 312–316.

American Psychological Association (1983). *Publication manual of the American Psychological Association* (3rd ed.) Washington, DC: author.

Belenky, M. F., Clinchy, B. M., Goldberger, N. R., & Tarule, J. M. (1986). *Women's ways of knowing: The development of self, voice, and mind.* New York: Basic Books.

Benoliel, J. Q. B. (1988). Some reflections on learning and teaching. *Journal of Nursing Education, 27,* 340–341.

Bevis, E. O., & Murray, J. P. (1990). The essence of the curriculum revolution: Emancipatory teaching. *Journal of Nursing Education, 29,* 326–331.

Cross, K. P. (1981). *Adults as learners: Increasing participation and facilitating learning.* San Francisco: Jossey-Bass.

Cross, K. P. (1991, May). Reflections, predictions, and paradigm shifts. *AAHE Bulletin,* 9–12.

de Tornyay, R. (1990). The curriculum revolution. *Journal of Nursing Education, 29,* 292–294.

Diekelmann, N. (1992, June). *Transforming RN education: New approaches to innovation.* Keynote paper presented at the conference, *Transforming RN Education: Dialogue and Debate.* Madison, Wisconsin.

Freire, P. (1970). *Pedagogy of the oppressed.* New York: Herder and Herder.

Hott, L., & Garey, D. (1988). *Sentimental women need not apply: A history of American nursing* [Film]. Los Angeles: Direct Cinema Limited.

Lazzari, M. M. (1991). Feminism, empowerment and field education. *Affilia, 6*(4), 71–87.

Mason, D. J., Backer, B. A., & Georges, C. A. (1991). Toward a feminist model for the political empowerment of nurses. *Image, 23,* 72–76.

McKeachie, W. J. (1986). *Teaching tips: A guidebook for the beginning college teacher.* Lexington, MA: Heath.

Melosh, B. (1982). *The physician's hand: Work culture and conflict in American nursing.* Philadelphia: Temple University Press.

Moccia, P. (1990). No sire, it's a revolution. *Journal of Nursing Education, 29,* 307–311.

Moss, L. (Producer/Director). (1987). *Nursing theory: A circle of knowledge* [Video]. New York: National League for Nursing.

Styles, M. M. (1975). Serendipity and objectivity. *Nursing Outlook, 23,* 311–313.

Tanner, C. A. (1990). Reflections of the curriculum revolution. *Journal of Nursing Education, 29,* 295–299.

Tennant, M. (1991). The psychology of adult teaching and learning. In J. M. Peters, P. Jarvas & Associates (Eds.), *Adult education: Evolution and achievements in a developing field of study* (pp. 191–216). San Francisco: Jossey-Bass.

Verduin, J. R., Jr., & Clark, T. A. (1991). *Distance education: The foundations of effective practice*. San Francisco: Jossey-Bass.

15

When It All Comes Together:
The Elements of a Successful
Clinical Experience

Gerry Chalykoff

INTRODUCTION

My interest in clinical course work experience and its effects on the baccalaureate registered nurse (BN/RN) student started three years ago during my first year as a university teacher. At that time, one of my students was involved in a clinical experience with a community social service agency. This was an experience which called for great autonomy and professional competence within crisis oriented situations. She would be the only RN in the agency. The student wondered how she would ever fulfill the requirements of this experience and hoped that the term would quickly pass. I watched as this student was transformed over that academic year from a somewhat anxious and skeptical student to someone beaming with pride over her accomplishment and her ability to contribute to the agency and to the clients. Her eyes sparkled during class discussions, she laughed more, and she supported other students. I wondered how this change occurred. Was it just a serendipitous event or could I try to have each student achieve this kind of success during their clinical course? I knew that this was a wonderful feeling to have as a teacher and I knew I wanted to feel it more often.

*The author wishes to thank Professor Linda S. Nugent, University of New Brunswick, Saint John Campus for her comments and review of this article.

I began to look for ways to improve my clinical teaching with BN/ RN students. Although I had clinical teaching experience as an instructor in a diploma nursing program and as a staff educator, this was different. The course requires students to nurse an individual, family, or group undergoing a stressful life event or crisis. Students are expected to use Hoff's (1989) crisis paradigm or an appropriate theoretical model to guide intervention. Each student chooses a particular patient or client population of interest and together we approach the most appropriate clinical agency. Students usually practice with one or two agency staff members. In this new situation, I was not in the clinical area with the student, and as well, would never achieve clinical competence in the varied areas of nursing in which students wanted to practice. I began to question what I wanted to achieve in clinical courses and how I could promote student success.

The purpose of this paper is to share concerns, ideas, and questions about clinical experiences in BN/RN programs. In particular, I will discuss the characteristics of a clinical experience which promote student success, and fulfill the educational vision. This will be explored from several perspectives; namely, the goals of clinical instruction for BN/RN students, a review of some of the literature, the findings of a pilot study on BN/RN clinical experiences, and a schematic framework developed to help me in teaching future clinical courses.

CLINICAL EXPERIENCE IN BN/RN EDUCATION

Clinical experiences involving BN/RN students are not regulated by faculty concern about preparing a student who will pass licensing examinations. Since the student is already a registered practitioner, the faculty assumes the student can function adequately in the clinical area. This can give a faculty member the freedom to design and implement unique clinical experiences, yet at the same time, leave one at a loss to describe what is to be accomplished in the clinical area. What are our goals for BN/RN clinical courses? What kinds of clinical experiences are necessary, and what does this mean for the clinical faculty?

Goals of the Clinical Experience

Most faculty would agree that BN/RN students should use research or theoretically based practice in their clinical experiences. Yet, is this expected in clinical experiences and, if so, do students feel their practice has changed for the better?

Results from the RN Baccalaureate Nursing Data Project by the Association of American Colleges of Nursing (cited in Redman & Cassells, 1990) indicated that many BN/RN students did not engage in clinical practice as part of acquiring their bachelor's degree. When asked questions related to professional and personal growth since entering the program, most students reported minimal improvement in clinical judgment and decision making ability. However, students did perceive an increase in skill level in community health, gerontology, and infectious/communicable disease care.

When asked about the adequacy of the BN program components, most students reported the relevance of clinical practice coursework as only slightly adequate. Although students reported an increased knowledge of nursing theories/models, little applicability of this content in their post-graduation practice was perceived. Does this indicate some "anti-theory" bias in the workplace or rather, some questions about the usefulness of theories/models in actual practice? The Data Project authors have called for a more in-depth study of the nature of clinical experiences for RN students, as well as a further exploration of lack of clinical application of models and its implication for professional studies.

Types of Clinical Experiences

Data from the aforementioned American study indicated that approximately 90 percent of BN/RN programs that include clinical coursework require some practice in the area of community health and family health nursing. Opportunities for independent clinical study were less frequently reported. In Canada, the clinical course requirements for BN/RN students are quite similar. A perusal of Canadian university calendars suggested that BN/RN students are required to take an average of four term courses of clinical practice during their programs. Nearly all programs required some clinical experience in family and community health nursing. Most programs also required some additional practice with specific client groups such as the older adult, ill adult, or child. About half the programs contained an upper-level course in which students focused on the application of a nursing theory, or the development of advanced professional skills in a practice area of their choice. A few programs offered the student specialized or innovative practicums such as critical analysis of a nursing field, development of a nursing contract with a high risk group, or implementing a quality assurance or health education project. The wide array of clinical courses available to BN/RN students indicates individuality in university curricular requirements. It also leaves one to question the type of experiences, besides those in family and community health, that should be a part of BN/RN education.

Adapting to the Needs of the BN/RN Student

The "typical" BN/RN student is a working parent with many professional and personal commitments. In addition, particularly in Canada, the student may live many miles from a university campus and be unable to travel the long distance for study. RNs have told us they want baccalaureate education that is flexible and geared to the special needs of adult learners (Pym, 1992). This situation has inspired many nursing educators to develop nontraditional, and often ingenious course delivery methods. RNs can now take baccalaureate courses through audio or videoteleconference and correspondence. This may mean that the faculty member has even less direct contact with the student in the clinical area and would need to rely on a number of different strategies such as preceptorship or learning contracts to provide clinical learning opportunities. The chance for a student to see the faculty member as a direct care provider "role model" during the clinical experience has become more unattainable and perhaps impractical and unnecessary for clinical learning.

These changes raise many questions including: how can we as clinical educators respond to these particular teaching challenges; what kinds of new clinical teaching skills must we develop to help students achieve success in nontraditional courses; and should some of our views about what constitutes an acceptable clinical experience be challenged?

LITERATURE REVIEW

The literature addressing clinical experiences of BN/RN students is fairly limited. Most authors focus on the educator's role and student opinion of such; the remainder look at clinical decision-making, developing course content, and designing new experiences. I have chosen to present a brief synopsis of some works which examined clinical teaching and innovative clinical teaching practices, as these speak to the major concerns of this paper.

Effective Clinical Teaching

Much of the literature on effective clinical teaching suggests the importance of valuing the student as a person during the experience. Farley (1990) calls clinical teaching a shared adventure in which the nurse educator coaches students to be the best they can be. Coaching is described as an art, involving a partnership with the student which empowers him or her to exceed previous levels of clinical expertise. Allen (1990) calls on nurse educators to reconceptionalize their view of the student as a person. This would mean seeing the student as a person with a rich history and a unique professional future, no longer simply "raw material" to be shaped into our images. In a review of literature on effective clinical behaviors of nursing faculty, Zimmerman and Waltman (1986) found that effective clinical teaching could not be described in one or two behaviors but in a collection of behaviors, which included availability to students, professional competence, interpersonal relations, teaching and evaluation practices, and personal characteristics.

In a study which explored the practice of nurse educators judged to be expert clinical teachers by their dean or chairperson, Hedin (1989) found that these nurse educators were directed by specific aims or goals. These aims or goals fell into the broad categories of providing good patient care, connecting/fitting the student to the experience, and enabling the students to develop questioning and judgment skills. In describing their clinical teaching, six general categories of faculty attributes or behaviors emerged from the data. These attributes were: a high level of self knowledge, sharing themselves as human beings, reflectiveness on teaching and clinical practice, characteristics such as a sense of humor and empathy, an attitude of respect for the learners, and confidence in their own clinical expertise.

A meta-analysis of the research literature on clinical teaching by Pugh (1986) revealed that research in this area was still in its infancy and limited in generalizability by sampling and methodological issues. To facilitate data review, studies were grouped into three broad categories: opinions of students, opinions of students and faculty, and investigations analyzing the process of clinical teaching. Much of the research was found to focus on the clinical behaviors of nurse educators. The desirable teacher behaviors which emerged from the review included acceptance of the student as a person, provision of fair feedback, and effective modeling of both the teacher and nurse roles by the nurse educator. However, in a 1980 study by Pugh which was included in the review, BN/RN students consistently ascribed less importance to the nurse educator's demonstrating how to function as a nurse than did basic BN students.

Clinical Experiences Designed for the BN/RN Student

To answer the question, what constitutes a good clinical experience, Mundt (1990) described three broad criteria: social, curricular, and instructional. First, a good experience makes a social statement about the nature of the profession's relationship to those it serves; whereby the student is encouraged to become an active contributor to social policy development and to come away with an understanding of his or her responsibilities for the protection of clients in the health care system. Secondly, a good clinical experience is philosophically consistent with the aims of the curriculum and provides the student with an understanding of how the experience fits into the curricular scheme and where they are expected to go from here. Lastly, a good clinical experience should be well matched to the learning needs of the student and the instructional aims of the particular course. The outcome of the effective integration of these criteria is a student who can articulate the experiences they have had, their level of proficiency and an action plan for continued learning (p. 79).

Several nurse educators have attempted to facilitate clinical learning for the BN/RN student by designing strategies which promote individualized achievement and build upon student experience. Ryan (1985) described how the use of learning contracts, personalized objectives, student profiles, and flexible clinical time schedules promoted a high degree of both student and faculty satisfaction with a medical-surgical rotation. The opportunity to apply change theory in the clinical setting, as part of a practicum to learn planned change, was found to be particularly beneficial by Olson and Cragg (1988). The practicum, carried out in a variety of clinical areas, gave students the chance to refine their leadership skills and recognize their strengths and weaknesses as change agents. Students reported feeling satisfied that they had made a contribution to the functioning of a nursing unit and more confident in their ability to carry out planned change projects in the future.

Peterson and Dyck (1986) used general systems theory to explore how nurse educators could facilitate BN/RN student practice during a self directed learning clinical experience. The authors found that specific educator activities before and during the clinical experience fostered equilibrium between the healthcare agency and nursing college subsystems. In preparation for the clinical experience phase, activities such as providing healthcare agency staff with adequate information about learning contracts as a teaching strategy, encouraging students to think realistically about objectives, and helping the student to develop objectives which were mutually beneficial seemed to increase the support the student received from the agency. During the actual clinical practicum, the role of the nurse educator became that of consultant. Students were encouraged to anticipate and solve problems using each other as valuable resources. According to the authors, this proactive and cooperative approach decreased the sense of competition between students and provided them with life skills applicable to many situations.

INSIGHTS FROM A PILOT STUDY

As part of end of term clinical evaluation discussions of the crisis course, I asked a small sample (n = 5, for each category) of students, agency staff, and fellow nurse educators to describe what they felt to be a successful clinical experience and what factors contributed to success. The course was graded as Pass or Fail (Credit/Noncredit). A synopsis of the salient points of these discussions follows.

Student Perceptions

Students described what they felt was a successful clinical experience, how they judged whether their experience was successful or not, and what factors they felt contributed to the success of the experience. These perceptions have been grouped into three categories: perceptions about themselves, influencing factors of the course and nurse educator, and influencing factors of the clinical agency.

Perceptions about Self.   Generally students felt that their clinical experience was a success if they achieved one or more of the following: they had put into practice what they had learned, developed confidence as a nurse, acquired an in-depth knowledge of some particular aspect of nursing, gave something important to the clinical agency, and/or improved their ability to function in their workplace role. Their feelings of accomplishment were shared in terms which were more self evaluative than reflective of the opinions of others. Consistently, the students stated that they believed they would succeed or that they viewed the experience as a challenge and liked challenges. All expected some negatives about the experience and visualized it as something that would not always go smoothly. They prepared for the experience by reading and expected to put much energy into it.

Course/Nurse Educator Factors.   All students verbalized the importance of choice in clinical setting. They found the option to practice in their area of interest as the main reason for clinical success. The option to self schedule clinical time was also seen as crucial to an effective experience. One student felt strongly that the number of clinical hours should be set by the students, not mandated by the program requirements. All felt having clear learning objectives or a mapped out plan which could be modified was helpful.

Feelings on the use of the Pass/Fail (Credit/Noncredit) grading system were mixed. Some felt this system to be quite helpful in taking the competitive edge and pressure off the experience. Others felt that they were "being robbed" of the chance to earn a good grade. They expressed frustration at not having their clinical strengths and time commitments formally recognized.

Students felt that the nurse educator contributed to their success by providing reassurance that they were doing the right thing, placing few limitations on them, and being available for questions and discussion of problems. Students seemed to see the nurse educator as a consultant.

Agency/Clinical Factors.   Students related that either the agency had a positive image of nurses or had given them the feeling that what they were doing would be of benefit to the agency. Most said that the agency had a fairly clear idea about what they could or could not do. One student expressed a feeling of complete freedom in the clinical agency. She felt trusted and supported in carrying out her project.

Healthcare Agency Perceptions

Although clinical personnel had completed short evaluations of student performance many were surprised when asked to describe what they felt to be a successful clinical experience. Their responses indicated that such discussions probably should have occurred much earlier. I found that adding this question to our regular "end of the year" discussion seemed to give agency personnel the chance to describe to me what they were really all about and what they wanted to achieve. Perceptions from the clinical agency personnel fell into the categories of what they saw as a successful student experience and what factors about their facility they felt contributed to student success.

The Successful Student.   Agency staff described a successful student in terms of behaviors related to the student his/herself, the student inter-actions within the agency, and the reactions of clients and their fami-lies to the student. They could feel a sense of excitement in the stu-dent. The students seemed to develop a sense of his/her own power over the term. They saw changes in perceptions, where the student questioned some preconceived judgments he or she had come with into the clinical experience. The successful student shared discoveries, participated in agency activities, and felt comfortable over time to chal-lenge or disagree with some staff decisions or policies. This student seemed to understand the experience of the client and the nurse's role in the agency. One unit manager found that she received consistently positive feedback about the student from client, family, and unit staff. This was important for her in evaluating how a student was doing. Interviewed staff in all the agencies felt strongly that the successful student was one who left with accurate judgments about the agency's values and what the staff were trying to accomplish. When a student left with a negative view of an agency, it was quite distressing, in that the student probably never had the chance to really work through his or her perceptions with the staff.

How the Agency Contributed to the Student's Success.   Most staff felt that the student benefitted from an organizational philosophy which valued personal opinions and nurses in general. Having a student was seen as a mutually beneficial and enjoyable experience. Agency per-sonnel looked for potential in the student and were willing to nurture the student throughout the experience. Each agency also allowed the student as much flexibility as possible in scheduling clinical time.

Perceptions of Nurse Educators

The nurse educators interviewed expressed ideas about what they felt constituted a successful clinical experience and what factors or behav-iors they used to evaluate an experience as such. Nurse educators also shared situations in which their perception and that of the student dif-fered about whether the experience was a success or not. Lastly, nurse educators identified which of their teaching behaviors seemed to contribute to success, and which behaviors they would change or add in future clinical courses.

Perception of a Successful Experience.   Nurse educators were very general in their descriptions of a ·successful clinical experience. Besides having met the desired learning objectives, successful students were described as transformed in thinking or being. Some transformations were manifested by distinct changes in student behaviors, while others were identified in simple student statements such as they had learned something about themselves. Most successful students were described as assertive, yet nonthreatening to the clinical agency. They were interested in understanding the client's experience and approached the agency staff in a nonjudgmental manner. The clinical experience became a process for students, something more than just putting in time. Students could control their time in the clinical area and did not appear pressured to fit into a rigid schedule.

Less than successful clinical experiences were described as ones in which the student's "heart really wasn't in it" or that the student "just didn't seem to have the time or the energy for the experience."

Teaching Strategies.   Various successful teaching strategies were mentioned. All educators emphasized the importance of giving students choices in clinical areas, allowing as much flexibility as possible in scheduling clinical time, continuing to give students the option to practice in their workplace, and providing consistent positive feedback. Behaviors which faculty would add or develop for next year included: challenging students with more probing questions, starting and stopping clinical discussion groups on time, and being more particular about pulling the common theoretical threads through the experiences.

There was a sense of frustration with how to help students who could not identify personal learning objectives. Often, it seemed these students felt a sense of inadequacy when they compared themselves to their peers. Although the individual nature of the experience was stressed, these students felt a competitive pressure to identify some extraordinary learning objectives.

Common Themes

Several common themes emerged from the interviews.

Clinical Experience as a Shared Process.   Students, agency staff, and nursing educators viewed a successful clinical experience as process.

This process included the development of confidence or comfort by the student with a specialized body of knowledge, and a sharing of that knowledge. The process was reinforced by agency staff and a clinical educator who valued the opinions and abilities of the student. The feeling of success was usually a shared one.

Flexibility and Choice.   Successful clinical experiences were marked by student choice in an area of practice and flexibility in scheduling clinical time. Flexibility in time scheduling gave the student more control in fitting the experience into a multitude of work, school, and family demands. Choice in clinical practice area seemed to promote a sense of usefulness, purpose, and enthusiasm in the clinical experience.

Congruency in Concept of Roles and Goals.   It was important that student, agency staff, and nurse educator were congruent in their concept of what the role of the student/nurse was in the agency, as well as what the roles of the nurse educator and agency staff were in helping the student to develop this role. In addition, all were working toward a common or complementary goal. Student and nurse educator were aware of the agency's special aims or visions.

IMPLICATIONS FOR CLINICAL TEACHING

We need to examine and continue to dialogue about what we want to achieve in the clinical education of BN/RN students. This is a need at the national educational and professional levels, as well as at the individual university or program level. We need to explore what elements are critical in clinical practice at the baccalaureate level and how this differs from clinical practice at the diploma or community college level. We need to ensure that students have an understanding of these goals and components, so that as Mundt (1990) so well articulated, they can describe where they have been and where they are headed.

In an attempt to make the faculty facilitator role more deliberate, I have developed a schematic framework which can be used in teaching clinical courses. This framework has been developed using results from the pilot study, literature review, and personal experience. The framework outlines a process in which the nurse educator, clinical agency staff, and student combine efforts to achieve a common goal, and ultimately a successful clinical experience. Each partner is aware of what the other brings to the experience, and of the role each one plays.

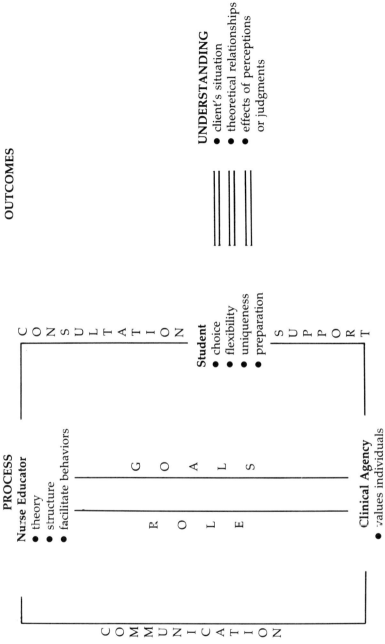

Figure 15.1 Facilitating a successful clinical experience.

Framework to Help Facilitate a Successful Clinical Experience

As depicted in the diagram, the successful clinical experience is a process whereby student, agency staff, and nurse educator come prepared to embark on a *shared* endeavor. The nurse educator comes into the situation with knowledge of the theoretical and structural components of the experience, as well as an understanding of the unique abilities of the student and goals of the clinical agency. The student comes to the experience with an accurate perception of his or her individual strengths, control and choice in the clinical setting, and some preparatory study about the client population. The staff in the clinical agency values the student's input and sees the process as a mutually beneficial one. All parties are knowledgeable of the roles one another will play.

During the experience, students receive adequate support from agency staff and consultative assistance from the nurse educator. The expected outcomes reveal students who have a greater understanding of their client's situation, the theoretical bases for nursing actions, and the effects of their preconceived perceptions and judgments.

REFERENCES

Allen, D. G. (1990). Critical social theory and nursing education. *Curriculum revolution: Redefining the student-teacher relationship* (pp. 67–86). New York: National League for Nursing Press.

Farley, V. M. (1990). Clinical teaching: A shared adventure. In *Curriculum revolution: Redefining the student-teacher relationship* (pp. 87–93). New York: National League for Nursing Press.

Hedin, B. A. (1989). Expert clinical teaching. In *Curriculum revolution: Reconceptualizing nursing education* (pp. 71–89). New York: National League for Nursing Press.

Hoff, L. A. (1989). *People in crisis* (3rd ed.). Don Mills, ONT: Addison-Wesley.

Mundt, M. H. (1990). Organizing clinical learning experiences in the baccalaureate nursing curriculum. In N. Chaska (ed.), *The nursing profession turning points* (pp. 77–83)). Toronto, ONT: C. V. Mosby.

Olson, J. K., & Craig, C. E. (1988). Learning planned change: A practicum for RN students. *Journal of Nursing Education, 27,* 178–179.

Peterson, J. M., & Dyck, S. (1986). Systems theory facilitates student practice in self-directed learning courses. *Nurse Educator, 11*(5), 12–15.

Pugh, E. J. (1986). Research on clinical teaching. In W. L. Holzemer (ed.), *Review of research in nursing education. Volume I* (pp. 73–92). New York: National League for Nursing Press.

Pym, F. R. (1992). Women and distance education: A nursing perspective. *Journal of Advanced Nursing, 17*, 383–389.

Redman, B. K., & Cassells, J. M. (Eds.) (1990). *Educating RNs for the baccalaureate: Programs and issues.* New York: Springer Publishing Company.

Ryan, M. C. (1985). Assimilating the learning needs of RN students into the clinical practicum. *The Journal of Nursing Education, 24*, 128–130.

Zimmerman, L., & Waltman, N. (1986). Effective clinical behaviours of faculty: A review of the literature. *Nurse Educator, 11*(1), 31–34.

16

A Profile of Preceptorships in Baccalaureate Degree Nursing Programs for Registered Nurses

Catherine O. Rosenlieb

INTRODUCTION AND LITERATURE REVIEW

The background of this study was the desire of the nursing faculty at a central western Pennsylvania university to obtain information about preceptorships for RN students with the possibility of adding preceptorships to clinical nursing courses. This descriptive study was conducted to describe and report a profile of preceptorships in RN baccalaureate programs.

In order to address the learning needs of the RN student population, it is incumbent upon nursing faculty to offer challenging clinical nursing opportunities that provide diverse learning experiences. Faculty must capture the moment and capitalize on the RN student's heightened motivation to learn new knowledge and skills. The RN student must be given choices—choices in courses and choices in clinical practica.

Preceptorships provide opportunities for choices. Corrigan (1992) concurs that a preceptorship program is a study/practice experience designed to offer a flexible, specialized, and independent learning opportunity for RN students. Corrigan asserts that preceptorships hold special advantages for students as they gain the opportunity to work with a clinically expert, active nurse. Kelly (1992) agrees that preceptorships with a staff nurse tend to enhance the student's learning.

Corrigan (1992) reviewed five university nursing preceptorships, all in rural settings, four in western states and one in an eastern state. She concluded that formal preceptorship programs take many shapes and that the five reported preceptorships provide valuable models to emulate.

Clayton, Broome, and Ellis (1989) examined the professional socialization behaviors of two groups of senior nursing students—one assigned to staff nurse preceptors and the other assigned to faculty. The researchers hypothesized that the students who practiced under the tutelage of a nurse preceptor would report significantly different professional socialization behaviors than the students with faculty. Completing Schwerian's Six-Dimension Scale of Nurse Performance as a pretest/posttest instrument, the preceptored group scored higher on socialization both immediately after the experience and six months after graduation than the group assigned to faculty. Lawless (1989) commented that preceptor programs, such as described in the above study, offer a mechanism for enhancing the transition of novice nurses into independent professionals.

Henry and Ensunsa (1991) critically reviewed 52 nursing journal articles about preceptors and preceptorships in nursing service and education. The articles spanned the years from 1975 to 1990. One of the major findings was that of belief in the value of preceptors. Additionally, their report calls for research in both nursing service and education. For nursing service they suggest research on patient outcomes as the measure of preceptorships' effectiveness. For nursing education they recommend studies of measurable changes in the RN learners' knowledge, skills, and behavioral performance.

Sheetz (1989), claiming that clinical competence is germane to professional nursing practice, contrasted clinical competencies of baccalaureate students who participated in a summer preceptorship (N = 36) to those who worked as nursing assistants (N = 36) in noninstructional clinical settings. Students in the preceptored group achieved greater increases in clinical competencies than those who worked as nursing assistants. Both groups, however, perceived their summer work as valuable and reported an increased level of self confidence in a nursing role. Laschinger and MacMaster's (1992) exploratory study suggested that their students' preceptorship experience had a significant impact on the development of senior students' adaptive competencies.

Andersen (1991) described the learning outcomes of students who participated in a senior preceptorship course. She also related how a preceptor used storytelling measures, sharing her own blunders in performing skills when she was a new graduate. Storytelling was effective in decreasing feelings of inadequacy in a student who was able to see that the preceptor had not long ago been a bit clumsy in performing her clinical skills.

Within the preceptorship literature there are claims that preceptorship programs benefit everyone (Heinecke & Martin, 1991); that preceptorships are good vehicles for recruitment, retention, stress reduction, and acculturation into the world of work (Turkoski, 1987; Woodtli, Hazzard, & Rusch, 1987) and that preceptorships can enhance collaboration and repair the rift between nursing service and education (Borland, Bone, Harlow, Parker, & Platon, 1991; Corrigan, 1992; Davis & Barham, 1989; Dunnum & Bailey, 1991; Lewis, 1990; Oermann & Navin, 1991; Rosenlieb, 1986).

The value of preceptorship programs has been widely acknowledged but, according to Lewis (1990), there are disadvantages for the institution and staff. Her article identifies several problems with preceptor programs and offers ten suggestions for preventing and/or solving problems.

Davis and Barham (1989) recommended getting the most from preceptorship programs. They proposed that nursing faculty and agency staff can maximize resources by collaborating on program design from the ground up.

Today, preceptorships are commonplace in nurse education programs, new graduate orientation programs (Henry & Ensunsa, 1991), and for seasoned nurses transferring to unfamiliar nursing units within their current health care institution. More broadly, the use of clinical nursing preceptorships is viewed as a major factor in the unification of nursing education and nursing service. Dolan (1984) asserted that preceptors project a sense of colleagueship with the experienced nurse, discuss different approaches to clinical practice, explore the context of a complex clinical situation, and trade paradigm cases. In so doing, preceptorships build bridges between education and practice.

The review of the literature, however, failed to produce any recent descriptive, empirical studies focused directly on the utilization and characteristics of clinical nursing preceptorships in RN programs. A study of this topic thus was timely and stimulated interest in the use of clinical nursing preceptorships in RN programs. The purpose of this study was to determine the utilization and characteristics of preceptorships in baccalaureate nursing programs for registered nurses. The study was organized around eight major research questions with multiple subquestions.

METHODOLOGY

This descriptive study used a mailed, self-administered questionnaire as the survey instrument for gathering data. The questionnaire, created by the researcher, consisted of 16 pages with 40 closed and open-ended items. The survey instrument, designed to address the research questions, provided data regarding the sample of RN programs and their faculty liaisons.

The population for this study consisted of 147 RN programs listed in the NLN publication, *State Approved Schools of Nursing–1990*. At the end of the initial data collection phase, the overall usable return rate was 131, of which 80 programs offered preceptorships and 51 did not. The 80 programs became the sample for this study. In the second phase of the survey, the faculty liaison's participation rate was 87.5 percent and the adjusted sample became 70 RN programs.

FINDINGS AND DISCUSSION

Characteristics of Preceptorship Programs

Ninety percent of the RN programs offering preceptorships were located in universities or liberal arts colleges; forty-seven percent were situated in public institutions. Fifty-one percent were located in private institutions of which 72 percent were religious and 28 percent were secular schools.

The majority (78 percent) of the RN programs offering preceptorships were two academic years or less in length. Although preceptorships have been included in RN programs for almost 20 years, the great majority (81 percent) of the preceptorships in RN programs were ten years old or less. The mean age of the RN preceptorships was 8.6 years.

Nearly 75 percent of the programs allotted up to ten semester hours to the preceptorships. The majority of the programs, however, assigned up to five semester hours (N = 45, 48 percent) to their preceptorships. The low number of semester hours apportioned to the preceptorships suggest that they are but one type of clinical nursing experience in RN programs.

Fifty-four percent (N = 38) of the RN programs allotted up to 25 percent of their clinical courses to preceptorships. Twenty-five percent distributed 51 to 100 percent of their clinical courses to preceptorships.

Fifty-two percent of the RN programs used 11 or more service agencies for their preceptorships. The mean was 17.5 service agencies.

Two-thirds of the respondents to this study reported intensive care and emergency care as the top choices of hospital clinical units. The remaining preferred clinical units were geriatric, medical-surgical, maternal-infant care, and psychiatric-mental health units.

It can be said the appeal of intensive/critical care nursing to RN students is the challenge of high risk patients and high technology command. The accessibility of intensive care units and emergency care departments can also account for the high usage of these clinical settings. The American Association of Colleges of Nursing (AACN, 1988) study supports this conclusion.

Home health agencies, community/public health agencies, school nursing, occupational health, and hospice care were the most accessible and the most frequently selected community settings used for the RN preceptorships. Two-thirds of the 70 RN programs in this study chose home health as their favored community agency. The data in this study reflected a growing interest in home health.

Responsibilities for Planning and Conducting a Preceptorship— Student, Preceptor, and Nursing Faculty Member

In the majority of the RN programs (N = 41, 59 percent), preceptors were selected jointly by the RN BSN student, faculty liaison, and service agency personnel. Collaboratively selecting preceptors with input from the faculty liaison, students, and clinical agency personnel should create a "good fit" learning environment. Input from all participants is an opportunity to consider needs and personal preferences. However, students are not always guaranteed specific placements. The final decision must depend on the educational goals to be achieved by the student and the identification of appropriate staff nurse preceptors (Waters, Limon, & Spencer, 1983). As a recommendation, the final activity in pairing of student and preceptor should be their interviewing each other for compatibility, as nurse managers interview new employees and vice versa. The sharing of observations and expectations should initiate good interpersonal relations, so critical to the success of the preceptorship. Corrigan (1992) asserted that preceptorships are founded on a collaborative independent relationship between the preceptor, student, and nursing faculty member. It is through this collaboration that many benefits are realized.

The RN student was responsible for coordinating his/her schedule with the preceptor's schedule in the majority of programs (58 percent). Eighty-three percent of the time the RN student's and the preceptor's schedules matched. The majority (53 percent) of the schedules were steady day time; 12 percent of the schedules were steady evening. All other varieties of shifts and weekends were less than 10 percent each.

Synchronizing the RN student's schedule with the preceptor's was the student's responsibility as reported by the majority of respondents (58 percent). Communication between student and preceptor must be direct in order to save time and allay conflict and confusion. Waters et al. (1983) stressed, "The fate of any joint endeavor rests on the quality of communication between partners" (p. 20). Therefore, scheduling by the partners themselves is essential to preceptorships.

An overwhelming 90 percent of the responses noted the ratio of preceptor to student was one-to-one, which is consistent with the literature on this topic. Henry and Ensunsa (1991) claim the most distinguishing characteristic of preceptor programs is the one-to-one relationship of preceptor and preceptee. Lewis (1990) suggested the one-to-one ratio of novice to expert commonly found in preceptor programs has obvious advantages for the RN student. Moreover, the one-to-one ratio allows the bond between the partners to develop and provides more time for the preceptor to teach and supervise the student. As the student's learning increases, less attention is taken away from the patient/client, the primary focus of the preceptor.

There are times when the preceptor cannot be present to the preceptee. Forty-seven percent of the programs indicated the student practices only when the preceptor is present and 24 percent indicated a substitute preceptor oversees the RN student. Cantwell, Kahn, Lacey, and McLaughlin (1989) related the practice of substituting another preceptor on the assigned preceptor's days off, or when he or she was reassigned to another clinical unit. Lewis (1990) said in certain circumstances the student should be sent home when the preceptor is not available to the student. Optimally the preceptor-preceptee dyad should keep the same schedule including shift rotations and days off (Cantwell et al., 1989; Greipp, 1989; Lewis, 1990).

An important factor to consider in a preceptorship program is the amount and variety of clinical experience students will be exposed to in preceptored assignments (Farnkopf, 1983). The quality of the experiences depends upon multiple variables—the number of students to accommodate, number of available skilled preceptors, variety of clinical nursing units, seasonal census cycles, illness patterns, competition with other nursing programs, students' goals for the experience, and the locus of clinical settings—rural, small communities, and urban. It is well known that sufficient time and significant clinical exposure are essential to meaningful preceptorship experiences (Rosenlieb, 1992).

Responsibilities of the Academic Institution and the Nursing Service Agency in Relation to the Preceptorships

Support for Preceptorships.   Obtaining administrative support is necessary when asking nursing service agencies to commit time, facilities, and personnel to preceptorship programs (Lewis, 1990; Radziewicz, Houk, & Moore, 1992). In this research the majority (51 percent) of responses indicated the highest level (service agency) nurse administrator as the person authorized to approve clinical preceptorships. This finding is similar to the Ohlone project (Waters et al., 1983), in which the highest level hospital nurse administrators were contacted early in the planning period for acceptance and approval of the project. When Radziewicz et al. (1992) elected to change a preceptorship to an elective perioperative course for nurses, they had to present it to their administrators. They invested thought and time into planning, preparation, and presentations of the proposal to ensure administrative support.

Similar to Corrigan (1992), this research found the use of staff nurse preceptors to supervise students fell within the scope of existing contractual agreements between the college and the hospitals in 57 percent of cases. The use of staff nurse preceptors was seen simply as an extension of general practice in which students were placed under the direction of staff nurses. Nonetheless, new contracts may be necessary for the preceptorship program, according to Davis & Barham (1989), because preexisting contracts for student education in a particular practice setting may not provide legal coverage for the altered student-faculty-staff arrangements of some preceptorship experiences. They recommended that this issue should be explored with legal counsel and risk management officials in both settings.

Two-thirds of the academic institutions demonstrated their support of preceptorships in giving faculty liaisons the same number of credits as they do with traditional courses. The faculty liaisons, the fulcrums of the preceptorships, reported spending enormous amounts of time and energy coordinating their preceptorship programs. Their workload was redistributed and far exceeded the expectations of classroom teaching. Preceptorships command the three "Cs"—commitment, coordination, and cooperation. For this the faculty liaisons must be appropriately compensated. The compensation is giving full credit toward teaching load for full service to the academic institution.

Training Sessions for Preceptors.   Sixteen percent (N = 11) of the respondents to this study reported the use of training sessions for preceptor preparation. Preceptor training sessions reported in this study were less than half a day in length. In the literature the most frequently cited length was two days (Lachat, Zerbe, & Scott, 1992; Modic & Bowman, 1989; Young, Theriault, & Collins, 1989).

The general purpose of preceptors' seminars is to meet the needs of faculty liaisons and preceptors. The seminars save time and energy for faculty liaisons because a group can be oriented to the preceptorship and its expectations in a few hours. One-to-one orientations are inefficient regarding time and travel to clinical sites (Schubert, 1983). To conduct a workshop or seminar for preceptors in less than half a day provides little time for the presentation of topics. However, the preceptors' time is limited and their being absent from the clinical setting is costly to the employer.

Nonclinical Activities.   About one-half of the non-clinical activities used by the RN programs were: (a) journals, logs, and diaries written by students (86 percent); (b) faculty liaison meetings held separately with students and with preceptors (67 percent); and (c) peer group meetings for RN students (67 percent). These are informal ways of conducting formative evaluation of the preceptorships and provide useful feedback to the faculty and nursing service. Writing in journals, logs, and diaries gives the students opportunities to share with others as well as to reflect and process their experiences.

The faculty liaisons reported that their role relationships with preceptors were to serve as educational resources, to identify appropriate learning experiences for the student, and to assist preceptors in their role transition. These role relationships reflected ordinary but necessary activities to support the preceptors, particularly new preceptors.

Peer group meetings, rather than individual meetings, "are opportunities to create a natural conversational setting for storytelling and to encourage participants to talk with each other as participants in natural practical discourse about particular clinical situations" (Benner, Tanner, & Chesla, 1992, p. 15).

Criteria for Selection of Preceptors

The majority (53 percent) of the preceptors required a baccalaureate or higher degree, although 19 percent of the respondents indicated that preceptors with baccalaureate degrees were not always available. The responses to Spears' (1985) study of preceptorships in generic baccalaureate nursing programs revealed that 70 percent of the respondents reported that they preferred/required baccalaureate preparation for preceptors. Length of clinical experience may be seen as an alternative to the BSN, as one's clinical world "is shaped by learning from experience" (Benner, Tanner, & Chesla, 1992, p. 27).

In about 40 percent of the RN programs, no specific number of years of full time clinical nursing were required for the experienced nurse to be a preceptor. Slightly less than 20 percent of the programs required two years of full time experience. The survey of nursing journals by Henry and Ensunsa (1991) revealed that the prerequisite amount of experience ranged from six months to two years.

In this research two methods most frequently used to select preceptors were personal interviews and supervisors' letters of recommendations (38 percent). The prominent write-in responses mentioned that faculty recommend preceptors and students request preferred preceptors (29 percent). This study did not discern the reasons for the difference in formality of methods used for selecting preceptors. A small number of respondents (N = 4) indicated that selected service agencies have built into their career ladder criteria that staff nurses become preceptors in order to achieve career advancement.

Rewards and Recognition for Preceptors

The major form of recognition/reward (29 percent) given by the clinical agencies to the preceptors were letters of commendation placed in the preceptor's personnel file. The academic institution used the same form of commendation, except the letters (60 percent) were sent to the preceptor and to the preceptor's supervisor. In Spears' (1985) study, the major (46 percent) self-recognition/reward given by the generic baccalaureate programs were letters and certificates of appreciation. Writing a personal letter of appreciation is a modicum of gratuity for the services delivered by the preceptors. It is understandable, then, for preceptors to dropout or stopout from preceptorship programs. Lack of reward and inadequate preparation for the role have been cited as potential causes for disenchantment with the preceptor role. Greipp (1989) reported that considering the nationwide nursing shortage, it would seem that nursing preceptors are at high risk of burnout from overuse, abuse, and devaluation of the role, to the point where they could view being preceptors as a burden.

Corrigan (1992) asserted that the most important function of the faculty member is facilitation. Agency personnel are willing to cooperate only as long as they experience faculty support in their preceptor role and easy access to faculty consultation and back-up. Greipp (1989) and Lewis (1990) suggested innovative rewards for preceptors and Alspach (1987) proposed a "Preceptor's Bill of Rights" in response to the belief that preceptors have rights as well as responsibilities.

In return for providing preceptors for nursing education programs, more than two-thirds of the clinical agencies required nothing of the academic institution. The RN students, however, do provide uncompensated patient care, and the academic institutions offer selected academic services (e.g., library and media resources, and sometimes a free annual attendance at a continuing education seminar, conference, or workshop).

Evaluation Procedures

The majority of responses (50 percent) indicated the student, the preceptor, and the faculty liaison all participate in evaluating the student's performance. The three participants had input into the evaluation process but the faculty liaison's assessment carried the most weight. Slightly less than twenty percent of the respondents reported only the faculty liaison evaluated the student.

The most frequently used evaluation strategies utilized by the participants differed according to their specific roles. The students were required to write journals, diaries, or logs to record and react to the experience. The subjective writing of narratives of daily or weekly experiences gave pause for reflection and internalization of events. The preceptors completed objective questionnaires which were focused on the preceptorship in general and required less time than subjective evaluations. The faculty liaisons' method of evaluating the preceptorships were small group conferences in which evaluation information was gathered with input from students and preceptors.

One-to-one conferences held between the student and faculty liaison allowed time to share observations, concerns, and feelings toward the preceptorship experience. One-to-one conferences between student and preceptor were times to plan, share feelings, and assess student progress. Faculty liaison and preceptor conferences were important times to share observations of the student's progress and discuss ways to improve his/her performance should this be a concern.

Corrigan (1992) described the evaluation process of a rural registered nurse preceptorship in northern Arizona. Informal evaluation took the form of dialogue between faculty, students, and preceptors. A written log was submitted weekly by the student to the community health faculty. The dialogue gives pause for reflection and storytelling and the evaluation gives insight to needs for improvement. This is also an opportunity to share the positive occurrences. Formal evaluation of the participants took place as the preceptorship experience came to a close. The evaluation processes described by Corrigan (1992) reflect those of this research—multiple strategies for evaluating the participants.

Benefits and Limits

Learning is the goal of preceptorships. This research found learning to be the most frequently cited benefit of preceptorships. This research also suggests that students gain quality learning experiences with individualized attention from preceptors who are active practitioners as well as role models. Quality was a concept that appeared in 90 percent of the responses to this study. Quality was not defined or described by the respondents.

Preceptorships build bridges between education and practice. This was evidenced by respondents who viewed collaborative relationships between education and practice as beneficial. The respondents frequently rated the preceptors as experts and as highly qualified professionals with specific expertise. The "experts" were also frequently referred to as role models for the RN students. All of the above characteristics reflect the literature about preceptors.

Teaching-learning led the perceived benefits to the clinical agency. Recall that the data in this study were provided by faculty liaisons and

RN education programs. The majority of respondents believed preceptors to have developed or improved their teaching skills, and gained opportunities for personal and professional role enhancement. This finding reflected Lewis' (1990) claim that the novice preceptee can act as a catalyst in rekindling interest in ongoing learning, in providing motivation for improved practices and behaviors, and in engendering the satisfaction that occurs as a result of helping another professional.

In some preceptorship programs students prepared and presented programs for clinical units or departments. Several faculty acted as consultants to the service agencies. The research literature supports these benefits to the clinical agencies.

Quality, another perceived benefit to the clinical agencies, spoke to what faculty liaisons saw as the upgrading of nursing care in the units in which preceptorships were functioning. Statements such as "students stimulate staff, keep employees on their toes, and infuse fresh blood" into the units were common comments. Collaboration was achieved through developing collegial relationships. These findings were congruent with the literature of preceptorships. Having registered nurses as students facilitated a collaborative and collegial ambience for personal and professional growth of both preceptors and students.

Recruitment benefits to the clinical agencies were possible outcomes but were not validated in this research. It could be that since most RN students are already employed, the clinical agency stands little chance of recruiting them. The AACN (1988) study reported 57 percent of RN graduates worked in the same RN job as they had before completing their BSN degree.

Role modeling, viewed as a positive entity, reflected Bergeron's (1983) belief, "If you value what you are doing, the student will most likely value it also" (p. 95). The literature is replete with role model information, a critical characteristic of preceptors.

With benefits there are limitations. The faculty liaisons perceived time as the major constraint, consistent with the literature. Loss of direct control of student learning was reported in this study, similar to Waters et al. (1983). There were also concerns about the quality of teaching by preceptors. Some preceptors were experts in their specialty but not necessarily good clinical teachers. Travel was problematic for some faculty liaisons (and students as well). The travel problems involved time and distance and varied among programs. For some programs travel and distance were problematic; for others they were an annoyance.

The major limitations perceived for the clinical agencies were also time constraints—preparing for the preceptorships, spending time with students, time away from primary assignments, time constraints when short staffed, and increased workloads for the preceptors. The faculty liaisons reported that expert preceptors and excellent evaluations of the preceptorships counterbalanced the effects of the negative aspects. The major negative aspect was coordination of the preceptorship—finding quality clinical sites and preceptors, and accomplishing all of this in a reasonable length of time. Not all faculty liaisons were satisfied with the episodes of ineffective teaching by certain preceptors and relinquishing control of students to preceptors. This was expressed by a minority of the respondents and revealed the reality that not every preceptorship is ideal. Nonetheless, the positive aspects of preceptorships outweighed the negative, which is definitely congruent with the literature.

The outstanding positive aspect of the preceptorships, with the faculty liaisons as the primary source of information, was the experience of the preceptorship itself. Positive comments of the preceptorship experience reflected the literature, such as: the "one-to-one" experience, the "real world" adventure, students "love" it, "wide variety" of experiences and options, and a "win-win" solution to limited resources. Learning followed the experience of the preceptorship as a positive gain for students as well as for faculty. For students the gain was flexible, unique, individualized learning with greater diversity in clinical specialities. For faculty the gain was increased student learning in a variety of settings without direct supervision by the faculty.

· CONCLUSIONS AND RECOMMENDATIONS

Based on the results of this survey and discussion of the results, it can be concluded that the majority (54.4 percent) of RN-BSN programs offer preceptorships. One hundred thirty-three deans and directors and 69 faculty liaisons requested a summary of the findings of this research, indicating interest in the preceptorship concept. The importance of this conclusion is that deans, directors, and faculty are examining multiple teaching methods to promote student interest and to extend learning experiences beyond what nursing faculty can provide.

Preceptorships in RN programs have increased significantly in the past decade and are located in public and private colleges and universities. With the shift of nurse "training" from service agencies to institutions of higher education, the service-education gap was created. Preceptorships were viewed as one way to close the gap, or to at least narrow the gap. This is achieved through collaboration, a working together of service and education. With the present shortage of nurse educators clinical preceptors could become a solution to this dilemma.

In this study, faculty liaisons referred to preceptors as experts but none of them explained what the concept "expert" meant to them. In Benner, Tanner, and Chesla's (1992) research, the clinical expert was described as having "at least five years of experience . . . and recognized by peers and supervisors as an expert practitioner" (p. 15). It is therefore recommended that precepted clinicals for all RNs be based on an understanding of Benner's (1992) model of novice to expert. It is equally important for the preceptors and faculty liaisons to be knowledgeable of Benner's levels of practice.

It is recommended that other researchers, using narratives and storytelling, conduct further investigations of RN programs to obtain information about preceptorships from students, preceptors, and administrators as primary sources. Another recommendation is to ask faculty liaisons to tell in their own words the perceived concerns of quality teaching by selected preceptors, and the loss of full control of students' learning.

It is suggested, also, that this study be replicated in associate degree nursing programs, RN to MSN programs, and in master's in nursing programs.

Limitations of this research were that all of the data were collected solely from faculty liaisons and that the results are generalizable to RN preceptorships only.

REFERENCES

Alspach, J. G. (1987). The preceptor's bill of rights. *Critical Care Nurse*, 7(1), 1.

American Association of Colleges of Nursing. (1988). *RN baccalaureate nursing education (1986–1988)—Special report*. Washington, DC: Author.

Andersen, S. L. (1991). Preceptor teaching strategies: Behaviors that facilitate role transition in senior nursing shortage. *Journal of Nursing Staff Development, 7*, 171–175.

Benner, P., Tanner, C., & Chesla, C. (1992). From beginner to expert: Gaining a differentiated clinical world in critical care nursing. *Advances in Nursing Science, 14*(3), 13–28.

Bergeron, B. A. (1983). Positive aspects of the preceptor role. In S. Stuart-Siddall, & J. M. Haberlin, *Preceptorships in nursing education* (pp. 83–88). Rockville, MD: Aspen.

Borland, K., Bone, C., Harlow, M., Parker, M. N., & Platou, T. (1991). Collaborating to develop a student intern program. *Nursing Management, 22*(10), 56–59.

Cantwell, E. R., Kahn, M. H., Lacey, M. R., & McLaughlin, E. F. (1989). Survey of current hospital preceptorship programs in the greater Philadelphia area. *Journal of Nursing Staff Development, 5*, 225–230.

Clayton, G. M., Broom, M. E., & Ellis, L. A. (1989). Relationship of a preceptorship experience and role socialization of graduate nurses. *Journal of Nursing Education, 18*, 72–75.

Corrigan, C. (1992). Implementing rural preceptorships in baccalaureate nursing education. In P. Winstead-Fry, J. C. Tiffany, & R. V. Shippee-Rice (Eds.). *Rural health nursing: Stories of creativity, commitment, and connectedness* (pp. 333–358). New York: National League for Nursing Press.

Davis, L. L., & Barham, P. D. (1989). Get the most from your preceptorship program. *Nursing Outlook, 37*, 167–173.

Dolan, K. (1984). Building bridges between education and practice. In P. Benner, *From novice to expert: Excellence and power in clinical nursing practice* (pp. 275–283). Menlo Park, CA: Addison-Wesley.

Dunnum, L., & Bailey, K. (1991). Trauma internship: A success story. *Journal of Neuroscience Nursing, 23*, 253–255.

Farnkopf, F. T. (1983). Criteria for evaluating a clinical setting for a preceptorship. In S. Stuart-Siddall, & J. M. Haberlin (Eds.). *Preceptorships in nursing education* (pp. 157–163). Rockville, MD: Aspen.

Greipp, M. E. (1989). Nursing preceptors: Looking back—looking ahead. *Journal of Nursing Staff Development, 5*, 183–186.

Heinecke, F., & Martin, A. (1991). Preceptor programs—everyone benefits. *Journal of Practical Nursing, 41*(4), 23–24.

Henry, S. B., & Ensunsa, K. (1991). Preceptorship in nursing service and education. In P. A. Baj, & G. M. Clayton (Eds.). *Review of research in nursing education, Volume IV* (pp. 51–72). New York: National League for Nursing Press.

Kelly, L. Y. (1992). *The nursing experience: Trends, challenges, and transitions.* (2nd ed.). New York: McGraw-Hill.

Lachat, M. F., Zerbe, M. B., & Scott, C. (1992). A new clinical educator role: Bridging the education-practice gap. *Journal of Nursing Staff Development, 8,* 55–59.

Laschinger, H. K., & MacMaster, E. (1992). Effect of pregraduate preceptorship experience on development of adaptive competencies of baccalaureate nursing students. *Journal of Nursing Education, 31,* 258–264.

Lawless, C. A. (1989). Commentary on the relationship between a preceptor experience and role socialization of graduate students. *JONA's Nursing Scan in Administration, 4*(4), 11.

Lewis, K. (1990). University-based preceptor programs. Solving the problems. *Journal of Nursing Staff Development, 6,* 17–20.

Modic, M. B., & Bowman, C. (1989). Developing a preceptor program: What are the ingredients? *Journal of Nursing Staff Development, 5,* 78–83.

National League for Nursing. *State approved schools of nursing—1990.* New York: Author.

Oermann, M. H., & Navin, M. A. (1991). Effect of external experiences on clinical competence of graduate nurses. *Nursing Connections, 4*(4), 31–38.

Radziewicz, K. M., Houck, P. M., & Moore, B. (1992). Perioperative education: Transforming preceptor program into perioperative elective. *AORN Journal, 55,* 1060–1069, 1071.

Rosenlieb, C. (1992). Preceptorships in baccalaureate nursing programs for registered nurses. (Doctoral dissertation, University of Pittsburgh, 1991). *Dissertation Abstracts International, 52,* 5194B.

Rosenlieb, K. O. (1986). Nursing service and education collaborate to enhance students' learning. In J. F. Wang, C. L. Nath, & P. S. Simoni (Eds.). *Living with change and choice in health* (pp. 367–373).

Morgantown, WV: Sigma Theta Tau, International Honor Society of Nursing, Alpha Rho Chapter.

Schubert, P. (1983). Preceptor seminars and their use in the nursing education program. In S. Stuart-Siddall, & J. M. Haberlin. *Preceptorships in nursing education* (pp. 191–200). Rockville, MD: Aspen.

Sheetz, L. J. (1989). Baccalaureate nursing student preceptorship programs of clinical competence. *Journal of Nursing Education, 28,* 29–35.

Spears, M. (1985). A study of senior preceptorships for generic baccalaureate nursing students in the United States. (Doctoral dissertation, George Peabody College for Teachers of Vanderbilt University, 1985). *Dissertation Abstracts International, 47,* 807A.

Turkoski, B. (1987). Reducing stress in nursing students' clinical learning experience. *Journal of Nursing Education, 26,* 335–337.

Waters, V., Limon, S., & Spencer, J. B. (1983). *Ohlone transition: Student to staff nurse.* Battle Creek, MI: W. K. Kellogg Foundation.

Webster's third new international dictionary of the English language, unabridged. (© 1966). P. B. Gove (Ed.). Springfield, MA: Merriam-Webster.

Woodtli, A., Hazzard, M. E., & Rusch, S. (1988). Senior internship: A strategy for recruitment, retention, and collaboration. *Nursing Connections, 1*(3), 37–50.

Young, S., Theriault, J., & Collins, D. (1989). *Journal of Nursing Staff Development, 5,* 127–131

Part IV

Creative Instructional Strategies

17

Understanding Caring Through Photography

Philip Darbyshire

Photographs, which cannot themselves explain anything, are inexhaustible invitations to deduction, speculation, and fantasy.*
— Susan Sontag

INTRODUCTION

This chapter outlines an approach to promoting understandings of caring which I believe helps to nurture and stimulate students' sense of "visual literacy."

To date, I have used the viewing and discussion of photographs with classes of mature students who are Registered Nurses and who have returned to our educational institution on a part-time basis to study for a BA (Honors) Degree in Health Studies. Beginning in 1992–93 these sessions were incorporated within a full course unit entitled "Understanding Caring Through Arts and Humanities." The discussion and viewing of photographs was also introduced to students in our undergraduate (baccalaureate) nursing degree program at that time.

The study and discussion of photographs allows teachers and stu-

---

*See *On Photography,* © 1973, p. 23.

dents to create a rich dialogue around selected visual images. Photographs are chosen for their ability to address particular aspects of the human condition that may disclose caring, or indeed its absence and breakdown. Photography offers students and teachers the chance to experience visually what can be difficult to articulate in words. This is not to suggest, however, that words are superfluous. The discussion of photographs helps the students to connect with and give voice to significant moments from their own clinical experience while also uncovering a wealth of other salient issues relating to our varied "patterns of knowing" (Carper, 1978).

VISUAL LITERACY IN A WRITING CULTURE

As nursing education within the UK has moved increasingly into the University and Higher Education sectors, the educational emphasis has correspondingly shifted. Within this ethos the student abilities which are promoted and valued are almost exclusively those related to academic reading and writing (Bezencenet, 1986, p.5). As part of a strong "word culture" it can easily be forgotten that nursing is an infinitely more complex practice than can be accommodated within such a restricted mode of understanding. We are also required to promote aesthetic awareness and ways of coming to know if caring is to be understood outside of the traditional technical-rational paradigm (Gendron, 1988; Smith, 1992).

Nursing education has largely ignored what has been called "visual literacy" (Highley & Ferentz, 1988, p. 112). This is surprising in view of nursing's expressive visual language which suggests that much of our everyday understanding of practice may have a strong visual and aesthetic dimension. We speak of someone being "the picture of health" or of a child being "the image of her parents." Interpretive phenomenological studies of nurses' expertise have shown the ways in which nurses' concerns are often alerted by seeing that a patient "just doesn't look right" (Benner, 1984; MacLeod, 1990). Nurses' narrative accounts of the perceptual knowledge embedded within their practices often highlight the profound visual impact that a particular patient's facial expression or a wider scene from clinical practice has had, upon both their understanding of nursing and other human concerns (Benner & Tanner, 1987). For example, in the UK, the "whistleblower," Mr. Graham Pink has described what, for him, was the final straw in his campaign to highlight staff shortages in the elderly care unit where he worked as a night duty Charge Nurse. This was when he came upon a confused elderly patient who had climbed out of bed, fallen to the floor, and was sitting and crying in a pool of urine (Turner, 1992). I suspect that this is very much an everynurse story and that we could all recall particular images or scenes from our practice; visual icons of caring or its breakdown, which have evoked paradigm shifts in our thinking (Benner & Wrubel, 1982).

PHOTOGRAPHY IN NURSING AND HUMAN SCIENCE

Photography has been used increasingly as a research approach within nursing and social sciences (see Collier & Collier, 1986; Higgins & Highley, 1986; Highley & Ferentz, 1988; Ziller & Smith, 1977). Researchers using photography have claimed that this can be a useful adjunct to ethnographic and other qualitative strategies designed to explore health and nursing phenomena, and have developed this approach in a diverse range of studies, for example, families of chronically ill children (Hagendorn, 1990) and elderly rural populations (Magilvy, Congdon, Nelson, & Craig, 1992).

Photographs have also been used in historical research in order to disclose "physical details and textures only implied in written and oral sources" (Apple, 1988, p. 40). Apple's work is particularly effective here in showing how historical photographs of nurses tend to ignore their caring practices in favour of more idealized posed representational images. Fox & Lawrence (1988) reveal a similar photographic trend where portrayals of nurses have moved from passive, wooden poses to equally stilted visual associations with education and science, e.g., the "nurse being taught in the laboratory," or the "nurse working with complex machinery" type of photographs.

HOW CAN PHOTOGRAPHY PROMOTE AN UNDERSTANDING OF CARING?

Highley & Ferentz (1988) delineate several uses for photographic nursing research. These have proved to be a valuable framework in the consideration of how photographs promote students' understandings of human caring. Among other uses, Highley & Ferentz suggest that photographs can help us learn more about ourselves and our work, sharpen our visual senses and generate new insights and understand-

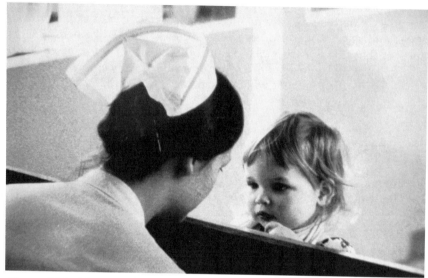

Figure 17.1 Nurse and child at the safety gate. Photograph by Philip Darbyshire.

ings. In the specific project of using photographs to help promote an understanding of caring, photographs have other valuable uses. They can stimulate students to tell their own stories or narratives of caring in practice. They can help students and teachers develop more interpretive understandings. They can highlight nurses' many ethical concerns and sensitivities. They encourage us to focus on the individual and their human experiences while also showing that these are rarely private or isolated from our wider common experiences.

1. Photographs Help Us Learn More About Ourselves and Our Work.

For too long, nurses' caring practices have remained undiscussed, invisible, and trivialized by a health care system which values instead, managerialism, abstract theoretical knowledge, and the seductive certainty of official policy documents. Photographs, if we accept the view that they represent a "slice" or "moment" of reality, draw us back to what Husserl (1982) called "the things themselves," the everyday human encounters where our traditions of caring are being lived out and developed.

In the discussion groups it is important therefore, that photographs are not selected on the basis of their instantly dramatic or shock value. It is often the most seemingly ordinary photograph which will evoke some of the most expansive discussion. As Susan Sontag has noted:

> *In teaching us a new visual code, photographs alter and enlarge our notions of what is worth looking at and what we have a right to observe.* (Sontag, 1973, p. 3).

For example, the photograph of the nurse and child at the safety gate (See Figure 17.1) has evoked students' memories of when they had been hospitalized as children. This photograph also stimulated discussion around questions such as how a small child sees an adult environment and world, caring communication with children, the place of parents during their child's hospitalization, and the nature of trust itself.

Similarly, the photograph of the little girl with a biscuit (See Figure 17.2) seems very ordinary. Yet discussions of this photograph almost inevitably focus on the child's eyes, which are taken to be very much "the windows to the soul." Several students have tried, with great difficulty, to articulate their awareness of what they felt was a similar "look" in the face and eyes of other children who have been the victims

Figure 17.2   Little girl with biscuit. Photograph by Philip Darbyshire.

of physical or sexual abuse, or of children who had been extensively hospitalized almost since birth. This is a "look" which appears to have too much of life, hardship, pain, and wariness for one so chronologically young.

2. Photographs Sharpen Our Visual Senses.

An essential element of nurse caring is the involved and engrossed stance which allows patients' concerns to show up. Integral to this is the nurse's perceptual ability, a developing expertise which goes beyond mere observation of discreet behaviors to a skillful grasping of the situation. In a recent study of experienced Ward Sisters in the UK, MacLeod (1990, pp. 173–175) stressed how these nurses' expertise enabled them to "notice the little things." They noticed expressions on patients' faces, their body posture, but perhaps most significantly, they noticed "wholes and discrepancies in these wholes."

Although photographs have a poor narrative sense, in that they are a moment in time, students can uncover a wealth of detail in a photograph. Photographs will also often evoke particular personal or clinical practice memories among students where a "little thing" is re-visioned and takes on a new salience.

3. Photographs Generate New Insights and Understandings.

One of photographic theory's most contentious issues is that of the meaning of a photograph. From a realist perspective, a photograph is a slice of reality, a form of documentary, factual proof that the imaged event occurred. This position is openly articulated by Collier & Collier (1986) who believe that "Photographs are precise records of material reality" (p. 10). However, such a "naive empiricism" (Beloff, 1985, p. 17) is surely as untenable as it is inhibiting. Phenomenological and qualitative researchers have long argued that there can be no external reality existing outside of our embodied involvement in the world. Similarly, there can be no "brute data" or uninterpreted human experiences.

So it is with photography. The photographer, like the researcher, the teacher, and the practitioner, is irrevocably implicated and involved in his or her practice; in this case, the production of the photograph. The group which discusses the photographs also brings to the discourse each person's understandings, perceptions, experiences, assumptions, and perhaps even prejudices.

In practice, this means that when students and I discuss photographs there are often marked differences in interpretations and understandings. For new groups this is often unsettling as a student may feel that they are failing to "get it," or not seeing something which everyone else seems able to see. They may also be concerned if their interpretation of the meaning of the photograph is diametrically opposed to others in the group.

For this reason, the discourse surrounding the photographs calls forth new ways for teachers and students to "be in the world learningly" (Diekelmann, 1989, p.38). Within such a student-teacher relationship, the concerns and perceptions which arise as we study the photographs are part of a different dialogue; one which seeks to avoid the numbing polarities of teacher/student, good/bad, right/wrong, valid/invalid, etc.

4. Photography Promotes Interpretive Understandings.

The Curriculum Revolution has encouraged us to promote more interpretive understandings of caring and nursing and the study of photographs offers a promising approach to developing these understandings. This is because photographs do not have a single meaning located either within the photograph itself, with the photographer, or within the audience. As Sontag has stated:

> Any photograph has multiple meanings; indeed to see something in the form of a photograph is to encounter a potential object of fascination. (Sontag, 1973, p. 23)

A good example of this has been students' discussions around the photograph by British war photographer, Don McCullin, taken during the Biafran civil war in 1969 (See Figure 17.3). It is described as a "Twenty-four year-old mother, her child suckling her empty breast" (McCullin, 1980, p.147).

This is an image which usually stimulates wide ranging discussion. It confronts us with the human cost, or perhaps more accurately, the cost to women and children, of men's wars.

Although a photograph is certainly a freezing of a moment in time, some photographs have a different temporality. Here, classes have noted that these horrors did not start or stop in 1969 and that this photograph could have been taken yesterday in many parts of the world ravaged by civil or economic war.

Many students have spoken of this woman's terrible beauty, her

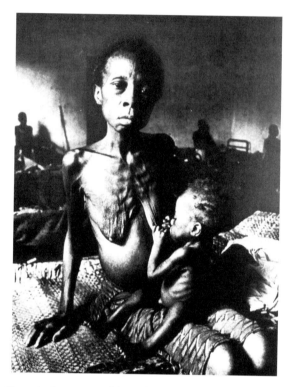

Figure 17.3 Twenty-four year old mother and child during Biafran Civil War. Photograph by Don McCullin in *Hearts of Darkness*, © 1980, London: Secker and Warburg. Reproduced by permission of Abner Stein.

quiet, strong human dignity in circumstances that we can scarcely begin to conceive of. They notice that she has her head held high despite being desperately weak and emaciated. But it is her eyes which speak most eloquently. We have considered that they disclose a dignity, a sorrow, a hope and a hopelessness, and some ineluctable, elemental spark of personhood and humanity.

Not all students read this photograph in this way. In one group a student argued strongly that the rest of the group were simply "imagining" this as his understanding was that this mother's face conveyed nothing but profound sadness and despair. He also argued that to speak of dignity and humanity in the context of this photograph was to somehow gloss over and miss its full horror.

Students are usually quick to see a clinical relevance in these interpretive disagreements and can often quickly connect the discussion with episodes from their practice where they had made an assessment or judgement of a patient on the basis of something as seemingly superficial and slight as a fleeting facial expression or the look in a patient's eye.

Another series of photographs which is particularly valuable in evoking a wide range of interpretive understandings are those contained in the book, *Gramp* by Mark and Dan Jury (1976). This is a photographic record of the dying and death at home of their grandfather, Mr. Frank Tugend, who suffered from Alzheimer's Disease. This series of photographs has been used regularly by Bertman (1991) as part of a wider arts and humanities approach to developing medical and nursing staff understandings of death and dying. Bertman reports that these photographs are usually well received by students and viewed as being a record of "a family's tender caring for a grandfather through senility and death" (p.67).

This, however, is in marked contrast to my own experiences of using the photographs and accompanying text in *Gramp*. Students have become extremely angry with both the content of these photographs and with what they often regard as their essentially exploitative nature. Although they are reluctant to criticize a family who takes on the difficult task of caring for a confused and deteriorating elderly relative at home, they see Gramp as having very little of the human dignity which the family was so concerned that a hospital or a rest home would have stripped him of.

The text tells of how, as his Alzheimer's Disease worsened, Mr. Tugend would strip off his clothes, destroy his bedroom furniture, and refuse food and drink. One particular photograph in *Gramp* shows one of the family trying to give Mr. Tugend a drink "on the run."

Looking at this photograph, students have engaged in deep interpretive debate as to what this is a photograph of and what it is about. Some students immediately notice the woman's facial expression and body posture which seem to shout out a revulsion and disgust. But with whom or what? With Gramp? With who or what he has become? With having to do this? Rather than the familial closeness which the book's text describes, this photograph shows a literal "arm's length" distance which seems symbolically much greater. Other nurses notice what they initially feel to be minor details—Mr. Tugend's disheveled and unkempt state, his stained and uncovered mattress. Students are often uncomfortable in mentioning these details of the photograph as they are reluctant to undermine the family's efforts by focussing on "trivia." However, in our discussions this point inevitably turns to a recognition of nurses' noticing and understanding what MacLeod (1990) calls the importance of the little things.

This particular photograph evoked the strongest of memories from one student who had visited her mother, who also had Alzheimer's Disease, in a hospital. As she approached her bed she saw her mother, standing against a wall being fed her lunch by a nurse who was breaking off pieces of food and offering them to her mother in this "arm's length" way. For this nurse, this was a visual exemplar of her mother's depersonalization and of the nursing practice of helping patients to eat and drink being reduced to a mere refueling stop.

In a vivid image, this nurse referred to the nurse as "feeding her mother like a pillar box." (In the UK, mail boxes are around 5 feet high with a slot-like mouth at the top.)

5.   Photography Promotes Ethical Awareness.

So often in education we imagine that our task as educators is to enlighten through informing and instructing. We then easily forget that in promoting understanding of the complexity of human caring, we must often leave students disturbed and confused (Watson, 1990, p. 20); puzzled but not paralyzed. This calls forth from teachers ways of helping students to develop ways of seeing, being, thinking, and understanding which are more meditative and contemplative than closure-producing or inappropriately analytic. For as Robert Pirsig (1974, p.77) has observed:

> *When analytic thought, the knife, is applied to experience, something is always killed in the process.*

The study and discussion of photographs offers one way to move our understandings of the ethics of caring beyond the disengaged, abstract reasoning which has been the foundation of traditional ethics teaching in nursing for so many years. One of the most insightful descriptions of ethical being is that the person is able to feel uncomfortable in the presence of the discomfort of others. Photography is assuredly capable of making us feel uncomfortable. It can shake our complacency, confront us with images of realities which we might otherwise choose to ignore, and urge us to reflect and dwell with thoughts of what it must be like for those other real people behind the image. As John Berger has said of the photographer, Donald McCullin, "McCullin is the eye we cannot shut" (quoted in Beloff, 1985, p.111). Perhaps the most vital ethical learning and understanding occurs not while students are looking at and discussing photographs in class but rather when they are sitting alone at home, wondering why they cannot blank a particular image from their mind, or debating with friends and colleagues about whether a particular photograph should have been taken at all.

In her seminal collection of essays *On Photography*, Susan Sontag (1973) seems to suggest that photographs can effectively "by-pass" real ethical discourse by showing people not so much as real people but as the subjects and objects of photographs. However, it has been my experience that students are often acutely sensitive to the myriad of ethical issues raised by photographs.

For example, we have discussed several of Diane Arbus's photographic portraits (Arbus, 1972) which seem to be either revered as showing moments of great intimacy between the photographer and the subject, or reviled as cynically manipulative attempts to ridicule and snigger at some of society's most marginalized and damaged people.

The series of photographs in *Gramp*, once again has evoked considerable ethical discussion. Nurses have questioned whether the photographs should ever have been taken, in that they may represent an exploitative manipulation of a person who could neither consent nor object to them. Students ask what this "shy" man, this "loner," as the text describes him (Jury & Jury, 1976, p. 14, 21) would feel about his deterioration, his nakedness, his defecating onto newspapers on the floor, his dependence, his very moment of death becoming public. We have also asked ourselves whether there are times when ethics demand the putting down as well as the picking up of a camera.

Listen now to the great photo-journalist, W. Eugene Smith describe his ethical comportment as he worked on the story of the Minamata disaster:

When you go to a city or village like Minamata, the great, the most grievous problem as far as I am concerned is how to reach the patients. How do you get them to accept you so that you can photograph? The question of photographing them is a question of intrusion; it is a question of depth; it is a question of learning your subject well enough to know how to photograph. I thoroughly believe that in all photography this is most important. I don't believe one should intrude when the intrusion is obnoxious, or dangerous, or it just truly is within the rights of the subject to object. I have complete sympathy with anyone who does object. Becoming closely enough acquainted with the subjects is a question that no one can tell you how to solve, but it is a question of how to be intimate enough so that they forget that you are a photographer to the extent that they will not be self-conscious when you are around. (W. Eugene Smith cited in Janis & MacNeil, 1977, p.105)

Students can gain a valuable insight into their own ethical comportment by re-reading this account as if it were being spoken by a nurse or nurse researcher about nursing or research rather than photography. In studying Smith's photographic essay on the plight of the people of Minamata in Japan (Smith & Smith, 1975) it seems no accident that such a sensitivity, respect, and humility in the face of others' tragedy produces photographs which have the power to move and touch us at a level which words alone can rarely do.

TOMOKO AND HER MOTHER'S GIFT

Susan Sontag (1973) has suggested that some photographs, by virtue of their emotive charge and our relevant and receptive political consciousness, become "ethical reference points" (p.21). She cites the "negative epiphany" (p.19) of the victims of Belsen and Dachau. In contrast, I suggest that W. Eugene Smith has given nursing and human caring an equally powerful but more "care-ful" and uplifting vision in his photograph from *Minamata* of "Tomoko in her Bath" (See Figure 17.4).

This is a photograph which demands that we do not simply look at it and play over its surface. This is a photograph to dwell with in order that we might better understand all that it discloses about human caring. Again, Sontag (1973) reminds us that:

The ultimate wisdom of the photographic image is to say: "There is the surface. Now think—or rather feel, intuit—what is beyond it, what the reality must be like if it looks this way." (p.23)

"Tomoko and her Mother" has, in my experience, been a profoundly moving and vivid emblem of human caring for students. Elements of caring which might have seemed in danger of being abstracted, instrumentalized, prescribed, costed and controlled are released and let be in

Figure 17.4   Tomoko in her bath. Photograph by W. E. Smith, © 1981, The Heirs of W. Eugene Smith. Photo courtesy of Black Star.

this photograph. In dwelling with this image, classes have spoken at length about the true meaning of comfort, of bonding, of mothering, of caring touch, of engrossment and attentiveness, of the nature of beauty and "normality" and of the saving power of love.

"Tomoko and her Mother" also speaks to us of other realms or "levels" of care. In our classroom discussions we have seen concentric circles of caring radiate from this photograph. At the photograph's heart there is the elemental and unconditional caring of a mother for her child, but within the wider context of the Minamata story, the photograph becomes a microcosm of the caring that the people of this small fishing village showed for each other at the community level.

When we consider that the Minamata mercury poisoning tragedy was the direct result of careless industrial pollution it becomes clear that this photograph discloses for us another dimension of caring— that of caring for our planet. Heidegger (1977) has suggested that our relationship with this Earth cannot be that of the technological project which seeks to subjugate and control our planet as a mere "resource" to be used.

The photograph of Tomoko and her mother may allow us to see the possibilities for letting caring be and letting it remain what it is with its own possibilities. To try to force human caring into a technological, instrumental, instructive or theoretical frame may be just one more violence against Tomoko and her mother which ultimately inhibits rather than nurtures caring.

CONCLUSION

Transforming nursing education will be a cynical chimera if it occurs only at the level of new course titles, altered timetables and "ideologically sound" curricular documentation. Hearts and minds are required to change, both ours and our students'. Alternative learning approaches are required which uncover, preserve and nurture our caring practices. Enabling and encouraging dialogue around photographs is potentially very valuable in developing students' visual literacy and aesthetic understandings of caring and their own practices.

Of course, photography seminars on their own will not transform nurse education, only people can achieve that. I am often asked when this revolution or transformation will begin, and reply that the transformation happens when enough people live and work as if it had already taken place.

REFERENCES

Apple, R. D. (1988). Photographs in the history of nursing. In A. H. Jones (Ed.), *Images of nurses: Perspectives from history, art and literature.* Philadelphia: University of Pennsylvania Press.

Arbus, D. (1972). *Diane Arbus.* New York: Aperture.

Beloff, H. (1985). *Camera Culture.* Oxford: Basil Blackwell.

Benner, P. (1984). *From novice to expert.* Menlo Park: Addison-Wesley.

Benner, P., & Wrubel, J. (1982). Clinical knowledge development: The value of perceptual awareness. *Nurse Educator, 7,* 11–17.

Benner, P., & Tanner, C. (1987). Clinical judgement: How expert nurses use intuition. *American Journal of Nursing, 87,* 23–31.

Bertman, S. L. (1991). *Facing death: Images, insights and interventions.* New York: Hemisphere Publishing Co.

Bezencenet, S. (1986). Photography and education. In S. Bezencenet and P. Corrigan (Eds.), *Photographic practices: Towards a different image.* London: Comedia Publishing Group.

Carper, B. (1978). Fundamental patterns of knowing in nursing. *Advances in Nursing Science, 1*(1), 13–27.

Collier, J., & Collier, R. M. (1986). *Visual anthropology: Photography as a research method.* Albuquerque: University of Albuquerque Press.

Diekelmann, N. L. (1989). The nursing curriculum: Lived experiences of students. In *Curriculum Revolution: Reconceptualizing Nursing Education.* New York: National League for Nursing Press.

Fox, D. M. & Lawrence, C. (1988). *Photographing Medicine: Images and power in Britain and America since 1840.* New York: Greenwood Press.

Gendron, D. (1988). *The expressive form of caring. Perspectives in caring,* Monograph 2, Toronto: University of Toronto Faculty of Nursing.

Hagendorn, M. (1990). Using photography with families of chronically ill children. In M. Leininger & J. Watson (Eds.), *The caring imperative in education.* New York: National League for Nursing Press.

Heidegger, M. (1977), Building, dwelling, thinking. In D. F. Krell (Trans. & Ed.), *Martin Heidegger: Basic Writings.* London: Routledge & Kegan Paul.

Higgins, S., & Highley, B. (1986). The camera as a study tool: Photo interview of mothers of infants with congestive heart failure. *Children's Health Care, 15,* 119–122.

Highley, B., & Ferentz, T. (1988). Esthetic inquiry. In B. Sarter (Ed.), *Paths to knowledge: Innovative research methods for nursing.* New York: National League for Nursing Press.

Husserl, E. (1982). *Ideas pertaining to a pure phenomenology and to a phenomenological philosophy.* The Hague: Martinus Nijhoff.

Janis, E. P. & MacNeil, W. (1977). *Photography within the humanities* Danbury, NH: Addison House Publishers.

Jury, M., & Jury, D. (1976). *Gramp.* New York: Grossman/The Viking Press.

MacLeod, M. L. P. (1990). *Experience in everyday nursing practice: A study* of *'experienced' ward sisters.* Unpublished PhD Thesis, University of Edinburgh.

Magilvy, J. K., Congdon, J. G., Nelson, J. P., & Craig, C. (1992). Visions of rural ageing: Use of photographic method in gerontological research. *The Gerontologist, 32,* 253–257.

McCullin, D. (1980). *Hearts of darkness.* London: Secker and Warburg.

Pirsig, R. M. (1974). *Zen and the art of motorcycle maintenance.* London: Bodley Head.

Smith, M. J. (1992). Enhancing esthetic knowledge: A teaching strategy. *Advances in Nursing Science, 14*(3), 52–59.

Smith, W. E., & Smith, A. M. (1975). *Minamata.* New York: Alskog-Sensorium/Holt, Rinehart & Winston.

Sontag, S. (1973). *On Photography.* London: Penguin Books.

Turner, T. (1992). The indomitable Mr. Pink. *Nursing Times, 88*(24), 26–29.

Watson, J. (1990). Caring knowledge and informed moral passion. *Advances in Nursing Science, 13*(1), 15–24.

Ziller, R. C. & Smith, D. E. (1977). The phenomenological utilization of photographs. *Journal of Phenomenological Psychology, 7,* 172–185.

18

RN Students Need To Tell Their Stories

Janalou Blecke
Margaret M. Flatt

Registered nurse (RN) students have been telling their stories at Saginaw Valley State University (SVSU) since the BSN program began in 1976; however, it took a long time to realize how meaningful and important their storytelling was—to them and to nurse educators. A brief account of the circumstances that contributed to this growth in awareness is necessary; SVSU's story illuminates those circumstances.

Initially, the numbers of RN students in the BSN program at SVSU were small; however, an outreach project implemented in 1983 had a significant impact on those numbers. The project included the appointment of a coordinator, and a portion of that role involved advising and counseling both new and enrolled students. The first person to hold the position noted differences in her relationship with these students. She knew more about them than she had ever known about any of the students with whom she had worked previously; however, the logical explanation for this was that she was working so closely with them in this concentrated effort.

One recommendation at the end of the project was to continue the coordinator role within the department; however, because the program had been established and resources were scarce in the mid 1980s, the traditional offices of the university assumed responsibility for the functions of the role. It was not long until it became clear that this arrangement was not going to work. Rumors had increased related to program

requirements and faculty were experiencing more difficulty with negative, and sometimes hostile, attitudes from the RN students. At one
point, a meeting of the students was initiated by two faculty to attempt
to identify issues and formulate recommendations.

The eventual outcome of the situation was the reappointment of the
RN Coordinator/Advisor. Release time was arranged for a faculty to
assume the responsibilities of the role which related chiefly to student
recruitment, progression, and retention. Fulfilling responsibilities in
these areas certainly meant attending to the numbers being generated
but, more importantly, it meant relating one-to-one with the students
and attending to what they had to say, i.e., listening to their stories.

DEFINITION AND FRAMEWORK

Initially, what the RNs were saying was not thought of as stories.
Awareness in that regard was the result of experience with Benner's
(1984) work and the growing emphasis in the profession on stories for
research and knowledge building (Benner, 1991; Boykin & Schoenhofer, 1991; Sandelowski, 1991). It became apparent that this strategy
had great potential for understanding and facilitating the educational
experience of the RN student. It was important, therefore, to clarify
first what was meant by stories and storytelling.

Briefly, for purposes of this paper, the definition of a story is relating an interpretation of the events or circumstances of an experience
that includes the factors of time and personal meaning; contained
within the story and its message are the teachings of the particular
culture. This definition is in line with what authors such as Coles
(1989) and Livo and Rietz (1986) described. The latter seemed more
process oriented:

> *"Story" is a mental program or structure, a way of organizing and
> understanding something. "Story" might very well be an invention of
> the human mind, which we impose upon events or information to create
> logic and sensibility. "Story" might not be outside the body, but inside
> it, an artifact of thinking. Storied information, which is "slotted" or
> reconfigured into story shape, is more easily remembered and can be told
> to others in a conventionally arranged manner.* (Livo & Rietz, 1986,
> p. 7)

Story is contrasted from storytelling by Livo and Rietz (1986), i.e., we
make our stories available to others through storytelling and our stories

are made through storytelling. There are aspects of the storytelling technique that also are applicable with RNs. For example, one's cultural history and awareness of the universe are made known through storytelling. Additionally, storytelling is dependent upon the situation, so factors such as the setting or time of day affect it.

Coles (1989), on the other hand, seemed more content oriented and indicated that stories are something we all carry with us on our journey through life. Story is "everyone's rock-bottom capacity . . . the universal gift, to be shared with others" (p. 30). As with Coles and the people who brought him their stories in the hope that he would interpret them correctly and understand the truth of their lives, so we likewise might think of students and the stories they have to tell. The truth of their lives, including their educational experience, is in their stories and it is up to us in the educational institution to seek the best or most correct interpretation of them in order to understand and facilitate this experience we share with them.

PROCEDURES

The data base for this paper was derived from both observations related to and accounts of RN stories that were gathered from a number of sources during the 1991–92 academic year at SVSU. The current RN Coordinator kept a record of RN stories from her contacts as the year progressed, and both the current and past RN Coordinators provided notes and observations recalled from their experiences since 1983. Additionally, both had roles as faculty at the senior level during the year and had contact with approximately 15 RN students each. Stories and observations from both classroom and incidental contacts were kept. At the end of the year, a memo was sent to the RN students in the senior semesters asking them to respond regarding our "hunches" about the importance and benefits of their stories. Similarly, faculty in the department of nursing were queried about their experiences and observations. The final data source was from a paper prepared by a graduate student with whom the past RN Coordinator worked during the 1991–92 academic year. The student had gathered stories from interviews with RN students during her involvement with the transition course of the BSN program. The RN students were informed about the purpose of her work and the benefits to the course and program. They also were informed that this activity was not related to evaluation of

their performance in the course, and they were not obligated to participate. Contributing the data was considered consent to participate.
Since the work was course related and these precautions were taken,
no additional institutional review was deemed necessary.

Data verification and analyses were completed both independently
and collaboratively by the current and past RN Coordinators. The phenomenological method as described by Giorgi (1985) and operationalized by Parse, Coyne, and Smith (1985) was utilized to guide the
data analysis. Through this method one comprehends a sense of the
whole and then themes are identified and synthesized from the subjects' descriptions, individually and collectively. It is in the final general synthesis that the various aspects of the meaning of the phenomenon are presented. In this situation the synthesis revealed the types of
stories RNs tell, the focus of their stories, and the purposes or outcomes of the stories.

TYPES OF STORIES

According to the data, stories from RNs occur in two basic ways—
formally or planned, and informally or spontaneous. Formal or
planned stories are generated from strategies such as the critical incident technique or journaling with paradigm cases. In contrast, the informal or spontaneous type of stories occur chiefly in class discussions
and during advising sessions.

Formal or Planned

Examples of the formal or planned type are derived from the project by
the graduate student. She participated in restructuring the transition
course for the RN students based upon the central concept of empowerment, a phenomenon of interest to her. The end-of-course evaluation which she then conducted, utilizing a phenomenological approach, revealed interesting stories in interviews with the students
(Bryant, 1991). One RN described the details of her "most horrifying
experience" in nursing school and the "mental torture for two years"
she shared with her peers of not knowing whether they would graduate, even at the very last minute. She expected the same when she
came to the BSN program. She said she thought, "you really had to
brown-nose, and sit up straight in your chair, and think hard about

making good comments or they might infer that you are probably not a good candidate and somehow you would be out of here." She added that "it isn't that way at all" and expressed amazement at how students she observed in another class spoke to the faculty. She concluded by saying, "this has been a real freeing experience."

Another RN the graduate student interviewed described herself as deeply depressed. She was "down from being despondent with nursing, with people, tired of the people dying, tired of the bureaucratic bull-shit. Just tired of all of it." She said she was:

> so depressed and angry that I didn't even recognize how far down I was until I started coming out of it and looked back . . . and [the faculty] and the class have helped stop, take a look at things, what's going on, look at my practice, what I like about it. It's been like a clarifying thing.

She continued later, "class has been really, almost like my savior at the right time." Her story was lengthy but she concluded with ways she was making changes in herself in relation to the practice situation which she formerly had found so intolerable.

A third RN intermingled some informal story telling with the formal in her interview response when she described her difficulty speaking out in class.

> . . . It's not that I don't want to. It's just that it's been difficult for me. Ten years ago I probably couldn't even sit here and talk to you. I've come a long way since I was in high school, you know. I had a bad experience when I was a teenager and it's been hard for me to get over that, talking in front of groups. It was a thing at church. It was a girls' thing. It was a step to step thing. When you were a 'queen,' you had to get up and give a talk in the front of church. And then, the next week, the pastor's son had taped and was playing back the tape for the class, you know and when he had got to my part . . . he sat there and laughed. And it was hard for a teenager to accept that at that time. They were laughing at you every time they played the tape back when it sounded so funny. I know it did sound funny but . . . you didn't appreciate being laughed at either.

Informal or Spontaneous

Examples of informal or spontaneous stories are derived from the daily contacts with RN students. One RN said she tells stories in class "to help basic students become aware of situations 'out there,' and the school clinical doesn't or can't prepare them for everything, to decrease their shock and help them deal with the situations." Not all stories related to class are told in the actual class session. It was necessary for one RN this past year to tell the faculty in both semesters about the tragedy of a child whose accident resulted in disability and necessitated the family's assistance for care. The situation had come to the point that it was causing potentially serious consequences for the student and her family. When the faculty asked about her resources, she shared her insights into the situation and indicated she already had sought help. The student wanted the faculty to know that she was trying to meet all expectations on time but she also needed the latitude to attend to other priorities.

Advising sessions with the RN Coordinator are full of stories. One RN recently reported dropping out of statistics after one week. Among other things, her son was graduating and she was concerned about the possibility of skewed priorities. This student's story apparently needed to include information about how the sermon she had heard on Mother's Day helped her make the decision to take a look at her priorities and commitments. She asked herself, "Am I missing the boat? It's time to step back," and decided, "you can't do everything."

FOCUS OF STORIES

In addition to the types of stories RN students tell, the analyses revealed the focus of their stories. All stories focused on experiences which were then placed in three categories. The first category is concerned with the students' experiences in nursing education; the second with their professional and practice related experiences; and the third with their family situations. Each category also tends to incorporate the element of time; past, present, and projected future experiences are interrelated to achieve coherency and integration.

Experiences in Nursing Education

Experiences with the institutions that provided their initial nursing education are of extreme importance to the RN students. Without prompting they often mention the institution and discuss their view of the quality of education they received. The strong feelings expressed in the process suggest that this earlier preparation has great worth to them and should be regarded similarly by the listener. The implication is that the experience in the current educational institution is being measured against that of the former. Additionally, they make it clear that they do not appreciate the prospect of repeating course content covered in their basic program.

Current experiences with higher education can be both positive and negative; however, RNs tend to share more of those that are negative and often what they share relates to their feelings about assuming the student role and the road blocks they perceive to advancing their education. Students who have attended or explored programs at other institutions are very critical of the shortcomings they perceive in them. They are sometimes troubled by misinformation, or what appears to be misinformation, received from colleagues or the various offices of the educational institution. They complain bitterly when the institution changes the rules after they have committed to pursuing the degree. They speak of conflicts between work and educational schedules; the message is clear that the educational institution should be more flexible and efficient in its planning related to the adult student. Those who have been out of the educational setting for a number of years are more prone to speak of fear related to their potential inability to succeed with current strategies such as gaining credit through examination.

In contrast, stories of more positive experiences reflect a level of satisfaction and appreciation. One RN said that due to her young children at home, she works second shift so her husband can care for the children. When she took the community health course, the faculty arranged an evening clinical for her which allowed her "to continue her same routine at home." She was "grateful" for that, as well as other flexible arrangements she was anticipating in the last three courses in the program.

Professional and Practice Related Experiences

The RN students share information about their current position, as well as information about work history and career goals. They speak of changes in their work situations and how they see themselves progressing and setting new goals which are in keeping with those of the employing institution.

When their current position, or another they are seeking, requires a higher level of preparation, they tend to want to talk about rapid advancement in the program in order to obtain the desired credentials. Students who do not feel the pressure to progress rapidly are more likely to speak of learning as their priority and the changes they have observed in themselves over time. For example, one student asked which bachelor's degree at the university would be "quickest" as she was teaching a nursing assistant class at a community college and needed a bachelor's degree to continue. In contrast, another student indicated she was in no hurry to complete the program and said, "I want to use my brain."

Stories also describe nursing colleagues from both the educational and service arenas whose support and encouragement are sought and cherished. One student indicated she considered not returning to complete her degree but was encouraged by co-workers who said she "shouldn't stop now with only senior nursing courses to finish." Colleagues are viewed as reliable sources of information, often more so than faculty members because they provide support as they share information about courses and policies. The concept of mentoring is implied frequently in reference to these relationships.

Experiences Related to Family Situations

In relation to family situations, there is great variation; however, the RN students state clearly that family life does not stop while one works on a degree. Some talk about decisions to take time out from their educational pursuits to bear and rear children. Others speak of moving from one location to another and the effect this has on their educational pursuits. The RN who dropped statistics concluded, "no one has a simple life anymore."

One RN who was considering dropping the program in her senior year felt the need to share the extreme complexities of her life. She indicated she was a single mother. She felt as if she was missing her son's junior high years because her schedule was so full of work, school, and studying. She said she had so little time with him that "he talks with me while I shower and he will sit by my bed and talk with me until I fall asleep." Additionally, she described the care needed by her elderly mother who has a chronic condition and is not handling it well. She promised her son she would take a year off from her studies before pursuing the MSN; however, she has mixed emotions about doing so because she feels she is "getting too old."

Families, both immediate and extended, are recognized for the support and encouragement they provide. The RNs describe changes in family roles and functions to accommodate their return to school. Children who are in high school or college are sometimes referred to as tutors, especially in areas such as math or chemistry. Overall, the assistance RNs receive from their families provides them with the freedom to grow and frequently they note changes in the family that they attribute to their own growth.

PURPOSES/OUTCOMES OF STORIES

Three basic categories of purpose or outcome are evident in the RN students telling their stories. The first category benefits the students themselves; whereas, the second benefits the nursing program. In the third category there are mutual benefits for both the students and the program.

Student Benefits

When senior RN students were asked about the value or importance of telling their stories, most interpreted the inquiry in the sense of the formal or planned type of storytelling and not the everyday relating of information to one another. One said that sharing experiences validates one's sense of professionalism, commitment, and ability to think and perform in a way that benefits the client involved. She also spoke of empowerment and stress relief as one debriefs and shares particularly significant events. She even thought that storytelling could be a "real stress reliever" and contribute to "improved clinical practice" if it was incorporated into end-of-shift reporting among peers. Additional benefits to this would be reduced animosity and improved relationships among peers, as well as new insight into clinical situations.

The theme of insight was present in the responses of others. Another said that through storytelling, she can look at things from a "fresh viewpoint," as well as gain support both from peers, who are not co-workers, and from educators. A third RN spoke of the importance of support from faculty when, due to her family situation, she needed flexibility with turning in assignments.

Program Benefits

One major purpose or outcome of benefit to the program is the evaluative data these stories provide. In a sense, continual monitoring of the stories is like prevention in that, as trends become evident, activities such as an RN Task Force can be initiated early in order to gather additional data and make timely recommendations concerning program direction. This strategy would be a useful supplement to the traditional, intermittent survey utilized for the purpose of program evaluation because it would be ongoing and individualized. It would satisfy a recommendation made by Beeman (1988) for educators to be aware of the diversity in the student population because a high degree of individual variance was noted in the responses to a survey.

Another benefit involves the relationship between education and service or practice. A clear understanding of one another is central to this relationship. Through listening to the stories from RN students, educators get a sense of what is happening "in the trenches." Not only is this relevant for knowing the level of care being practiced, but also for knowing the impact the educational program is having. Additionally, through the strategy of stories, educators get a sense of the extent and accuracy of the information about the program that is being promulgated, as well as how it is being perceived.

Mutual Benefits

A benefit to the program from RN students telling their stories is support for the RN Coordinator role in the department. Simultaneously, the RN students benefit from the services provided through the role.

In addition to multiple system involvements, several other factors make the RN student's situation unique. For example, the majority of students do not take full course loads, and it is not uncommon for them to stop out for a semester, so their student support group may change every semester. Additionally, over the period of time it takes them to complete the program, policies and procedures change, resulting in the need for alteration of their short and long term plans. These factors can create a sense of disjointedness and frustration which challenge the coping and integration skills of the RN students. Certainly, supportive family and colleagues help the RN students with such things as maintaining their morale and reorganizing their activities. Additionally, by listening to the stories, supportive faculty facilitate their progression in courses and contribute to their development of a sense of coherence.

It seems, however, that the students benefit from something more; someone who provides the elements of continuity and consistency they need in order to cope in the multiple systems in which they are involved and to integrate their experiences as adult learners. The RN Coordinator role includes these elements, as well as a third element suggested by Diekelmann's (1990) work, namely, caring that fosters a sense of connectedness that all humans need. In the case of the RN students, this sense of connectedness facilitates their progress through the transition process. One major way educators communicate the caring that promotes such connectedness is to use the strategy of stories.

LEARNING TO USE STORIES

Several valuable lessons have been learned in using the strategy of stories with RN students. Some of these relate to the time and effort it takes to master the process, for all parties concerned. To illustrate, one of the authors recently had a larger than usual number of RN students in the class with the basic senior students. These RN students represented a wider range of nursing roles than usual so the faculty viewed them as a rich resource for stories to illustrate course material. They also were more vocal than some in the past had been, so they required very little prompting to contribute. Within a very short time the faculty noted a change in the tone of the stories; they ceased to be reflections of experience and began to sound like "preaching" directly to the basic students. The basic students were responding with verbal and nonverbal behavior that reflected anger and frustration. Faculty intervention was necessary to help both parties in the storytelling process. The RN students needed more and better direction in the requests to relate their stories and the basic students needed more and better assistance in listening to the stories in order to learn from them.

An experience described by another faculty revealed other lessons related to stories. She had always had a few RN students in her class of basic students and decided to try an all RN section. She had utilized storytelling (unknowingly) in the past when she asked the RNs to share their experiences to illustrate a point. Now, however, faced with only RN students in the group, she said she was "scared to teach the course. I thought I would be tested and scrutinized by the group." What she discovered after the first session was "that the ten of us with all our varied backgrounds (ICU, Psych, Adult Health, Pediatrics, Hospice, OB) were going to have a good and challenging class." She noted that all of the "students achieved an A."

It is clear from these experiences that it not only takes time and practice to become proficient with the strategy of stories, but also takes care in planning and implementation similar to that required for any other educational strategy. Additionally, from her experience with the use of stories, the graduate student noted that one needs to be aware of the wide variation in response that is possible to a single question.

SUMMARY AND CONCLUSIONS

Finally, what is it about RN students' experiences in the transition process in nursing education that makes their stories *need* to be told? Actually this question is asked from both the side of the RN students who are the learners and need to tell the stories, and the side of the educator/advisor who needs to have the stories told. In short, the answer to both is that these stories reveal very graphically and meaningfully what is happening in the learning and professional development processes and, simultaneously, they facilitate the progression of those processes. The RN students seem to have an innate sense about what telling their stories will do for them in relation to their learning and professional development processes. They require very little encouragement to prompt their story telling. For the educators/advisors, no other strategy is as adaptable and achieves as much in relation to facilitating the learning and development processes. For both parties, the graphic revelations in stories paint a picture of how past, present, and future blend together to form a meaningful, coherent view of a position in the world. According to Antonovsky's (1979) work on stress and coping, such a view is necessary if stress is to be resisted and health maintained. A final statement in one RN's story illustrates and sums this up well:

> When I first started at SVSU way back in 1981, I needed 122 credits. I am a diploma graduate. My first class was a challenge, not the studying or tests or whatever homework, but I was older, had two small children and worked full-time. When I walked into the classroom and saw all those young faces I wanted to turn and leave, but then in walked another nurse who faced the same thing and I jumped about and welcomed her. We have gone through this whole program together. She graduated this December. Looking at my grades I can tell my life story by the grades I have. Two C's represent a tumor removed from my breast and my father's death. I kept plugging away and for the most part I am very grateful that you have instructors in the nursing program that have

helped me get through the rough times with their understanding and caring.

REFERENCES

Antonovsky, A. (1979). *Health stress and coping: New perspectives on mental and physical well-being.* San Francisco, CA: Jossey-Bass.

Beeman, P. (1988). RNs' perceptions of their baccalaureate programs: Meeting their adult learning needs. *Journal of Nursing Education, 27,* 364–370.

Benner, P. (1984). *From novice to expert: Excellence and power in clinical nursing practice.* Menlo Park, CA: Addison-Wesley.

Benner, P. (1991). The role of experience, narrative, and community in skilled ethical comportment. *Advances in Nursing Science, 14*(2), 1–21.

Boykin, A., & Schoenhofer, S. O. (1991). Story as link between nursing practice, ontology, epistemology. *IMAGE: Journal of Nursing Scholarship, 23,* 245–248.

Bryant, J. (1991). Unpublished interview data for paper prepared for N650, Advanced Clinical Nursing, MSN program, College of Nursing and Allied Health Sciences, Saginaw Valley State University, University Center, MI.

Coles, R. (1989). *The call of stories: Teaching and the moral obligation.* Boston: Houghton Mifflin Co.

Diekelmann, N. (1990). Nursing education: Caring, dialogue, and practice. *Journal of Nursing Education, 29,* 300–305.

Giorgi, A. (1985). Sketch of a psychological phenomenological method. In A. Giorgi (Ed.), *Phenomenology and Psychological Research* (pp. 8–22). Pittsburgh, PA: Duquesne University Press.

Livo, N. J., & Rietz, S. A. (1986). *Storytelling: Process and practice.* Littleton, Colorado: Libraries Unlimited, Inc.

Parse, R. R., Coyne, A. B., & Smith, M. J. (1985). *Nursing Research: Qualitative Methods.* Bowie, Maryland: Brady Communications Co.

Sandelowski, M. (1991). Telling stories: Narrative approaches in qualitative research. *IMAGE: Journal of Nursing Scholarship, 23,* 161–166.

19

The Teacher-Student Relationship: The Heart of Nursing Education

Judith Buchanan

Through reflection on my learning episodes, I have come to realize that my style of learning is based on pragmatic needs growing out of work related and personal experiences. I learn best when setting my own goals and when given guidance and support to meet these goals. Real learning experiences for me have always been either participatory in nature or have offered the challenge of independent discovery; as well as respected my way of learning.

The intention in this paper is to discuss the teacher-student relationship from a perspective born out of this personal reflection on learning, coupled with a belief that the nature of teacher-student relationships can be understood within Peplau's (1988) interpersonal relations framework. If one subscribes to this framework, then one operates from the assumptions that nursing education is an interpersonal, investigative, nurturing process through which the teacher fosters the development of the student's personality and selfhood in the direction of maturity. The work that the student does to contribute to meeting personal learning goals is accomplished within an interactive teacher-student relationship. All teacher-student interactions are opportunities for learning.

The discussion which follows is based on the author's[1] three years

---

[1]Note: To remain congruent with the personal nature of this discussion, the teacher will not be de-gendered. Teacher will be referred to using the female pronoun.

of experience as a participant-observer in the educational journeys of BN/RN students who are in a bridge course. This course is a two se-mester, introductory nursing course within a baccalaureate curriculum for registered nurses. The contexts of these journeys have been class-room settings and distance education (via audio teleconferencing) sites.

As a point of clarification, participant-observer in this framework is Peplau's (1988) term for the source of interpersonal data. When applied to the situation under discussion here, participant observation implies that the teacher-student interaction can be studied as a between-per-sons phenomena. What occurs between student and teacher can be observed, explained, and understood as to the ways in which it evokes learning and growth for both parties. The teacher is not a spectator.

PROFILE OF THE NURSE STUDENT

Registered nurses often return to school with confused spirits and loss of confidence which stems in part from nursing's collectively low self-concept and depleted self-esteem (Valiga, 1989). Roberts (1983), in her seminal work on nursing as an oppressed group, presents the view that in the systems where many nurses work, behaviors representative of powerlessness are the very behaviors that are seen as right and de-sirable within the system. Such behaviors are quiescence, passivity, and subservience to power and authority, all of which reflect that there is a value more dominant than nursing's that is in control.

Dykema (1985), using a specific theory of powerlessness as a frame-work, explains nursing's difficult past and present position in the patri-archal health care arena. Her contention is that the dominant/legitimate value (i.e., medicine's value) has insidiously supplanted the less wor-thy nursing values, and she speculates that the debates over the layers of nursing education have helped to lull nursing into a powerless pos-ture. Unpalatable as this view may be, there is a legitimized power, and nurses are in a deficit position in relation to it. Many nurse authors speak of this patriarchal dominance (see for example Ashley, 1980; Chinn 1991; Chinn & Wheeler, 1985; Doering, 1992; Mason, Bacher, & Georges, 1991; Pitts, 1985; and Watson, 1990, to name but a few). Nursing's "co-optation into the unhealthy environment of the current health care sys-tem" (Chinn & Wheeler, 1985, p.77) where power, authority, and status are primarily associated with the physician, continues to consign nursing knowledge and nursing practice to a secondary rank.

The educational traditions in nursing have supported the tendency "to limit the recognition, scope, and expansion of nursing knowledge" (Doering, 1992, p.31). Nursing curricula and the conventional process of nurses' training have helped to foster and maintain the oppressed and self-effacing nurse (Bevis & Murray, 1990; Doering, 1992; Pitts, 1985; Richardson, 1988). The training ground for many nurses has been predominantly teacher-centered, behaviorist, and mechanistic in nature. In this scenario the teacher is viewed as powerful and in control, and the student is viewed from a dependent and personally powerless position. Compliance is reinforced, and task mastery is emphasized at the expense of conceptual competence or analytical skill. In teacher-centered learning, teacher-student relationships are easily distorted and become such that they can "oppress students and discourage learning and clinical responsibility" (Diekelmann, 1992, p.79). Teacher-centered learning contributes to the perpetuation of the subservient role that the nurse occupies in a patriarchal health care system which negates nursing values (Mason et al., 1991; Watson, 1990).

Many, if not most, of the nurses returning to school were trained in traditional nursing schools which support authoritarianism, and now work in the paternalistic, rule driven health care system which devalues nursing's role. It can be assumed from this that nurses entering the university are usually well schooled in rejecting the search for discovery, creativity, and caring professional relationships. The revolution in nursing education is in part an attempt to assist nurses to "recognize the value and legitimacy of their own voices" (Mason et al., 1991, p.76), and their own ways of knowing. Many of the ways of knowing needed to reform the policies and politics of health care are those associated with femaleness in a paternalistic framework and with servility in oppressive professional relationships (Chinn, 1991).

AN EVOCATIVE MODEL OF TEACHING

What is needed is an educational environment that will free the oppressed or alienated nurse "to be fully human, to be fully a participating subject of the world" (Hedin, 1986, p.56); an environment that will encourage the nurse to begin to value what has been devalued as knowledge (Chinn, 1991), such as caring and intuition. Such a conviction commits the teacher to enter into, and to share the world of the student; to create a climate that will summon the student to confront and to explore new perspectives, and to develop a relationship with personal creative processes and diverse talents.

At its root, such a climate could be termed evocative. To evoke implies that possibilities need to be continuously explored, summoned up, or provoked into being. An evocative model acknowledges the central role of experience, and therefore the curriculum needs to be grounded in the real day-to-day experiences (past and present) of the nurse-student. The evocative process is one whereby the teacher draws forth from the student unrecognized or unacknowledged ideas, information, or other situational configurations. An assumption underlying the evocative process is that relevant strength and data for learning lie dormant in any individual. Summoning this strength and data can vitalize the input of new information.

Central to the establishment of an evocative, educative learning climate is a philosophy of student-centered teaching which fosters the growth of the "scholar clinician that will mark the future" (Bevis & Watson, 1989, p.3). This philosophy is key to understanding the interpersonal relationship between student and teacher.

A PHILOSOPHY OF STUDENT-CENTERED TEACHING

Clarifying one's philosophical position is a means of disentangling and understanding one's own personal values in regard to education. The expression of values and guiding principles regarding student-centered education allows for a synergistic relationship between the student and the teacher. Indeed, much of the current thinking concerning student-centered teaching can be traced to its humanistic roots where ethical, aesthetic and spiritual growth is nurtured, and the tendency toward self-actualization becomes a goal (Richardson, 1988).

In this paradigm the teacher becomes truly present to the student, and intentionally uses *self* as a positive motivating force in the educational alliance. The term "use of self" espoused here indicates that the teacher applies self-knowledge to the teacher-student relationship. Ongoing development of self-knowledge imbues in the teacher a greater capacity to be a sensitive observer of the interpersonal phenomena in which she participates (Peplau, 1989, p.49).

The teacher-student relationship focuses on helping the student gain personal, intellectual and interpersonal competencies beyond those which were held at the point of entry into the educational system. Teaching strategies will be emancipatory (Bevis & Murray, 1990). These perspectives presume that both student and teacher can grow through the learning process, that the teacher-student relationship is based on mutuality, and that the student must be given a considerable degree of freedom and autonomy in the educational experience (Hiemstra, 1988).

Watson (1989) suggests that the overall goals of traditional nursing education have come to neglect the moral imperative of nursing itself, which is caring. She argues for a nursing education which is holistic, recognizing "that learning is subjective, contextual, dialogic, and values driven" (p.1). She sees the moral context for nursing education being a reflection of the professional nurse-client relationship, and that "knowledgeable caring" (p.2) *is* professional nursing.

THE NURSE-TEACHER

One can begin to appreciate the notion that the teacher is, relative to the process of learning, no different than the student. Thus a complementary pattern (i.e., "in which the fit is hand-in-glove" [Peplau, 1992, p.17]), where one is seen as teacher and one is seen as student, becomes inappropriate. Perhaps one could replace the word teacher with translator, which bespeaks rather pointedly of the process of being guided along the educational way (an idea adapted from Carlsen, 1988).

In the role of one who evokes learning possibilities, the teacher attempts to draw the student toward the summation of individual potentiality and self-actualization. By recognizing and identifying that there are constraining factors, reasonable expectations for the student can be established.

As with any professional interpersonal relationship, there is an element of risk. This risk can be reduced when the teacher has an understanding of her values and beliefs and is able to articulate these. By viewing the teaching process as a shared person-to-person experience, the teacher will more readily see the professional role and the personal role as congruous. The teacher will attempt to fully express the complexity of herself and will not circumvent this expression in her role as teacher.

In this view, the teacher's connectedness between personal experiences and how they affect the teaching role will be appreciated. Encounters with the student marked by authentically shared experiences can move the student toward an expanded sense of self and can affect that student's self-image. In subscribing to the value of human nature as capable and indeed desirous of achieving growth and wholeness, the teacher will experiment with innovative teaching methods that will achieve the goal of contributing to the growth of the student. Reflecting on one's own storehouse of knowledge and experience is an essential component for maintaining teacher effectiveness in an egalitarian atmosphere where both teacher and student share in the process of learning. Thus professional effectiveness can be linked to a base notion of self-discovery and a belief in the centrality of learning to the practice of teaching (Diekelmann, 1992; Powell, 1989).

MODEL OF AN EVOCATIVE TEACHING PROCESS

The form, quality, and process of the teacher-student relationship is guided through phases to become "a journey that nourishes the student's selfhood" (Bevis cited in Bevis & Watson, 1989, p.32). Interlocking and overlapping phases of teacher-student relationships have been observed by this author and are consistent with the phases of the nurse-client relationship described by Peplau (1988). The phases are discernible as orientation, working, and resolution phases (Forchuk, 1991). The phases are not equal in length or intensity, and differ qualitatively from each other. Peplau's phase theory, a developmental theory, may be viewed as a metaphor for the passing of seasons.[2] The educational experience becomes a "sequential unfolding of particular demanding situations" (Carlsen, 1988, p.39) or transitions, to which the student must respond. Development, the major process evoked, involves creating new ways of being and knowing to address the changing rhythms of the educational milieu. This perspective is congruent with the concept of the teacher as one who evokes forward movement, or growth, within the student.

Table 19.1, a model of the teaching process constructed for the purposes of this paper, corresponds with an educational philosophy of student-centered teaching. Obviously a number of relationship variables and situational influences will impact on this process. One can

---

[2]This metaphor for a phase theory is liberally adapted from Carlsen, 1988, p.39, and may be used here in a different context from that intended.

Table 19.1   An Overview of an Evocative Model of Teaching[1]

I.   ORIENTATION PHASE

    A.   Establishing a climate of trust ——————— (ongoing) ——► Teacher is
    B.   Establishing liberating uses of power   —— (ongoing) ——►   the
    C.   Establishing structures that are enabling — (ongoing) ——► translator

II.   WORKING PHASE

    A.   Assessment and Goal Setting

- Creating learning situations that will require that the student engage in reflection, self assessment, and hypothesizing.
- Exploring and clarifying learning needs.
- Setting goals based on active understanding of the learning situation (shared decision making is the basic mode of planning).
- Mutually formulating learning objectives through a learning contract.

    B.   Strategy Selection and Implementation

- Guiding the student through transitions using support strategies:
  —Listening
  —Adapting structure
  —Expressing positive expectations
  —Sharing of self, self-disclosure

- Providing challenge in learning experiences:

  —setting tasks, and providing choice and options that enhance creative development
  —engaging in discussion, debate, and inquiry
  —setting high standards
  —giving feedback creatively and consistently

- Providing a vision through learning experiences:

  —offering new ways of looking at nursing situations and suggesting ways of 'being' in nursing
  —providing opportunities for reasoning through real situations

- Evaluating outcomes and reformulating learning needs

III.   RESOLUTION PHASE

    A.   Establishing a climate conducive to terminating:

- Encouraging student to synthesize what has been learned—process and outcomes

Table 19.1 (*cont'd.*)

- Guiding exploration of how experience may enrich future career goals

- Promoting reflection on the manner, quality, and patterns of change in critical thinking, problem-solving and interpersonal competencies.

B. Mutually evaluating teacher-student relationship, as well as learning experience itself.

---

[1]*Note*: Adapted from Arms et al. (1984), Barrows (1988), Bevis & Murray (1990), Bevis & Watson (1989), Daloz (1986), Ferguson (1991), Glen (1990), Langenbach (1988), Wlodkowski (1985).

never assume that the student wants to accept the responsibility inherent in student-centered teaching (Burnard, 1990), or to offer the level of involvement required for active learning experiences.

The Phases

Throughout "the unsettling first steps of the educational journey" (Daloz, 1986) the teacher's initial task is to create a rich learning environment. The adult student flourishes when the learning climate is mutually respectful, collaborative, and supportive, and one in which personal potential can be visualized. The latter point may be credited to Norris (1982), the others being well accepted principles of adult learning.

The *orientation phase* is critically important as it sets the stage for the work that is to follow. The orientation phase begins with the first encounter between teacher and student. The task here is for teacher and student to come to know each other as persons, and to understand each other's expectations. The centrality of the student is acknowledged. The teacher's belief that each student brings unique characteristics and learning needs to the class is put forth as a value of profound importance. Tasks of this phase involve orienting the student to the process of the learning. Clarity on the part of the teacher is essential in describing the dimensions of the teacher's role.

At this point the teacher is generally stereotyped as a "supervisory personification" (Peplau, 1992, p.15) which is a consequence of earlier, traditional nursing education. The student thus assigns any concomitant distortions held about persons in authority to the teacher (Norris, 1982). The student usually does not trust the initial description of the values, beliefs and process of this educational experience and expects rather to meet with behavioral objectives, and knowledge testing. The orientation phase is relatively brief, lasting usually through one to two encounters. The bond between the teacher and the student initially is fragile though cordial.

The student has perhaps entered the course feeling anxious and inadequate. These feelings become increasingly compounded as the student's identity becomes even more threatened. The stresses become less manageable as the reality of the student role gets placed into the configuration of other life roles. Thus, the student often enters the *working phase* frustrated, confused and unknown, that is to say without an established identity in the present learning situation. The student may be overwhelmed with a sense of unknowing, in that prior experiences do not seem to exist to support this present student role. The student may fear failure, or may fear success. The teacher must intervene in a manner that will effectively assist the student through this period. The anxiety expressed now is almost guaranteed to resurface in some form at some later point.

The conditions for learning as thinking are really nourished in this phase. The perspectives noted in Table 19.1 are, no doubt at this juncture, incomplete. Given more time with students, the author may come to more accurately reflect a responsiveness to the interactions between timing and contextual conditions inherent in the teaching process. What is now in hazy focus within Table 19.1, may move to the foreground. New features may well get highlighted as the model becomes crystallized; a more reasoned structure may emerge over time. Be that as it may, the strategies and activities endorsed through this model are validated by other more seasoned educators (see for example, Allen, Bowers, & Diekelmann 1989; Beeman, 1990; Eyres, 1992; Fulwiler, 1982; Gussman & Hesford, 1992).

In the working phase, the teacher needs skill in working with the anxiety of the student and in using the energy derived from it in creative and constructive ways. If the anxiety is not acknowledged, the student may attempt to avoid the challenges and struggles inherent in the learning, or may hide from them.

Assessment and goal setting. As the working phase unfolds, the student begins to identify with the learning, issues can be examined, and there is a move toward planning for assignments. The student starts to use the conditions and resources (including the teacher) of the learning environment. This component of the working phase is identified as assessment and goal setting. The student at this time needs to gain further perspectives on being a student and being a nurse. Examples from the classroom are used here in an effort to more cogently bring Table 19.1 to life. The reader is invited to merge all of this with the discussion on trust, power, and structure found within this chapter, which permeates the entire teaching process.

I persist in my quest to integrate a personal philosophy of teaching with an actual practice of teaching in a way that is clearly congruent to the student and is at the same time practical and understandable (e.g., the lecture format is a rare event in the classroom; seminar style and experiential learning episodes are the norm). This philosophy is discussed in the initial class, and class time is given over to people learning about each other. Expectations, beliefs, and assumptions about the student and about the educational experience are clearly documented components of the course syllabus. My perceived need to keep the course readings current sometimes borders on compulsive, however it does serve to underscore the necessity of remaining aware of the debates, discussions, and dissentions in the world of Nursing. Suggested (i.e., additional) readings are chosen with a view to the varied interest and/or scholarly levels of the particular student group. In this way, the individual student can know in advance that there should be at least one complementary reading that will capture her or his attention on the subject. This is essential for distance learners who do not have the library resources available in the same way as do on-campus students.

I have endorsed the concept of a learning contract and have adapted the work of Knowles (1986) to the way in which the contract is developed and used. The contract is used in teleconferenced courses as well as on-site courses. The student feedback has been such that I have maintained the practice. Though the students generally value the contract, the majority still choose the standard contract as opposed to developing their own.

Strategy selection and implementation.

a. Guiding—Certain students in any group of the first year nursing course level are still looking for a teacher with the mystique of an all-knower. Definitely a teacher who allows herself to become at times confused about what she is supposed to know, and one who regards the syllabus as merely "an inventory of themes of understanding" (Schon, 1983, pp.332–333) is not yet a comfortable enough guide to the structured education which many still desire. However this is addressed openly. An excerpt from an end of term feedback letter to students (dated Apr. 21, 1992) follows, which illustrates openness to the issue.

All things considered, I can say with conviction that we've been through an experience of mutual learning over the past two semesters and have weathered our journey well. Many in our group entered N2014 with a perceived need for structure, a clearly etched out course (education) path, and a teacher who would be in "charge." The initial exposure to the teaching philosophy which I espouse caused many to be anxious for a time. The feedback (end of this term) has made that point. But I think that by now you have come to realize that there was a structure; not a content structure, but rather a process structure. I did assume responsibility for that process (and I did know what I was doing!).

Also in respect to guiding, I have kept my hours of availability to students generally unrestricted, although I have learned from experience that I must guard my home life from the available times. As nurses work shiftwork, this has meant that I have had to schedule student appointments at some unlikely hours (e.g., 7 a.m. or 7 p.m.). Also, due to the impersonal nature of the telephone added onto the already rather detached teleconference medium of teaching, I am not above making "house-calls" in certain critical instances. A portion of the times spent with students one-on-one is given over to matters directly related to assignments, learning contracts, and the like. However, consuming more of the time are the occasions of student advising and of student anxiety or anger, or sometimes both.

b. Challenging—Journals have been used to foster student self-awareness, but even more critically to enhance the interpersonal nature of the teacher-student relationship. Distance education compounds the challenges in meeting the prescriptions of this model. This "exploratory discourse of the self" (Gussman & Hesford, 1992, p.32) allows students to reflect on content, and to use language in their own way and in a way that is safe from criticism. Through the journals I can get to know which students are having difficulties with concepts and can track the learning progress of students. Fulwiler (1982) provides a valuable discourse on journaling in the context presented here. Rather than respond to each individual student's journal, which is far too cumbersome a task, I developed a system of writing a generic response based on the themes which emerge from the collectivity of journals. My intention in this is to reinforce the learnings, draw upon the richness of the students' writings, and expand the conceptual material beyond the boundaries of its presentations in the combined classroom/journal context. A reference list is always a component of the response, and serves to identify further resources on the topic, including student resources. A brief excerpt from one of the generic journal responses follows:

> *The journey inward to deal with much of the material covered in class exercises, in the journals, and in certain of the readings was the most difficult component of this course for some of the N2014 group. As Mary put it, however, believing that the teacher and the student are essentially no different is helpful when trying to understand that we are all trying to put our own unique stamp on this experience. Some of the concepts were difficult to swallow. Some good came out of something initially thought negative for some (e.g., "I can actually use rejection or failure as a learning tool."). I urge you to apply certain therapeutic principles to your self, as you would apply them within the context of the nurse-client relationship. These are unconditional acceptance and positive regard (Thanks to Melissa for the reminder). You're worth it!*

c. Vision—Serendipitous learning experiences are intended. I attempt to use active teaching strategies as much as possible, and often take an exercise from a source and rework it to suit my own style or to create more than focus from the experience. One example is a case study ostensibly developed to have the students consider, in small groups, the nursing diagnosis of non-compliance. Although the diagnostic label is value laden to begin with, I created five additional Mr. Cohens (the "client" in the case study). Each Mr. Cohen had a component of his family constellation or of his personhood that would potentially create certain attitudes toward the client by the nurse. These attitudes could color the nurse's frame of reference as she approached the tasks associated with the exercise. I have also used photographs to draw out values issues, and am consistently pleased with the discussions that emerge.

d. Evaluating/reformulating—As a matter of general principle, I have modified the syllabus of the Nursing Concepts course each year based on feedback received from the students. The feedback form is given out during the first class of the semester, and the student is expected to briefly critique class content immediately following each class. The form also has sections for comments on the required texts, reserved readings (both required and optional), assignments, and other comments that may need to be stated.

The transition to the *resolution phase* begins with the completion of the final assignment. It is a phase of termination and involves self-evaluation (student and teacher) and course evaluation. Often the student will acknowledge some degree of transformation and an openness to further transformative experiences. Usually the student will have connected to the teaching principles and strategies and will have found a way to personally affirm some measure of success as a learner. The relationship culminates with the teacher and the learner at a precipice, ready to move on to new understandings and new realities.

In beginning to establish a climate conducive to terminating, direction and guidelines for a self-evaluation process are given on the standard learning contract. Although I respond to each student individually on the content of the self-evaluation, I do so with a general opening. This is done as an attempt to link the student back to the beginning of the term, and to provide a conduit for some reflection on where we had travelled. A portion of one such feedback letter follows as an illustration:

> *As this term ends I trust that you do see yourself more-or-less as a self directed learner. Malcolm Knowles (1975) who is the guide for me on this matter states that "one of the competencies possessed by self-directing learners is a concept of themselves as nondependent and self-directing persons" (p. 64). Perhaps by now you are at, or even beyond, having a clear picture of "being able to visualize how you would feel, how you would think, what you would do if you were completely self-directing" (p. 64). If then, as one in our group wrote on her self-evaluation "you only get out of independent learning what you put in," the onus thus remains with you to keep going and growing. Actually I could borrow from Peplau (1988, p. 12), and with a few minor word changes construct the following:*
>
>> *Self-directed learners participate with their teacher in the organization of conditions that facilitate forward movement of the personality in the direction of creative, constructive, productive, and personal thinking and learning.*
>
> *As you continue on your educational journey, I want to draw you back onto a memory of the "Returning-to-School Syndrome" (Shane, 1980). You are likely, as you go into subsequent nursing courses, to slip back into a stage of disintegration again, with its concomitant threat to your self-confidence and perhaps some feeling of inadequacy. If your self-image is severely threatened for even a temporary period, your ability to learn may be inhibited or limited (Callin, 1983). Pondering this in ad-*

vance may prevent you from remaining stuck in the mire. And also take heed, you may be leaving behind the traditional culture of nursing (which encourages you to be dependent and powerless), and could be envisioning an emerging culture of nursing. The old rules may no longer work for you, yet you possibly have not yet figured out the new ones. The angst will be well worth the joy in your discovery of a fuller professional you.

TRUST, POWER AND STRUCTURE

The relationship enhancer of trust, the issue of power, and the use of structure are the key constructs in establishing the evocative educational climate. Although the stage is set in the orientation phase for a beginning endorsement of these, they remain critical factors through the entire teacher-student relationship.

Trust.   Engendering horizontal trust is essential to the development of any helping relationship. In the initial stage of the teacher-student relationship, the student's trust owes its strength to readily accessible descriptive cues, specifically the legitimate role of the teacher. As the teacher-student relationship burgeons, the distance between the two should narrow if the student perceives the teacher to be trustworthy. Perceived trustworthiness is generally based on the teacher's reputation for honesty, sincerity and openness, and lack of ulterior motives. "As greater intimacy develops, some of the student's unreflecting deference to authority may diminish. No longer based on superficial trappings, the relationship has the potential to be transformed into something more profound and powerful" (Daloz, 1986, p.127).

Trust has been built when, for example, the student comes to understand that to posit opinions, ideas, or possibilities freely is welcomed, even when that student is not totally confident of the correctness of the input. It is important for the student to feel that there is nothing wrong with not knowing, and that through dialogue and discussion, the unknown will be identified for further inquiry or searches.

Power.   Power, like trust, is commonly an issue in setting the stage for a professional relationship. A teacher needs to be wary of a power which reflects authority (Bevis & Murray, 1990; Glen, 1990). In the evocative model, the teacher uses "restrained power" (Bevis & Watson, 1989) or a power which supports and encourages the energy, intellect, and creativity of the student. Power is dependent on the trustworthiness of the teacher. "The power is that of expertise in content, in how to learn, in inquiry, and in scholarly pursuit. It is power that relies upon the consent of the learner and rests in mutual respect" (Bevis & Watson, 1989, p.169).

Power in this view is, for example, using one's own deliberations, reflections and hunches as a framework for guiding the students through the process of inquiry and problem solving. It is important for the teacher to admit to not knowing everything about the content, yet to demonstrate expertise in the process of learning (Valiga, 1989).

Structure. Although structure in any teaching relationship can be oppressive, some forms of structure are liberating. An empowering structure is one which provides informational conditions within the learning environment that motivate the student in a self-directed fashion. Planning is part of structure, but the teacher will realize some built in contradictions in this method of student-centered teaching (Langenbach, 1988). Within a flexible learning environment independence in learning is expected and creative growth and cognitive development are nurtured. Valiga (1989) proposes that in the structuring of the unstructured environment competition and cooperation will be encouraged, scepticism and inquisitiveness will be fostered, and freedom of choice will exist.

A practical example of structure would be the teacher's initial directiveness in regards to modelling the inquiry and reasoning process. As the students are guided through repeated practice in the process, they will gradually acquire the skills of self-directed study. The teacher compliments this process by gradually backing away and becoming far less directive in guiding the students to the recognition and acquisition of the knowledge they require.

OUTCOMES

Regardless of the terms used to describe student outcomes, increased competencies as scholars and as clinicians should result from the educational journey for the returning-to-school nurses. The quality and scope of education must enable the nurse to assume a professional nursing role that can be expected within an evolving health care system.

Stark and Lowther (1988) describe competencies which are of primary concern to educators in all professional fields. From their work critical outcomes for BN/RN education can be identified. In particular, four broad categories of competencies are expected, and have been described by BN/RN students taught by this author in summative evaluations. The competencies are: (a) conceptual competence, understanding nursing from nursing theoretical perspectives and endorsing nursing values, as opposed to understanding nursing from medical or institutional models; (b) technical competence, particularly therapeutic communication, increasing one's professional nursing skills; (c) integrative competence, the blending of both theoretical and technical skill in the clinical setting; and (d) professional sensibility, or professional identity. The latter refers in part to affective outcomes. Nurses express this as confidence, self-assurance, pride and respect for self. This competence is also reported by Nielson (1989). In a research study designed to test androgogical concepts in a post basic program in oncology nursing, Neilson (1989) unexpectedly found that the nurses perceived the most valuable outcome to be that which happened within themselves.

Peplau's perspective on competencies, although not written for an educational context, could just as easily be adapted to become the competencies of concern to the nurse educator. These "are generally categorized as intellectual, problem solving, and interpersonal. Competencies are evolved from capacities that are put into use and practice" (Forchuk, 1991, p.57).

SUMMARY

This author has witnessed many nurses entering the university unhappy, feeling an outside pressure (e.g., the nursing profession) rather than a personal need, to do so. Nurses return to school often at great personal expense, adding one more role to an already full family and work life. Most nurses study part-time, and do not necessarily have the support of their peers in the workplace as they embark on this journey. A tradition of expecting authority, and a technical training background are added to the factors that create a profile which is not atypical of a returning-to-school nurse. Assisting these nurses to continue to grow and to flourish as nurses, as learners, and as persons involves a reframing of the process and the products of learning. Teaching must become a process of evoking possibilities and meaning for the individual student, while validating and using the richness of the experience that the student brings to the setting.

The concepts and views expressed in this paper have been a compository of personal beliefs about nursing education and of a way of being a teacher of adult students who are nurses. This is a view of teaching as a three phase process of person-to-person interaction where the primary function is to build on an effective teacher-student relationship. The process is guided by Peplau's (1988) interpersonal relations framework. Outcomes for the student are increased competencies as a scholar-clinician.

Central to the evocative model of teaching is the belief that the teacher can use herself as an instrument to evoke learning potential. Achieving a sense of harmony between what I profess to believe about teaching and learning and what actually happens in the classroom is an ongoing goal. The potential for achieving the goal will always be colored by the particular configuration of personalities, learning styles and lived realities of the group that converges to become "a class" at any one time. I include myself in this equation.

The vitality of the teacher-student relationship is connected by a "gossamer thread that weaves itself through the various characteristics" of both the teacher and student who are involved in the learning experience (Galbraith, 1989, p.10). This relationship is the very heart of nursing education.

REFERENCES

Allen, D. G., Bowers, B., & Diekelmann, N. (1989). Writing to learn: A reconceptualization of thinking and writing in the nursing curriculum. *Journal of Nursing Education, 28,* 6–11.

Arms, D., Chenevey, B., Karrer, C., & Rumpler, C. (1984). A baccalaureate degree program in nursing for adult students. In M. S. Knowles and Associates (Eds.), *Andragogy in action.* San Francisco: Jossey-Bass.

Ashley, J. (1980). Power in structured misogyny: Implications for the politics of care. *Advances in Nursing Science, 2*(3), 3–22.

Barrows, H. (1988). *The tutorial process.* Springfield, IL: Southern Illinois University School of Medicine.

Beeman, P. (1990). Brief: RN students in baccalaureate programs: Faculty's role and responsibility. *The Journal of Continuing Education in Nursing, 21*(1), 42–45.

Bevis, E., & Murray, J. (1990). The essence of the curriculum revolution: Emancipatory teaching. *The Journal of Nursing Education, 29,* 326–331.

Bevis, E., & Watson, J. (1989). *Toward a caring curriculum: A new pedagogy for nursing.* New York: National League for Nursing Press.

Burnard, P. (1990). The student experience: Adult learning and mentorship revisited. *Nurse Education Tomorrow, 10,* 349–354.

Callin, M. (1983). Going back to school. An open letter to a nurse thinking of returning for further education. *The Journal of Continuing Education in Nursing, 14*(4), 21–27.

Carlsen, M. B. (1988). *Meaning-making: Therapeutic processes in adult development.* New York: W. W. Norton.

Chinn, P. (1991). Looking into the crystal ball: Positioning ourselves for the year 2000. *Nursing Outlook, 39,* 251–256.

Chinn, P., & Wheeler, C. (1985). Feminism and nursing. *Nursing Outlook, 33,* 74–77.

Daloz, L. (1986). *Effective teaching and mentoring: Realizing the transformational power of adult learning experiences.* San Francisco: Jossey-Bass.

Diekelmann, N. L. (1992). Learning-as-testing: A Heideggerian hermeneutical analysis of the lived experiences of students and teachers in nursing. *Advances in Nursing Science, 14*(3), 72–83.

Doering, L. (1992). Power and knowledge in nursing: A feminist poststructuralist view. *Advances in Nursing Science, 14*(2), 24–33.

Dykema, L. (1985, September). Gaventa's theory of power and powerlessness: Application to nursing. *Occupational Health Nursing,* 443–446.

Eyres, S. (1992, June 19). Women's ways of knowing and teaching RN students. Presented at the conference *Transforming RN Education: Dialogue and Debate,* in Madison, WI.

Ferguson, L. M. (1992). Teaching for creativity. *Nurse Educator, 17*(1), 16–19.

Forchuk, C. (1991). Peplau's theory: Concepts and their relations. *Nursing Science Quarterly, 4*(2), 54–60.

Fulwiler, T. (1982). The personal connection: Journal Writing across the curriculum. In T. Fulwiler & A. Young (Eds.), *Language connections: Writing and reading across the curriculum* (pp.15–30). Urbana, IL: National Council of Teachers of English.

Galbraith, M. (1989). Essential skills for the facilitator of adult learning. *Lifelong Learning AAACE, 12*(6), 10–13.

Glen, S. (1990). Power for nursing education. *Journal of Advanced Nursing, 15*, 1335–1340.

Gussman, D., & Hesford, W. (1992). A dialogical approach to teaching Women's Studies. *Feminist Teacher, 6*(3), 32–39.

Hedin, B. A. (1986). A case study of oppressed group behaviour in nurses. *IMAGE: Journal of Nursing Scholarship, 18*, 53–56.

Hiemstra, R. (1988). Translating personal values and philosophy into practical application. In R. Brockett (Ed.), *Ethical issues in adult education*. New York: Teachers College Press.

Knowles, M. (1975). *Self-directed learning: A guide for learners and teachers.* New York: Cambridge, The Adult Education Company.

Knowles, M. (1986). *Using learning contracts.* San Francisco: Jossey-Bass.

Langenbach, M. (1988). *Curriculum models in adult education* (pp. 163–175). Malabar, CA: Robert E. Krieger.

Mason, D., Backer, B., & Georges, C. (1991). Toward a feminist model for the political empowerment of nurses. *IMAGE: Journal of Nursing Scholarship, 23*, 72–77.

Neilsen, B. (1989). Applying andragogy in nursing continuing education. *The Journal of Continuing Education in Nursing, 20*, 86–90.

Norris, C. (1982). Facilitating student learning through the teacher's use of self. In S. Smoyak & S. Rouslin (Eds.), *A collection of classics in psychiatric nursing literature* (pp.50–56). Thorofare, NY: Charles B. Slack.

Peplau, H. E. (1988). *Interpersonal relations in nursing: A conceptual frame of reference for psychodynamic nursing* (reissued from 1952). London: Macmillan Education.

Peplau, H. E. (1989). Interpersonal relationships: The purpose and characteristics of professional nursing. In A. O'Toole & S. Welt (Eds.), *Interpersonal theory in nursing practice: Selected works of Hildegard E. Peplau* (pp.42–55). New York, NY: Springer.

Peplau, H. E. (1992). Interpersonal relations: A theoretical framework for application in nursing practice. *Nursing Science Quarterly, 5*(1), 13–18.

Pitts, T. P. (1985). The covert curriculum: What does nursing education really teach? *Nursing Outlook, 33,* 37–39, 42.

Powell, J. H. (1989). The reflective practitioner in nursing. *Journal of Advanced Nursing, 14,* 824–832.

Richardson, M. (1988). Innovating androgogy in a basic nursing course: An evaluation of the self directed independent study contract with basic nursing students. *Nurse Education Today, 8,* 315–324.

Roberts, S. (1983). Oppressed group behavior: Implications for nursing. *Advances in Nursing Science, 5*(4), 21–30.

Schon, D. (1983). *The reflective practitioner: How professionals think in action.* New York: Basic Books.

Shane, D. (1980, June). The Returning-to-School Syndrome. *Nursing 80,* 70–71.

Stark, J., & Lowther, M. (1988). *Strengthening the ties that bind: Integrating undergraduate liberal and professional study.* (Report of the Professional Preparation Network.) Ann Arbor: University of Michigan.

Valiga, T. (1989). Curriculum outcomes and cognitive development: New perspectives for nursing education. In *Curriculum revolution: Mandate for change.* New York: National League for Nursing Press.

Watson, J. (1989). A case study: Curriculum in transition. In *Curriculum revolution: Mandate for change.* New York: National League for Nursing Press.

Watson, J. (1990). The moral failure of the patriarchy. *Nursing Outlook, 38,* 62–66.

Wlodkowski, R. (1985). *Enhancing adult motivation to learn* (pp.281–291). San Francisco: Jossey-Bass.

20

Distance Education for RN Students

Betty J. Paulanka

INTRODUCTION

The competitive demands of today's complex society have compelled both health care and academic institutions to confront important educational and economic constraints related to survival in a highly technological environment. These combined constraints have motivated health care providers and educators to become partners in meeting the educational needs of registered nurses (RNs).

More specifically, the increased demand for highly skilled nurses coupled with evidence of declining enrollments in baccalaureate nursing programs in the 80s necessitated the use of more innovative approaches to RN education. The timing and environment were right for more flexible approaches to a Bachelor of Science in Nursing (BSN) for registered nurses. Nurse educators must work to reduce the barriers for adult learners and nurses while providing respect for the unique contributions returning registered nurse students can offer to the academic setting. The task was to do this without sacrificing the quality of course offerings.

The College of Nursing at the University of Delaware offers a four year BSN curriculum designed to meet the needs of the traditional college student and the returning RN student. Faculty believe that while the goal of a BSN education is similar for both groups of students, mechanisms for meeting behavioral outcomes for each group can be adapted within the same curricular structure. RNs enrolling in this program meet the same course requirements as the basic nursing student.

However, RN students have more flexibility in their choice of courses designed to meet curricular requirements. Additionally, the RN student is allowed to use a credit-by-examination option to meet all but two of his/her nursing course requirements. One introductory nursing course and one clinical nursing course must be completed by all RN students. Most students are encouraged to enroll in the nursing research course in addition to these nursing requirements. The demanding nature of on-campus courses has limited the enrollment of RN students in this program. The national nursing shortage and increasing demands for sophisticated nursing care in the hospital and in the community have created an impetus for change in our education program.

To this end, partnerships between major university constituents (the College of Nursing, the Division of Continuing Education, and the Vice President of Special Services in the Office of the President) and surrounding health care agencies were developed. These partnerships facilitated the use of University of Delaware resources to serve the educational needs of RNs in health care institutions. At the onset the program was designed to serve approximately 200 nurses throughout Delaware and the adjoining states of Maryland, New Jersey, and Pennsylvania. It was estimated that at any one time, one half of this number would include matriculated, part time RN students. The remainder of the students would consist of RN students participating in courses offered through the Division of Continuing Education prior to their admission to the nursing program. It was projected that the typical RN student would be between the ages of 25 and 40, married with children, and exhibit a high degree of personal, professional, and academic competence. The majority of the pool would be employed either full or part time in hospitals and related health care settings.

Partnerships with the Division of Continuing Education (CE) and the Office of the President resulted in an expansion of learning opportunities available to off-campus RNs and employed a variety of educational delivery options. Distance learners could avail themselves of credit-bearing nursing and support courses videotaped in the University's "state of the art" Instructional Television (ITV) studio and, through the Division of CE, the tapes would be delivered directly to the student's worksite. External studies courses from CE and credit-by-examination options for testing nursing competencies were other existing alternatives for returning RNs to earn academic credit. All distance students were supported by an individualized counseling and advisement support system that is coordinated by selected faculty within the Department of Nursing Science. The primary goal was to maintain quality educational standards while meeting the varied needs of RN students.

Getting started consisted of five phases: (1) Developing Partnerships, (2) Selecting a Model to Reduce Barriers, (3) Preparing Faculty, (4) Operationalizing the Program, and (5) Evaluation.

DEVELOPING PARTNERSHIPS

Step one focused on the need to integrate multiple University resources throughout the campus by developing internal partnerships. The first partnerships formed were with the Division of Continuing Education (CE) and the Vice President for Special Services who controlled the use of the Instructional Television Studio classrooms. These internal partnerships facilitated consideration of the mutual needs of faculty and administration in the policy development process. The Division of Continuing Education served as the coordinator of services while the College of Nursing and a representative from the Office of the President addressed educational policies and advisement concerns associated with providing courses at distance sites. As a result of this program, partnerships with other colleges within the university continue to develop.

The University outreach program, Flexible Options for Continued University Study (FOCUS), was established in the Division of Continuing Education to provide distance education services. The coordinating services provided by CE included marketing activities in the dissemination of all FOCUS informational materials, receipt and return of course tapes and related coursework materials, and general University advisement and registration procedures. The College of Nursing assumed responsibility for the selection of courses appropriate for videotaping and the development of an advisement system to meet the needs of off-campus RN students.

These relationships proved to be quite enlightening for purposes of resource sharing. Optimizing the use of educational and institutional resources available through the Division of CE provided a variety of economic benefits. Nursing students became eligible for incentive scholarships from CE that provide funding for the first and last three credits in the program. Flexible contracts between CE and selected institutions for fee payment allowed some students to enroll in University courses without the up-front cost of registration. The use of educational technology to provide quality courses at distance locations with expanded support of nursing faculty for RN education were critical factors in the success of this initiative.

Support from the Office of the President was the key to overcoming many burdens that often result from institutional bureaucracy. The ability to change fee structures for distance sites proved crucial to the survival of the video delivery alternative. Opportunities for staff education in the television studios and the expansion of job descriptions for several key people in both departments were exciting. Nursing's role as a leader in this University endeavor provided a new level of respect for faculty and the nursing program.

The next task consisted of developing important external partnerships and nurturing existing relationships with clinical agencies. Regional luncheons and presentations were offered to introduce health care agencies to the concept of distance education and clarify proposed responsibilities of each partner. Once contracts with health care agencies were confirmed, the agencies identified site coordinators to facilitate the ease of transfer of tapes and course work materials to RN students at participating work sites.

Initial partnerships were established primarily with hospitals in the tri-state Delaware Valley region. One local, long term care facility and a community health agency also participated. The largest enrollments came from out-of-state hospitals in New Jersey and Pennsylvania.

The development of policies and procedures for working with partners in this joint educational venture resulted in a mutual understanding between and among internal and external partners. Providing role definitions and expectations promoted positive relationships. Policies were developed to address the number of nursing courses that could be taken through the FOCUS alternative before matriculating in the nursing program. Worksites developed their own procedures for handling the tapes and course materials. The College developed various printed materials to assist RN students in the proper sequencing and selection of courses. The Division of CE shared in the recruitment and advertising expenses associated with this venture.

News releases were used to increase visibility and support for the program. The program started in September of 1988 with 46 RN students, 9 of whom enrolled in two courses. Three different courses were offered at 12 of the original 35 sites identified within the first year. Today, the program has approximately 76 sites in four different states, of which an average of 50 sites offer courses during any one semester. At this time about one fourth of the RNs enrolled in the FOCUS delivery alternative are matriculated in the College of Nursing's BSN program.

SELECTING A MODEL TO REDUCE BARRIERS

Reducing the institutional, situational, and dispositional barriers to education frequently encountered by RNs was the next priority. Surveys and interviews with RN students and Nursing Administrators implied that the time factor associated with University courses was the primary situational barrier to university education. Cost effectiveness was viewed by the College as a potential institutional barrier. Using these two factors as major criteria for decision making, a time shifting approach utilizing a "candid camera" classroom format was selected to address the most pressing situational and institutional barriers. This approach attempted to respect the needs of RNs and health care agencies by capitalizing on the technological resources of a major university. It also respected the University's need to minimize costs. The time shifting approach allowed videotapes of a typical, three credit, live class to be delivered to student worksites for an approximate university cost of $5000 per course. While other more interactive approaches were available, the cost of such technology in the late 1980s was prohibitive.

Methodology for distribution of tapes at the worksite became the prerogative of the site coordinator. The site coordinator was a nurse appointed by the agency to facilitate learning at distance sites. Having on site coordinators employed by the agencies increased the autonomy of agencies participating in the program.

PREPARING FACULTY

The challenge facing faculty was to deliver quality educational opportunities through a different modality that supports the pursuit of a rigorous baccalaureate degree program. A major objective was to respect the students' competing demands on time and resources, while respecting the faculties' concerns about control over the teaching process. Resolving such multiple and complex problems required integrating quality instruction with appropriately tailored delivery technologies that allow for up-to-date instruction and advisement not only where, but when required.

Recognizing the unique needs of the RN as an adult student, an attempt was made to orient faculty to the need for more flexible approaches to teaching. Malcolm Knowles' theory of adult learning provided the basis for changes in instructional and advisement strategies. Knowles' four basic concepts related to self concept, experience, readiness to learn, and time perspective/orientation to learning were used to differentiate between adult (andragogy) and child (pedagogy) learning (Knowles, 1980).

Using this approach allowed faculty to increase their awareness of the primary differences between adult learners and traditional students. Developmental needs and conditions that surround adult learners were contrasted to the needs of the typical on-campus students. The importance of valuing these differences in the educational process when working with adults was emphasized to guide faculty in their approach to student interactions.

Although many faculty had experience working with RN students enrolled in our on-campus, basic nursing curriculum many did not anticipate the differences that would be encountered when working with all RN classes. The vulnerability of the RN's self concept and the importance of respecting the individual's personal and professional experiences in life and nursing were discussed in relation to addressing the diverse needs of RN students. The immediacy of the needs of this group in conjunction with their willingness to challenge the system were contrasted to the behaviors of the typical on-campus student. This brief orientation to the behavioral differences in adult and typical basic students allowed many faculty to be prepared for the influx of questions, curricular challenges, and innovations that this new population of RN students created in our existing system. Concerns about the needs of this growing group of students prompted the development of an ad hoc committee to address curricular issues related to their diverse needs. As a result of this process course requirements and sequencing for RN students were evaluated and restructured.

However, this orientation did not prepare faculty for the long term effects of larger numbers of RN students in the program. While faculty verbalized that they understood the differences in the two types of students some faculty remained inflexible in their individual approaches to RN students who attempted to meet behavioral objectives through more creative alternatives. Concerns related to these issues are ongoing. Faculty are currently exploring the idea of developing a separate curriculum for RN students.

OPERATIONALIZING THE PROGRAM

Initiating the first distance education FOCUS courses in nursing was both exciting and frustrating. Faculty and the Division of Continuing Education staff were committed to making these course offerings a success. The high level of motivation and enthusiasm for the project provided the peer support and energy needed to make things work despite unpredicted problems.

The program began with 46 different RN students enrolled in three courses at 12 different sites. Course selections consisted of two non-clinical nursing courses and a chemistry lab course. The largest class, a nursing pathophysiology course, enrolled 24 distance students and the smallest class, chemistry, consisted of seven distance students. All students enrolled in the chemistry section were required to attend lab sessions offered at in-state, off-campus, distance sites on a weekly basis. Four new courses were offered the following semester along with a repeat of the original three courses that were described as "canned" courses.

Enrollment numbers decreased to 38 RN students despite the fact that the number of off-campus sites and course offerings increased. Only ten students participated in summer session through the FOCUS delivery option. This decline in enrollment numbers was a marketing puzzle since students were overwhelmingly favorable in their evaluations of the courses and the video delivery mode. The new challenge was to identify reasons for decreased enrollment numbers and provide incentives to encourage faculty and site coordinators to offer "canned" versions of courses throughout the year.

The faculty role in offering a course in the video delivery mode includes grading papers, communicating with off-campus students, the Division of Continuing Education and site coordinators at active distance sites, as well as other course coordination activities required with live courses. The complication arises in terms of faculty workload. To resolve this conflict all faculty teaching in video delivered courses, live or canned, were paid on S-Contracts from the Division of Continuing Education, in addition to their usual University salary. The difference in payment for live or canned courses was that live course S-Contracts had to be paid in a Professional Development Fund to be used by faculty for special purchases or professional travel. Faculty coordinating canned courses could be paid directly through an S-Contract or voluntarily deposit money in their Professional Development Fund. Reimbursement rates for S-Contracts varied with rank and the number of students enrolled through the distance alternative.

At the outset of the program many faculty were apprehensive about their appearance on the TV monitor and later the videos. Needless to say, on taping days faculty appeared to be particularly well dressed and color coordinated (joking comments were not unusual). More importantly, faculty paid increased attention to the quality of their lectures, overheads, and audio visuals in general. Pride in their lectures was clearly evidenced in the faculty's response to videotaped classes. While this overall effect is good, it did create an unanticipated departmental expense and an increased workload for the Instructional Resource Department. Videotaping also heightened faculty awareness of copyright laws related to the distribution of educational resources and fair use practices. Legal opinions were sought to clarify faculty concerns. Many of the copyright issues are still being discussed. The outcomes of these responses to videotaping have served to strengthen faculty presentations and the quality of materials used throughout the curriculum. Overall it has been a real plus for the program.

Student/faculty interaction issues resulted in fewer problems than anticipated. Faculty were provided with answering machines and attempted to return calls in a timely fashion. Telephone tag became a game for some, but faculty quickly learned that many calls had to be returned during evening hours. Work conditions for most nurses are not amenable to academic discussions during on-the-job hours.

Some faculty are still attempting to adjust to the unique personal differences in the RN students. The urgency of their seemingly routine problems, their demands for immediate answers and willingness to question "so-called authorities" frequently frustrates some faculty, while others find it challenging and rewarding to work with adult students. The enthusiasm and motivation of this group tends to stimulate faculty to keep abreast of changes in the health care system.

Unfortunately, the majority of drawbacks and frustrations identified with the initiation of the FOCUS delivery alternative were experienced by the distance students. Primary problems centered on the delivery of course materials, books, videos, etc. in a timely manner. An influx of late registrations provoked a shortage of texts and course materials in some areas. Videotape delivery time initially projected to result in a one week lag time for distance students often resulted in a two to three week lag time before reaching site coordinators. Although the University and the United Postal Service maintained a strict plan to keep on schedule, many hospital delivery systems were slow in getting materials to site coordinators in a timely fashion. Thus, materials arrived late or were identified as lost for short periods of time.

To compound this problem, course syllabi were designed to address the needs of on-campus students. Due dates, reading assignments, and test dates printed in initial syllabi became very confusing for distance learners who were supposedly working one week behind the on-campus class schedule. Despite the fact that faculty were extremely flexible with distance learners, students became frustrated and always felt they were in a "catch up" mode. Faculty learned quickly that course materials for distance students needed some modification.

EVALUATION

Academic outcomes were a primary factor used to determine the success of this alternative learning mode. Learning effectiveness was assessed by comparing grades earned by the on-campus students to the grades earned by the distance RN students. These findings confirmed the findings of similar research studies in other disciplines, i.e., there is little, if any, statistically significant variation between on-campus and video based off-campus student performance (Paulanka & Stone, 1990; Dutton, 1988). Table 20.1 describes the details of the first year's Comparative Performance Analysis.

Questionnaires, course evaluations, and student interviews were used to measure student responses to the FOCUS alternative. Student satisfaction outcomes emphasized the fact that many RNs would not have been able to return to school for their degree without the video option. Viewing courses in the privacy of their homes or the agency library with the option to rewind to review specific content was identified as a major advantage. Many recognized the need to be self-motivated and the importance of avoiding the temptation to procrastinate.

Table 20.1   Comparative Performance Analysis

Course		On-Campus Mean Performance	N	Off-Campus Mean Performance	N
Nursing	205	2.64	64	2.58	12
	312	2.82	85	2.90	21
	314	2.69	81	2.12	25
	332	2.90	84	3.42	7
Chemistry	105	2.14	88	2.17	6
	106	2.27	97	2.86	7
Philosophy	102	2.76	70	3.67	3
Aggregate		2.58	569	2.63	81

(Paulanka and Stone, 1990, p. 11)

Some students even organized small study groups in their work site. However, time saving and convenience of the video system were repeatedly identified by students as the motivating force that encouraged them to return to school.

Another real and unpredicted faculty problem was dealing with the on-campus students' responses to courses being videotaped. Open forum meetings were held with on-campus students to address their concerns. Many suggested that ITV classrooms inhibited faculty spontaneity. There was an overwhelming resentment about the flexibility of course times offered to distance students but not offered to the traditional student. This complaint resulted in a decision to make tapes available to on-campus students in the library resource room, a factor that did not generally affect class attendance, much to the surprise of faculty.

Despite favorable evaluations of courses by distance students, enrollment numbers remained constant. Marketing experts were forced to seek reasons for limited enrollment increases. The reality that video courses are not for everyone was factored into the analysis but the major issue turned out to be money. Besides an additional $75 video course delivery fee, the majority of distance students were out-of-state residents paying almost triple the tuition required of in-state students. Since many of the work related reimbursement programs had a $1000 cap on course expenditures or required students to provide the upfront money demanded by the University at the time of registration, costs quickly became prohibitive. A second limiting factor was the inflexibility of curricular requirements in the nursing program and University bureaucracy related to course transfer policies.

Recognizing barriers specific to RN students was a beginning step toward guaranteeing the continued success of a distance education alternative for RN students. Negotiations for policy changes to reduce student costs while ensuring cost effectiveness for the University were initiated at administrative levels and approved by the Board of Trustees.

The results of these efforts culminated in a new pricing system for video courses. Students now pay a designated site registration fee for FOCUS courses which is much more competitive with in-state tuition fees. Special contracts have been established with selected medical centers to arrange up-front payment alternatives for course registrations. The entire registration process has been simplified to improve access for distance students.

Ad hoc committees within the College of Nursing were formed to address course selection and transfer concerns without sacrificing the integrity of the curriculum. It was quickly recognized that the realities of providing an entire program to distance learners was much more complex than simply providing access to a limited number of course offerings in a video format.

The Nursing Department's ad hoc committee worked to resolve curricular problems and issues related to transfer of non-nursing credits. More flexible course substitution policies were initiated to meet the needs of all RN students. Opportunities for on-campus weekend experiences were built into the BSN for the RN Option. Efforts were aimed at providing support systems for distance students. Problems and complexities related to providing equal services to distance and traditional students still exist. Efforts to make educational access less complicated for distance students have been successful. Changes needed to address the concerns of on-campus RN and basic students have been much slower. Frequent communication with Continuing Education staff about real and potential problems is a continued necessity.

PROGRAM OUTCOMES

Four years later the FOCUS course delivery alternative continues to flourish. In the Fall of 1991, there were 215 RN students enrolled in

Table 20.2   FOCUS Course Distribution: Fall 1991

	Course	# Sites	Enrollments
N			
U	Societal Context	30	45
R	Psychopathology	11	12
S	Pathophysiology	9	10
I	Pharmacology	7	7
N	Research	7	7
G			
S			
U			
P	Chemistry	10	14
P	Philosophy	24	35
O	Math	6	10
R	Nutrition	36	75
T			
	Totals	*51 Sites	**215 Enrollments

Five Nursing Courses
Four Support Courses

*51 FOCUS sites participated in Video Delivery course offerings.
**Eight students enrolled in two courses.

nine different courses. Table 20.2 reflects course distribution for enrollments in the video-delivery alternative. Fifty of these RN students
were directly enrolled in nursing courses and the other 165 RN students were enrolled in support courses required by the nursing curriculum. Approximately 55 of these students are matriculated in the nursing program and many others are waiting for confirmation of their
acceptance. Spring of 1992 saw the first graduates of this initiative. Until this year most students concentrated on completing their prerequisites. Students are often encouraged to complete support courses at
local community colleges to enhance convenience and reduce costs.
Currently, large numbers of distance students are completing the
credit-by-examination option available for most nursing courses.

Besides the obvious benefits provided to returning RN students, the
videotaped courses have also offered some unexpected program benefits. The "canned" versions of non-clinical courses allow the college to
offer all non-clinical courses whenever and wherever there is a demand. Ready access to course content increases learning resources for

Table 20.3   RN Enrollment in FOCUS Courses   1988–1992

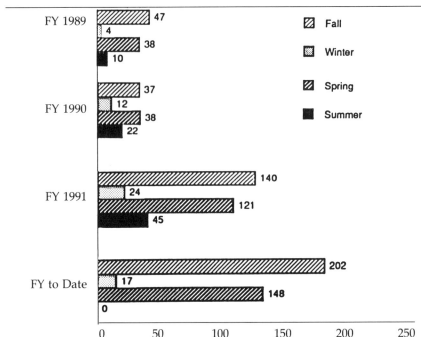

on-campus students who may miss a class, fail a course, or simply want to review some content.

Enrollment numbers in the video delivery alternative have almost quadrupled in the past four years. Table 20.3 summarizes course enrollment numbers over the past four years. The number of worksites has more than doubled in the past two years. In most instances, health care institutions contact us to become a worksite.

Table 20.4 identifies the number and locations of current active worksites. Overall there are 76 potential worksites, however many sites do not offer courses every semester. The advantage of this system is that you can offer a course at as many sites that wish to participate with as many or as few students who wish to enroll in a specific course.

Faculty have benefitted from the canned versions of courses in numerous ways. First, lectures are readily available for peer or self-evaluations. In emergency situations faculty have used canned lectures in

Table 20.4   FOCUS Worksites

State	'91 Fall	'92 Spring*
DE	10	12
PA	19	14
NJ	22	20
MD	1	3
Total	52	49

*Six new sites for '92 Spring.

order to avoid cancelling and rescheduling classes. Canned versions of a live class serve as an excellent resource to validate test questions. Most often faculty have used video courses to augment teaching in a seminar format.

The faculty determine the shelf life of a course depending upon content and currency issues. Generally, each nursing course is retaped every two years. This allows the Division of CE to make a profit and at the same time, it keeps the content up to date. In rare instances some individual lectures were retaped to ensure content validity. For example, the information on the diagnosis and treatment of AIDS in the late 80s changed so rapidly that course lectures related to this information had to be retaped.

The College has made an educational decision not to expand beyond the limitations of its faculty resources. Maintenance of this decision requires close communication and coordination of mutual recruitment efforts with Continuing Education staff. Current economic limitations and a need to restructure workload issues have somewhat limited the potential growth of the FOCUS alternative. Faculty are pleased with the format for reimbursement. Most choose to deposit their money in the tax free Professional Development Fund. Access to the fund allows them to augment college support for continuing education programs and educational travel.

The numerous partnerships developed as a result of the FOCUS initiative have been a positive experience. These experiences have enhanced public relationships both within and outside of the University community. The College of Nursing and the Division of Continuing Education at the University of Delaware view this alternative course delivery mode as a major success. At a time when many University enrollments are diminishing due to the limited population of traditional college age students, these partnerships have allowed increased numbers of RN students to enroll in a quality baccalaureate degree program. More importantly, this flexible delivery alternative has provided increased access to a Bachelor of Science in Nursing that would not have been possible without the use of video technology and supportive nursing faculty.

In the Fall of 1989, the National League for Nursing reviewed the FOCUS alternative as part of the accreditation review. League reviewers were very impressed with the quality of the canned courses. One reviewer compared a taped class with the live class she evaluated. Her notes implied that there was minimal difference between live and canned class presentations. Faculty were commended on the quality of their lectures.

Evaluation data and program outcomes imply that the candid video delivery system for RN education at the University of Delaware is both a profitable and viable mode to meet the needs of self-directed, returning RN students. The "time shifting" approach with creative fee structuring was a key element in this successful, distance education initiative. The partnerships the College of Nursing developed in this joint venture have strengthened relationships both within and outside the University.

REFERENCES

Dutton, J. C. (1988). A comparison of live and videotaped presentations of a graduate ME course. *Engineering Education, 1,* 243–246.

Knowles, M. S. (1980). *The adult learner: A neglected species.* (3rd ed.) Houston: Gulf.

Paulanka, B. J., & Stone, H. R. (1990). *Selecting a model to maintain nursing professionals.* Unpublished manuscript, University of Delaware, Newark.

21

The RN Mentor Program:
An Exercise in Leadership

Genevieve E. Chandler

Typically, when RNs enter the Mobility Program at the University of Massachusetts they come looking for something more, something new and something different. Yet in the beginning, few are able to put their finger on what that something is. The entering students have achieved a level of excellence in their nursing career and know that another job change will not provide the different perspective, broader view, or intellectual challenge they are interested in. Actually, most of the RNs have already tried the change of job approach and some are at the point of considering a change in career. Their commitment to nursing, however, runs deep and rather than move on or leave altogether they decide to take on the challenge of academe and invest the time, money, and energy to learn more about their chosen profession.

At the University of Massachusetts, RN to BSN Mobility Program faculty offer students the opportunity to develop and expand their knowledge base through theory, research, and clinical experiences. Within the program, one extremely successful component has been the RN-Sophomore Mentoring Program. This unique one day clinical exchange offers both RNs and sophomores an opportunity to apply the skills and knowledge that they have accumulated throughout the year. The enthusiastically positive evaluations speak to the benefits achieved by each class of students. For the RNs it brings together the "something" they came into the program looking for. In the following paragraphs the setting, structure, process, and outcomes are described in detail so faculty from other returning RN programs will have the information necessary to incorporate this exciting experience into their own curriculum.

THE SETTING

Recognizing that the ever changing needs in health care spur on the requirement for advanced knowledge and skills in nurses, the RN Mobility faculty have worked to develop a smooth transition from RN to BSN. Knowing that the health care system also demands a lot from its nurses, the faculty have created a sound educational program that provides the information, resources, and support today's nurse needs. The RN TO BSN Mobility tract was designed with both the needs of the health care system and the needs of the individual nurse in mind.

The nursing program is located within an internationally prominent University located in a rural setting. The returning RNs travel up to two to three hours coming from five surrounding states in order to enroll in the courses. The Mobility Program is designed so that all non-nursing coursework can be completed at the college of the student's own choosing. The University program itself can be completed in one calendar year. Faculty recognized that to meet the diverse needs of this population the classes had to be accessible and affordable for working, family-oriented RNs. In an attempt to design a suitable course load, all of the required nursing classes are offered in one day, the same day throughout the year. The circumscribed schedule makes it possible for the students to plan school, work, and home life in a predictable manner. This intensive program provides the basis for a cohesive student group. Many of the students carpool long distances together, spend time between classes, and move through the curriculum as a group. The result has been the creation of a team spirit of "all for one and one for all." Students say that they started together and they *will* finish together!

An assumption of the UMass program is that the majority of RNs return to school after achieving a level of expertise in their practice. Their decision to enter a bachelor's degree program is motivated by a desire to enlarge their view of health care and their practice of nursing so that they can expand their current role and be more mobile in preparation for future positions. During the intensive year of undergraduate study students have the opportunity to read, write and reflect on past nursing experiences, and to develop career plans for their future nursing practice. In preparation for graduation all RN students are required to enroll in the leadership course. The leadership course provides the context for the RN Mentoring experience.

THE PREPARATION

Leadership

The assumption of the Leadership course is that one cannot lead alone but must empower others to participate in leadership. Kouzes and Posner (1989) have developed a leadership framework that describes the critical variables necessary for empowering leaders to be effective. The framework for the leadership course is built on five practices identified as most common to the achievements of leaders. These practices are: challenging, inspiring, enabling, modeling, and encouraging (Kouzes & Posner, 1989). The results of their study indicated that leaders empower subordinates to meet organizational goals by operationalizing these leadership practices.

In class, students begin by assessing their own knowledge and abilities in each of the five areas. Individual and group exercises are employed to assist students in examining the development of their current leadership styles and in designing preferred leadership styles. The content areas of organizational theory, management strategies, decision making, change, conflict, power, and communication are taught through the lens of empowerment. For example, in studying organizational theory students would learn the type of structures that empower nurses to enable patients, the health care team, and the organization. On the subject of conflict, students analyze their usual conflict style and learn how to develop a cadre of conflict approaches that promote staff and patient interaction. The philosophy of the class is that leadership starts with self. In order to gain the trust and respect of others one must first be aware of one's own perceptions, attitudes and behaviors. Kouzes and Posner state: "the self confidence required to lead comes from learning about ourselves—our skills, our prejudices, our talents and our shortcomings" (p.36).

The following description of each of the five leadership practices offers the basic content of the conceptual framework for the course:

Challenging: Leaders search for opportunities to challenge the status quo, to experiment and take risks. The format of the class is designed to assist students in challenging their own process, the status quo of their workplace, and that of the health care system. Through group dialogue, case studies, and student debate the individual's and the systems' processes are examined and critiqued while new visions for the future are created.

Inspiring: Inspiration begins by leaders envisioning an uplifting future and enlisting others to commit to their goals. Once a dynamic vision is created it must be communicated in an exciting way that will inspire commitment by members of the organization. When the students have developed a vision that is consistent with their values they learn communication techniques to enact their vision.

Enabling: Leaders enable others to act. Good leaders know they cannot do the job alone. They need to create a team and foster team work by convincing the members to commit to a common vision. Successful leaders develop collaborative goals and cooperative relationships through trust. They strengthen others by sharing power and information. The enabling process begins in class with students working collaboratively with each other and the professor to design the course process and content. Involvement and cooperation is expected.

Modeling: Leaders must model the way for others by practicing what they preach. They must devise a plan and provide a map for others to follow. Leaders need to set the example and plan small wins for accomplishments that will further the vision. Kouzes & Posner (1989) describe leaders as modeling the way by laying down milestones and putting up sign posts. They create opportunities for success. Through assignments students begin to "model the way" in class by developing management strategies and career goals that are consistent with their values. The mentoring experience provides an ideal situation to "model the way."

Encouraging: Leaders encourage honest involvement by recognizing contributions and celebrating accomplishments. They design rewards that are linked to performance. In class students are recognized and rewarded for their performance. Celebrations are a regular part of the process.

The teaching method of the professor is to lead the class by challenging, inspiring, enabling, modeling, and encouraging. The goal of the

Table 21.1   A Comparison of Successful Leader and Mentor Characteristics

LEADER	MENTOR
(Kouzes & Posner, 1989)	*(Vance, 1982)*
Enabler	Teacher/Guide
Encourager	Sponsor
Model	Exemplar
Coach	Counselor
Visionary	Visionary

leadership course is to build competence and confidence in each student so they are enabled to undertake the responsibilities inherent in the leadership role of the baccalaureate degree nurse. The role of a mentor is consistent with the leadership framework. Mentoring is a vehicle for developing one's abilities to challenge, inspire, enable, model and encourage. The senior nurse as mentor is a theme that is developed in class and encouraged in practice.

Mentoring

Mentoring is one approach to creating a nurturing support system. The result of Kanter's work with empowering organizations indicated that to progress in one's career one needs, in addition to a role model, a system of mentors and sponsors (1977). A mentor acts as a teacher, sponsor, host, guide, exemplar, and counselor (Vance, 1982). The characteristics of a mentor are remarkably similar to the five leadership practices (see Table 21.1).

As a more senior person, the mentor shows the mentee the ropes, includes them in professional networks, introduces them to colleagues and guides them through the organizational culture. The organizational culture is referred to as the shadow structure. With the organizational structure being the written policies and procedures, the culture is the unwritten, oral network of myths, norms, values, and roles. The mentor nurse makes known the unknown culture for the novice nurse. To prepare the RN student for the mentor role there are two critical assignments: the care diary and media training.

The Assignments

With the returning RNs practicing less by rules and maxims and moving more into the realm of intuitive knowledge, it is important to coach the student in developing an awareness of interventions and approaches to colleagues and patients that have become natural and automatic for the RNs. Two assignments that assist RNs in recognizing their intuitive knowledge are the care diary and media training.

The care diary is a weekly narrative of a caring situation in which the nurse participated. The description of caring incidents takes the usual, expected, natural behaviors of the nurse and highlights how they made a difference. Benner stated, "When experts can describe situations where their interactions made a difference, some of the knowledge embedded in their practice becomes visible. And with visibility, enhancement and recognition of expertise becomes possible" (1984, p.36). Writing the care diary enables the RNs to develop a heightened awareness of their usual activities that go unrecognized and undocumented. The effects of their caring then become part of the student discourse. When the RNs meet with the sophomores they are better prepared to discuss the caring process and its outcomes. The care diary consists of three parts: the description, the analysis, and the definition. The first component, the description, is a brief story of an incident that demonstrates caring. The second step is a content analysis of the caring incident. In this process the key variables that indicate caring are extracted from the description for the definition of caring. Caring is then defined from this one nurse-patient incident. The care diary was developed as a mechanism for the students to recognize, identify, and articulate the intuitive, hidden aspects of their practice that staff nurses have described as essential and empowering (Chandler, 1992a).

The purpose of the media training is to raise nurses' awareness of their responsibility to inform the public of a nursing perspective. The media awareness assignment has two distinct parts: a survey of printed news media, and a letter to the editor or an editorial. In the first part of media awareness the students conduct a six week survey of the local and national news coverage of health care issues. The assignment is to identify when and where nurses are mentioned in the printed news media. Inevitably the results from the survey are similar to other studies (Berush, Gorden, & Bell, 1991; Chandler, 1992b): nurses are not in the news. The student then chooses one of the articles for review to identify where it would have been beneficial to have a nurse's input. The class is taught the format and ingredients for a letter to the editor and an editorial. The assignment is to succinctly describe the nurse's role in relation to the specific health care issue they have chosen to write about, and send their comments as a letter to the editor. The issues the RNs have responded to range from premature infant care to condom use to hospice care. The letter is a vehicle for the nurse to explain to the reader the essential role nurses play in today's health care system. The students are told that this is no time for modesty, let the truth be known! The result of the effort has been that more than two thirds of the letters have been published with one or two feature articles on the role of nurses in health care. As the result of being published, the students feel very successful and report that the experience leaves them feeling that they can make a difference and that they do have some influence. The director of the Mobility program, the dean, their employers and families all get copies of the letter. It is an empowering experience for the student and a boost in the public's awareness of the effects of nursing care.

Both the care diary and media awareness training are designed to assist the student in articulating the hidden, intuitive aspects of nursing care. With this preparation, when the RNs meet with their sophomore students the RNs are prepared to describe their practice.

THE PROGRAM AND STRUCTURE

In addition to studying leadership and mentoring, a requirement for both the RNs and sophomores is to become familiar with Benner's work on skill acquisition (1984). The RNs use *From Novice to Expert* (Benner, 1984) as a resource in their initial nursing process class. The sophomores have been exposed to the five stages of skill acquisition and have been required to read *How Expert Nurses Use Intuition* (Benner & Tanner, 1987). What follows is a brief description of the information that the students have prior to the mentoring experience.

Benner (1984) has described the nursing skill acquisition process by applying the Dreyfus model to clinical situations. According to this model persons pass through graduating levels of proficiency from novice to advanced beginner, to competent, to proficient, and finally to expert. The student's ability to perform skills increases with experience. The novice stage represents the new nurse with no experience in clinical situations within the health care context. In the educational setting rules are decontextualized and theories are objectified to provide a base the novice student can build on. The advanced beginner has accumulated enough practical experience so that he or she is able to recognize patterns and significant situations. The third stage, competency, refers to the two- to three-year post graduate nurse who is familiar with the job requirements. They are able to see the patient from a long term perspective, analyze the current situation and design a comprehensive plan of care. The fourth stage, the proficient nurse, has accumulated enough experience so that he or she can attend to the patient holistically, predict events, and modify the plan accordingly. The expert performer, the fifth stage of skill acquisition, has enough of an experiential base so that the nurse no longer practices clinically by rules and maxims but has an intuitive and informed grasp of the situation.

The sophomore students, whose knowledge has been developed in the classroom, lab, and in focused clinical experiences, would fall into the novice stage. From the perspective of the sophomore, the RN mentors resemble what they have read about expert nurses. In the clinical situation the sophomores observe the RN from the perspective of skill acquisition as well as for the six key aspects of intuitive judgement (Benner, 1984). Intuitive judgment consists of pattern recognition, similarity recognition, common sense understanding, skilled know-how, sense of salience, and deliberative rationality.

Pattern recognition is the ability of the expert nurse to perceive connections between disparate parts of a situation. The context of the patient situation is not simply a backdrop for the clinical realities but it is part of the pattern. It takes experience to consider the whole, the context, the past and present situation, the patient, and to identify patterns. The second aspect of intuitive judgment, similarity recognition, is the intuitive ability to recognize relationships between situations despite objective differences in the current case. Commonsense understanding is defined as an intimate sense of the language, culture and history of each patient and their illness. It is the ability to take in patient history, family interactions, and the current situation to create an understanding of the patient's world. Skilled know-how is defined as the physical ability that comes with practice and experience. The routine technical procedures become so familiar that they are second nature to the expert nurse. Sense of salience is defined as an innate ability to differentiate what is important from what is not as pertinent at the time. The better the nurse knows the patient the increased possibility of an appropriate sense of salience. Deliberative rationality is a method used to prevent tunnel vision by getting some distance on the situation to consider other possibilities. Deliberative rationality is the act of introducing the role of the devil's advocate by "trying on alternatives, allowing the expert to maximize judgment without being limited to one interpretation" (Benner & Tanner, 1987, p.29). When the sophomores meet with the RNs they observe the RNs' practice for intuitive judgements. When both groups are familiar with the stages of skill acquisition they each have a grasp of one another's abilities and a language to describe the practice.

The mentoring program is instituted late in the spring semester when the undergraduate sophomores have completed two semesters of basic nursing skills, nursing process, and nursing diagnosis. The RNs have essentially completed the BSN program. The actual experience takes place in one day during a shift of the RN's choosing. The individuals from these two diverse groups of students are matched by a professor who has taught both groups. The sophomore students submit clinical and geographic preferences for the location of the experience. Each sophomore spends one shift, day or night, 8 hours or 12 hours, observing an RN during the RN's actual work day. This is a voluntary experience with no grade attached to either student's performance. Faculty preparation for the clinical experience includes contacting the agencies, requesting student demographics, and administering pre and post questions to each group.

In preparing for the mentoring experience RNs are asked for their name, workplace, type of unit, shift, work phone, home phone and the VP of Nursing's name and correct title. The sophomores and RNs are matched by considering the sophomore's clinical and geographic preference. Once they are paired, it is the sophomore's responsibility to contact the RN and arrange a day for their visit. Faculty recommend a preferred week and the students attempt to arrange their schedules accordingly.

The Vice President of each clinical agency of nursing is sent a letter explaining the program, its past success, and the necessity in these days of complex technology and constrained budgets to maximize and expand clinical learning opportunities. It is suggested that it might also be an opportunity for the Vice President to showcase their facility in the interest of recruiting future baccalaureate prepared nurses. The letter is sent at least one month prior to the experience.

THE PROCESS AND OUTCOMES

To prepare the RN for spending a day as a mentor/leader and the sophomore as a novice/observer each group is administered a pre-test.

Sophomore Pre-test Questions:

1. How would you define an expert nurse?

2. What behaviors that typify an expert nurse (Benner level V) do you expect to see?

3. What do you expect to learn from the experience?

The sophomores have had the opportunity to live a day in the life of a nurse in the emergency room, neonatal ICU, labor and delivery, infection control, middle management, intensive care, home health, and oncology. The breadth of the experience covers the scope of nursing.

During the day with a sophomore student the RN demonstrates the role of teacher, negotiator, advocate, comforter, questioner and decision maker. One sophomore wrote:

> *Prior to my novice experience I had a strong desire to go into the community aspect of nursing. After spending the day with my expert I made up my mind to definitely pursue a nursing career in community nursing. Kim talked to me extensively about her job and rewarding experiences.*

> *P.S. I found this experience to be invaluable. My expert opened my horizon and expanded my knowledge. She was a perfect example of what I thought an expert should be.*

This quote is not an exceptional response, this enthusiasm is typical of the results. The ownership, "my expert," "my novice," occurs for both the RNs and the sophomores. It is part of the chemistry that makes the match work. One sophomore responded to the question "How were the roles of teacher, sponsor, host and guide, exemplar, or counselor demonstrated by your expert?" with the following comment:

> *The expert I followed during the day was great. He explained why and how he did everything. He was more than willing to teach me about all his individual patients and their needs, and explained his rationale behind all his interventions. He was a fine example of an expert nurse and a great host because he explained about the hospital, special rooms etc. He was also great with his patients and was a good counselor in that he knew just what to say to them.*

It is easy to hear how seriously the RNs take their role as mentor. Many worked on very busy units but they still took the time to teach, counsel and demonstrate procedures. One student commented:

> My expert answered all questions I had—she made sure that she clarified everything for me. She made me feel very comfortable by introducing me to the staff, who were all very friendly. She showed me how to perform certain procedures (although I wasn't able to perform them on the babies). And took things step by step. I was allowed to hold one of the babies though!

Another student commented:

> My expert demonstrated the role of teacher by teaching an Alzhiemer client's spouse how to get her to take in more fluids by using a straw as a dropper in her mouth. The next day the client's dehydration had been eliminated. She was successful in her teaching.

In the post-test the sophomores were asked to identify how the expert nurse demonstrated Dreyfus' six aspects of intuitive judgment (Benner & Tanner, 1987). Some examples follow:

Pattern recognition: The experts understood the responses that their clients made. They knew what to expect, and recognized all their clients' needs.

Similarity recognition: Since most of the men in the V. A. hospital had similar health needs, one may intervene all in the same way. The expert knew, however, that even though they had the same problems, they had different needs.

Commonsense understanding: When the experts had new admissions, they were right there to find out what clients needed, where they were before the V. A. hospital, if they had eaten in the last couple days, drank, showered etc.

Skilled know how: The experts had an intelligence in all that they did, and really knew all about what they were doing. For example— they knew when it was time to take a patient off oxygen for a while, to see if the patient could learn to be without it since he had quit smoking.

Sense of salience: One time a patient didn't want his normal routine followed for the day, my expert knew he was up to something because the patient wanted to be left alone. So we checked up on him a couple of minutes later and he was drinking alcohol in his room. The expert knew the patient must have received it from a visitor.

Deliberative rationality: The expert nurses didn't take it for granted when a patient said he was doing fine, they still took their pulses and temperatures etc. and interpreted the situation themselves—and deal[t] with the problems that may have been found selectively. All patients were treated uniquely, even though a lot of the men had the same problems; and the expert wasn't drawn into 'tunnel vision,' because different daily needs were recognized.

The sophomores had the opportunity to witness and discuss the gamut of ethical concerns from confidentiality to forced medication, HIV patients, drug addicted mothers and babies, pain management, physician caused hemorrhage, patient competency, and differences between the patient's and the nurse's values. One sophomore wrote, in response to the post-test question about what ethical concerns arose during the experience and how the expert resolved them:

> During my Clinical Experience, I had expected there to be some ethical concerns, however, I had no idea they would be so complex in nature. As soon as I arrived I had to sign two forms on confidentiality. As in any other field of nursing, I did not take these forms lightly. I was at a detox, in which people from all walks of life seek treatment. The expert nurse was faced with many ethical dilemmas. She is the nurse who decides who should get what amount of medication and this is a difficult decision. When people call for admission, she makes the decision on who to accept and who to turn away. She said, "It can be emotionally straining sometimes because I want to admit everyone, but we only have so many beds. It's tough. Also, I think about the people who are turned away. What happens to them?" She also has a person with HIV virus, who she must treat the same as any other patient. This is also difficult to do.

Another student in the NICU wrote:

> One of the infants was suspected of having drug withdrawal symptoms, and was at high risk for being HIV positive, but my expert nurse did not treat this infant any differently than the others.

The sophomores are overwhelmingly in support of having the opportunity to share in the role of an expert nurse. Prior to the experience one concern that was expressed by several students was that they were worried that their expert might be clinically and technically competent but no longer caring and compassionate. The students were pleasantly surprised to see such genuine caring, understanding, and connection between the RN and the patient. They said they were surprised by the active involvement the nurse required of the patient. In addition the sophomores observed two areas that are so difficult to teach in class: prioritizing and time management, qualities that one can only gain from experience.

In preparation for the experience the RNs also responded to the pre-test questions:

RN Pre-test Questions:

1. How do you define an expert nurse?
2. How do you expect to demonstrate roles of the mentor (teacher, sponsor, host and guide, exemplar, counselor) to your novice?
3. What do you expect to gain from this experience as mentor?
4. Which nursing theory is most influential in directing your practice?

From the RN perspective their evaluations of the experience were no less enthusiastic than the sophomores'. Their roles as mentor and leader came through loud and clear. One RN wrote:

> *I answered many questions. I helped my novice to see that many decisions in nursing come with time and experience and not necessarily from a book. She couldn't understand how I knew a patient was in trouble, before the patient knew she was in trouble.*

Another nurse reported:

> *In operationalizing my role, I allowed the protege to fail, to venture a guess, yet still feel safe with me. I demonstrated delegating authority, giving feedback to LPNs, and provided information and knowledge to other staff RNs. The protege was able to visualize the multi-faceted role of the professional nurse.*

The experience gave the RNs an opportunity to demonstrate their expertise. In this case the sophomore spent the day with a nurse manager:

> *My nurse made rounds to each patient's room in the morning and talked for a minute to each patient. In that time she assessed the patient; how they were feeling, eating, etc. She knew each of the patients' histories and personalities—a sign of commonsense understanding. In one case today a patient was suffering from respiratory distress. Immediately my nurse stated this when she saw the bluish hue of the woman's face and put her on a respirator immediately. She checked the woman's blood gases and sure enough—her PCO2 was very high. By the end of the day her blood gases had returned to normal, thanks to my expert nurse's skilled know-how, intuition, and similarity recognition.*

The RNs shared their wisdom with their novices as demonstrated by this student comment:

> *My expert nurse talked to me about what makes an excellent nurse. She said the key is to never stop asking questions. She said you will never know everything, and you will never stop learning. She also said that if you think you know everything, then you're in trouble and you're not going to go any further.*

One mentor reported that his student was able to get a better sense of the bigger picture because she was not bogged down with her own assignment. The RNs took good care of their students:

> *I have chosen a day for us with a nice team. I switched days off to have the particular doctors who will treat the student well. I have given the student a list of the surgeries we will be in on and explained them to her.*

In addition to successfully functioning in the role as mentor these RNs were able to articulate how they personally benefited from the novice experience:

> *Seeing the energy of youth in the nursing role was enlightening. She was bright, caring, and inquisitive. This experience allowed me to see I have something to share and see I really do have reasons to do what I do—they were just buried in the hustle of the floor life.*

> *An expert nurse knows how to give power away. In giving that power, the experts become empowered themselves.*

> *I was able to look at what I do through "new eyes." Dee helped me realize that it is the little things that make the difference.*

This experience allowed me to develop my talents for teaching and expression. It helped me define my role in the acute care setting. It left me feeling powerful and able to make a difference beyond the hospital.

The RNs recognized they had a lot to teach and were comfortable in the role. One reported that the student witnessed 42 procedures in one shift!

A serendipitous result of this experience was the RN appreciating how knowledgeable a sophomore was, after only two years of liberal education. This observation reinforced their already formulated opinion regarding the necessity of a BSN degree. The individual RN's description of his or her student included such comments as: "Very smart, good communicator, very caring and professional with tremendous potential." This response was typical of RNs who were as different from each other as thirty people could be. They each felt they had mentored an exceptional student.

Learning about leadership, empowerment, and mentoring in class raised the RNs' awareness of the knowledge and skill they possessed and some they needed to strengthen. The mentoring experience afforded the RNs the opportunity to practice with new appreciation for the important roles they assume in their every day work. For both the sophomores and the RNs it is a very meaningful and memorable experience. Seventy-five percent of the RN students mention this day on their class evaluations.

CONCLUSION

The advancement in health care knowledge, the explosion of scientific information, the pervasiveness of life style related illness and chronic disease all guarantee a role for educated nurses. There has never been a more opportune time to pull all the factions of nursing together. Educators can be leaders in this process by creating a collegial, mentoring experience while students are in school. The RN mentoring program is one model of nurse empowerment that inspires the integration of our tremendous nursing resources.

A recent graduate wrote in a letter, "I especially enjoyed the expert to novice program with my sophomore student. After one day my job no longer seemed so dull and routine. It was refreshing to have someone else see what I do and find it so exciting!"

One day can make a difference.

REFERENCES

Benner, P. (1984). *From novice to expert: Excellence and power in clinical nursing practice.* Menlo Park, CA: Addison-Wesley Publishing Company.

Benner, P., & Tanner, C. (1987). How expert nurses use intuition. *American Journal of Nursing, 87,* 23–31.

Berush, B., Gorden, S., & Bell, N. (1991). Who counts in news coverage of health care? *Nursing Outlook, 39,* 204–207.

Chandler, G. (1992a). The source and process of empowerment. *Nursing Administration Quarterly, 16,* 65–71.

Chandler, G. (1992b). Nurses in the news: From invisible to visible. *Journal of Nursing Administration, 22,* 11–12.

Kanter, R. M. (1977). *Men and women of the corporation.* New York: Basic Books, Inc., Publishers.

Kouzes, J., & Posner, B. (1989). *The leadership challenge.* San Francisco: Jossey-Bass Press.

Vance, C. (1982). The mentor connection. *Journal of Nursing Administration, 4,* 7–13.

22

Creation of Visual Metaphors in RN Education

Sally A. Decker
Janet E. Bryant

Registered nurses (RNs) returning to school to obtain their BSN degree need mechanisms to help them reframe their experiences of nursing. They need to recognize the value of their experience and use it as a tool for new knowledge development. The abstract reasoning required for reconceptualization of their nursing role and reframing their nursing experiences is frequently difficult for RNs. Instead of being empowered by a new way of conceptualizing their role, they have believed that they are being asked to "give up" a way of thinking. The concrete world in which they have practiced offers little foundation for the creativity and abstract reasoning needed to reframe their experiences and feel empowerment in the educational setting.

In the process of redesigning a course for RN students returning for their BSN degree, the course was built around the concept of empowerment and metaphors were used as a means of assisting students to think abstractly and creatively about nursing. We redesigned the course in our roles of senior faculty member and graduate student. Both of us became members of the class.

We gratefully acknowledge the help of Hideki Kihata, Associate Professor of art, and the members of N300, Nursing Transition, class of 1991, Saginaw Valley State University.

This project was partially supported by a Teaching Innovation grant, Saginaw Valley State University.

355

This chapter presents the use of visual metaphors as a mechanism for helping students with the process of transition to the BSN role. The total experience can be viewed as a case study of a class in which the specific experience of transition, or a change in thinking, was lived by the group. The visual images created by the class and the students' experience with this process are viewed as a source of knowledge about transition to the BSN role.

This source of knowledge, or path of discovery using visual metaphors, can be labeled as "esthetic knowing," as identified by Carper (1978). Photographic experiences as esthetic inquiry offer both power in creativity and a way to conceptualize the beauty and unity of an experience. These esthetic paths focus on a unity of experience in the domain of nursing that is creatively and imaginatively expressed (Sarter, 1989, p.110).

THEORETICAL FRAMEWORK

Using photographs as a means of esthetic inquiry requires that the purpose of the photographs be defined and the framework out of which the visuals evolve be understood (Highley & Ferentz, 1989). In this classroom study, the purpose for the creation of the photographs was to help students understand the process of transition to the BSN role and increase the students' creativity using visual metaphors to expand their ways of knowing the world of nursing. The framework from which the project emanated was a combination of the empowerment philosophy utilized for the total class experience and Szarkowski's (1978) framework for analysis of modern photography.

Based on the concept of empowerment, three sets of assumptions were used to guide the redesign of the course. In the first set, experience was identified as a valuable teacher. This assumption included recognizing that each student's experience enhances self-esteem (Benner, 1984; Friere, 1970), and that keeping the students' experience at the center of the learning process sparks the quest for learning (Cantor, 1953). In the second set of assumptions the importance of caring and collegial dialogue within a learning environment was identified. More specifically, these assumptions were: 1) dialogue is helpful in creating an atmosphere for critical thinking (Friere, 1970); 2) collegiality is valuable and can be nourished (Hedin & Donovan, 1989); 3) horizontal learning (teaching/learning) is empowering and preferred (Friere, 1970); and 4) caring is a moral ideal (Watson, 1985). Most directly influencing the photography experience was the final set of assumptions relating to the creative process and the process of constructing meanings. These assumptions were that creativity can be encouraged through creative exercise (Bevis, 1989) and what one comes to know through the process of learning evolves from the thought that goes into efforts to construct meaning (Smith, 1992).

Building upon the empowerment assumptions, one segment of the course used photography as a means of assisting students to construct meanings about transition in nursing education. Students were introduced to contemporary photography and the critical analysis of John Szarkowski (1978). Szarkowski selected 127 pictures that he considered exemplary of American photography and divided them into two dichotomous groupings: photography as a means of self-expression and photography as a method of exploration. In explaining this, Szarkowski used the differences between the world views of the romantic and realist visions of art.

The romantic view is that meanings are dependent upon our understandings; thus, an object has meaning only in terms of the human-centered metaphors that we assign to them. The realist view is that the world exists independent of human understanding and it contains specific patterns of meaning. In the romantic vision, the photographer is the actual subject of the photograph. In the realist vision, the objective structure is the subject (Szarkowski, 1978, p. 19). Szarkowski contends that no photograph represents entirely one or the other category of photograph, but these world views and goals of the photographer are distinctions of mirror and window categories of photographs.

Other distinctions between mirror and window photographs as described by Szarkowski (1978, p. 25) are the angle of view, light, and degree of concrete representation. In mirror photographs the angle of view is narrower and closer, as less information needs to be organized and abstract simplicity is desired. A wider angle is used in the window photographs. The image being conveyed is more abstract in the mirror photographs and more concrete in the window photographs. The mirror photographs are also darker in nature as they are more involved with suggestion than description. Szarkowski points out that photographs can thus be viewed as either mirrors (reflections of the photographer) or as windows through which one might better know the world.

REVIEW OF LITERATURE

Metaphor

The mirror and/or window photographs in this project were intended to be visual metaphors of the process of transition to the role of BSN-prepared nurse. Metaphors can help to explain the transition process and show students other possible patterns of meaning. Metaphorical thinking involves multiple patterns of perception and flexibility. It involves a broadening of perspective to reveal patterns not evident in a narrowly focused view. This broadening of perspectives can increase one's effectiveness in interpreting and interacting with reality (Pugh, Hicks, Davis, & Venstra, 1992, p. 13). We believe that the process of creating metaphors can empower students by helping them reframe their ideas.

The ability to reframe is the ability to step outside and see a situation in a new way (Pugh, Hicks, Davis & Venstra, 1992, p. 73). It is the ability to change the shape of a problem and visualize new solutions. In RN education, helping students see that there are other ways to interpret the reality of their nursing experiences is important to learning. Helping them to experience change in perspective is empowering and is a function of the use of metaphors.

A great deal has been written about literary metaphor over the years. While Aristotle's claim that a good metaphor implies an intuitive perception of similarity in the dissimilar is important, there are those that claim that metaphors do not let us perceive similarities, but instead create something altogether new (Harries, 1978). Metaphors probably do both in that they create similarities and dissimilarities. They also create convergence and new images. Pugh, Hicks, Davis, and Venstra (1992) state that through metaphorical thinking divergent meanings become unified into patterns that constitute our conceptual understanding of reality.

Expanding on the function of the literary metaphor, Ricoeur (1978) wrote that metaphor may provide some untranslatable information, thus yielding some true insight about reality and how this is attached to image and feeling. The use of metaphor can create new patterns of unity in the experience of transition for the RN student. It also can promote the linkage of new knowledge to the experienced reality of the student. "In a changing world, metaphor renders the truth of experience as the truth of knowledge, for it is the means of passing from individual immediacy to an established public world: the new must be linked to the old, and the experiences of any individual must be connected with that of his [sic] society" (Shiff, 1978, p.106).

As a tool in RN education, metaphorical thinking can cut across discipline boundaries, making knowledge in one domain a guide for comprehending knowledge in another. A transfer of meaning takes place in the direction of both domains. To be a metaphorical thinker, therefore, is to be a constructive learner, one who actively builds bridges from the known to the new (Pugh, Hicks, Davis, & Venstra, 1992, p. 5). In RN education, we bridge the old and the new, relating new ideas to experienced reality and yielding new insights for nurses to use in their practice.

Gordon (1978) has suggested that metaphor is the pattern by which people communicate their experience of the world. The metaphor is, therefore, the way we use our unique model of the world, found in our stored experiences, to make sense of new information. Just as stories can communicate our reality using verbal metaphors, photographs can communicate using visual metaphors.

The primary function of metaphor and kindred images is to express some ideas not adequately expressible otherwise—at least to the speaker's knowledge (Brown, 1927, p. 75). Brown noted that "every object in the universe may be said to have a twofold significance, a significance in itself as a fragment of reality—that is necessarily, a fragment of goodness, truth, and beauty, and a significance as symbol, emblem, or image of something other than itself" (p.23). The parallels to the critical framework of Szarkowski and to the unity of similarity and dissimilarity can be seen in these statements by Brown. Each object can be seen to have meaning in more than one way. The photographic experience encourages students to experience these multiple views while expressing a unity of thought not expressible otherwise: a representation of the transition to the BSN role.

In the nursing literature, metaphor has been used by Watson (1987, 1990) and Munhall (1986). Watson used selected literary metaphorical vignettes to depict the expressive elements of caring. She argued that if tacit knowledge is expressible, it is through metaphor. Munhall used the metaphor of wax apples in T. S. Eliot's (1936) poem, "The Love Song of J. Alfred Prufrock," as a way to look at the search for knowledge in nursing. Munhall used Eliot's description of the wax apple, ". . . tasteless, dry, but perfect in stability and lifelessness" (cited in Munhall, 1986 p.3), to communicate vividly her perceptions about research methods and their search for structural truth as opposed to meaning.

Visual Metaphor

Imagery can be used to move the concept of metaphor from the written or spoken word, the more common language of metaphor, to a visual form. Imagery can be created in the mind of the reader of the written word. It can also be created using a visual medium, and, hence, the bridge is from literature to art. Hausman (1989) wrote that the structure of verbal metaphors is a feature of certain phenomena that exhibit meaning or intelligibility. Based on this, he proposes that metaphor is integral to all art forms, including the visual arts (p. 8).

From the earliest records of humankind, mingled with the ordinary figures of men, animals, and representations of events, there are other drawings, paintings, or carvings that are symbolic. These forms of art stand for something other than an objective structure. They represent an abstract idea or a concept of the mind that belongs to the world of imagery (Brown, 1927). Both metaphor and imagery involve using material objects as images of immaterial, spiritual things (Brown, 1927).

Arnheim (1969) argued that visual perception is not a passive recording but an active concern of the mind. As an example he suggests that the perception of shape consists of the application of form categories referred to as visual concepts. Arnheim's argument is that thinking takes place in the realm of images, in the realm of the highly abstract, and frequently in the realm below the level of consciousness. At best, mental images are hard to describe verbally and drawings may better relate to such images (Arnheim, 1969). While drawings (in this case photographs) still may not be replicas of mental images, they may share some of the properties of the image, such as color, form, or object. Arnheim concludes that "pictorial representations are suitable instruments of abstract reasoning and point to some of the dimensions they can represent" (p. 116).

Metaphors in Education

Sticht (1979) suggested that teaching students to produce and comprehend metaphors is an important tool of communication and thought. The metaphor becomes a tool to extend student capabilities in educational settings. Sanders and Sanders (1984) have suggested that in the pursuit of lineal knowledge educators have forgotten the effectiveness of strategies that teach through devices that are creative and metaphorical. Activities to help students in metaphorical thinking have been identified, suggesting that this is a process that can be learned (Pugh, Hicks, Davis, & Venstra, 1992; Sanders & Sanders, 1984).

Petrie (1979) referred to the many roles of metaphor in education. These roles include: 1) metaphor as a heuristic aid that is useful and ornamental but not essential to learning; 2) metaphor as a method for the transfer of learning and understanding from the well-known to the less well-known in a vivid and memorable way, thus enhancing learning; and 3) metaphor as means for understanding the very possibility of learning something radically new. These last roles claim that metaphor makes intelligible the acquisition of new knowledge (Petrie, 1979). A metaphor can be thought of as a rational bridge from the known to the radically unknown and as a way to change the context of understanding. According to Ortony (1975), metaphors are able to bridge ideas and increase learning because they are compact, vivid and inexpressible.

PROJECT PROCEDURES

The photography project can be thought of as a case study of a class experiencing the transition to the BSN role. The students were asked to create at least one photograph, in slide format, that represented the concept of transition. To prepare for the assignment, students were introduced to Szarkowski's (1978) work on mirror and window photographs and shown examples of these photographs by Hideki Kihata, a photographer and member of the fine arts faculty. Students were given answers for their many practical questions about photography and obtaining film development. Over the next several weeks following the assignment, all members of the class (faculty and students) showed their slides (from 2–11 per member) and talked about the process of transition reflected in the slides.

At the end of the semester, students created a final series of photographs that reflected the process of transition for the class. The class members viewed all of the photographs together and rated the slides on a scale of 1–4 for inclusion into the final series. The photographer who worked with the class was also given an opportunity to select images for inclusion. Those photographs with the highest inclusion rating (setting the cutoff at a level so that at least one photo from every student was included in the final grouping) were included in the final series of images. The students decided the photographs should be shown once with a musical background of Michael Jackson's "Man in the Mirror" (in itself an interesting metaphorical suggestion of change and responsibility for change) and once with an explanatory narration from each class member. As pointed out by Highley and Ferentz (1989), narration using a photograph as a means of exploration is a rich source of information.

EVALUATION PATTERNS

This photography project became a means to "presence" nursing faculty with students. Hedin and Donovan (1989) wrote about the need to "transform" nursing education with the aim of the educational environment being the freeing of students to become fully human (p.9). Being fully human was explained by these authors as being in a state in which people critically engage in the reality around them. This photography project used visual metaphors created by all class members (student and faculty) to help students engage in the reality of transition and bridge nursing education and nursing practice.

No attempt has yet been made to analyze the actual content of the photographs. The comments of the students about the process of creating the photographs are the unit of analysis that will be presented. One of the authors, a graduate student exploring the phenomenon of empowerment in students, interviewed several class members at the end of the semester. She had no evaluation responsibility for the students and students consented to the interview process. Students were asked to tell her what they had experienced in the class. No specific questions regarding the photography experience were asked. The experience of empowerment emerged in the students' descriptions as moving from positions of powerlessness, alienation, and lack of control over their education and practice to mutual support (collegiality) and increased control. Comments relating empowerment themes identified in the interviews and the photography experience were found in the interview data (Bryant, 1991).

One student felt angry, despondent, and depressed about her nursing practice prior to the course. She felt that the photography session was a boost to her ego, and helped her to look at nursing in a new way.

The class has really helped me stop, take a look at things, what's going on, look at my practice, what I like about it. It's been like a clarifying thing . . . The experience with the camera and the slides was really amazing. It gave me a way to look at things in a different way—mirrors and windows! His explanation was just excellent. But I don't agree that everything [in mirror photographs] has to be dark. We don't have to agree with everything. But I looked at things in a different perspective. I looked at my practice through it and nursing in a different perspective . . . It has made me look at myself in a new light, maybe something I didn't like about myself in a non-threatening, healing kind of way.

Another student described the photography experience as a new way of communicating.

It has been hard for me to get over that, talking in front of groups. What I really enjoyed in this class was the photo journals—it was really neat. I just liked taking pictures. And seeing other peoples' pictures, and their perceptions of pictures—what you get out of them, and the positive things that were said about our pictures. When she first said that we had to do a photo journal, I thought oh, my gosh, what am I going to take a picture of? I had no idea of where to start. And then Janet [a peer in the class] gave me a lot of ideas. And so, all these things clicked.

The metaphorical process within this educational experience enhanced empowerment for these students as they became more aware of their feelings and communicated them in images. Individuals became more assertive in action and more engaged in their work. Empowerment was described in student comments such as "freeing," "healing," and "enjoyable."

The photography project, being a unifying experience for the entire class, helped all class members learn more about themselves and their work. Everyone learned to communicate in a new medium, generating new insights and understandings of clinical practice and transition. Faculty and students worked together to explore visual metaphors as enjoyable, enlightening, and empowering.

It is possible to capture some of this experience in one final metaphor. Brown (1927), in a collection of illustrative metaphors he encountered in one year, recorded this metaphor of a photographic plate by George Wyndham, "Above all, must the mind be disencumbered, clean, and plastic when, like a sensitive [photographic] plate, it is to receive the impression of a work of art" (p. 288).

REFERENCES

Arnheim, R. (1969). *Visual thinking.* Berkeley: University of California Press.

Benner, P. (1984). *From novice to expert: Excellence and power in clinical nursing practice.* Menlo Park, CA: Addison-Wesley.

Bevis, E. O. (1989). The curriculum consequences: Aftermath of revolution. In *Curriculum revolution: Reconceptualizing nursing education* (pp. 115–133). New York: National League for Nursing Press.

Brown, S. (1927). *The world of imagery: Metaphor and kindred imagery.* London: Routledge and Kegan Paul.

Bryant, J. (1991). Unpublished interview data from paper prepared for N650, Advanced Clinical Nursing, MSN Program, College of Nursing and Allied Health Sciences, Saginaw Valley State University.

Cantor, N. (1953). *The teaching-learning process.* New York: Holt, Rinehart, and Winston.

Carper, B. A. (1978). Fundamental patterns of knowing in nursing. *Advances in Nursing Science, 1*(1), 13–23.

Eliot, T. S. (1936). *Collected poems, 1909–1962* (pp. 3–7). New York: Harcourt, Brace and World, Inc.

Friere, P. (1970). *Pedagogy of the oppressed.* New York: Seabury Press.

Gordon, D. (1978). *Therapeutic metaphors.* Cupertino, CA: META Publications.

Harries, K. (1978). The many uses of metaphor. In S. Sacks (Ed.), *On metaphor* (pp. 165–172). Chicago: University of Chicago Press.

Hausman, C. R. (1989). *Metaphor and art.* New York: Cambridge University Press.

Hedin, B., & Donovan, J. (1989). A feminist perspective on nursing education. *Nurse Educator, 14*(4), 8–13.

Highley, B., & Ferentz, T. (1989). Esthetic inquiry. In B. Sarter (Ed.), *Paths to knowledge: Innovative research methods in nursing* (pp. 111–139). New York: National League for Nursing Press.

Munhall, P. (1986). Methodological issues in nursing research: Beyond a wax apple. *Advances in Nursing Science, 8*(3), 1–5.

Ortony, A. (1975). Why metaphors are necessary and not just nice. *Educational Theory, 25,* 45–53.

Petrie, H. G. (1979). Metaphor and learning. In A. Ortony (Ed.), *Metaphor and Thought* (pp. 438–461). Cambridge: Cambridge University Press.

Pugh, S. L., Hicks, J. W., Davis, M., & Venstra, T. (1992). *Bridging: A teacher's guide to metaphorical thinking.* Urbana, Illinois: National Council of Teachers of English.

Ricoeur, P. (1978). The metaphorical process as cognition, imagination, and feeling. In S. Sacks (Ed.), *On metaphor* (pp. 141–158). Chicago: University of Chicago Press.

Sanders, D., & Sanders, J. (1984). *Teaching creativity through metaphor.* New York: Longman.

Sarter, B. (1989). *Paths to knowledge: Innovative research methods for nursing.* New York: National League for Nursing Press.

Shiff, R. (1978). Art and life: A metaphoric relationship. In S. Sacks (Ed.), *On metaphor* (pp. 105–120). Chicago: University of Chicago Press.

Smith, M. J. (1992). Enhancing esthetic knowledge: A teaching strategy. *Advances in Nursing Science, 14*(3), 52–59.

Sticht, T. G. (1979). Educational uses of metaphor. In A. Ortony (Ed.), *Metaphor and thought* (pp. 474–485). Cambridge: Cambridge University Press.

Szarkowski, J. (1978). *Mirror and windows: American photography since 1960.* New York: Museum of Modern Art.

Watson, J. (1985). *Nursing: Human science and caring.* Norwalk, CT: Appleton-Century-Crofts.

Watson, J. (1987). Nursing on the caring edge: Metaphorical vignettes. *Advances in Nursing Science, 10*(1), 10–18.

Watson, J. (1990). Caring knowledge and informed moral passion. *Advances in Nursing Science, 13*(1), 15–24.